Schuessler, Wilhelm Heinrich

Abridged Therapeutics founded upon histology and cellular Pathology

Schuessler, Wilhelm Heinrich

Abridged Therapeutics founded upon histology and cellular Pathology

Inktank publishing, 2018

www.inktank-publishing.com

ISBN/EAN: 9783747785348

All rights reserved

This is a reprint of a historical out of copyright text that has been re-manufactured for better reading and printing by our unique software. Inktank publishing retains all rights of this specific copy which is marked with an invisible watermark.

ABRIDGED THERAPEUTICS

FOUNDED UPON

HISTOLOGY AND CELLULAR PATHOLOGY

WITH AN APPENDIX:

GIVING SPECIAL DIRECTIONS FOR THE APPLICATION OF THE INORGANIC CELL SALTS, AND INDICATIONS OF THE UNDERLYING CONDITION OF MORBID STATES OF TISSUE.
BIOCHEMIC METHOD OF SUCCESSFULLY TREATING DISEASE.

BY

DR. MED. SCHÜSSLER,
OF OLDENBURG.

AUTHORISED TRANSLATION
BY M. DOCETTI WALKER, M.D.

FIFTEENTH EDITION,
ADDENDA EMBODIED.

LONDON: AUG. SIEGLE, 30, LIME STREET, E.C.
DUNDEE: THE BIOCHEMIC DISPENSARY.
CHRISTCHURCH, N.Z.: TRUTH AND HEALTH PUBLICATION OFFICE,
194 HEREFORD STREET.

079

INTRODUCTION.

Moleschott, Professor of Physiology at the University of Rome, says in his work on "*Vital Circulation*": (Kreislauf des Lebens).

"The structure and vitality of the organs depend "upon the presence of the necessary quantities of the "inorganic constituents.

"On this fact is based the high estimation in which "of late years the subject of the relative proportions "of the inorganic substances to the individual parts of "the body has been held.

"This estimation neither proudly despises any fact, "nor fosters, on the other hand, futile hopes; but "promises both to Agriculture and Medicine a brilliant "future.

"In the face of such positive facts, it can no longer "be denied that the substances which remain after "incineration or combustion of the tissues—the ashes "—are as important and essential to the inner com-"position, and consequently to the 'form-giving' and "kind-determining' basis of the tissues, as those "substances which are volatilized during combustion.

A

and is turned into sulphuric acid. The latter combines with the bases of the carbonates, and turns into sulphates by driving off the carbonic acid.

Under the influence of the oxygen which has reached the tissues, a transformation takes place of those organic substances which are to enter into the composition of new (young) cells. The products of the transformation are: muscle, nerve, connective-tissue substance, (glue-furnishing substance), and mucin. With these substances (which are not present in the blood, but are only formed in the tissues from the albumen), the inorganic substances unite by reason of chemical relations and affinity. Whilst the formation of new cells is going on under the influence of oxygen so also the destruction of old cells takes place. Through the transformation of the organic substances, sulphuric acid, above named, is formed, as also urea, uric acid, carbonic acid, water, etc.

The final products of the metamorphosis are, urea carbonic acid, and water. These products leave the tissues along with the salts which have been set free, and give place to those organic substances which have not yet reached so high a degree of retrograding transformation, so as to allow these also to undergo their final metamorphosis The products of the Retrograde Metamorphosis are removed from the system by the lymphatics, the connective tissue, and the veins to the gall bladder, to the lungs, to the kidneys, the bladder, and the skin, and are eliminated from the organism together with the urine, the perspiration, fœces, etc.

Concerning the important function of connective-tissue (connective-substance) Moleschott thus expresses himself:—"It is one of the grandest conquests of "modern times, to which Virchow and Von Recklinghausen have paved the way, that this connective-"substance has been elevated from the indifferent and "secondary position formerly allotted to it, to one of "fertile activity hitherto unsuspected. That which "was formerly considered simply as a padding, a filling-" in, or protecting covering, now appears as the nidus "(bed) of the most minute sap-streamlets of blood to the "tissues, and from them back to the blood-vessels; "and, at the same time, as one of the most important "breeding-spots, of young cells, which are capable of "rising out of the embryonic undeveloped youthful "forms into the most characteristic formations of the "body."

An individual is in a state of health, when by the proper digestion of the solids and fluids of the food taken, the blood receives due compensation for the losses sustained in giving off the materials for the nutrition of the tissues, and when the nutritive material is present in the proper places and in the requisite quantities, and no disturbance occurs in the molecular movement,[1] and when the building up of new cells, and the disintegration, breaking up of old cells, as well as the elimination of useless material is carried on normally.

A disturbance in the molecular movements of any of the inorganic salts of a tissue produces a disease. For the healing or cure of such, the giving of a minimum dose of the identical inorganic substance suffices, because the molecules of that substance, administered as medicine, fill up the gap in the chain of molecules of that particular cell or tissue salt.

"Disease is an altered state of cell," says Virchow. Health therefore is the normal state of cell. The constitution of the cell is determined by the composition

[1] Spectrum Analysis has opened a new field of truth, showing matter to be capable of division to an extent of which we could form no comprehension. While speaking of the action of molecules of a minimum dose, a statement by Darwin is subjoined, referring to much more minute quantities than those used by Dr. Schüssler. He says in his work on Insectivorous Plants:—"It is an astonishing fact, on which I will not here enlarge, that so inconceivably minute a quantity as one 20,000,000th of a grain of ammonia phosphate should induce some changes in a gland, sufficient to cause a motor impulse to be sent down the whole length of the tentacle; this impulse exciting movements through an angle of about 180°."

of its environments, immediate surrounding, as much as the thriving of a plant depends on the quality of the soil around its root fibres.

The *Agricultural Chemist* speaks of the "Laws of the Minimum" in accordance to which the plant nutriment present in the soil in the minimum, must be applied as manure: he requires only three manure essentials, either nitrogen combined with hydrogen (ammonia) or *Calcium phosphate* or potash. The other substances forming plant food are present in the soil in sufficient quantities.

The "Law of the Minimum" is also applicable in the biochemic measures (remedies).

Example.—In the fostering soil of the bones in a child suffering from rickets, a want of the phosphate of lime has occurred, through a disturbance in the molecular movements of its molecules.[1] The quantity of phosphate of lime intended for the bones, which cannot reach its destination, would form a surplus (excess) if not carried off with the urine. The office of keeping the blood in its integral composition devolves upon the kidneys. They have therefore to eliminate every foreign substance and every surplus component.

The cure of rickets can take place only after the disturbance in the motion of the molecules in the said fostering soil has been adjusted by means of minimal doses of *Calcium phosphate;* after this the *Calcium phosphate* can pass into the normal current.

Every normal cell possesses the capacity of taking up and casting off substances. This power is diminished or suspended, when the cell has suffered a loss in one of its salts in consequence of an irritation (over stimulation.) The *status quo ante* can be re-established

[1] The rate at which molecular movements travel through a nerve has been measured, and found to be about 100 feet per second, or somewhat more than a mile a minute, in the nerves of a frog. In the nerves of a mammal it is just about twice as fast.

as soon as the deficiency has been made up with the homogeneous material from the immediate nutrient source. When the supply does not arrive spontaneously, it is to be assumed that the special salt is only present there in the minimum, or that the diseased cells have suffered besides the deficiency, also a physical alteration, which will not permit of the entering of the special blood salt.

In such a case higher grades of reduction or trituration of the salt are required. When the cells have received compensation for the loss and thus regained their integrity, they are in a condition to perform their normal function, and by it to effect the removal of disease products (exudations, transudations), by chemical processes. The Biochemic method of cure aids nature in her efforts of cure by furnishing her with the natural remedial means which are lacking in certain parts, namely, the inorganic salts. The direct aim in Biochemistry of covering a deficiency is thus achieved. Other methods of cure in which remedies are used heterogeneous to the constituents of the human organism reach their aim indirectly.

Those who, with unbiased mind, will consider this aim, and the means and ways by which it is achieved, will acknowledge that the Biochemic Remedies are sufficient to cure all diseases which are curable by internal means when applied in conformity with a correct diagnosis.

Some medical men have proposed that the Biochemic Remedies should be proved on healthy persons, and that symptoms thereby produced, should be considered the indications for their use. This is fundamentally false. The indications of the Biochemic Remedies must be derived from physiological and pathological chemistry respectively, by the results of their application in diseases. Who could believe that it would be possible that with large or small doses of cell-salts given to healthy persons, conditions of disease could be produced which have a similarity to puerperal fever, typhus, acute articular rheumatism, hygroma patellæ, etc. etc.

The Biochemic Remedies are given in minimal doses, as they are *not* selected on the principle of similars. Biochemistry is not Homeopathy.

The curative effectiveness of small doses may be deducted from these facts. Nature works only with atoms and groups of atoms termed molecules. The growth of animals and plants is a synthetic process, atoms or groups of atoms joining the already existing mass of molecules.

That infinitely small particles of matter which cannot be weighed can have an effect in the organism, cannot be contradicted in the face of such a fact, that waves of light, which are also unweighable, cause movements in the substances of living, green parts of plants in consequence of which carbonic acid is decomposed into carbon and oxygen. The use of small doses is a chemico-physiological necessity for the healing of diseases by means of the biochemic cure. For instance, when Glaubersalt is to reach the blood, this cannot be done by giving it in a concentrated solution. The latter has only an effect on the intestinal canal, where it excites a watery diarrhœa purge, and leaves the organism with these same evacuations. But a diluted solution of (glaubersalt) *Sodium sulphate* will enter into the blood and into the other intercellular fluids, and there effects by the hygrometric (water attracting) property of this salt, a passing over of the excess of water from the tissues into the venous blood and an increase of the secretion of urine.

These obviously different effects have their foundation in the following physiological relations:—The epithelial cells of the lining of the intestines cause the water to pass *from* the intestinal tube into the blood.

When the function of the epithelial cells suffers an interference by irritation, an opposite current is set up, water passes *from* the blood into the intestinal canal. A concentrated solution of glaubersalt irritates the epithelial cells, a diluted one does not.

Every biochemic remedy must be diluted, so that the function of healthy cells is not disturbed, and so that functional disturbances when present can be corrected.

In healthy people, animals and plants, the salts are contained in diluted proportions which correspond to the third, fourth, and fifth decimal medicinal degree of dilution. The following analysis of blood cells regarding the human organism will show this.

In a thousand grammes of blood cells the inorganic substances contained are at this rate—

Iron, - - - - - -	0·998
Sulphate of potash, - -	0·132
Potassium chloride, - -	3·079
Potassium phosphate, - -	2·343
Sodium phosphate, - -	0·633
Sodium, - - - -	0·344
Calcium phosphate, - -	0·094
Magnesium phosphate, - -	0·060

See Bunge's Manual of Physiological and Pathological Chemistry, p. 219.

Compare with the above analysis that of milk. One liter (1000 grammes) of milk contain of inorganic substances—

Potassium, - - -	0·78	grammes.
Sodium, - - -	0·23	,,
Lime, - - - - -	0·33	,,
Magnesia, - - -	0·06	,,
Iron, - - - -	0·004	,,
Phosphoric acid, - -	0·47	,,
*Chlorine, - - -	0·44	,,

*vide Bunge, p. 97.

Milk contains besides these, traces of Fluorine and Silica. One litre (about a quart) of milk suffices for the daily food of an infant, weighing about 1 stone.

If 6 centigrammes of Magnesia suffice to cover the necessary supply of Magnesium in an infant, how very small will be the dose of magnesia, by means of which an attack of neuralgia can be cured, which is caused by an almost inconceivably small deficiency of this salt in a most minute portion of the nerve tissue.

The percentage of the mineral substances in a cell is extremely minute. By weighing, measurement, and calculation, the German physiologist, C. Schmidt, has found that one corpuscle (blood-cell) contains about one billionth part of *Potassium chloride* The billionth part of a gramme equals the 12th or 6th cent. trituration or delution.

The dose of a Biochemic Remedy is not decided by the quantity of a disease product; for instance through the lack of a very minute quantity of *Sodium chloride* in the cells of the epithelial layer in a serous sac, an extensive serous exudation may result and a minute supply equal to the want of *Sodium chloride* molecules can effect the resorption of the exudation.

Guided by the relative quantities of the cell-salts given as above, each physician can base the selection of the dose.

In my practice I usually select the 6th dec. trituration, of which I dissolve a small quantity in water, and give it as the urgency of the case may require every hour or two, or 3 to 4 times daily. In suitable cases an external application is also effective.

One milligramme of a substance is estimated to contain 16 trillion of molecules; this quantity is more than sufficient for the restitution of a disturbance of the molecular-motion in the tissues.

Silica, which is insoluble in water, must be triturated up to the fourth or fifth degree, so that it may be dissolved in the water, and thus find its way to the destined pores in the walls of the capillaries.

The objection might be raised that the molecules of the salts taken as medicines would unite with those homogeneous salts contained in the blood, and therefore the aim of the cure would be illusiory. In reply to this objection, it must here be stated specially that this supposed union will not take place, as the molecules of carbonic acid serve as the isolating medium of the molecules of the salt.

The inorganic substances which serve as means of nutrition respectively of function of plants are taken up by them also, only in minimal quantities. Liebig says:—"The strongest manure, sulphate of iron coarsely powdered, can scarcely be compared in its effects with a far smaller quantity of the same in a state of infinitesimal subdivision, which in consequence of its fineness will be more generally diffused, so that some particles will be found in all parts of the soil. One single root fibre requires but extremely little nourishment where it is in contact with the soil, but for the welfare of its function and its existence it is requisite that this minimum must be present exactly in that spot."—See Liebig's Chemical letters, vol ii. p. 295.

In the 3rd edition of the Guide to the Mineral Baths (Bäder-Almanach) for 1886 we find the following remarks, page 121 :—" To judge by the results and the existing analysis, the waters of Rilchingen also contain chiefly those constituents with which, according to Dr. Schüssler's Abridged Therapeutics, all curable diseases are cured in the biochemic manner. In the waters of Rilchingen some of the mineral substances—as, for instance, *Magnesium phosphate,* is present only in the 8th, *Potassium chloride* in the 5th, and *Silica* in the 6th decimal attenuation or dilution."

Dr. Behneke, in his balneological letters, writes as follows :—" Relative proportion is a thing always of importance : it is the degree of concentration in which the salt solutions are present in the waters for use in the human organism. I am convinced that many of the most famous mineral springs owe their good results to the fact that the curative constituents are only present in weak dilution. This experience seems to me a very important one, that very minute doses, as we would think, of effective or beneficial constituents, produce often *the most* excellent results."

It may not be out of place here to quote some words of professor Huxley on "Cellular Pathology," from his address at the International Medical Congress, London.

PROFESSOR HUXLEY ON THE CONNECTION OF THE BIOLOGICAL SCIENCES WITH MEDICINE.

"I trust I have not been mistaken in supposing that an attempt to give a brief sketch of the steps by which a philosophical necessity has become a historical reality may not be devoid of interest, possibly of instruction, to the members of this great Congress, profoundly interested as all are in the scientific development of medicine.

"The greatest physiological and pathological work of the seventeenth century, Borelli's treatise 'De motu animalium,' is, to all intents and purposes, a development of Descortes' fundamental conception; and the same may be said of the physiology and pathology of Boerhaave[1], whose authority dominated in the medical world of the first half of the eighteenth century.

"With the origin of modern chemistry, and of electrical science, in the latter half of the eighteenth century, aids in the analysis of the phenomena of life, of which Descartes could not have dreamed, were offered to the physiologist. And the greater part of the gigantic progress which has been made in the present century is a justification of the prevision of Descartes. For it consists, especially, in a more and more complete resolution of the grosser organs of the living body into physico-chemical mechanisms. * * 'To apply

[1] Whose lineal descendant is Professor Moleschott, Senator of Rome, author of "Kreislauf des Lebens."

the physical sciences to physiology is to explain the phenomena of living bodies by the laws of inert bodies.' * * * It is not too much to say that one half of a modern text-book of physiology consists of applied physics and chemistry; and that it is exactly in the exploration of the phenomena of sensibility and contractility that physics and chemistry have exerted the most potent influence. * * 'All animals,' says Bichat, 'are assemblages of different organs, each of which performs its functions and concurs, after its fashion, in the preservation of the whole. There are so many special machines in the general machine which constitutes the individual. But each of these special machines is itself compounded of many tissues of very different natures, which in truth constitute the elements of those organs.'[1] (*l.c.* lxxix.) 'The conception of a proper vitality is applicable only to these simple tissues, and not to the organs themselves.' (*l c.* lxxxiv.)

"And Bichat proceeds to make the obvious application of the doctrine of synthetic life, if I may so call it, to pathology. Since diseases are only *alterations* of vital *properties*, and the properties of *each* tissue are *distinct* from those of the *rest*, it is evident that the diseases of *each* tissue must be different from those of the rest. Therefore, in any organ composed of *different tissues* one may be *diseased* and the other remain *healthy*; and this is what happens in most cases (*l.c.* lxxxv.) * * In a spirit of true prophecy, Bichat says, 'we have arrived at an epoch, in which pathological anatomy should start afresh' For as the analysis of the organs had led him to the tissues as the physiological units of the organism, so, in a succeeding generation, the analysis of the tissues led to the cells as the physiological element of the tissues. * * * * In fact, the body is a machine of the nature of an army, not of that of a watch, or of a hydraulic apparatus. Of this army, each *cell* is a soldier, an organ a brigade, the central nervous system the head-quarters and field telegraph, the alimentary and circulatory system the commissariat. Losses are made good by recruits born in camp, and the life of the individual is a campaign, conducted successfully for a number of years, but with certain defeat in the long run. * * * Hence

[1] Anatomie Générale.

the establishment of the cell theory, in normal biology, was swiftly followed by a "cellular pathology,' as its logical counterpart. I need not remind you how great an instrument of investigation this doctrine has proved in the hands of the man of genius,[1] to whom its development is due. * * Henceforward, as it appears to me, the connection of medicine with the biological sciences is clearly defined. Pure pathology is that branch of biology which defines the particular perturbation of *cell life* or of the co-ordinating machinery, or of both, on which the phenomena of disease depends. * * * Those who are conversant with the present state of biology will hardly hesitate to admit that the conception of the life of one of the higher animals as the summation of the lives of a cell aggregate, brought into harmonious action by a co-ordinative machinery formed by some of these cells, constitutes a permanent acquisition of physiological science. * * * There are some * * who look, with as little favour as Bichat did, upon any attempt to apply the principles and the methods of physics and chemistry to the investigation of the vital processes of growth, metabolism, and contractility: they stand upon the ancient ways.

"Others, on the contrary, supported by a robust faith in the universal applicability of the principles laid down by Descartes, and seeing that the actions called 'vital' are, so far as we have any means of knowing, nothing but changes of place of particles of matter, look to *molecular* physics to achieve the analysis of the living protoplasm itself into a molecular mechanism. If there is any truth in the received doctrines of physics, that contrast does not exist between living and inert matter, on which Bichat lays so much stress. In nature, nothing is at rest, nothing is amorphous; the simplest particle of that which men in their blindness are pleased to call 'brute matter' is a vast aggregate of molecular machanisms, performing complicated movements of immense rapidity and sensitively adjusting themselves to every change in the surrounding world. * * * * Living matter differs from other matter in degree and not in kind; the microcosm repeats the macrocosm; and one

[1] Rudolf Virchow, Professor at the University of Berlin.

chain of causation connects the nebulus original of suns and planetary systems with the protoplasmic foundation of life and organisation.

"From this point of view, pathology is the analogue of the theory of perturbations in astronomy; and therapeutics resolves itself into a discovery of the means by which a system of forces competent to eliminate any given perturbation may be introduced into the economy. And as pathology bases itself upon normal physiology, so therapeutics rests upon pharmacology; which is, strictly speaking, a part of the great biological topic of the influence of conditions on the living organism, and has no scientific foundation apart from physiology. * * * * It will, in short, become possible to introduce into the economy a molecular mechanism which, like a very cunningly contrived torpedo, shall find its way to some particular group of living elements, and cause an explosion [*i.e.*, absorption and molecular motion] among them, leaving the rest untouched.

"The search for the explanation of diseased states in modified cell life in the ætiology of disease, the elucidation of the action of medicaments by the methods and the data of experimental physiology, appear to me to be the greatest steps which have ever been made towards the establishment of medicine on a scientific basis. I need hardly say they could not have been made except for the advance of normal biology."—*Extracts from the Address.*

The most famous scientist in this country advances suggestions arrived at from his point of view, as seen by the above, which are in singular agreement with Dr Schüssler's views and experiences on the subject of scientific medicine.

Biology shows Biochemistry to be a science. The practical counterpart of the abstract science of Virchow's Cellular Pathology is formed by "Cellular Therapeutics," or the system of introducing molecular cell-salts. The one, indeed, is the forerunner of the other; the former science investigating the morbid states of tissue-cells; the latter a system by which the natural action of force—fixed by a law of chemical affinity—of any of the inorganic constituents is systematically employed to eliminate any given disease or perturbation from any of the tissue-cells by means of molecules of special adequate proportion, which, finding their way by affinity to the particular group of (diseased) living elements, set up molecular motion and equilibrium of balance in the economy of the cells. But only the non-functional tissue cells are acted upon, leaving the rest untouched! In health restored, the physiological laws are suffered to resume their normal course. Law is law, and in nature unalterable. If man is not the casual production or conjuction of atoms, one may not pass by this wondrous phenomenon which he presents, without acknowledging that this finely wrought composition of organic and inorganic atoms is regulated by a universal law, the teachings of which are far-reaching. By them we arrive by induction at the grand science of "Cellular Therapeutics." Biochemic treatment is the outcome of the teachings of Biology and those sciences which of late years have disclosed Nature's ways and footsteps, by aid of the microscope and spectroscope.

Let every medical man, every student test this law, and conscientiously apply the molecular tissue cell-salts under given abnormal conditions as indicated here, and he will not fail to attain good results. The action by chemical affinity of these triturated molecules of cell-salts is certain, because fixed by that law. Nature's laws appear profoundly simple, yet are they in simplicity profound. "Close observation of little things is the secret of true science." None who watch the wonderful results in Nature from infinitely minute causes will doubt the power of little things. Little bits of experience gathered up carefully and arranged systematically make up the store of our knowledge.

Surely those scientists who do not hail so great an event as the opening up of "Cellular Therapeutics," truly scientific medicine, do not comprehend the deep meaning of their own teachings in this direction, the possibility and rationale of a defined general Law of cure on these lines. Under the advance of Histology, Analytical Chemistry, Cellular Pathology, etc., it has become possible to group the tissues by their special constitution of definite organic and inorganic substances. Consequently, to apply to each kind of tissue its own general, definite, and peculiar cell salts, according to its requirements in disease.

The promoters of the sister sciences of medicine have made it possible for the physician in future to *depend* on the method of operation of his medicines in the living organism, when these are skilfully selected and scientifically applied. By the distinctive symptoms he is guided in his choice of the *particular* cell salts required—the immense varieties and complications of morbid states, offering vast scope for exact medical practice, wherewith to build up the great pyramid of scientific medicine of this advanced era.

The Biochemic treatment of disease must not be confounded with Homœopathy, which rests on the law of "Similia" and Symptomatology. Some would fain call it Homœopathy; but Dr. Schüssler is not a Homœopath. His new remedies owe their new development largely to Biology and its Cell-theory, and to Cellular Pathology, of which the necessary and natural counterparts are Cellular Therapeutics or Biochemic Treatment of Disease.

One of the most attractive and promising features of the above method is, that it is in no degree antagonistic to the medical science of the present day—is in every way complementary of it, and thus may be advantageously studied by all intelligent minds, and practically adopted in our schools of medical thought.

THE TRANSLATOR.

CHARACTERISTICS OF THE INORGANIC TISSUE-SALTS.

Ferric Phosphate = (*Ferrum Phosphoricum*).[1]

IRON is a constituent of the blood-corpuscles, and of the muscle-cells, etc. When the equilibrium of the iron molecules in the muscular fibres is disturbed, the latter become relaxed. When such a disturbance of proper balance takes place in the fibres which are circularly arranged round the blood-vessels, the vessels dilate, become distended, and an accumulation of blood arises in the vascular parts so affected. When, in consequence of an increased pressure of blood, a rupture of the walls of the blood-vessels ensues, hæmorrhage [bleeding] will follow.

When the muscles of the intestinal villi [absorbents] suffer a functional disturbance of their iron molecules, loose evacuations will follow.

When, in consequence of a disturbance of the proper balance of the iron molecules, the muscular fibres of the intestinal walls become weakened, then the vermicular action of the intestines proceeds with less activity, and a tendency to constipation arises.

Iron molecules, therapeutically employed, allay the pathological functional disturbance.

Thus iron, in restoring the blood-vessels to their normal condition, when dilated by disease, is dispelling

---

[1] As the most modern scientific terms have been adopted, read always instead of

Calcarea	Calcium ; for
Ferrum	Ferric ;
Kali	Potassium ;
Magnesia	Magnesium ;
Natrum	Sodium.

the irritation-hyperæmia [local excess of blood], which is the primary cause of the first stage of all inflammations.

Hyperæmia caused by an injury (accident), is cured by iron; and fresh non-suppurating wounds are quickly healed by this remedy.

Iron and the iron salts possess the property of attracting oxygen. In this fact consists their utility to the respective tissue-cells. I use the *Ferric phosphate* or phosphate of iron.

Upon my recommendation several farmers have given Ferric phosphate, with uniform success, to sows possessed with the mania of eating their own young. This disease (mania transitoria) arises from hyperæmia of the brain.

Magnesium Phosphate = (*Magnesia Phosphorica*)

Is the earthy constituent of muscle and nerves, and occurs also in the bones. As a nerve remedy it furnishes most excellent results. The nerve pains which are healed by *Magnesium phosphate* are generally of a shooting character, like lightning, boring, or with a sensation of being tightly drawn together, or grasped by a tight band: they readily change their location, and are somewhat relieved by warmth and pressure.

Headache, face-ache, toothache, epigastric pains (pit of stomach), stomach-ache, and pains of the above description in the limbs, I have frequently cured by this remedy. The pains of the stomach [bowels] generally radiate from the umbilicus (navel), they are sometimes accompanied by loose motions, and are eased by pressure with the hand, by warmth, or by doubling up. In face-ache [neuralgic or rheumatic], which at its height is accompanied by an increased flow of tears, *Magnesium phosphate* is not suitable, but *Sodium chloride.*

The action of Magnesia is the reverse of that of Iron. By functional disturbance of the iron molecules, the muscular fibres relax ; through the functional disturbance of the magnesium molecules they contract. Therefore, *Magnesium phosphate* is the remedy for all cramps : spasms of the glottis, cramps of the legs, tetanus, lockjaw, St. Vitus's dance, spasmodic ischury [stoppage of urine], etc.

Farmers give *Magnesium phosphate*, with very prompt results, for spasms and flatulent colic in horses, and for the acute tympanic [drum-like] swellings of cattle, arising from green, unsuitable fodder. The inflammatory colic of horses requires *Ferric phosphate* ; should mortification commence, *Potassium phosphate*.

Potassium Phosphate = (*Kali phosphoricum*)

Is a constituent of the brain, the nerves, the muscles, and the blood-corpuscles. A disturbance of the function of the molecules of this salt causes

(*a*) In the Brain—according to locality, extension, or intensity of disturbance :

- (1) Mental depression, manifesting itself by irritability [excitability]; over-sensitiveness ; tendency to weeping ; timidity, shyness, dread ;
- (2) Softening of the brain.

(*b*) In the Nerves : laming pains, mostly felt during rest ; better from movement without exertion ; feeling of lassitude and exhaustion.

(*c*) In the Muscle-cells : fatty metamorphosis. In the juice of muscle or flesh : putrid decomposition.

(*d*) In the Blood corpuscles : too rapid decay of the same.[1]

[[1] See "Outlines of Physiology, Human and Comparative."—J. Marshall, F.R.S., Professor in University College, London. Vol. I., Chemical Composition of the Tissues.]

Therefore, *Potassium phosphate* cures the following conditions of disease: Septic hæmorrhage, scorbutic bleedings, mortification, cancrum oris, gangrenous, croup, phagedenic chancre, putrid-smelling diarrhœa, adynamic, typhoid conditions, etc.

It will also be found useful in concussion of the brain, symptoms of collapse, and shocks of paralysis.

Calcium Phosphate = (*Calcarea Phosphorica*)

Is a constituent of the teeth, the bones, the connective-tissues, the blood-corpuscles, etc.

It is the specific remedy for rachitis (rickets), cranial tabes (wasting of the cranial bones), pallor, anæmia (bloodlessness), chlorosis, and hydrocephalus. It also assists the new callus formation of fractured bones and in teething.

It also cures those pains arising from anæmia, which are usually accompanied by a creeping sensation and a feeling of numbness or coldness.

By reason of its specific relation to the albuminous bodies, *Calcium phosphate* assists resorption of albuminous exudations and transudations. Therefore it cures hydrops genu, hygroma patellæ, and tumor albus (white swelling). It cures also various scrofulous affections, chronic glandular swellings, goitre, etc.

Those cramps which attack scrofulous persons are not always curable by *Magnesium phosphate*, in which case *Calcium phosphate* is to be used.

Calcium phosphate is a restorative after acute disease.

Sodium Chloride = (*Natrum Muriaticum*).

By its volumetric force the carbonic acid which is in our blood drives off the chlorine of the *Sodium chloride* which is contained in the epithelial cells of the salivary glands, and the Sodium thus set free unites with the carbonic acid, and this combination enters into the blood, whereas the chlorine which was driven off, combined with hydrogen and dissolved in water, enters the stomach as hydrochloric acid.

When by reason of a deficiency of *Sodium chloride* in the epithelial cells, no hydrochloric acid is formed, then the alkaline mucus secreted by the upper layer of the epithelial cells of the mucous membrane is increased. If in such a case we were to reduce the secretions of this mucous membrane by the action of hydrochloric acid, the procedure would only be a palliative one. But to effect a rational cure it behoves us to adjust or correct the disturbance in the nutrient fluid of the salivary glands themselves, and to promote the molecular motion of the molecules of *Sodium chloride* by prescribing or introducing homogeneous molecules.

Sodium chloride is also the functional remedy of mucin contained in the epithelial cells of all mucous membranes. It cures catarrhs of all the mucous membranes where the secretions are watery, transparent, glairy, glassy. The hydrochloric acid formed in the epithelial cells of the salivary glands reduces or limits to the normal quantity the alkaline mucous secretions of the upper layer of epithelial cells, so hydrochloric acid contained in the mucin of all mucous membranes splitting off from *Sodium chloride*, their functional remedy, can already in this nascent condition reduce or limit the mucous secretion.

But not only by the volumetric force of the carbonic acid, but also by the volumetric force of the water[1] present, can hydrochloric acid be driven off from the *Sodium chloride.*

[1] When Sodium Chloride is dissolved in water the latter contains, besides NaCl, a small quantity of HCl and NaOH (*vide* Bung's Lehrbuch der physiologischen und pathologischen Chemie).

In the former case, Sodium having lost the chlorine, combines with carbolic acid, and this combination enters into the blood; in the latter case arises Sodium hydrate, which dissolves the mucin and increases the secretion of mucus. Hence the occurrence of catarrhs from damp air.

Sodium chloride corresponds as remedy to watery secretions which are sometimes irritating and scalding; further, in headache, face or toothache, with an involuntary flow of saliva or tears, or when accompanied with vomiting of watery fluids.

When the *Sodium chloride* contained in the epithelial cells of the serous membranes suffers a disturbance in its molecular motion, then a serous effusion is the result.

Potassium Chloride[1] = (*Kali Muriaticum*).

Potassium chloride is to be found as a constituent in the blood corpuscles in muscle, nerve and brain cells, as well as in the intercellular fluid. When the motion of the *Potassium chloride* molecules has been disturbed in the walls of the blood or lymph vessels, and in consequence a lack or minimum has resulted, an exudation of fibrin and of white blood or of lymph corpuscles takes place. But when the integrity of the tissues has been restored by giving doses of *Potassium chloride* in molecular form, resorption or casting out of the exudation can take place. The one or other of these processes will take place, probably by the splitting off of a portion of the chlorine from the *Potassium chloride*, which, uniting with hydrogen, and in a nascent condition as hydrochloric acid, acts as a solvent upon the fibrin.

Potassium chloride cures Dysentery, summer

[1] This salt (KCl) must not be confounded with Potassium Chlorate ($KClO^3$).

Diarrhœa, Diphtheria, membranous Croup, croupous inflammation of the lungs, fibrinous exudation in the interstitial connective-tissues (*e.g.*, Mastitis), acute infiltration of the lymphatic glands, infiltrated inflammation of the skin, with or without vesicles, (blistering Erysipelas), etc. *Potassium chloride* is the surest remedy for many diseases, especially of Eczema, which has been developed after vaccination with bad vaccine lymph.

Calcium Fluoride[1] = (*Calcarea Fluorica*)

Is to be found in the surface of the bone and in the enamel of the teeth. On the grounds of therapeutical experiences I assume that it is also a constituent of the elastic fibres, and that the proper function of these is promoted by this salt.

Elastic fibres are found in the epidermis (skin), in the connective-tissue, and in the vascular walls.

A disturbance of the equilibrium of the molecules of Calcium fluoride causes a continued dilatation, or chronically relaxed condition of the implicated fibres. When the elastic fibres of any portion of the vessels of the connective tissue or of the lymphatic system have arrived at such a condition of relaxation, the absorption of a solid exudation in such a part cannot take place. In consequence, induration (hardening) of the parts set in. When the elastic fibres of the blood-vessels suffer from a disturbance of the molecules of Calcium fluoride, such pathological enlargements of blood-vessels take place, which make their appearances as: hæmorrhoidal tumours, varicose (dilated) veins and vascular tumours.

Sodium Phosphate = (*Natrum Phosphoricum*).

Through the presence of *Sodium phosphate*, lactic acid is decomposed into carbonic acid and water. The

[1] Fluor spar.

Sodium phosphate possesses the property of fixing or absorbing the carbonic acid in proportion of two parts of carbonic acid to one of phosphoric acid. When it has fixed the carbonic acid it thus carries the same to the lungs. It is contained in the blood corpuscles, muscle, brain, and nerve cells, and in the intercellular fluids.

The oxygen inhaled by the lungs liberates the carbonic acid only loosely fixed by the *Sodium phosphate;* the carbonic acid is given off in the expiration and exchanged for oxygen, which in its turn is taken up by the iron of the blood corpuscles.

Uric acid is readily dissolved by the presence of *Sodium phosphate* at the normal temperature of the body. From the preceding the indications for *Sodium phosphate* result.

Therefore, it is the remedy of those diseases which arise from an excess of lactic acid (pertaining to milk). It is specially suited to the troubles of young children who have been fed with too much sugar and milk, and suffer from acidity.

The symptoms which indicate the use of *Sodium phosphate* are: Acid risings—vomiting of sour fluids or curded masses; yellow-greenish diarrhœa (stools appear chopped); pains in the bowels, cramp, with symptoms of acidity.

Sodium phosphate is also indicated in the uric acid diathesis, podagra, gout, as also in acute and chronic articular rheumatism.

The Sulphates.

The sulphuric acid arising from the oxidation of the albuminous bodies would, as such, destroy the tissues, did it not, by driving off the carbonic acid, unite in its nascent condition with the bases of carbonates.

Sodium Sulphate = (*Natrum Sulphuricum*).

Sodium sulphate is not present in the cells; only in the intercellular fluids. It regulates and promotes the elimination of the excess of water; for instance, such as has arisen in consequence of the decomposition of lactic acid, brought about by the *Sodium phosphate.* Through a disturbed and only partial elimination of it by the skin œdema arises; also œdematous inflammations of the skin, smooth erysipelas; through disturbances in the biliary course arise vomiting of bile, bilious, watery diarrhœa, etc.

Potassium Sulphate = (*Kali Sulphuricum*).

The sulphates which are met with in the earth's crust and the oxide of iron (iron oxydul) serve as carriers of oxygen. When a sulphate and an oxide of iron come in contact simultaneously with an organic substance in a state of decomposition, they give off their oxygen, and sulphate of iron is thereby formed. The latter is decomposed by the presence of air; sulphuric acid and oxide of iron result, which under favourable conditions become again carriers of oxygen.

Similar processes may occur in the human organism. Among the sulphates the *Potassium sulphate* seems to play an important part, because it is contained in cells as well as in intercellular fluids, whilst the *Sodium sulphate* and *Calcium sulphate* are only present in the intercellular fluids.

When the molecules of the *Potassium sulphate* suffer a disturbance the following diseases arise: Pains which are intermittent change their location, are worse during rest, with warmth towards evening and in close rooms, but cease in the open air, in a cool atmosphere rich in oxygen. Excessive desquamation of the epidermis (skin), catarrhs with yellow slimy secretions, etc.

Calcium Sulphate = (*Calcarea Sulphurica*).

Calcium sulphate stands in close relation to suppurations. It cures mattery discharges from the mucous membranes and mattery exudations in serous sacs, as well as tubercular ulcers or abscesses of the intestines, and ulcers of the cornea, etc.

Silica = (*Silicea*)

Is a component part of the connective-tissue, the epidermis, the hair, and the nails.

The effect attributed to it upon the brain, spinal marrow, and nerves, must be referred to the connective-tissue covering of the nerve fibres.

A functional disturbance of Silica molecules causes a swelling of the affected portion of connective-tissue cells. This swelling may remain stationary for some time, become absorbed, or end in suppuration.

Silica, like *Calcium sulphate*, is connected with suppuration, the difference between the two remedies being that *Silica*, by promoting suppuration, or the formation of pus, brings an abscess to maturity, whilst *Calcium sulphate* heals suppurating wounds by checking the suppuration.

As long as there are infiltrated parts in a suppurating wound which have to be emptied by continued suppuration, *Silica* is the remedy required, and the healing of the wound proceeds with the decrease of these infiltrated parts. When no such swellings or infiltrated places are present, and the wound does not heal on account of the torpidity of the tissues, *Calcium sulphate* is the remedy indicated.

The inorganic substances present in the blood and tissues are sufficient to heal all diseases which are curable at all.

The question whether this or that disease is or is not dependent on the existence of germs, microbes, or bacteria, is of no importance in biochemic treatment. If the remedies in the following Special Guide are used, the therapeutical aim—that of curing disease—will be gained in the shortest way.

Long-standing chronic diseases, which have been brought on by over-dosing, excessive use of medicines, as quinine, mercury, etc., can be cured by minute doses of cell-salts.

The symptoms [or indications of the underlying morbid states of tissues] decide the selection of the remedy.

But although the above-named diseases, caused by the abuse of medicines, can be cured by taking cell-salts, it is self-evident that acute cases of poisoning by arsenic, phosphorus, etc., must be treated according to the well-known principles on poisoning relating to such conditions.

Several doctors have supposed that the organic combinations of the human organism ought also to be comprised in the biochemic therapeutics. Such views are erroneous, which I shall endeavour to show.

Biochemic Therapeutics, as has already been indicated, is the Analogue of Agricultural Chemistry. When a plant possesses the necessary inorganic substances intended for it by nature, it is in a position to make for itself all the organic combinations which are necessary for its organism. A plant is not provided or manured with chlorophyll granules to make the leaves green, because one knows that the iron contained in the plants effects itself the formation of the green colour of its leaves. One does not nourish the plant with a compost or manure of lecithin, nuclein, etc., to supply it with these phosphoric combinations; but manure it if necessary with phosphate of lime. The plant abstracts from the *Calcium phosphate* the phosphoric acid, and binds it with the remaining substances necessary for the constitution of lecithin, nuclein, etc.

Should anyone raise the objection that the agricultural or horticultural chemists were in the wrong, believing as they do that only three manure essentials could suffice, but that all organic substances should be taken into consideration as regards the manure, *e.g.*, such as chlorophyll, gum, resin, oil, starch, grape sugar, pommic acid, etc., the scientist would smile at such a sage.

When the human organism contains organic substances, such as albumen, fat, carbo-hydrates, besides the necessary inorganic cell-salts in sufficient quantities in the right places, all necessary organic substances must form by reason of the oxygen, and the consequent subdivisions and syntheses, constituting the health of the individual.

Syntheses, which were formerly only accredited as the exclusive privilege of the plants, are also carried on in the human and animal organism.

To those who believe that the organic substances should also be included in my Biochemic Therapeutics, belongs Dr. Ring, Ward's Island, New York. He finds fault that the primary or elementary combinations are not included in my system of therapeutics, among other things, "The organic substances, such as keratin, tyrosin, creatin, creatinin, etc., are normal constituents of those tissues, in and upon which cancer tumours form, and we are therefore justified to accept that, by a correct preparation and correct choice, these will exert a special influence upon those allied or related tissues."

This is partially true, but mostly untrue. It is true that keratin is a normal constituent of some tissues, but creatin and creatinin are not constituents of the tissues. They are as products of the retrograde cell-metamorphosis. All organic combinations, which, like creatin, creatinin, urea, and uric acid, etc., are eliminated in normal urine, must be considered as the last stages of the oxidation of the organic nutrient substances. They may be compared, as regards their uselessness for the human organism, with the resin which is being eliminated by some plants as a useless product.

The idea of curing a diseased tissue with a healthy one, which is related to it, is very strange. Cartilage tissue is related to the mucous tissue. The functional remedy of both is *Sodium chloride.* Would anyone think of trying to cure a cold with a preparation of cartilage, when it is curable with *Sodium chloride?*

Ten years ago Dr. Constantine Hering thought of the plan of trying the horny tissues as a remedy. He and his friends tried on both horses and men prepared castor equorum, the horny excrescences on the legs of horses. In the index of symptoms relating to this, the statement runs:—"An old frail horse has grown twenty years younger." In spite of this promising symptom, which stamps this castor equorum as a renewing mill for old age, the remedy has sunk into oblivion.

Dr. Ring and *confrères* are having those substances prepared they have in view. Their undertaking will call forth symptom manufactories. We will probably read of very funny symptoms.

If the chemico-physiological views of these gentlemen were a little clearer, they would see that their enterprise is a very useless pastime.

For instance, when they use lecithin, they can at most get the effects of a phosphate; when keratin, which is rich in sulphur, they obtain nothing more than the effects of a sulphate. Why wander in the dark when Biochemistry offers already 5 phosphates and 3 sulphates.

When an inorganic salt is voided in excess in the urine, a deficit of the same salt exists in the immediate provisionary store of such a tissue, and the identical salt is indicated as a remedy (*vide* Rachitis, rickets, p. 21). When the urine contains albumen, sugar, etc., then a nutrient inorganic salt corresponding chemico-physiologically to these substances is present in the minimum, and the homogeneous or self-same salt is indicated as the cure or remedy. A minimum can only occur in the provisionary store of a cell-salt, never in the organic substances; therefore the organic substances are excluded from the curative remedies or therapeutics.

Whoever doubts this can try whether any disease can be cured by means of glue substance, mucous substance, tyrosin, elastin, sugar, fat, etc. The result will be a negative one.

For the synthetic formation and the preservation of the human organism, the following substances are required:—Oxygen, fat, albumen, glue-furnishing substance, mucous substance, keratin, elastin, hæmoglobin, lecithin, nuclein, cholesterine, water, and the inorganic salts.

Albumen forms the principal portion of the blood-plasma, and of the lymph. It is contained in the muscular fibres, the axes cylinders, the nerve fibres, and in the protoplasmic body of all the cells. The organic framework of the bones consists of glue-furnishing substance, so also cartilage, tendons, and the connective tissue.

The mucous substance is contained in the epithelial cells of the mucous membranes. Keratin is the organic basis of the epidermis, the hair, and the nails; elastin is in the elastic fibres.

The glue-furnishing substance, the mucous substance, keratin, and elastin are products which form under the influence of the oxygen during the splitting up of the albumen.

The hæmoglobin of the blood cells or corpuscles is the combination of an albuminous body with a body containing iron, namely hæmatin.

Lecithin and nuclein arise from albumen, fat, and a phosphate, in consequence of a special arrangement of molecules.

Whatever else is found in the tissues besides the above-mentioned organic and inorganic synthetic materials must be considered products of the retrograde metamorphosis of the cells and the breaking down of the albumen: substances which through the activity of the cells must be eliminated.

To the products of the retrograde metamorphosis of the cells belong, as stated, creatin, creatinin, etc.; to the products of the decomposition or the breaking down of the albumen belong tyrosin, leucin, etc.

Albuminous substances and fats are means of repair and sources of force. Oxygen, carbo-hydrates, and gluten (not to be confounded with glue-furnishing substance) are sources of force. The inorganic salts are means of repair and regulators of the functions.

The equalizing or adjusting of functional disturbances is synonymous with the restoring of health. This aim and object will only be reached through the Biochemic means and ways of the inorganic salts. The expectations of Dr. Ring and *confrères* of curing diseases by means of tyrosin, keratin, creatin, etc., is based on an illusion, a phantom, which disappears when physiologically illumined.

Each inorganic substance has special passages of transit through the walls of the capillaries.[1] Thanks to this provision each tissue receives only those mineral substances which pertain to it. The connective tissue *Silica;* the mucous tissue *Sodium chloride,* etc. Without such arrangement there would occur such confusion in the intercellular fluids that the building up of new cells would be impossible.

In healthy cells and their intercellular fluids the salts are in such favourably local relations to each

[1] Outlines of Physiology, Human and Comparative. J. Marshall, F.R.S. Vol. I., p. 60.

other that they cannot bear any improper or undue influence upon each other. Without such favourable relations contrary combinations (transpositions) would take place. If, for instance, *Sodium chloride* and *Potassium phosphate* are dissolved in one liquid, a new chemical combination by double decomposition will take place, and in consequence *Potassium chloride* and *Sodium phosphate* will form.

Such processes must not be disregarded by those who wish to use two Biochemic remedies together or at the same time.

When the two specified salts are dissolved in one liquid in ponderable quantities, the combination by double decomposition is but a partial one; but when minimum doses come in contact with each other in a relatively large quantity of fluid, complete (rearrangement of molecules) may take place.

C

SPECIAL GUIDE:

When to Use the Inorganic Tissue-Formers.

Febrile and Inflammatory Conditions.

For inflammatory and catarrhal fevers *Ferric phosphate* is the remedy.

Potassium phosphate is the remedy for nervous fever, characterized by high temperature, quick and irregular pulse, nervous excitement, or great weakness and depression, etc.

Exudations.

(*a*) Fibrinous exudations require *Potassium chloride.*
(*b*) Serous, poor in albumen—*Sodium chloride.*
,, rich in albumen—*Calcium phosphate.*
(*c*) Serous-mattery—*Potassium sulphate.*
(*d*) Serous, tinged with blood, } *Potassium phos-*
,, ichorous, fœtid, } *phate.*
(*e*) Mattery, } *Calcium sulphate.*
,, tinged with blood, }

When a fibrinous exudation in the subcutaneous or interstitial connective tissue is not absorbed by the action of *Potassium chloride*, and suppuration ensues, *Silica* should be employed. This promotes suppuration, and in most cases matter breaks through to the outside. When this has taken place, or the abscess has had to be opened by an incision, the use of *Silica* must be continued as long as it is indicated by the existence of infiltrated parts in the abscess. When suppuration and discharge of matter continues in the absence of such parts, *Calcium sulphate* is then the remedy. When the matter becomes ichorous and of bad odour, *Potassium phosphate* should be used.

When a fibrinous exudation is not dissolved by suppuration, but has become hardened, *Calcium fluoride* must be given.

Inflammation of the Serous Membranes.

In Meningitis, Pleurisy, Pericarditis, Endocarditis, and Peritonitis, *Ferric phosphate* is required in the first stage: for further treatment see under "Exudations."

Pneumonia—Inflammation of the Lungs.

Congestion, pleurisy, pleuro-pneumonia, and Costal pleuritis, all require:

In the first or hyperæmic stage, *Ferric phosphate*. For further treatment see under "Exudations."

Bronchitis.

Ferric phosphate in Bronchitis or inflammation of the bronchial tubes or windpipe (chronic or acute). For further treatment, the same remedies apply as in "Diseases of the Mucous Membranes."

Articular Rheumatism and Gout.

Acute Articular Rheumatism and Gout require *Sodium phosphate*. This remedy applies also in chronic rheumatic-gouty swellings of the joints.

Muscular Rheumatism must be treated by the remedies indicated in the paragraph "Rheumatic pains in the limbs and back, etc."

Diseases of the Kidney.

Inflammation of the Kidney—*Ferric phosphate, Potassium chloride.*

Bright's Disease—*Calcium phosphate, Potassium phosphate.*

Disease of the Kidneys after Scarlatina—*Potassium sulphate.*

Gravel of the Kidneys—*Sodium phosphate.*

Puerperal (Childbed) Fever.

The specific remedy of this disease is *Potassium phosphate.*

Typhus Fever.

The specific remedy for typhus fever is *Potassium phosphate.* Low delirium or stupor require *Sodium chloride* as secondary remedy.

Typhoid or Enteric Fever.

In typhoid the following remedies have to be considered :—*Potassium phosphate, Ferric phosphate, Potassium sulphate, Potassium chloride,* and *Calcium sulphate.* Compare "Typhoid adynamic symptoms."

Typhoid Adynamic Symptoms.

When, during an acute disease, accompanied by fever, such as diphtheria, scarlatina, small-pox, and so on, sopor (drowsiness) set in, or there be parched tongue, twitchings, watery vomiting, etc., *Sodium chloride* will be required. If there be sordes, a brown dirty-looking deposit on the teeth, putrid-smelling stools, septic bleedings, *Potassium phosphate* must be given.

Diphtheria.

Ferric phosphate subdues the fever, *Potassium chloride* the plastic exudation, deposit on tonsils and throat, or false membrane.

When vomiting of watery fluids, or watery diarrhœa set in, *Sodium chloride* must be given, or *Sodium sulphate* when there are symptoms to indicate it, and when the water vomited is greenish.

Potassium phosphate is indicated in decidedly foul gangrenous conditions.

This remedy cures the phenomena of paralysis, which often remain after an attack of diphtheria: *e.g.*, speaking nasally, squinting, etc.

Under no circumstances should other remedies, such as Lime Water, Carbolic Acid, Iced Water, etc., be used along with these remedies, because they may interfere with the proper action of these salts. Should an affection of the larynx have set in, in consequence of neglect or inappropriate treatment, *Calcium phosphate* or *Calcium fluoride* must be given.

Croup.

First of all give *Potassium chloride*. If this remedy does not suffice, *Calcium phosphate* or *Calcium fluoride* may be considered necessary as indicated by the symptoms.

Dysentery.

Ferric phosphate and *Potassium chloride* suffice in most cases.

Should delirium or tympanitis supervene, and the stools have a putrid odour, then *Potassium phosphate* suits; as also, if there be no symptoms of decay, but pure blood is passed with the stools.

For crampy, abdominal pains, when warmth, pressure, and doubling up are agreeable, give *Magnesium phosphate.*

Scarlet Fever (Scarlatina).

In mild cases *Ferric phosphate* and *Potassium chloride* are alone sufficient. Malignant cases must be treated by reference to the remarks under the headings "Diphtheria" and "Typhoid adynamic symptoms."

Post-scarlatinal Dropsy requires *Potassium sulphate.*

Small-pox.

Potassium chloride is the principal remedy. When adynamic symptoms arise, and those indicating blood decomposition, *Potassium phosphate* must be given. Confluence of pustules, salivation, and sopor require *Sodium chloride.*

Measles.

The symptoms which accompany measles must indicate the remedies.

Generally *Ferric phosphate*, *Potassium chloride*, and *Potassium sulphate* have chiefly to be considered.

Head and Face Aches [Neuralgic Rheumatic].

Stitching pain, pressure, or throbbing, aggravated by shaking of the head, by stooping, or, in fact, by every movement—*Ferric phosphate.*

Pains, accompanied by flushing and heat of the face —*Ferric phosphate.*

Pains, with vomiting of bile—*Sodium sulphate.*

Pains, with vomiting of transparent phlegm, mucus, or water—*Sodium chloride.*

Pains, with vomiting of food—*Ferric phosphate.*

Pains, with vomiting, hawking up of white mucus—*Potassium chloride.*

Pains, vivid, shooting, darting—intermittent and changing about—*Magnesium phosphate.*

Pains, of pale, sensitive, irritable [excitable] persons —*Potassium phosphate.*

Pains, fits of, with ensuing exhaustion—*Potassium phosphate.*

Pains which are worse in a warm room, and in the evening; better in the open, cool air—*Potassium sulphate.*

Pains, accompanied by the appearance of small lumps, nodules the size of a pea, upon the scalp—*Silica.*

Pains, with frothy, clear mucus covering the tongue, and torpid [constipated] bowels—*Sodium chloride.*

Pains, periodic, daily recurring, with an abundant flow of scalding tears—*Sodium chloride.*

Intermittent fever (veiled), showing itself as neuralgia of the head or facial neuralgia—*Sodium sulphate* or eventually *Sodium chloride.*

Pains with a creeping sensation, feeling of coldness or of numbness—*Calcium phosphate.*

Children's headaches, as a rule, are readily cured with *Ferric phosphate.*

Head, Scalp.

Dandriff and falling off of the hair require *Potassium sulphate* and *Sodium chloride* externally.

Alopecia areata—*Potassium phosphate.*

Herpes tonsurans—*Sodium sulphate.*

Comotio Cerebri (Disturbances of Brain Functions).

In concussion the functional *depression* of the affected brain-cells may require *Potassium phosphate.*

Hydrocephalic conditions—*Calcium phosphate.*

Hydrocephalus, chronic—*Calcium phosphate.*

Cephalatomata—*Calcium fluoride.*

Cranial tabes—*Calcium phosphate.*

Fontanelles remaining too long open—*Calcium phosphate.*

If in any of these diseases putrid-smelling stools occur, *Potassium phosphate* must be given as an intercurrent remedy.

Delirium Tremens.

Most cases are readily cured by *Sodium chloride.* Should the latter not suffice, give *Potassium phosphate* alternately.

Vertigo (Giddiness),

if occasioned by pressure of blood, is cured by *Ferric phosphate;* nervous vertigo by *Potassium phosphate.* The coating of the tongue must also be considered, if there be any gastric (stomach) disturbance.

Ears.

Ear-ache, noises in the ears or dulness of hearing, arising from hyperæmia (excess of blood), requires *Ferric phosphate.*

Nervous affections must be individualized, and may require *Magnesium phosphate, Calcium phosphate, Potassium phosphate.*

Inflammatory ear-ache requires *Ferric phosphate.*

Inflammatory swelling of the external meatus—*Silica.*

Discharge of thin yellow fluid from the ear—*Potassium sulphate.*

Discharge of thick yellow matter—*Calcium sulphate* and *Silica.*

Deafness, caused by swelling and catarrh of the Eustachian tubes and external meatus—*Potassium chloride, Sodium chloride.*

If reasons exist to surmise that the dulness of hearing is caused by an indurated (hardened) exudation of the inner ear—*Silica* and *Calcium fluoride* have to be given.

Mumps.

Potassium chloride; and with abundant saliva—*Sodium chloride.*

Should metastasis (orchitis) occur, *Sodium chloride* must also be taken.

Toothache.

With involuntary flow of tears—*Sodium chloride.*

With abundant flow of saliva—*Sodium chloride.*

With swelling of the gums—*Potassium chloride*, and if necessary, *Silica;* when the swelling is as hard as bone, *Calcium fluoride.*

With pains which change or dart about, are intermittent and easier with warmth—*Magnesium phosphate.*

Pains, which are easier with pressure but improved by slight touch—*Magnesium phosphate.*

With pains which are aggravated in the warm room, and in the evening, but better in the open cool air—*Potassium sulphate.*

With flushed cheek, aggravated by warm, relieved by cold fluids—*Ferric phosphate.*

With easily bleeding gums, or if gums have a bright red seam—*Potassium phosphate.*

When the aching tooth is loose; when the slightest touch on the surface of the tooth is painful—*Calcium fluoride.*

Complaints of Children during Dentition.

For difficulty in cutting of teeth—*Calcium phosphate* and especially *Calcium fluoride.*

When fever is present—*Ferric phosphate.* Cramps with fever—*Ferric phosphate.* Cramps without fever—*Magnesium phosphate* and *Calcium phosphate.* Inflammation of the eye—*Ferric phosphate, Calcium phosphate.* Dribbling [at mouth]—*Sodium chloride.* Spasm of the glottis—*Magnesium phosphate.* Spasmodic cough—*Magnesium phosphate.* Spasm of the bladder—*Magnesium phosphate.* Diarrhœa, see heading "Diarrhœa."

Eyes.

On the eyelids specks of matter—*Potassium chloride;* on the eyelids yellow crusts of matter—*Potassium chloride, Potassium sulphate.*

On the cornea a blister—*Potassium chloride, Sodium chloride.*

Flat abscess of cornea, proceeding from a blister—*Potassium chloride.*

Deep ulcer of the cornea—*Silica, Calcium sulphate.*

Spot on the cornea—*Sodium chloride.* The spots must be sprayed or moistened several times a day with a dilute solution of *Sodium chloride.* The molecules of this salt which remain on the spot cause, by their hygroscopic nature, a gradual moistening and absorption of the spot.

Secretion of yellow, greenish matter—*Potassium chloride, Potassium sulphate.*

Yellow, creamy secretions—*Sodium phosphate.*

Inflammation in the eyes of new-born infants—*Sodium phosphate* internally and externally.

White mucous secretions—*Potassium chloride.*

Inflammation of the eyes in the strumous or scrofulous—*Calcium phosphate.*

Light, transparent, mucous secretion, with acrid, smarting tears—*Sodium chloride.*

Yellow, slimy matter—*Potassium sulphate.*

Thick yellow matter—*Calcium sulphate, Silica.*

Great redness with severe pain, without mucus or matter—*Ferric phosphate.*

Pains in the eye, recurring daily at certain times, with flow of tears—*Sodium chloride.*

Styes [hordeoli], small lumps and indurations on the eyelids—*Silica.*

Spasms of the eyelids [cramps]—*Magnesium phosphate* and *Calcium phosphate.*

Spasmodic squinting—*Magnesium phosphate.*

Diplopia, sparks and rainbow colours before the eye, seeing many colours—*Magnesium phosphate* and *Sodium phosphate* used internally and externally.

Weak sight after diphtheria—*Potassium phosphate.*

Sensitiveness to light from exertion of the sight—*Potassium phosphate* internally and externally.

Weak sight, after suppression of perspiration of feet—*Silica.*

Hypopion—*Calcium sulphate, Silica.*

Retina, exudation—*Potassium chloride.* In the first stages of the inflammation of the retina, *Ferric phosphate.*

Inflammation of the cornea—*Potassium chloride* exudation white or grayish white; gold colour—*Sodium phosphate.*

Cavity of Mouth.

CATARRHAL INFLAMMATION of the MUCOUS MEMBRANE covering the soft palate, tonsils, and pharynx.

If there is dry redness [inflammatory] or violent pain—*Ferric phosphate.*

If white exudation—*Potassium chloride.*

If a creamy, golden-yellow exudation—*Sodium phosphate.*

If transparent, frothy mucus—*Sodium chloride.*

If tonsils are enlarged or swollen—*Potassium chloride* will suit best, if there is a white or grayish-white coating on the tonsils.

If suppuration threatens and matter forms—*Silica.*

In chronic enlargement of the tonsils the proper remedy is *Calcium phosphate.*

Inflamed Uvula requires *Sodium chloride.*

INFLAMMATION OF TONGUE.—If much swollen and of a deep, dusky red, *Ferric phosphate.* In most cases this will suffice. If not, *Potassium chloride.* When matter discharges—*Calcium sulphate, Silica.* For indurations—*Silica, Calcium fluoride.*

Scurvy; gangrenous—*Potassium phosphate.*

Cancrum oris (canker of the mouth)—*Potassium phosphate.*

GUMS.—If the gum be pale—*Calcium phosphate* is specially indicated: if it has a bright red edge, *Potassium phosphate* is required. The latter medicine is also required in bleeding and hæmorrhage from the gums.

Coatings of the Tongue.

A white, not slimy, covering requires *Potassium chloride.* Slimy coating, and small bubbles of saliva on the edges—*Sodium chloride.*

Tongue clean and moist, slimy—*Sodium chloride.*

Tongue if dirty brownish, grayish green, with a bitter taste in the mouth—*Sodium sulphate.*

Tongue, as if spread with liquid dark mustard, brownish, and offensive breath—*Potassium phosphate.*

Tongue covered with yellow slime—*Potassium sulphate.*

The coating of the tongue does not always wholly influence the choice of a remedy in all affections of the tissues. It has, however, to be taken into consideration in those cases where I have taken note of it in this volume. If anyone who is suffering from a chronic catarrh of the stomach, takes also another (acute) disease, the coating of the tongue will not always have that peculiar appearance which will indicate the remedy suited to the acute disease.

If any disease—particularly of a chronic nature—shows itself without decisive symptoms, then the coating of the tongue will, in most cases, guide in the choice of an appropriate remedy.

Aphthæ and Stomatitis require *Potassium chloride, Potassium phosphate;* and *Sodium chloride* when there is much dribbling of saliva.

Noma requires *Potassium phosphate.*

Vomiting.

Vomiting of food—*Ferric phosphate, Calcium fluoride.*

Vomiting of food and acid fluids—*Ferric phosphate.*

Vomiting of bile—*Sodium sulphate.*

Vomiting of stringy transparent mucus—*Sodium chloride.*

Vomiting of watery fluid—*Sodium chloride.*

Vomiting of blood—*Ferric phosphate, Potassium chloride,* and *Sodium phosphate.*

Hawking up of white mucus—*Potassium chloride.*

Vomiting of acid fluids or curdy masses—*Sodium phosphate.*

Jaundice.

In every case give *Sodium sulphate* first. In most cases of Jaundice this will suffice. Next rank *Potassium chloride, Potassium sulphate,* and *Sodium chloride,* which have to be given according to the secondary symptoms.

When it arises from a gastro-duodenal catarrh, *Potassium chloride* and *Sodium chloride* will be required. The coating of the tongue must determine the choice of either remedy.

Pains in Stomach and Abdomen.

GASTRITIS.—Acute Inflammation of the Stomach, with violent pains of the distended organ, vomiting, and fever—*Ferric phosphate.*

When a case has come too late under treatment, and there are symptoms of exhaustion, dryness of tongue, etc., *Potassium phosphate* will have to be given.

ACUTE AND CHRONIC PAINS OF THE STOMACH, which grow worse on taking food, or by pressing on the pit of the stomach, and particularly when vomiting of food occurs—*Ferric phosphate.*

Spasms, cramping of the stomach, with clean tongue, requires *Magnesium phosphate.*

Pains with a crampy [spasmodic] tight drawing lacing sensation as of a band—*Magnesium phosphate.*

Pains of the stomach, with accumulation of water in the mouth—*Sodium chloride.* If this does not altogether suffice, there exists generally a coating of the tongue, which requires *Potassium sulphate* or *Potassium chloride.*

PRESSURE, and a SENSATION OF FULNESS, with YELLOW SLIMY coating of the tongue—*Potassium sulphate.*

Gnawing pains in the stomach, with flatulence [short belching of wind], affording no relief—*Magnesium phosphate.*

Colic, which is relieved slightly by eructations, by doubling up the body [bending double], rubbing, and by hot applications, requires *Magnesium phosphate.*

Colicky pain about the umbilicus, obliging the patient to bend double—*Magnesium phosphate.*

Flatulent colic of little children, which causes them to draw up their legs, with or without diarrhœa—*Magnesium phosphate ;* and if there be acidity—*Sodium phosphate* must be given.

For pains of indigestion, accompanied by vomiting, the nature of the ejected matter indicates the remedy.

Gastric affection, with predominating acidity, heart-burn—*Sodium phosphate.*

Ulcers, gastric, ulceration of stomach—*Sodium phosphate.*

Diarrhœa.

Diarrhœa—watery, slimy, transparent evacuations—*Sodium chloride.*

Diarrhœa—evacuations like rice-water—*Potassium phosphate.*

Diarrhœa—putrid smelling—*Potassium phosphate.*

Diarrhœa—watery, bilious—*Sodium sulphate.*

Diarrhœa—mixed with blood or blood and slime—*Potassium chloride.*

Diarrhœa—mattery, or blood and matter—*Calcium sulphate.*

Diarrhœa—stools of undigested food—*Ferric phosphate.*

Diarrhœa—caused by excessive acidity—*Sodium phosphate.*

Worms.

Sodium phosphate is of use in many cases for thread or round worms, probably by destroying the lactic acid which seems to be necessary for the life of these worms. [After a course of this remedy for obstinate acidity a dead tape-worm was passed.]

Hæmorrhoids (Piles).

The principal remedy is *Calcium fluoride.* (See p. 24.) As a rule, besides the local Hæmorrhoids, there are present disturbances in the function of the liver, the digestive organs, etc.; these stand in close connection with the former; attention must be paid to those disturbances if a radical cure of hæmorrhoids (piles) is to be ensured.

Calcium fluoride has, therefore, to be taken alternately with another remedy, the choice of which is determined by the characteristics of the secondary symptoms. The remedies which will have to be most frequently considered are:—*Ferric phosphate, Sodium chloride, Sodium phosphate, Sodium sulphate,* and *Potassium sulphate.*

Magnesium phosphate dissolved in water and applied externally or locally will relieve excessive pain.

Diabetes Mellitus.[1]

Sugar must be decomposed into carbonic acid and water by oxygen which is being liberated. (See p. 25.)

[1] This disease was without its specific remedy in the Abridged Therapeutics until I brought it in my Index before the profession.

Boericke and Dewey, Philadelphia, have issued a book called "The Twelve Tissue Remedies," in which they copy from my translation although copyright. They give Dr. Schüssler as the authority, and the quotations they make are from *my* Therapeutical Index,

The sulphates as carriers of oxygen. Perhaps *Potassium sulphate* and *Calcium sulphate* may also serve as remedies in Diabetes.

---

p. 54, but *wrongly* quoted. Neither they nor Dr. S. seem quite clear on what I stated there as regards the pathological and chemico-physiological conditions which underlie Diabetes, else they would have given them correctly, or would probably before this have devoted some lines to this important and hitherto incurable disease. It may be interesting to some to know that breathing carbonic oxide can set up glycosuria.

In my Index I state that lactic acid (composed of carbonic acid and water) has to be decomposed on its way to the lungs. This we know is done in health by *Sodium phosphate*, which, after fixing loosely the carbonic acid, carries it to the lungs to be exhaled and exchanged for oxygen. But where an excess of lactic acid is being decomposed, there arises also an excess of water, the elimination and regulation of which is controlled and effected exclusively by *Sodium sulphate*. If the liver is also at fault, as some pathologists affirm, *Sodium sulphate* molecules again will allay any such disturbance. Dr. Charteris and others state that a uric acid condition in which uric acid is in excess and deposited in the urine always precedes the developed stage of Diabetes mellitus. Hence *Sodium phosphate* may be indicated as a prophylactic.

Sodium sulphate, the specific remedy for Diabetes, not only regulates the waste water, but under certain conditions can give off additional oxygen to the blood. Oxygen is necessary for the process of decomposing the sugar. This sulphate is one of the salts which can serve as a carrier of liberated oxygen of the blood.

I have lately given *Ferric phosphate* and *Sodium phosphate* to diabetic patients before and after food as an additional tonic, and with very good results, and *Potassium phosphate* as indicated in Therapeutical Index, under section No. 6, for *sleeplessness*, etc. The strict *regimen* in diet had only to be insisted on for a little time. The cures have been complete in each instance. *Sodium sulphate* was given as the chief remedy. Here dilutions are preferable without any sacchar lactis.

An objection has been made to my giving in the Therapeutical Index *Sodium phosphate* for a certain "Headache." In that Index I give *Sodium phosphate* for headache which arises from taking thick sour milk. (What objection can be taken to this?) Lactic acid is in excess in such milk, and *Sodium phosphate* is the cell salt which decomposes lactic acid, whether the latter be in the intercellular fluid, the blood corpuscles, the muscle, or nerve or brain cells. Those very depressing headaches which are frequently located on the fontanelles or at the back of the head, also those called "gouty headaches," often affecting the eyeballs, come under this category. I have cured such and others by *Sodium phosphate*.

M. D. Walker.

I have used *Sodium sulphate* with success for this complaint. My experience is confirmed—

(1) By two successful cures communicated to me from Scotland.

(2) By a notice in an Italian work, by Dr. Brentano, saying "Il dottor Aegidi l'amministro con pieno successo in un caso di diabete mellito:" Dr. Aegidi administered *Sodium sulphate* with complete success in a case of diabetes mellitus.

Coryza, Nasal Catarrh, Cold in the Head.

Cold in the head, stopped, dry, stuffy, requires *Potassium chloride* and *Calcium fluoride.*

Fluent coryza or running cold, with watery or clear slimy secretion—*Sodium chloride.*

Secretion, yellow slimy—*Potassium sulphate.*

Secretion, thick, mattery—*Calcium sulphate.*

Ozæna requires *Potassium phosphate* internally, and also applications of the same on the mucous lining of the nose, when the disease is seated in the membrane. When the disease is located in the periosteum or in the sub-mucous connective tissue—*Silica.* If the diagnosis be doubtful, the remedies should be used alternately.

Hoarseness.

Simple hoarseness from cold—*Potassium chloride;* rarely *Potassium sulphate* is required. When caused by over-exertion of the vocal organs (as in speakers, actors, singers), *Ferric phosphate* is most useful; if necessary, also *Potassium phosphate.*

Coughs.

Short, acute, spasmodic, very painful, require *Ferric phosphate,* then *Potassium chloride;* the true spasmodic cough—*Magnesium phosphate.*

D

Cough with expectoration of mucus, etc., see section on "Diseases of the Mucous Membrane."

Asthma.

The remedies for nervous asthma are *Potassium phosphate* and *Magnesium phosphate;* the latter particularly when troublesome flatulence occurs. In asthma, with much excess of mucus, *Sodium chloride* must be used when the mucus is transparent or frothy; *Potassium chloride,* when the mucus is yellow and easily coughed up; *Potassium chloride,* when the secretion is white; and *Calcium fluoride,* when after great exertions small yellowish lumps (plugs) are brought up. *Sodium sulphate* is the remedy when the expectoration is green.

Whooping Cough.

In the inflammatory catarrhal stage, *Ferric phosphate;* for the nervous, spasmodic affection, the whoop—*Magnesium phosphate. Ferric phosphate* must be taken when there is vomiting of food. According to the nature of the mucus there may have to be chosen *Potassium chloride, Sodium chloride,* or *Potassium sulphate.*

Special symptoms may necessitate the intercurrent use of a special remedy—such as *Potassium phosphate,* or *Calcium phosphate.*

Acute Œdema of the Lungs.

Dyspnœa, lividity of face, spasmodic cough with frothy expectoration of serous masses, require *Potassium phosphate* and *Sodium chloride.*

Diseases of the Mucous Membrane.

The colour and the consistency of the secretion discharged from the mucous lining must decide the choice of the remedy.

Secretion when fibrinous—*Potassium chloride.*
,, ,, albuminous—*Calcium phosphate.*
,, ,, yellowish with small tough plugs, lumps—*Calcium fluoride.*
,, ,, yellow, like gold—*Sodium phosphate.*
,, ,, yellow—*Potassium sulphate.*
,, ,, green—*Sodium sulphate.*
,, ,, clear, transparent—*Sodium chloride.*
,, ,, mattery—*Calcium sulphate.*
,, ,, very offensive smelling — *Potassium phosphate.*
,, ,, causing soreness and chafing—*Sodium chloride* and *Potassium phosphate.*

The choice of the remedies has to be made in accordance with the above distinctions or differentiations in Coughs with expectoration; Leucorrhœa or "whites"; Coryza or Cold in the head, and Bronchial catarrh or Cold in the chest, etc.

Inflammation and Catarrh of the Bladder.

In acute cases, first of all *Ferric phosphate,* then *Potassium chloride.* Chronic cases require *Sodium chloride* or *Potassium sulphate.* See above, "Diseases of the Mucous Membrane."

Suppression of Urine.

When spasm, cramp, is the cause of the retention or suppression of urine, *Magnesium phosphate* is the remedy. *Ferric phosphate* cures the suppression of urine, accompanied by heat, as in little children.

Involuntary Micturition at Night.

If the complaint is due to an affection of the nerves *Potassium phosphate* and *Calcium phosphate* must be used; if of the muscles—*Ferric phosphate.* In most cases *Potassium phosphate* is suitable. For children who suffer from worms—*Sodium phosphate* may be given.

Eczema. Diseases of the Skin.

The remedies recommended for the mucous membrane are equally suitable for the diseases of the skin. Eczema, lichen, etc., are included. Eruption of Vesicles (blisters) with

Serous-fibrinous contents	...	*Potassium chloride.*
Albuminous ,,	...	*Calcium phosphate.*
Clear, watery ,,	...	*Sodium chloride.*
Yellow,honey-col'red,,	...	*Sodium phosphate.*
Yellowish, watery ,,	...	*Sodium sulphate.*
Mattery ,,	...	*Calcium sulphate.*

Vesicles containing blood or ichor—*Potassium phosphate.*

Pustules on an infiltrated base containing matter require *Silica.*

The scaly condition of the skin after the vesicles have burst, when forming into large or small scales or crusts (scabs) requires the following treatment:—

Deposit flour-like ...	...	*Potassium chloride.*
Yellowish-white crusts	...	*Calcium phosphate.*
White scales	...	*Sodium chloride.*
Yellow, honey-coloured	...	*Sodium phosphate.*
Yellowish scales ...	...	*Sodium sulphate.*
Scabs, crusts of yellow matter		*Calcium phosphate.*

Crusts of yellow pus (matter) on an infiltrated (festering) base—*Silica.*

Offensive-smelling greasy scales or scabs—*Potassium phosphate.*

Epidermis, skin, peeling freely on a sticky base or surface—*Potassium sulphate.*

Hard skin on the palms of the hands, with or without fissures, cracks—*Calcium fluoride.*

Swelling or enlargement of sebaceous glands—*Sodium chloride.*

Inflammation and suppuration of the same—*Silica* and eventually *Calcium sulphate.*

Eczema eruptions which are moist require one or other of the Sodium salts ; the distinctive colour as given above must decide the choice.

Eczema or eruptions occurring after vaccination with unhealthy vaccine lymph require *Potassium chloride.*

Soreness, chafing of skin, as in little children, requires *Sodium phosphate* or *Sodium chloride.* When an offensive-smelling diarrhœa accompanies this soreness of skin *Potassium phosphate* must be given.

Nettle-rash requires *Potassium phosphate.*

Itching of the skin — *Magnesium phosphate* and *Potassium phosphate.*

Cracks of the skin, chaps, fissures—*Calcium fluoride.*

Erysipelas, " Rose."—The œdematous puffy inflammation of the skin requires *Sodium sulphate;* infiltrated or blistering erysipelas is cured by *Potassium chloride.*

Herpes zoster (shingles) requires *Potassium phosphate* and *Sodium chloride.*

Severe symptoms of fever and inflammation may accompany erysipelatous affections, and thus require *Ferric phosphate.*

Potassium sulphate assists desquamation, scaling of the skin.

Pemphigus.—Common pemphigus, blisters (blebs) of various sizes, with yellow watery contents and tense surface, requires *Sodium sulphate;* clear watery contents— *Sodium chloride.* Malignant pemphigus (blisters with watery - bloody contents and withered, wrinkled surface) requires *Potassium phosphate.*

Burns and Scalds, of the first and second degrees, require *Potassium chloride.* If suppurating, *Calcium sulphate.*

Chilblains, when recent (new) *Potassium phosphate.* If suppurating, *Calcium sulphate.*

When at the commencement of any inflammation of the skin or subcutaneous tissue, *Ferric phosphate* is given, the disease can be prevented, or blighted in the onset. If that stage has passed in which this remedy is indicated, *Potassium chloride* must be given.

Suppurating (matter forming) requires *Silica, Calcium sulphate.* When the pus is ichorus, dirty-looking, or has a heavy smell, *Potassium phosphate* must be given. Proud flesh requires *Potassium chloride.* Inflammation of the fingers is treated in the same manner.

Carbuncles require *Potassium phosphate.* Whitlow —*Silica.* Hard scorbutic infiltrations of subcutaneous tissues are cured by *Potassium chloride.* Scorbutic hæmorrhages require *Potassium phosphate.*

Ingrown toe-nails require *Potassium chloride* and local surgical treatment.

Lupus—*Potassium chloride* and *Calcium phosphate,* also externally.

Epithelioma—*Potassium sulphate.*

Effects of the bites or stings of insects—*Sodium chloride* (used externally).

Warts on the hands—*Potassium chloride.* Dissolve a quantity as large as a pea of the triturated powder in a tablespoonful of water, and moisten the part with this solution.

Mastitis, Inflammation of the Breasts.

Potassium chloride is indicated for the hard swelling of the breasts before matter has formed ; when it has formed, and during its discharge, *Silica* is indicated. (For further treatment, see Exudations, p. 34.)

Lymphatic Glands.

For acute infiltration (swelling), *Potassium chloride.* Chronic cases of swollen glands require as chief remedy—*Calcium phosphate.* If inclined to suppurate —*Silica;* and during suppuration, *Calcium sulphate* is required; and *Calcium fluoride* when the edges round the suppurating parts are callous (hard).

Bronchocele, goitre, require *Calcium phosphate, Sodium chloride.*

Chancre and Gonorrhœa.

CHANCRE.—The principal remedy for the soft chancre is *Potassium chloride;* the phagedenic—*Potassium phosphate;* the hard—*Calcium fluoride.* These remedies externally and internally.

Chronic syphilis requires *Potassium chloride, Potassium sulphate, Sodium chloride, Sodium sulphate, Calcium sulphate, Silica,* and *Calcium fluoride,* according to the symptoms.

Gonorrhœa, the chief remedy—*Potassium chloride.* When the secretion consists of blood and pus—*Calcium sulphate;* when yellow slimy—*Potassium sulphate.*

Discharge of blood requires *Potassium phosphate;* later stages, gleet—*Sodium chloride, Calcium phosphate.*

Besides the external use of the remedy corresponding to the symptoms, it is advisable, after urination, to bathe and syringe the parts twice daily with the same remedy dissolved in tepid soft water.

Orchitis requires *Ferric phosphate, Potassium chloride,* and possibly *Calcium phosphate.*

Induration (hardening) of testicles—*Calcium fluoride.*

Scrotal œdema—*Sodium chloride.*

Preputial œdema—*Sodium sulphate.*

Gonorrhœa glans penis, blanitis—*Potassium phosphate* externally and internally.

Hydrocele—*Calcium phosphate;* of old standing—*Calcium flouride.*

Accidents. Mechanical Injuries.

Bruises, cuts, and other fresh wounds, and sprains, require, at once, *Ferric phosphate.* If, after the use of this, any swelling of the contused parts remain, give *Potassium chloride.* If suppuration sets in, in neglected cases, give *Silica,* or, if necessary, *Calcium sulphate.* Ichor or mortification necessitate *Potassium phosphate;* exuberant granulations or proud flesh—*Potassium chloride.*

Fractures of bone require (along with surgical treatment) at first, for injuries of the soft parts—*Ferric phosphate;* then *Calcium phosphate* to promote the formation of callus, or new bony matter, to unite the fractured bone.

TENALGIA CREPITANS (painful crackling of the tendons), which occurs on the dorsal side of the lower arm above the wrist in the case of carpenters and other artisans, by pressing the chisel or other tool too hard in a rotatory motion against the material on which they were working: I cured this rapidly in two cases by means of *Ferric phosphate.*

A third case, which had become chronic under ordinary treatment, I cured easily with *Potassium chloride,* after *Ferric phosphate* proved ineffectual.

Ulcers of the Lower Limbs.

Under this head any of the remedies given for Diseases of the skin and mucous membrane may be required.

Calcium fluoride cures varicose ulceration.

Diseases of the Bone.

When the surrounding *soft parts* are red, inflamed, hot, and painful, use *Ferric phosphate.* Against ulceration of bone—*Silica, Calcium sulphate,* and

Calcium phosphate. Exudations from the bone, forming hard, rough, corrugated elevations on the bone surface require *Calcium fluoride.* This remedy is even better than *Silica* in cases of Cephalhæmatomata (so-called blood-tumours) on the parietal bones of new-born children.

RICKETS—*Calcium phosphate.* If atrophy ensues, with foul diarrhœa, this condition must first be subdued by *Potassium phosphate.* Should there be any excess of acidity, it must be removed by *Sodium phosphate.*

Some physicians, *e.g.*, Dr. Kassowitz, of Vienna, and Professor Hagenbach, in Berne, use phosphorus[1] in minimum doses as a remedy for Rickets.

R. Phosphori. - - -	$\frac{1}{100}$ grain.
Solve in Olei. amygd. dulc. -	10 grains.
Pulv. gumm. arab. - -	5 grains.
Syr. simplex. - - -	5 grains.
Aqua. destill. - - -	80 grains.

The above prescription is of a strength corresponding to a third decimal dilution; taken in teaspoonfuls the quantity of phosphorus per dose is even less.

When such a phosphorus solution is used the cure is not direct, but is effected in the following way:

The phosphorus molecules unite in the organism with molecules of oxygen and form phosphoric acid. The latter unites with the molecules of the *carbonate* of lime, and then only by driving off the carbonic acid becomes *Calcium phosphate.*

This treatment agrees both quantitatively and in its general character with that given in this book, when *Calcium phosphate* is taken in the third decimal trituration or solution.

But as some of the molecules of phosphorus or phosphoric acid find an opportunity while on their

[1] Sidney Ringer, M.D., London, finds even $\frac{1}{30}$ gr. of phosphorus to cause sickness and jaundice, and often to injure the lungs.

way to the rickety bone to combine with molecules of various carbonates (*e.g.*, of sodium, magnesium, or potassium), perhaps only a quarter of the dose of phosphorus intended for the diseased bone reaches it. The possibility of the *carbonate* molecules using up all the phosphorus may explain the failures which occur in this treatment. If *Calcium phosphate* itself be administered there is less likelihood of failure, because it does not enter into combination with *any* of the above-mentioned salts.

Hip-joint disease—*Ferric phosphate* first, then *Silica.*

Spina ventosa—*Calcium fluoride* alternately with *Magnesium phosphate.*

Anæmia, Chlorosis (Bloodlessness).

The remedy of genuine *anæmia* and *chlorosis* is *Calcium phosphate.*

Conditions resembling chlorosis require *Sodium chloride* and *Potassium phosphate*, the choice to be decided by the characteristic accompanying symptoms.

Potassium phosphate cures pallor or bloodlessness, which has been caused by long-continued strain depressing the mind.

Hæmorrhage (Bleeding).

Blood, red, readily coagulating into a jelly-like mass —*Ferric phosphate.*

Black, thick, tough blood requires *Potassium chloride.*

Black red or blackish-red, but thin and watery, not coagulating—*Potassium phosphate* and *Sodium chloride.*

Epistaxis, bleeding from the nose (in children), is, as a rule, generally cured by *Ferric phosphate.* Predisposition to nasal hæmorrhages—*Potassium phosphate.*

Uterine hæmorrhage, chiefly *Calcium fluoride* and *Potassium phosphate.*

Hæmorrhoidal bleedings—*Ferric phosphate, Potassium chloride* and *Calcium fluoride.*

Menstruation.

The remedies for Menstrual disorders must be selected in accordance with the attending symptoms, such as colour, consistency, etc. In leucorrhœa, "whites," then the peculiarity of the discharge must indicate the remedy.

Labour Pains.

Irregular, weak pains require *Potassium phosphate.*

Spasmodic, crampy pains—*Magnesium phosphate.*

Menstrual Colic.

Magnesium phosphate suits this colic generally. *Potassium phosphate* suits sensitive, irritable, pale, or lachrymose persons.

With accelerated pulse, increased redness of face, etc.—*Ferric phosphate* is to be given.

VAGINISMUS—*Ferric phosphate, Magnesium phosphate.*

Neuralgia, Rheumatic Pains in the Limbs, the Back, and the Nape of the Neck.

Pains only felt during motion, or made worse by motion—*Ferric phosphate;* second remedy—*Potassium chloride.*

Pains which are laming, making the parts affected feel powerless, gentle movement gradually lessening the stiffness and pain, yet too much exertion increasing the pains (such as walking too far); this kind of pain is always worse after rising from a sitting position at the commencement of movement, and requires *Potassium phosphate.*

Pains, with a feeling of numbness, coldness, or with a creeping sensation worse in the night and during rest, require *Calcium phosphate.*

Pains, vivid, shooting, boring, intermittent, shifting, neuralgic, require *Magnesium phosphate.*

Lumbago—*Ferric phosphate, Calcium phosphate.*

Sciatica—*Potassium phosphate, Calcium phosphate,* as the nature of the pain may be; chronic cases require *Silica.*

Pains which are worse in warm rooms, and in the evening better in open cool air—*Potassium sulphate.*

Pains which the patient cannot describe very clearly, accompanying symptoms must decide the remedy, such as an eruption, coating of the tongue, etc.

Fungoid swelling of the joints, *e.g.,* tumor albus (white swelling), requires *Calcium phosphate.*

For suppurations of the joints—*Calcium sulphate* and *Silica.*

Hygroma patellæ, "Housemaid's knee," requires *Calcium phosphate.*

Hydrops genu—*Calcium phosphate.*

Cysts—*Calcium phosphate.*

Spasms and other Nervous Affections.

Palpitation of the heart requires *Ferric phosphate, Potassium chloride, Sodium chloride, Potassium phosphate, Potassium sulphate,* etc., according to the nature of the accompanying symptoms.

Potassium chloride is almost a specific for epilepsy.

Spasms, fits of anæmic and scrofulous persons require *Calcium phosphate.*

Spasms of the glottis, tetanus, lockjaw, cramp in the legs, St. Vitus's dance, etc., require *Magnesium phosphate* and *Calcium phosphate.*

Ague. Intermittent Fever.

The remedy for ague is *Sodium sulphate.* The applicability of this remedy is shown by the following physiological or pathologico-chemical conditions. In patients suffering from ague the quantity of water in the blood corpuscles and in the blood serum is increased, and consequently less oxygen is taken up by the blood. It has been shown (page 26) that *Sodium sulphate* promotes the removal of excess of water from the organism. When by its action the proportion of water in the blood corpuscles has been made normal, the corpuscles are again able to take up the full amount of oxygen and distribute it to the cells of the tissues.

As the tissues are in this way brought back from their pathological to their normal physiological condition, they are enabled to remove out of the organism the cause of the ague—be it marsh-gas (miasma) or bacteria (fungi).

The quotidian (daily recurring) and the tertian fever require *Sodium sulphate;* the quartan, *Sodium chloride.*

Dry mountain air, which is rich in oxygen, itself can cure ague spontaneously, because the organism takes in a large amount of oxygen and gets rid of much water by exhalations, evaporation.

Ague patients must abstain from milk diet, buttermilk, eggs, fat, and fish.

Dropsy.

Dropsy, if caused by loss of blood or other vital fluids—*Calcium phosphate.*

Post-scarlatinal dropsy—see Disease of the Kidney.

Dropsy, œdema, of the areolar tissues has to be treated with *Sodium sulphate* and *Sodium chloride.*

In dropsy occasioned by cardiac disease, liver, or other diseases, the remedy has to be selected according to the prominence of the accompanying symptoms.

REFUTATION OF OBJECTIONS.

DIFFERENT objections have been made by physicians, who have arraigned my *Abridged System of Therapeutics* before the bar of their judgment, which I now take occasion to refute.

The late Dr. Constantine Hering, of Philadelphia, who informed the American medical profession of the tenor of my therapeutical system in a pamphlet entitled "*The Twelve Tissue Remedies,*" is of the opinion that I should also have embraced carbon and nitrogen among my therapeutical agents. It is, however, well known that neither carbon alone, nor nitrogen alone, enter into the composition of tissue-cells. Carbon and nitrogen are integral parts of the organic substances which form the organic basis of cells. The organic substances are only influenced by inhaled oxygen and by the inorganic salts. Nitrogen and carbon, therefore, remain useless as therapeutical agents.

If, in the animal organism, nitrogen should, or could be wanting, then albuminous substances would be wanting, of which nitrogen is an integral part. Albuminous substances can only be introduced into the body by means of food.

Dr. Hering, also, misses the organic acids in my system of therapeutics. How the organic acids, lactic acid and uric acid, are produced, is already noticed in the paragraph on combustion or oxidation, page 3. —No agricultural chemist would think of giving to a sickly vine the organic acids of the grape, because he knows that an inorganic salt (Potassium carbonate) will be the proper remedy.

Only indistinct conceptions of the chemico-physiological processes of the animal organism could have induced Dr. H. to raise such objections.

Dr. H. further insists that spectroscopic analysis would, in course of time, discover several other as yet unknown substances in the tissues of the human body, which would have to be incorporated among the factors of the tissue-therapeutics.

This assertion would seem as intended, in fact, to render the completeness of my therapeutics unattainable for a long time to come.

If, indeed, spectrum analysis could yet discover substances which do contribute to the formation of tissues, such substances would, of course, have to be incorporated among the agents of the tissue-therapeutics. The inorganic cell-salts already known are, however, able to perform, directly or indirectly, all the functions of the organism.

Another critic insists that there cannot be a strictly defined system of therapeutics applicable to all parts of the world, since each quarter of the globe had its peculiar diseases. To this I must reply that it is not a question of medical nomenclature; but rather that, in a system of tissue-therapeutics, only it is the tissues and their functional disturbances which are to be taken into consideration.

If an Ethiopian has muscles, he certainly has *Potassium chloride, Magnesium phosphate,* and *Iron* in them. A disturbance of the molecules of *Magnesium phosphate* in the muscles of an Ethiopian will produce the same phenomena as in those of a European.

The same critic thinks that all diseases might be cured with oxygen, carbon, nitrogen, and hydrogen, better than with my proposed twelve inorganic tissue-salts. These four elements may, perhaps, suffice in the hands of a necromancer, but they would certainly leave a physician in the lurch.

A third opponent, Dr. von Grauvogl of Munich, has been so warped by his persecuting zeal as to fail to notice the contradictions in which he is involved by his own statements.

He says that with local pathology and local therapeutics no lasting good is accomplished; that disease is not confined to any one part of the organism, but that the whole organism is, in fact, the disease; even tumours, evidently local, could thus be understood. So he speaks, and, in spite of it, treats chondroma with *Silica,* because this substance is contained in the bones. This, surely, is local therapeutics. It cannot be doubted, however, according to my way of thinking, that local therapeutics are correct. If one has dissipated irritation - hyperæmia by its appropriate remedy, the symptoms dependent upon it—pain, fever, general malaise—have disappeared. If, in consequence of an irritation-hyperæmia, an exudation has taken place, again local treatment is required in order to get rid of the exudation, and after its removal the secondary symptoms cease.

If, as Dr. von G. asserts, the whole organism is the disease, then death must, of necessity, be the result of every illness. On page 38 of his book, speaking of the Law of Similars, he says: "From these propositions it follows that the curability or incurability of disease does not shape its course according to its intensity merely; but principally according to the quality, quantity, and relation of the remaining healthy parts." If, according to Dr. von G., the whole organism is the disease, how can there be any talk of "remaining healthy parts"?

Dr. von G. further says that, according to Gorup Besanez, the physiological localities of the chemical constituents of the body were, on the whole, yet unknown, therefore a physiological principle could not be perfected. If Dr. von G. shares these views, what, then, induces him to adopt the expression, "relation of *Silica* to the bones," and consequently to use *Silica* as a remedy in chondroma and rachitis?

"All means of nourishment are also means of function," says Dr. von G. Soon after he thus expresses himself: "Therefore, one can speak of substances as means of function only so far as they are not constituent parts of the body." How does that harmonize?

Dr. von G.'s hobby-horse, "Logic," seems not to be so well ridden by him as he himself believes.

That all inorganic *means of nutrition* are at the same time *means of function* is a proposition which I endorse. It never occurred to me to undertake for practical purposes a definite division of the cell-salts into means of function and of building material. I call them building material, in so far as they occupy a place in the organic basis of the cells; and means of function, in respect of their chemico-physiological action.

Dr. von G. says, "Schüssler demands that facts should shape themselves according to his theories." Not at all, honoured sir! My therapeutical system has arisen between theory and practice constantly and mutually controlling and correcting each other. Not I, but Dr. von G., demands that facts should shape themselves according to his ideas. To cure chancre he uses Glauber salt, but the disease steadily resists. This, at least, is averred by physicians who have made similar experiments.

Dr. von G., after a long *raisonnement* about means of adaptation, imbibition, effusion, etc., insists that there can be only a system of molecular—not cellular—therapeutics. Despite Dr. von G.'s disquisition, I shall retain the term Cellular Therapeutics, since I consider it as more correct.

For instance, you supply iron molecules to the blood-cells in need of iron; you render a service to the respective cells, and such service carried out for the benefit of these cells may, without solecism, be termed

E

a system of Cellular Therapeutics. If one causes, by therapeutical means, iron molecules to enter the cells through the molecular interstices of the blood-cell membrane, the service is rendered not to the iron molecules, but to the cells. To dispute whether one should call it a system of Cellular—or Molecular—Therapeutics is simply a piece of ridiculous pedantry.

To the critics who have hitherto arisen against me I quote the words of Voltaire, in *La Pucelle d'Orléans*:

> " Censeurs savants, je vous estime tous ;
> Je connais mes défauts mieux que vous."

MORE OBJECTIONS BY A HOMŒOPATH.

REFUTED BY DR. SCHÜSSLER, THE FOUNDER OF THE NEW OR BIOCHEMIC SYSTEM.

(Published separately some time ago.)

Dr. von Grauvogl, retired Surgeon-Major of the Staff, 1 Cl., at Munich, has attacked my Abridged Therapeutics a second time in the General Homœopathic Journal. His first objections I refuted in the Third Edition of my book; and on the second I will throw some light in these lines.

Dr. von Grauvogl is the author of several homœopathic works: one of these, "The Fundamental Laws of Physiology, Pathology, and Homœopathic Therapeutics," has been criticised by Dr. Roth mercilessly, but not unjustly. In Hirshel's Zeitschrift für Hom. Clinic, under the title "Parænesis ad aliena à medica Doctrina arcenda," Dr. Roth says there, that Dr. von Grauvogl has cemented together Mechanics, Chemistry, Rademacher, Priessnitz, and Fuchs' lung-idiopathy with scholastic Philosophy; by so doing the most nonsensical book was compounded.

Although his book is a collection-surium of the kind above alluded to, Dr. von Grauvogl maintains the rudiments of my Therapy were contained in it. He is mistaken in this. I never hesitated to give the names of those men from whose writings I drew my idea. If I had borrowed anything in any way from Dr. v. G.'s work, his name should stand foremost with an epitheton ornans and shine in my opusculum. His elaborations were, however, entirely useless to me. I do not comprehend why he, as philosopher, should rise against me with so much ire.

But I will pass on to the points at which Dr. v. G.'s attacks are aimed.

Dr. v. G. misses in my writings a definition of the meaning "curable."

If I had happened to be a philosopher newly off the irons, he might have expected from me an attempt at such a definition. But my ordinary common-sense tells me that every sensible man knows what is to be understood by curable and uncurable. It is not clear to me why Dr. v. G. considers the absence of the thought of such definition a kind of back-door or loophole.

Dr. v. Grauvogl, who likes to define, says: "Therapeutics is a science, a complete subordination of the special to the general, in natural laws, by which the connections of the phenomena of each separate case can be given and explained. From this it is evident that there can be no abridged science."

This is genuine pedantry. In my Therapeutics, it is all important practically to find out whether my twelve remedies meet all requirements or not. This cannot be done by æsthetic philosophizing. Dr. v. G. thinks my Therapeutics would leave me in a difficulty in cases of abnormal substitutions, *e.g.*, when mucous tissues are metamorphosed into bony or fatty tissues, or when muscular tissues are forming where they should not be. My reply is: In these cases the functional remedy is required which has degenerated and become abnormal of those tissues. When a tissue performs its function normally, no new formations can develop in it. It is requisite and necessary, therefore, to correct the abnormal function of the above tissue by means of the respective functional remedy.

I do not know why Dr. v. G. considers himself justified in insinuating that he can give me a piece of information in these words: "May it be told once for all to Dr. Schüssler, that the deficiency of a substance in the organism can never be its own cause?" Have I ever made a statement to the contrary to this notorious truism?

When I apply *Potassium chloride* therapeutically for the cure of an exudating inflammation of the skin, caused by boiling water, I know that the irritation on the skin from the hot water caused a disturbance of the proper balance of the molecules of *Potassium chloride* in that part in which they are biochemic functionaries.

Dr. v. G. asserts I had come into serious conflict with Moleschott, and as proof of this assertion he quotes this from "Kreislauf des Lebens," by Moleschott: "Physicians know how frequently one has to change the course of action of the digestive organs, and foremost that of the liver, before one is in a position to offer iron successfully to the blood." The serious conflict is a product of art of Dr. v. G.'s desire to criticise.

As *exact* individualization has been emphasized by me as an indispensable requirement necessary in the manipulation of my Therapeutics, it was not necessary for me specially to say that *anæmia* arising from disease of the liver is curable indirectly by means of the functional remedy for the *liver* disease.

Virchow's teaching Dr. v. G. supposes me not to have considered in the conception of my Therapeutics. In support of this he cites the following from Virchow: "The individual cell within a tissue is not being fed, but it feeds itself; it abstracts from the nutritive fluids, which are in its environments, the parts required by it;" and Dr. v. G. adds, "*i.e.*, as long as they are healthy: when diseased, that is, changed in any way in their molecules, the commencement of acute diseases, namely, fever, at once proves that the diseased parts, yea the whole body, can no longer take up nutrient materials, and it is often unable to master those forced upon it."

Dr. v. G. has forgotten I do not pretend or profess to feed, but endeavour to correct errors of function (faulty functions), and this task is and must be as easily performed "at the commencement of acute diseases" as in a later stage.

When sulphur is used for tests in repeated large doses, the organism will be found to exert itself to get rid of the burden by the channel of oxidation. Thus a surplus of Sulphuric acid must arise, and increased formation of sulphates, as well as an increased giving off of carbonic acid. In the organism, processes take place the same as in a chemical laboratory despite Dr. v. G. With mathematical formulas—which he likes to parade—he may catch simpletons.

What Dr. v. G. says about inflammations and hyperæmia is partly indefinite or only partially pertinent. "The cause of inflammatory processes is essentially a physical or chemical alteration of the vascular walls of the blood-vessels respectively, the blood itself." These are his words. As the word alteration means nothing further than change, he should have defined more clearly the changed vascular walls. Alas! he does not even know whether it is a physical or a chemical change. Rideo quandoque bonis dormitat philosophus.

Dr. v. G. declares, "That dilatation of the blood-vessels did not depend on a diminution of the tensile power of their muscular circular fibres, but on a paralysis of the nerves of the vessels." By this he has only hit one half of the truth. Dilatation of a vessel can be caused by paralysis of the nerves of the blood-vessels; it can, however, also be the after effect of an irritation, over-stimulation, to which the muscles of the vessels were exposed. Dilatation of the first kind extends itself over a larger area of vessels; a dilatation of the second kind may be more circumscribed, being dependent on a small number of those relaxed muscular fibres which are circularly arranged round the walls of the blood-vessels.

It is true that a hyperæmia need not of necessity have an inflammatory exudation as a consequence; on the other hand, an inflammatory exudation may exist without hyperæmia having preceded it.

When in consequence of intense stimuli, or too strong an irritation whether internal or external, a disturbance of the molecular balance occurs in the molecules of the *iron* of the circular fibres, the vessels dilate; when too strong an irritation strikes the *Potassium chloride* molecules of a tissue, an inflammatory exudation ensues.

I admit that hyperæmia may sometimes be of short duration; but that it may also last for some time, every practitioner knows. That many acute diseases can cure themselves, or, as is often said, can be cured by Nature, is known to everybody. But that their duration can be shortened therapeutically cannot be denied either. The possibility of Nature curing is frequently quoted by opposing schools.

Dr. v. G. utilizes the possibility of spontaneous resolution or disappearance of a hyperæmia, as an argument against my *Ferric phosphate*, and to a larger extent even against my entire Abridged Therapeutics, where he fancies he has discovered a great many ifs and buts. He even casts this as a reproach at me, that several laymen in Hungary, not practitioners, were astonished at the effects of *Calcium phosphate*, which not I, but a Hungarian homœopath, had prescribed from reading my Therapeutics.

If anyone dares to say or do what does not agree with v. Grauvogl's views, on him he tries to imprint the stamp of ignorance, and when he wishes to prove anything he simply refers to the books written by himself. This proceeding would be perfectly correct if Dr. v. G. were possessed of infallibility instead of imagination of infallibility. Under these circumstances I do not feel called upon to "correct the errors" he imputes to me.

He asserts that if I had but once proved one drug on myself—for instance, *Silica*—I could not for a moment doubt that every local disease was only a symptom of the alteration (change) of the entire organism. For by such a proof he thinks I would surely have experienced that long before symptoms were perceptible in the bone-system, the rest of the whole organism had set up action against this substance by a number of symptoms. Therefore *Silica* could not be indicated locally except in the case of Chondroma.

To this my reply is: All the results effected by tests made with *Silica* can in nowise shake my firm belief in the possibility of local Pathology and Therapeutics. *Silica* is a physiological means of function of the connective tissue. The sphere of action of *Silica* is therefore very large, and when given so as to study the action of this drug, it may produce symptoms in all the organs. But it does not follow that in Chondroma, which has its seat in the framework of connective tissue around the bones, a functional disturbance of the molecules of *Silica* in all the connective tissues of the said organism must have preceded it. It is more readily conceivable that an irritation, when set up in the connective tissue surrounding bone, could cause Chondroma. A proof to the contrary, made up of philosophical baubles, cannot hold good.

In saying that what is peculiar to the whole, points with certainty to the peculiarity of the individual, Dr. v. G. expresses simply a well-known platitude.

Every shepherd knows that it would be impossible for him to recognise the individual sheep of his flock if he did know the peculiarity of sheep in general.

If, as Dr. v. G. declares, the whole organism were the disease—for instance, in intermittent fever, chlorosis, dysentery, etc., the whole of the bony framework, as well as the crystalline lens, would have to be diseased, also. No one has, however, cataract or bone-disease, chlorosis or dysentery, etc., as inseparable concomitants of intermittent fever; for the crystalline lens and bone-tissues are among the parts which are found to be left healthy in those diseases.

As he will not suffer any "double meaning" in science, he says that the conceptions of means of nutrition and means of function cover each other. If two conceptions cover each other, they are equal to each other. Soon after he speaks of the difference between nutrition and function. He also believes that there are tissues which have no functions (do not participate in function). A tissue which does not participate in function and is not functional is dead.

If anyone wishes to study nutrition and function, he must not take Moleschott or Virchow as authorities, but inquire of Dr. v. G.

What, indeed, could one learn of Moleschott ? Moleschott is, as v. G. says, *only* an author for the people (a man who writes for many), and v. G. has only a limited circle of readers ; whilst Moleschott is a Professor, an academical teacher, and one of world-wide fame who enjoys " a somewhat greater reputation in science than von Grauvogl."

Regarding the sublime theory of the connective tissue channels, I must appeal to the writings of Virchow, v. Recklinghausen, and Moleschott.

Moleschott says, in the latest edition of his "Kreislauf des Lebens" : " It is one of the grandest achievements of modern times, to the knowledge of which Virchow and v. Recklinghausen have paved the way, that the connective tissue has been raised from the secondary part, which at first was allotted to it, to one of productive activity such as was never anticipated. What appeared formerly only designed as a protecting covering or padding, appears now as the bed of the most minute and secret streamlets of juices or sap from the blood to the tissue, and back from these into the blood-vessels, and at the same time as one of the most important nidi (breeding places) of new cells, which, developed from the embryonic early shapes, can rise to form the most peculiar and special structures of the body." (Isomeric transpositions, differentiating Albumen.)

In relation to this, I say, p. 10 of my Third Edition :

"As the connective-tissue channels carry the nutrient fluid to the tissues on the one hand, they on the other hand carry back into the circulation the waste or *débris* of those tissues which have been broken up and have undergone disintegration by the continuous influence of the oxygen. Importation and exportation taking place side by side, special connective tissue channels must exist for the purpose of carrying the *supply*, and others for carrying the *waste*. For unceasing traffic in two directions cannot take place on the same set of rails."

Dr. v. G., to whom the above-cited from Moleschott is surely unknown, confuses connective-tissue channels with capillary vessels. He reproaches me with not being versed in this special line of literature.

Those questions regarding lactic acid and the constituent parts of the ash of the tissues cannot be settled definitely. Marchand and others consider lactic acid, and Bencke considers oxalic acid, the cause of Rachitis (Rickets).

Sodium phosphate cures all such diarrhœa which arises from an excess of lactic acid. In Rachitis (Rickets) this remedy is useless. Excess of lactic acid would therefore not seem to be the primary agent of this disease.

Dr. v. G. says: "When a theory is false, then the practice resting on it must be false too." The sentence might perhaps be reversed. "If the practice be correct, the theory must be correct too." And many have practically convinced themselves that the Indications in my Therapeutics are correct.

From the following passage in my first article against Dr. v. G., he concludes that I must be an empiricist of the first water. "He who does not know the sphere of action of my twelve remedies in its full range is not in a position to judge whether they can meet all therapeutical requirements or not." Dr. v. G.'s counter-statement is therefore a weak one if he infers that my method is empirical. Truly, the premises leading to such a conclusion do not lie in the above words, for in them it is not stated in which manner I acquired the knowledge of the effects of my twelve therapeutical agents, whether by experiments or provings on the healthy, or *ex usu in morbis.*

None but a prejudiced mind, such as that of Dr. v. G., could have seen in the words an indirect challenge to allow himself "to be led on to the slippery ground of empiricism by me." As there is no lack of doctors who have regard to my Therapeutics in their practice, it is immaterial to me whether the number be increased or not by the unit represented by Dr. v. G. His favour or disfavour will have no influence on the future fate of my Therapeutics. If he thinks that "aspiring youth" has to be deterred from following my teachings, and that this duty has been imposed upon him, it is questionable whether the "aspiring youth" feel so little self-dependent that they require his guardianship or tutorage. Who opposes Dr. v. G. is, in his ideas, a stranger in the precincts of logic.

Moleschott says: "Thus logic became a formula of scholasticism which the assiduous and eager students consider a thorny roundabout road towards development and advance."

But Dr. v. G. considers that if anyone has not crammed himself with a formula of thought, he is perfectly unfit to think. With as much reason he could have asserted that if anyone does not know the physical laws of hearing and sight, he must be blind and dumb. Experience teaches the opposite. Indians and other uncivilized nations can compete for acuteness of their organs of hearing, etc., with the most learned Professor of Physics. Just as a healthy man sees and hears aright without having learnt a formula on sight and hearing, so a healthy and sound man thinks aright without having impressed upon his memory a formula of thought or an elementary book of logic.

Every sensory perception excites a thought, which must be correct in itself and in the relation to another, as long as the organs of sense and the brain are normal or healthy. Regarding this assertion I find myself at one with Dr. v. G. in spite of himself, for he says if I had tested the effects of *Silica* on myself, my opinion regarding it would not differ from this. The errors he imputes to me could therefore not simply rest on an error of thought—even if they had been committed by me—but must have arisen through want of experience. It is plain, therefore, I could not have sinned against the formula of thought.

Formulas of thought are, however, as superfluous as a fifth wheel to a carriage. For if a man were not able to understand and order aright his own thoughts, he would be far less able to understand printed logic, the products of the thoughts of others.

DR. SCHÜSSLER.

[The following numbered Clinical cases have been collected from various Medical Journals, and from the practice of qualified Medical Practitioners.

It will be seen that most of the cases which Dr. Schüssler has put on record here have been treated by other medical men. These give conclusive proof of the merits of the Biochemic treatment of disease.]

CLINICAL CASES.

1. APRIL, 1879. M.K., æt. 16, has suffered for years from periodically returning headaches. The pain is concentrated in the right temple, and of a boring nature, as if a screw were being driven in—as the patient expresses herself. Preceding this pain there is a burning sensation at the pit of the stomach, bitter taste in the mouth, and lassitude. These symptoms are only felt at night, or in the morning. When the attack comes on, the patient is quite unable to attend to any ordinary duties. General vomiting of bile follows, and then improvement sets in. *Sodium sulphate*—daily; as much as a bean, dissolved in water, and taken repeatedly, cured the young lady entirely.

---

2. M. L., a gentleman æt. 38, took a chill while in a state of perspiration. He suffered in consequence from tearing pains in the limbs, noises in the ears, with dulness of hearing and frontal headache. These pains were accompanied by fever, and although he had night-sweats, they brought no relief. The appetite was poor, and the tongue covered with a white coating. I gave a small quantity of *Potassium chloride*—in water every two hours. A rapid and general improvement set in, but pains and numbness in the feet were still present. Also the habitual perspiration of feet was still absent. At this stage the patient received *Silica*—2 doses daily for a week. Perspiration of feet was re-established, and on the reappearance of this, the rest of the ailments left him, and health was quite restored.

---

3. May, 1879. J. D., a man of 69 years of age, had been complaining for several weeks of pains in the limbs, which settled in the right leg, from the hip down to the ankle, but were worse at the joints, being of a shifting nature—

intermittent—sometimes shooting and darting like lightning, causing the patient to change his position frequently. Warmth gives him relief. He is unable to leave his bed; is almost in despair, thinking he is dying. *Magnesium phosphate*—a dose every three hours. The improvement on taking this remedy was marked and rapid. But whenever he stopped with the medicine, he felt worse again. By continuing daily with *Magnesium phosphate*, a complete cure was effected.

---

4. I was called to attend a girl 12 years of age. She had had, some time ago, an attack of rheumatic fever. I found the little patient, who had been taken ill the previous day, in bed. The joints of both knees were swollen, somewhat red, and very painful. The joints of the vertebræ at the nape of the neck were implicated, and every movement out of the constrained position of the neck and back was very painful. Her friends expected that salicylic acid would be applied, which they had already seen used, but I gave *Ferric phosphate*—and *Potassium chloride*—alternately every three hours. Next day, to the astonishment of her friends, the fever and pains were less, and knees were quite free from pain. Now I ordered *Potassium chloride* to be given alone for the swelling, and the next morning on my return I found all the symptoms worse. I repeated the *Ferric phosphate* again, and there was a rapid improvement. But in the same degree as the pains were leaving and the swelling decreasing, spasmodic pains in the abdomen set in. There was also an occasional vomiting of bilious matter. As soon as these latter symptoms came on, I ordered the little patient some *Magnesium phosphate* dissolved in water, in frequent sips, which removed all these symptoms in 24 hours. *Ferric phosphate* and *Potassium chloride* were continued in less frequent doses. Six days after my first visit the patient was able to leave the bed, and was quite well.

Dr. SCHLEGEL.

---

5. Notes by the Editor of the "Monthly Medical Journal."—From this clinical report it is very evident that the proper application of Dr. Schüssler's method has surpris-

ingly favourable results. We have repeatedly occasion to recommend these medicines, as they are so reliable in cases of muscular rheumatism.

---

6. December, 1879. A little girl, aged 9, had recovered from Diphtheria and Scarlatina rather easily, and was allowed to be in the convalescent room. Suddenly she began to swell without any apparent cause. Her face became puffy; the feet also œdematous to above the ankles. Urine scarcely decreased; containing no albumen. No pain over kidneys on pressure. Pulse somewhat feverish; but appetite, sleep, and stools still natural. I gave three different medicines — amongst these, Aconitum — without success. Dropsy (anasarca et ascites) is increasing rapidly; urine scanty; only very small quantities occasionally, being slightly turbid, and containing much albumen. Whether any epithelial sheathings were present was not ascertained. Kidneys were now more sensitive to pressure. Occasionally delirious. *Sodium chloride* alone cured this case in about a fortnight.

DR. KHON.

FROM THE "CLINICAL TIMES."

7. In August, 1877, a young man who had suffered from sciatica some years ago, and had been in the habit of having subcutaneous injections of morphia, developed a boil on the seat. This discharged freely, and would not heal. When at last it seemed to be healed and was comparatively well, the patient took cold. While at a military review he was caught in heavy rain. Suppuration began again, and this time the discharge was excessive. His mother became alarmed, as he was very weak, and had no appetite. His sleep was disturbed, and he felt a constant thirst. I prescribed *Silica*—a dose every morning on an empty stomach. After one week the mother was able to furnish the very favourable report: "The discharge of matter has been reduced so much that at one time it seemed gone altogether. The great thirst has left him, and his appetite has returned; his sleep is sound, and the shivery, chilly feeling he had has completely gone." *Silica* has here furnished a brilliant demonstration of its power over suppuration, with its characteristic accompanying symptoms. DR. GOULLON, JR.

8. Dr. F. of Alsò, Hungary, reports : I was requested to go into the country to see a man who had been suffering the last three days from spasmodic convulsive hiccough. He was lying in bed. Subcutaneous injections of morphia, friction with chloroform and sinapisms (mustard poultices) were all of no use. Although the spasm was mitigated for two or three hours, it returned with more violence than ever. I gave him a powder of *Magnesium phosphate*—in half a tumblerful of water. After the second tablespoonful the hiccough ceased altogether, to the astonishment of all those present.

---

9. A hard swelling under the chin about the size of a pigeon's egg disappeared completely in about four weeks under the use of *Calcium fluoride*. Both old and new school medicines have failed to cure.

DR. F.

---

10. In Diphtheria (maligna), where every known remedy failed, *Potassium phosphate*—and *Potassium chloride*—with, and sometimes without, *Sodium chloride*, effected subsidence of malignity, and hastened the cure.

DR. F.

---

11. In Paralysis after Diphtheria, I know of no better remedy than *Potassium phosphate*.

DR. F.

---

12. A very interesting case came under my treatment, which deserves the attention of the profession. I was called to a lady advanced in years. She had been suffering for nearly five weeks from fearful attacks of convulsive spasms. During the last twenty-four hours she had had 30 attacks. The spasms darted through her body like an electric shock so that she fell to the ground. The attack lasted a few minutes, after which she felt well enough, but rather exhausted. The sufferer did not venture to leave her bed now, afraid of being injured. She had been treated by her first doctor with Flor. Zinci., Fowler's Solution, and friction, but with-

out success. When I saw the lady I thought of trying Schüssler's functional remedies. Knowing that *Magnesium phosphate*—and *Calcium phosphate*—are the two prescribed for allaying spasms (cramp), I chose the latter, *Calcium phosphate*, under these circumstances. Next day, to the astonishment of those about her, I found the old lady walking about the room. She met me with a smile, exclaiming: "Ah, Doctor, my spasms are cured." And so it was. She had not had another attack.

Dr. FECHTMANN.

---

13. Reuter, a master shoemaker of Berlin, æt. 40, was taken ill, after catching cold, as he stated. There was fever and violent pains in the right shoulder. The first visit I paid was on the third day after he had been taken ill, Nov. 21st. Temperature high, pulse full and quick, thirst, and loss of appetite. The right shoulder was very red, and sensitive to the touch. He was not able to lie in his bed, as the pressure of the pillows was unbearable. He was lying on the sofa, supported with cushions, so that the shoulder should be free from pressure. I gave my patient *Ferric phosphate*, as much as would cover a sixpenny piece. This was dissolved in a large glassful of water, and a teaspoonful of the solution given every hour. Improvement was felt even after a few hours. During the night the patient was able to sleep, and on the following day the fever abated. On the 25th Nov. the patient was able to move the arm pretty freely. Nov. the 28th he tried to work; but feeling the weight of his hammer too much, he rested a few days longer, when he felt himself quite well.

Dr. L. SÜLZER.

---

14. March 2nd.—Dr. Fisher was consulted by a lady (*enceinte*) who was suffering from a cough which caused great inconvenience, as with every cough there was emission of urine. *Ferric phosphate* cured her very speedily. A short time ago the lady, under similar circumstances, was again troubled with a cough. *Ferric phosphate* this time also cured her speedily.

F

15. Dr. Köck, of Munich, reports:—In thirty-five cases of measles which came under my treatment, coryza and bronchial catarrh were very slight in the promonitory stage. Conjunctivitis and intolerance of light along with it were the most preminent symptoms. Within a few days after, the rash appeared, lasting five or six days, and then disappeared. But either during the blush of the rash or the fading of it, painful swelling of one or both glands below the ear set in. The children again became feverish, and were crying and moaning both day and night. The remedy which I now chose was *Ferric phos.;* and according to the violence of the fever, I ordered a spoonful of the solution every hour or two. I gave it at the premonitory stage, and when I saw that it proved very satisfactory, I looked for no other remedy. For this glandular swelling, external redness and painfulness, I used the same medicine, and my cases ended very satisfactorily.

---

16. In September last autumn I was in the Highlands. The dairymaid of a farmer there spoke to me, saying she had hurt her thumb while sharpening a scythe. The case proved to be this:—The whole thumb of the left hand was swollen, and of a bluish-red colour, and very painful when touched, much inflamed, and there was a small wound at the extensor side at the joint above the nail. On pressure there was a white-yellow discharge mixed with white shreds. Both phalanges were easily displaced, and a peculiar noise was heard, which I had observed before in similar cases. This fact made me decide on giving *Calcium fluoride.* The medical man in the village, whom the farmer had consulted, said amputation was the only thing that could be done for the case. She took *Calcium fluoride;* and some time after, the farmer had occasion to see me, when he informed me that the servant's thumb was quite well.

---

17. A woman, aged 56, from Simbach, who always wore blue spectacles, came to see me, as she had become blind of the right eye. The cause and consequent suffering were as follows:—Three years ago, on the 15th Jan., at twelve o'clock noon, she was walking from Arnstorf to Simbach. The

whole of the meadows were covered with snow, on which the sun was shining brightly, causing a strong refraction. Suddenly she felt a severe pain in the right eye, and immediately discovered that she had lost the sight of it. She took some snow and held it over her eye, which she thought did her some good. On reaching home she sent for the doctor, who put a leech to the right temple, and gave her a strong purgative. She had to keep her bed for three weeks. The pain subsided, but her sight did not return. Some time after, she travelled all the way to Passau, to consult Dr. E., the occulist. He gave a laxative and some ointment to be rubbed all round the eye (*Ungnt. Hydrarg.*). As the ointment affected the gum and loosened her teeth, she stopped using it, her sight being no better. Later on, when she heard that Professor Rothmund had operated on the pastor of Landau for cataract, she went to see him. "If this medicine won't help you, you will remain blind for life," were the Professor's words. His prescription was Potassium Iodide. After having had the prescription made up three times, and using it steadily, she felt no improvement, and was quite inconsolable. With her right eye she saw nothing —all seemed smoke and mist; and the other eye was becoming weaker and weaker from month to month. External examination showed the conjunctiva intact, as also the cornea, iris, etc. All pointed to internal disease of the inner medium of the eye. I could see but little of the retina, as there was a kind of mist over it, which seemed to spread from the vitreous humour over the background of the eye. I introduced the rays of light in different directions, and by this means I was better able to obtain sight of the retina. It appeared dim and misty, the veins were clearly seen forming a dark network. In some places there were distinctly defined spots, some larger than others, appearing to me like the residue of extravasated blood. The arteries were scarcely visible, and seemed to me pale and more contracted than in the normal condition. The necessary therapeutic treatment clearly indicated to me was to produce absorption of the exuded substance, this being the cause of the dulness of sight. According to Professor Rothmund's opinion, inflammation of the retina always arises in the connective tissue, and as this exuded substance appears of a coagulating nature, which no doubt is fibrinous, and, as is well known, can be hypertrophied, and is capable of fatty degeneration, I found that of the remedies I could think of, the most suitable seemed to be *Potassium chloride.* I now gave the woman eight powders, each containing two centigrams; the powder to be dissolved in half a wineglassful of water, a tablespoonful to be taken night and morning. A fortnight after, the patient came back, saying, "I don't think I am any worse; please to give me some more of these powders." She received a dozen, with the same directions. One morning she called quite early, and told me in great glee that on rising that morning she could see the window-sash quite distinctly. I tested her sight from different distances, and found that she had really improved. "I can see pretty well through the mist," she said. *Potassium chloride* was continued in small doses, and in four months her sight was restored.

---

18. June 16th.—Dr. Köck writes:—An old woman came to me, 72 years of age. She had worn a green shade over her eyes to my recollection since my younger days when as a student I spent my holidays at Simbach with my grandparents. This person complained of a constant burning sensation in her eyes, causing a continual flow of smarting tears. This commenced at eight o'clock in the morning and lasted till sunset. During the night it was better. She had much thirst, but little appetite. Externally the conjunctiva palpebrarum was in a chronic state of inflammation. On either side of the nose there was excoriation and eczema of the skin, caused by the flow of acrid tears. The punctæ lachrymosa were dilated; but the tear ducts were unobstructed. I hesitated whether I should give *Sodium chloride* or Arsenic; but Dr. Schüssler's special mention of *Sodium chloride* in regard to these excessive lachrymal secretions determined my choice, and I gave *Sodium chloride* in water; one teaspoonful three times a day. In three weeks the symptoms all greatly subsided, and shortly after entirely disappeared.

---

19. August 17th.—Dr. Köck informed us that a farm-servant came to him, and he said he could not see. Some

time before this a piece of wood had struck him in the eye. He had been treated for it; had had purgatives, leeches, and cold water applications, and now his sight was quite gone. The particulars of the case were these. The bulbus was infiltrated through vascular engorgement. The conjunctiva was swollen, and the eyelid also in an irritated and inflamed condition. The cornea was dim, with a smoky appearance of the anterior chamber (*i.e.*, between the cornea and iris), and some matter could be seen floating quite distinctly. I found no foreign body. The subjective results were—severe burning pain in the eye as if from a foreign body, and continuous flow of tears. The man had to keep his eye tied up. His appetite was good, and pulse normal. As to therapeutic treatment, I had evidently to deal with two different affections—Hypopium (matter in the eye) and conjunctivitis.

First of all, I gave *Ferric phosphate* every two hours, and in a week the burning pain and watering of the eye were less. One week after this the man complained that his sight had not improved. Now, I had the task of absorption of the matter before me, as well as the clearing of the cornea. To meet the first condition I gave Hep. sulph., but after a fortnight I could recognise no special progress. I felt rather in a fix with the case, as absorption would not take place. Remembering an expression of Dr. Quagleo, at M., that he considered Schüssler's *Calcium sulph.* a still more powerful medicine, I gave three doses of *Calcium sulphate*—to be taken in water. Scarcely a week after, the man came to me greatly delighted, saying that he could see gleams of light in the right eye. Positively, I found the cornea less cloudy, and could observe that some of the matter had been absorbed. Whenever I find improvement certain, I decrease the dose. I now gave him a dose only night and morning. In three weeks absorption was complete, and dimness of the cornea quite removed, and his sight restored. Besides this, all the inflammation of the conjunctiva was also cured.

---

20. August, 1880.—A swelling under the chin the size of a pigeon's egg was considerably reduced by *Potassium chloride*, but still there was induration (hardness) and an uneven surface. *Calcium fluoride*, taken for a few days, caused it to

disappear altogether. Shortly after its disappearance the patient had slight conjunctivitis with swelling, which *Potassium chloride* soon cured.

---

21. At a Meeting of Medical Men at Schaffhausen, Professor Dr. Rapp said :—" In my opinion the greatest merits of Dr. Schüssler's method lie in the introduction of *Potassium phosphate* and *Magnesium phosphate.* In ordinary stomatitis, with swelling of the gums, deposit on the teeth, and foul breath, *Potassium phosphate* has given very satisfactory proof of its value."

---

22. In Asthma, when the patient's attack comes on after taking food, and his colour becomes bad, or when there is rapid emaciation or the eyes appear sunken, Dr. Rapp recommends the *Potassium* remedies.

---

23. December, 1879. — Dr. Crüwell reports on incontinence of urine :—" When I became acquainted with Dr. Schüssler's preparations, I was very anxious to test the effects of *Potassium phosphate,* as Dr. Schüssler recommends this against paralysis and paralytic conditions. Whoever has been occupied with the study of psychology is naturally ready to suspect paralysis everywhere. I acknowledge I may have given *Potassium phosphate* too frequently, as I was desirous to find out what it could do. For various reasons it led me to give it for incontinency of urine. I gave it three to four times daily in a little water. In five cases, two of which I treated without good results, *Potassium phosphate* brought about amazingly rapid improvement. With a young girl of seven I had until lately to repeat the remedy every time it was given up, as the incontinency always returned when it was discontinued. The most successful case was that of an old gentleman of sixty. No doubt in this case there existed a sub-paralytic condition of the sphincter muscle. Some months after treatment he called back to say he was perfectly cured, but desired to have some of the powders, simply by way of precaution."

24. A lady, 29 years of age, of sanguine temperament, with rather high colour of face, has been suffering the last five years from the following indigestion troubles, which she contracted by a draught of very cold water whilst in a state of heat and perspiration:—She has no desire to eat; great dislike to milk. After food, nausea and vomiting of food, which is so acid that it sets her teeth on edge. She can take nothing sour. Meat, and also salt herring, cause much pain, and so do cake and coffee. The sickness and retching occasionally come on before breakfast; otherwise only after food. To this is added Cephalalgia. She feels a beating pain in her forehead and temples—formerly on the left, now more on the right side. This pain is most violent. Catamenia appears every three weeks, with much loss; dragging pain in lower abdomen and lumbar region. The motions are normal, the sleep is disturbed by anxious dreams, and she feels in the morning as though she had been beaten. In the evening she feels oppressed and swelled, so that she has to loosen her dress; she cannot wear it in the least tight. Her pulse is accelerated 100 per minute. As a girl, she was quite healthy, and had never suffered from anæmia. On the whole, the lady was not much emaciated, in spite of her ailing so long. This was the description the patient gave of her case. The leading symptoms of this case led me to choose iron. I ordered her a dose of Dr. Schüssler's saccharated trituration of *Ferric phosphate* to be taken before meals, about the size of a bean, three times daily. When I saw her again she was able to give me the very satisfactory report that her ailments were cured. DR. MOSSA.

---

25. MARCH, 1880.—Dr. Mossa, Bamberg, reports:—Towards the end of last year I received a letter with the following details, and asking me to forward some medicine:—"My boy, a child of seven, hitherto healthy and strong, has been suffering from pains in the stomach for some weeks. Latterly he has vomited all his food, sometimes immediately after taking it, and at other times not till during the night. The child has now become very emaciated. Last week he was frequently fevered. This has, however, not returned since taking the medicine our doctor here has given him.

The boy complains of much exhaustion." To form a strictly scientific diagnosis of the case on such information was clearly impossible. But as it was not convenient for me personally to examine the case, I had to do my best with the details furnished. The nature of the abdominal pains pointed to swelling and enlargement of the organs of the viscera—liver, spleen, &c.; also the feverish attacks, probably subdued by quinine, and the vomiting of food, all coincided with my surmises. As to the selection of the medicine I hesitated considerably, and then decided to give *Ferric phosphate*—twelve powders, one night and morning. The report some time after was very favourable. The fever had not returned; the vomiting of food and pains in the stomach had quite ceased soon after taking the medicine. The little fellow was feeling so much stronger that he attended school again.

---

26. Dr. Goullon, jun., who used *Potassium chloride* with much success in a swelling of the feet and lower extremities, adds the following particular indications for its use. The remedy in question appears indicated in chronic persistent swelling of the feet and lower limbs, when the swelling is soft at first, afterwards becoming hard to the touch, without pain or redness. It is, however, itchy; and at one stage may be termed snowy white and shining. Lastly, the swelling becomes less perceptible in the morning than in the evening; but may acquire such dimensions as to cause great tension, with a feeling as if it would burst.

---

27. A case from a contributor may here be mentioned, which was cured by *Potassium chloride*:—A lady, Mrs. B., suffering from swelling of the leg below the knee, had been seen some months by her doctor, who had poulticed it, and had opened it with the lancet; but there was no discharge. She was unable to walk. It was then painted with Iodine without effect; then bandaged to reduce the excessive hard swelling, and cold water poured over it thrice a day. Some parts were blue-looking on removing the bandage. It felt cold and very hard, and looked as if ready to burst; almost

twice its usual size. Warm fomentations and *Potassium chloride*, taken internally and applied externally, cured the leg in three weeks.

---

28. July 29, 1879. From the reports of a Medical Congress at Dortmund, by Dr. Stens, junior:—I should like to report on a case of rheumatism, which was cured by *Ferric phosphate* in a very short time, after having tried several of the most reputed remedies which seemed indicated. A lady of about forty-two years of age (catamenia normal, though scanty) had been treated by me for the last few years. She suffered from digestive derangement, and sometimes from violent attacks of megrim. This lady awoke one morning with an acute pain in the right upper arm and region of right shoulder, being of a tearing nature. She had walked the previous evening through a damp meadow, getting her feet wet. The pains were worse if she moved her arm quickly; not as bad on moving it very gently. She was therefore careful to use gentle motion. The parts affected were painful on being touched. Several nights perspiration had been excessive, and afterwards made its appearance every morning between two and six o'clock, when the pains were always worse. The patient complained also of a pain in the right hand and powerlessness, which prevented her from lifting anything heavy. She often felt rather exhausted, and had to lie down. I gave her no less than five remedies, which seemed to suggest themselves, but without success. From the lady's anæmic condition, and partly Dr. Schüssler's recommendation, I was led to think of iron. I prescribed his own preparation of *Ferric phosphate*—as much as would cover a sixpence, to be taken night and morning. The result was that after taking the medicine for six days, the pains, with their accompanying symptoms, did not return, even though soon after this wet weather set in, when she had generally felt her pains to be much worse.

---

29. Report from the Archives of Medical Men of the Rhinelands and Westphalia.—Dr. Brisken mentions three cases of rheumatic fever. One case was that of a bookbinder, middle-aged, whom Dr. Brisken had treated three

years previously for this malady. On that occasion his recovery took from eight to ten weeks. The patient was again attacked in the joints of the hands and knees, when he received *Ferric phosphate* every hour ; and as the fever had abated, *Potassium chloride* was given the same way. On the fifth day he was able to return to his work.

---

30. The second case was that of a gentleman, aged 70. He had acute rheumatism in the shoulder and elbow joints. He had been cupped, which made him worse. His joints were wrapped in waldwolle (turpentine wool) with no effect. He had not been in bed the last two nights, as on lying down and getting warm the pains were worse. On the third day he came under Dr. Brisken's treatment. After giving him *Ferric phosphate* the fever ceased in a few days, after which *Potassium chloride* was given. In a short time complete recovery resulted. When these remedies do not cut short the attack, *Sodium phosphate* must be given as chief remedy.

---

31. To a third case Dr. Brisken was called on the eighth day after seizure. Some of the joints were swollen, and the patient had not been able *to stay in bed* a single night. In the morning he received *Potassium chloride*, with such good results that during the next night he was able to stay in bed, and in twelve days was completely cured.

---

32. Dr. Orth relates :—Elizabeth F., a widow, aged 70, consulted me on April 5th, on account of an epithelioma seated on the right cheek, reaching from the lower eyelid to the nostril. It was almost circular, and about the size of a florin. The epithelioma had existed for some years, and was at the stage of forming an ulcer, with hard base and callous edges. I ordered *Potassium sulphate*—a powder every evening, and lint saturated with a lotion made of *Potassium sulphate* for external application, to be changed frequently. On May 6th I noticed that the ulcer had visibly diminished, and on May 23rd the ulcer had cicatrized to the size of a sixpenny piece. A few days later the lady left to return home, and I regret I have not heard from her since.

33. William W., a factory worker, came to me on September 4. He suffered from epithelioma, which was situated on the right side of the nose, almost immediately below the corner of the eye, and about the size of a two-shilling piece. The eye itself seemed to be sympathetically affected, whether through the irritation of the discharge, which might have found its way into the eye from the edge of the eyelid, which, however, was not greatly destroyed. Be that as it may, there were conjunctivitis palpebrarum and bulbi, with dulness of the cornea. The ulcer at the side of the nose had existed for four years. At first there was a slightly red spot, which was a little raised and swollen. Later on it became covered with a horny-like scab, which after a time fell off, and left a sore. This spread slowly, but steadily. The patient had through the whole time of its existence consulted a great number of doctors. He had also been treated for two months by a specialist for the eye, after it had become implicated, but all without effect. *Potassium sulphate* was now given him, a dose night and morning, and externally a lotion of *Potassium sulphate* was used. After only a few days the inflammation disappeared. The ulcer began also to heal under the steady treatment. By the 8th of October, the sore had cicatrized so that only a speck was left, when the patient was able to resume work again on the 6th of October.

---

34. The following is the case of a lady, aged 44. Dr. A., of Arnsberg, writes :—I saw, on the 6th of February, a lady who was suffering from mental derangement.

Religious melancholia was at the root, although before this occurrence she had not inclined to religious excitement. She now declared she was lost for ever, lamented, cried, wrung her hands, and tore her clothes, or pieces of paper which were laid about to prevent her tearing her garments. She did not know those around her, and was unable to sleep. Her eyes had an unconscious stare, and frequently it required two people to hold her down. Only by holding her nose and by force a little food or medicine could be put down her throat. I prescribed *Potassium phosphate*—as her condition, though one of excitement, was pathologically one of depression, to which *Potassium phosphate* is suited. Dr. Schüssler says in his book:—"A functional disturbance of the molecules of this salt causes in the brain mental depression, showing itself in irritability, terror, weeping, nervousness, &c., as well as softening of the brain." She took *Potassium phosphate* with excellent results. A former experience gained by this remedy led me to select it.

On that occasion it was in the case of an old man aged eighty. He suffered from mental derangement, which showed itself in the form of intense Hypochondriasis and Melancholia. He was tired of life, but had a fear of death. For weeks he had been treated to no purpose with many remedies apparently called for, as Nux vomica, Aur. Bromide of Potassium in allopathic doses. But he was rapidly cured by the continuous use of *Potassium phosphate.* Even after eight hours from the commencement of the treatment, a certain feeling of calmness was experienced, and that night he had a quiet sleep. I had, therefore, no reason to regret the treatment I selected, as the improvement continued steadily, so that on the 25th of February I discontinued my professional visits.

I have seen my previous patient frequently, busily engaged in her home with her usual cheerfulness, and she speaks quite calmly of her past illness.

From an Address given by Dr. Schlegelman at R., 1875.

35. A. S., the child of a post official visiting here, was taken ill with an attack of very slight scarlatina. The rash had disappeared after scarcely twenty-four hours. The throat symptoms, at first threatening to be severe, disappeared in three or four days. On the seventh day almost complete retention of urine set in, as in twenty-four hours only a very small quantity was passed, although the child drank a good deal. The urine contained some albumen, the feet were swollen, the abdomen very much distended. As the child was all this time in high fever, and at night delirious, I advised the parents on my visit on the morning of the eighth day to consult a second physician. Dr. Gerster, who was called in to consult with me, agreed completely

with my diagnosis. When I told him that I had not had any results from any of the medicines, such as belladonna, cantharides, and arsenic, we agreed to give *Potassium chloride* —every two hours a small powder. In the evening the little one was already better. She had passed a tolerable quantity of urine free from albumen; the pulse steadier, the skin moist. The following night the little girl slept quietly for several hours. In the morning almost free from fever, and could be considered convalescent. We continued the use of *Potassium chloride*, and a few days after she was able to return home perfectly well.

---

36. A boy, W. T., æt. 11, had been treated here by Dr. Fuchs for acute inflammation of the bowels. During the course of the disease I had been called in. When convalescent we had allowed him to return by rail to his home at B. A week after he contracted there inflammation of the peritoneum, with high fever and acute pains. My colleague Fuchs and I prognosed the case as rather hopeless, as he had been so much reduced by the disease he had just passed through, being constitutionally delicate. Having found atropine, aconite, etc., as well as strapping, of no avail, we decided upon *Ferric phosphate*, as a last resource—a dose of about ten grains per hour. The effect was a brilliant one. The fever abated; the pains decreased rapidly. This medicine we continued till the fever had quite subsided, and profuse perspirations commenced. At this stage we gave *Potassium chloride*, which caused the absorption of the rather profuse effusion.

---

37. A very nervous lady, 26 years of age, who suffered continually either from headache, toothache, face-ache, and pains in the limbs, or spasms, cramps of the stomach, indigestion, flatulence, and colic, was tormented day and night with a spasmodic cough, suppression of urine, want of sleep, and so on. In short, every day she complained of some trouble or other, and in reality suffered from it. This case almost brought me into despair. All my exertions were in vain. All the best remedies known left me in the

lurch. Almost every day a letter or telegram informed me she was getting worse, and summoned me to call. I had the happy thought of looking at Schüssler's book. I found under the head of *Magnesium phosphate* all her symptoms grouped together. I gave her this medicine, and from that moment we both had peace. "This medicine has done me no end of good," she said. And although formerly she had to keep her bed for weeks, she soon after was able to go into the garden, and later on visited a watering-place. I had to give her, however, plenty of the good remedy before leaving. DR. F.

---

38. A young lady of 17, M. M., consulted me on account of an obstinate acrid leucorrhœa. I tried the whole series of remedies indicated for such cases. All were without effect, so that I could not but wonder at the patience and perseverance of the patient whom I saw once a week. In this case Schüssler again helped me out of the dilemma. *Potass. chloride* effected a quick and permanent cure. DR. S.

---

39. In the year 1875, Dr. Schlegelman reports from Regensburg:—D. A., aged 20, a delicate lady, who suffered in her childhood a good deal from scrofula, was attacked last winter by a severe pain in the back, in consequence of catching cold. The third to the fifth ribs were very sensitive to pressure. Violent trembling of the right foot, and at the same time of the right arm, set in, the moment she attempted to move the arm or extend the hand, and thus made all work impossible. The patient was all the more depressed about this, as in her vocation she had a good deal of writing to do. I gave my remedies—pulsatilla, rhus. tox., belladonna, nux vomica, platina, etc., all without effect. I sent the young lady into the country; her condition remained the same. New remedies had no better results. At last I thought to have found her remedy in zinc. met., as I had heard nothing from her for four weeks. How astonished was I to find my patient, whom I thought cured, entering my consulting-room on 30th Sept. trembling worse than ever.

On my inquiry why she had not called sooner, she told me somewhat timidly she had gone to Mariabrunn to see a herbalist, and used the cure during the time. The result, as I could easily see, had not been successful. Consequently she placed herself under my treatment again. I told her I was willing to treat her, and opened Schüssler's Therapy. I chose *Magnesium phosphate*—and had no reason to regret my choice, for after the first few doses (three times a day, ten grains) a decided improvement was noticed, of which I heard on the 11th October, when I saw her again. At this date not even a trace of the trembling could be observed.

She had written repeatedly after this, and even then had experienced no trembling whatever. The cure was complete, as up to date she had been doing all kinds of needlework and a great deal of writing, without any recurrence of the affection.

---

40. Dr. Schlegelman writes, Jan., 1876 :—I was attacked with muscular rheumatism the latter part of November, travelling by rail, sitting close to the window of a draughty carriage. My whole right side was affected going, and on returning the pains were very severe; especially *worse* on *every movement* I made. Bryonia eased me temporarily. I only reached home at midnight, and had a very bad night. Bryonia was of little use now. I applied the electric current next morning repeatedly, but it was of no avail. I then took a pinch of the *Ferric phosphate*, and, as if by magic, the pains disappeared, and did not return.

---

41. Dr. Fuchs, of Regensburg, reports :—In August, 1875, I cured a lady 40 years of age, who had suffered for a considerable time from an effusion in the bursa of the knee-cap. Twelve doses of *Calcium phosphate*—two doses per diem, according to Dr. Schüssler—removed this chronic condition of housemaid's knee.

Dr. Schlegelman reports the following seven cases :

42. L., of Regensburg, a strong healthy man of 26 years of age, had taken cold during a state of perspiration, and contracted acute rheumatism of the joints. At first the right shoulder was attacked. The patient had violent pains and high fever. Bry., which seemed decidedly indicated

here, had no other effect except that the pain on the next morning had changed its seat, and had appeared in the left knee. In this way he continued for several days, under the use of various medicines. Either the one or other of several joints were affected. The most distressing pains continued day and night, and evidently the patient was greatly reduced. At last I decided to test Schüssler's medicine. I gave *Potassium sulphate.* The result was very favourable. The wandering pains ceased changing their location, and the pain confined itself to the right shoulder again, but was far less violent than before. Under the continued use of this medicine, the fever and pains gradually disappeared. Sleep and appetite returned, and no other joints were implicated. Eight days after giving the first dose of *Potassium sulphate*, the patient was dismissed as convalescent. No relapse occurred.

---

43. I have made very little use of Dr. Schüssler's *Potassium phosphate*, but have, notwithstanding, effected a few very interesting cures.

A woman, aged 64, came under my treatment, who had been for many years treated without success. She had taken steel baths, a great many steel pills and drops, and quinine. She complained of severe vertigo, felt mostly on rising from a sitting position, and on looking upwards. She was constantly in dread of falling, and did not venture to leave her room. I gave her all the usual remedies without any benefit. At last I gave her, in May, 1875, two doses daily of Dr. Schüssler's *Potassium phosphate.* I had the pleasure of seeing a rapid and decided cure following this. The patient can attend to her domestic duties; she can go out alone, even to distances, and is almost completely cured of her painful sensation of giddiness. Dr. S.

---

44. I have hitherto only given *Sodium phosphate* in scrofulous subjects, and only then when my old remedies calci. carb., etc., failed.

One case was particularly striking on account of its being cured so rapidly. In May last a little girl of eight was brought to me who suffered from severe conjunctivitis, with great dread of light. She had been treated for some time by an ordinary practitioner, but without effect. I ascertained that her eye affection dated from the time she had had measles some years previous. Calci. carb. and other medicines proved ineffectual. The enlargements of the glands of the neck, and the creamy secretion of the eyelids, led me to try *Sodium phosphate*—of which I administered a dose three times daily. A week later on, the child was brought to me, her eyes bright and perfectly cured.

---

45. A landed proprietor, 44 years of age, wrote to me a few weeks ago:—"The medicine I have taken very steadily, and for a long time attended strictly to my diet. In spite of this, my trouble is not better; I may almost say it has become worse."

The conditions were these:

"1. I feel almost constantly a taste as of bile.

"2. My tongue is covered with a curdy, bitter coating.

"3. During the day, especially after food, I suffer from eructations of gases, which have either a bitter taste or are tasteless.

"4. My complexion is rather yellow.

"5. The appetite very poor; no thirst. My favourite beverage, beer, is distasteful to me.

"6. I incline to shiver, and am somewhat faint.

"7. My head is but little involved, but feel a constant pressure over one eye.

"8. Stools are normal, but scanty, on account of spare diet.

"The whole condition discloses that I have bile in the stomach." Thus far the patient's own report. To this I may add that the patient in question had already taken by my orders nux. vom. and pulsatilla. He had used the waters of Marienbad the previous summer on the recommendation of another medical man.

I sent him now Dr. Schüssler's remedy, *Sodium sulphate*, with the request to take daily three doses of this powder. The gentleman came six or seven days later to my consulting-room to thank me for the valuable medicine. "The powder," he said, "has really worked wonders. All my ailments have disappeared as if by magic, and I feel at last perfectly well."

G

46. I have used *Sodium chloride* repeatedly with excellent results, and especially in obstinate cases of salivation. One case in particular was cured with remarkable rapidity by this remedy. A young lady, aet. 20, who suffered from severe inflammation of the tonsils, so that she could scarcely swallow milk or water, had received from me a preparation of mercury.

The inflammation of the tonsils was reduced very quickly, but another evil set in, namely, violent salivation. The gums were loosened, bleeding easily, and standing back from the teeth, and the teeth were slackened.

I thought of curing this affection also with mercury, with which I had often before succeeded in such cases; but by continuing this remedy the evil was only increased. Now I ascertained from the patient that in the previous summer she had been ill at N., and the doctor had given her a good deal of calomel, which caused fearful and long-continued salivation. She was afraid the evil would again become very tedious, as it had been so bad at N. I now stopped the mercury, and ordered *Sodium chloride*—a dose the size of a bean every two hours.

The success surpassed my most sanguine expectations. In twenty-four hours the swelling of the glands had distinctly diminished, and in three days a complete cure was effected.

---

47. D. R., a boy of 7 years of age, who took spurious croup whenever there was a sharp, keen north-east wind, having had a few years before a very severe attack of true croup, this past autumn had again an attack, with fever, and a loud barking cough.

Aconite and liver of sulphur, which had been recommended by so many authors against spurious croup, produced no change whatever, so that I prepared myself, in the case of this boy, for a continuance of the affection, as usual, for several days. The nights especially were very restless, with much coughing, rough and hard, so that his relatives were very anxious. There were dry heat and great oppression present. I changed my Hep. sulph. for *Potassium chloride*—and gave every two hours a full dose. After a few doses the cough became loose, lost completely the barking sound, and the whole of the following night my little patient slept quietly, so that on the following morning he awoke able to get up quite lively and well.

---

48. A. R. v. G., a young lady of 18, had visited a hydropathic establishment, along with her mother, in the past summer (1875). Without being ill, she had used the baths, even during her catamenia. Immediately after this, she took violent spasms or cramps, which set in daily, and continued after having returned home. A medical man was consulted, as the disease increased in spite of the different medicines she took. A second doctor was consulted, who quite agreed in the diagnosis as well as the treatment adopted by his colleague. Injections of morphium, very strong and repeated several times daily, were the main remedies applied, but the distressing ailment could not be removed; on the contrary, the cramps increased in violence and frequency. The medical men in attendance finally declared that there was no chance of improvement until the patient would take some steel baths in the spring. The parents were afraid that their daughter would not live to see the spring, and if she did, that she would not be fit to be removed. They therefore telegraphed requesting a visit from me.

On the 6th of September last I saw the patient for the first time. I had known her formerly, and was astonished to see, instead of the blooming healthy girl as she had been, a pale emaciated figure whom I should not have recognised. During my presence she had an attack; her features were distorted, the eyes turned upwards, froth came to the mouth, and then a fearful paroxysm of beating and striking with the hands and feet such as I had never seen before. This was only the commencement. Suddenly the trunk of her body was contorted in an indescribable manner; the back of the head pressed deeply into the pillows, the feet forced against the foot of the bed, her chest and abdomen became arched like a bridge, drawn up almost half a yard. In this unnatural position she was suspended several seconds. Suddenly the whole body jerked upwards with a bound, and the poor sufferer was tossed about for some seconds, with her spine drawn in.

During the whole attack, which lasted several minutes, she was quite unconscious; pinching and slapping had no effect; dashing cold water in the face, or applying burnt feathers to the nostrils, were ineffectual; the pupils were quite insensible to light.

Ignatia, which I ordered, had no effect; cupr. metal. acted better, but only temporarily; Belladonna, Ipec. and Pulsatilla (the latter for suppressed catamenia), were of no use. The attacks did not increase, neither did they decrease in the least degree. The morphium injections, too, were continued at the desire of her friends.

When at my visit on the 4th of October, the spasms came on again with such violence that the bedstead gave way, I consulted Schüssler's Therapy, and now ordered her to have —*Magnesium phosphate*.

After taking this remedy, on the 10th of October the catamenia appeared; but her condition otherwise was in no way changed. The spasms continued with the same violence. Then remembering Schüssler's injunction to use *Calcium phosphate* where *Magnesium phosphate*, though indicated by the symptoms, proves ineffectual, I gave her *Calcium phosphate*—on the 16th of October, a full dose every two hours. Immediately the spasms became less frequent. On the sixth day there was an attack, weak and of short duration. From this date she had peace until the 6th of November, the day of the return of the catamenia, which was preceded by a short slight attack.

On the 14th of December I had a call from the young lady, looking well and blooming, who wished to consult me for a slight bronchial affection. She told me that she was completely cured of her attacks, and that at the beginning of December she had been quite regular, without experiencing any inconvenience.

---

49. Dr. Schlegelman reports:—*Potassium sulphate*, I have repeatedly tested in wandering rheumatism, and have had very favourable results.

---

50. Dr. S. writes:—Mrs. S., aged 24, of Regensburg, who had been suffering for several years from lichen (skin affec-

tion) had used various well-known medicines which had done her no good. I tried various remedies, and at last cured her. A few months ago she came again, and the lichen was worse than ever. My former remedy had no effect; and with several others, arsenic, etc., it was no better. I gave her *Calcium sulphate* night and morning, in quantities as large as a bean, and in a fortnight the cure was complete.

---

51. Silica has proved an excellent remedy. Within the last few months I was able to cure a young lady, 16 years old, who lives in the country. I did not see her myself. The mother of the girl came to me almost crying, and told me her daughter had been suffering for the last few months from her right foot. The medical men treating her there declared that the foot must be amputated. It was fearfully swollen; the discharge of matter was excessive; her leg was almost bent to a right angle at the knee-joint, and could absolutely not be stretched out. I advised her to give up all internal as well as the external remedies, and prescribed *Silica* to be taken once daily. Three months later the patient came herself, walking without any assistance. The foot was almost completely healed, with only a slight discharge of matter.

Thus I succeeded, also, in a case of discharge from the ear, which had been treated for a long time ineffectually, and had caused the patient severe pain day and night. This case was also cured with *Silica.*

---

52. From the Rundschau: Magnesium phosphate for Whooping Cough. In the spring of 1881, when there was an epidemic of whooping cough amongst the children here, a little child of ten months was given up by the family doctor. I heard this from the father of the child, who was in great grief. He mentioned that the spasms, which occurred about ten times in the course of the day, were so severe that the little face became quite livid, blue, and swollen. I at once gave *Magnesium phosphate.* One single powder moderated the spasms so forcibly that they returned only occasionally, and the attacks were quite mild. Five days later I gave some *Potassium phosphate,* but without beneficial effect, then

Calcium phosphate, and it had no effect, as the paroxysms grew only worse for want of *Magnesium phosphate.* I ordered it to be taken again, and in a very short time the spasms and whoop were gone, and the child recovered rapidly.

A FEW CASES FROM THE AUTHOR'S PRACTICE.

53. Feb., 1880.—In a village a few miles from the town of Oldenburg, a child was taken ill with Diphtheria, which at an early stage was complicated by an affection of the larynx. The child was treated by the ordinary methods and died. Almost at the same time a child of another family in the village was attacked by Diphtheria with the same complication. The father of the latter child came to me. I prescribed *Potass. chloride* for the disease in the first instance, and *Calcium phosphate* for the affection of the larynx to be taken alternately. I requested the father to inform me without fail of the result, which he promised to do. Two days after, I received a letter from him, in which he informed me that the child had completely recovered.

---

55. A young man complained of an unnatural appetite. He had to eat almost every hour, feeling such an intense craving for food, yet he felt exhausted and languid. There were no secondary symptoms present. The tongue was clean, the urine was not increased, evacuations normal. *Potassium phosphate* cured the patient in the course of two days.

---

56. A lady felt for two days a drawing laming pain in the sole of her foot. The affected spot, about the size of a florin, had a bluish appearance. Pressure, or a blow, or other mechanical influences, had not preceded it. A dose of *Potassium phosphate* subdued the pain in about half an hour.

---

57. An old lady had become bedridden for the last fortnight on account of the following ailment. She felt a considerable pain in the lower part of the thorax on the left

side, which increased when she coughed. The cough was a slightly catarrhal one. The invalid felt very exhausted, and had no appetite. The tongue was dry, the pulse frequent, weak, and intermittent. *Potassium phosphate* cured her in the space of a week.

---

58. To the above I add another important effect of *Potassium phosphate.* By the use of it, spurious labour pains subside, weak pains are stimulated by it, and often in the shortest space of time the desired effects are produced with most favourable results.

---

59. An old man was attacked by severe vomiting and diarrhœa, accompanied by exceedingly painful cramp in the calves. Evacuations had the appearance of rice-water. I undertook the treatment about six hours after the beginning of the attack, and one dose of *Potassium phosphate* effected a cure. The speedy cure of this case of choleraic diarrhœa would justify the belief that *Potassium phosphate* is a specific against cholera.

W. H. SCHÜSSLER, M.D.

From the Eclectic Medical Journal, Cincinnati, Ohio, July, 1884:—

Rheumatism: A Splendid Cure with the Tissue Remedies. By E. H. Holbrook, M.D., Baltimore, Md.

Miss A. W., 10½ years old, was taken with a chill on January 1st, 1884. The next day I found her with very high fever, pulse 120; severe pains in back and limbs; nausea and vomiting; joints, small and large, greatly inflamed; hands, feet, and limbs œdematous. Could not bear to be touched or moved. Great sensitiveness in every part of the body and limbs. Pains became very much *worse at night*, increasing to such an extent that her screams could be heard by the neighbours on either side of the house. Constant cry for cold water; vomiting of food and drink almost as soon as swallowed. Tongue coated yellow, with horribly bitter metallic taste. Great prostration. Hereditary gouty-rheumatic and dropsical diathesis. Has had for some time back a ravenous appetite, especially for sweet things, which were freely indulged in.

Treatment.—After wasting much of the first week with various remedies with no improvement, I determined to adhere to the system of Schüssler. For the fever, vomiting of food and drink, and the inflammation, I gave *Fer. phos.*—6x. Pains aggravated at night, *Calc. phos.* 6x.; for rheumatic-gout, œdema, dropsy, yellow-coated tongue with bitter taste, *Sodium sulph.*—3x., about 10 grains in half a goblet of water, a teaspoonful every other hour in alternation with the first two, which were given dry and at the same time. From the commencement of this treatment decided improvement began, and by the fourteenth day of her sickness she was able to sit up. Previous to her sickness she had become so stout she could not stoop to button her shoes, and her cloak could scarcely be buttoned around her. Indeed it was so uncomfortable buttoned that she would go with it open almost all the time. After her recovery she was able to stoop, and her cloak could be lapped several inches.

Among the first cases in which I tried these remedies was a negro child, about two months old. The following are about the symptoms presented :—Painful diarrhœa, constant rolling of the head, eyes turned up, tongue brownish-yellow, no desire to nurse for some time. The mother said it had been sick for a week, and she had been giving it different things ; but as it got worse, she called me. I told her I was afraid there was little chance for its recovery, but I would do what I could for it.

Prescribed *Magnesium phosphate* and *Calcium phosphate* in alternation every fifteen minutes. This was about 9 or 10 o'clock a.m. I returned about 3 o'clock p.m. to see if it was still alive, and to my astonishment found it better. It had ceased rolling its head, eyes were natural, had nursed once or twice, and was sleeping. Ordered the medicine to be continued at longer intervals. The next morning it was considerably better. At this visit I found the tongue covered with a thick *white* coating, and the mouth sore. I now prescribed *Potassium chloride*, the remedy for this condition, in place of the *Calcium phosphate*, to be alternated with the *Magnesium phosphate* every hour. The next day the tongue was clear, and after leaving a few more powders, to be continued for a day or two longer, the case was dismissed.

Neuralgia.—Since writing the above I have had to treat a severe case of neuralgia of the head. The lady had come sixty miles to attend a musical entertainment, and was compelled to go to bed on account of the pain. After suffering several hours I was called, and relieved her completely in an hour with *Mag. phos.*—6x., a dose every ten minutes.

The better acquainted I become with this system the more pleased I am with it. In labour, when the pains are too weak and irregular, I have seen nothing act more promptly and effectually than *Potass. phos.* For spasmodic, crampy pains, *Mag. phos.* is a gem. After delivery I give *Fer. phos.* where I used to give Aconite and Actea Racemosa, to be followed or accompanied by whatever may be indicated. I also use as a wash 3x. to the vulva and abdomen, and for syringing the vagina morning and night. The parts heal quickly under this treatment, and with the use of other remedies as indicated, the patient makes a good recovery.

Another case was that of a lady with bilious colic. I was sent for in the night, and for particular reasons did not go. I, however, sent what I thought would relieve her. Early in the morning her husband was again at my office, saying she was no better, but suffering terribly. I gave him a different remedy to be administered until I could get there. About half-past nine I arrived at the house, and found her still suffering excruciating pains. Ascertaining that she had vomited bile, and had a very bitter taste in her mouth all the time, I administered a powder of *Sod. sulph.* in a little water. In about two minutes after taking it she said she was considerably relieved for the first time since eleven o'clock in the night. In about five minutes she had a free movement from the bowels, and she continued to improve, and was up and about the next morning.

A case of neuralgia was relieved with one dose of *Magnesium phosphate.* A bad case of asthma was cured with *Potassium phosphate.* Other cases might be stated, but those will suffice to show the value of the system.

I would advise every reader to purchase the book and study it well. It will be found a great aid in very many cases.

For some time I used only the 3x. and 6x. (coarser preparations), but of late have been using some of the remedies in the centesimal trituration as prescribed by Dr. Schüssler. I believe those I tested act certainly better in his trituration.

E. H. HOLBROOK, M.D.

Of the many successful cases at the Dispensary, 9, Perth Road, Dundee, a few are given here, which may be of some interest.—M. DOCETTI WALKER.

In the case of a little boy, seven years of age, who had concussion of the brain, from a fall, meningitis (inflammation of the covering membrane) set in, with its characteristic symptoms, and the first medical man's prognosis was adverse. *Ferric phosphate* carried the day. On the third night, however, there was a change; the pulse being in the morning 100, having been 125 on the day before, fell to 49 per minute. *Potassium phosphate*, a dose every quarter of an hour, raised it steadily, though slowly, up to 57, where it remained for two days. After that it rose, and the case mended very satisfactorily, the now threatening symptoms, stupor, dilated immovable pupils, etc., disappearing. A perfect recovery resulted at the end of a fortnight. The remedies given were *Ferric phosphate*—*Potassium phosphate*—a few doses of *Potassium chloride* and *Calcium phosphate*.

Lizzie Macquillen was brought to the Dispensary on October 15. Four years of age, to all appearance an imbecile; her head large, broad and flat, but the rest of the body undeveloped like that of an infant, denoting her disease to be a case of rickets; also curvature of the long bones, etc.; the face pale and triangular; no teeth; the neck too weak to keep the head steady; constant movement of the eyes, showing no intelligence. The mother stated the little girl seemed to be well enough till four or five months old, when she took fits till the end of the twelfth month. Since then she had scarcely grown any bigger; never had the power of holding anything in her tiny hands, and if food was held to her, did not know it was for eating; had to be fed; never attempted to use her legs; could only sit when resting her elbows on the flat cross-bar of her chair, fixing her mouth on the knuckles of her hands. In bed she could not turn herself over. She had frequently been under medical treatment, but without benefit. The mother persisted in the statement that she had lost her first and second set of teeth. The case seemed a very hopeless one. Having great doubts of doing much good, prescribed *Calcium phos-*

phate—in alternation with *Potassium phosphate*—a dose every hour, and told the mother to come back in six weeks, as I would give her an additional remedy then. She called back at the appointed time, quite proud of her little thing. The change was marvellous, scarcely any rocking of the head, and as I turned over the leaves of the entry-book the little creature looked up wistfully, bent over and stretched out her hand to take hold of it. The mother expressed her gratitude for the change in her child, saying the last week or two many neighbours had called to see little Lizzie, and the father now happy to dandle her on his knees. To continue another six weeks the remedies *Calcium phosphate* daily, alternate doses of *Potassium phosphate* and *Potassium chloride* day about. The improvement has continued steadily, she nibbles crusts out of her own hand, the intelligence developing apace, she begins to say some words, can now stand holding by her chair, which she pushes before her and moves through the room. To crown all she has cut two front teeth. January 21st.—The biochemic remedies to be continued, about three or four doses a day, for some time.

W. Watson, aged 40 years. Ulceration of stomach, vomited all his food, and latterly all the egesta had the appearance of coffee grounds. He had suffered from vomiting and indigestion more or less for fourteen years, had seen many doctors, and taken much medicine without avail. I advised him to take *Ferric phosphate*[6]—and *Sodium phosphate*[6]—in usual quantities, and a tablespoonful every two hours alternately for a fortnight. On his second visit he was free from vomiting, had little pain, and felt greatly better. He continued another ten days with the same remedies, and returned quite well. On making special inquiry if he had nothing troubling him, he said, "No, the only thing I sometimes trouble myself about, is thinking after taking any kind of food, whether it will trouble me, but it never does." His cure has proved permanent, as it is now nearly two years since, and he is still keeping well.

Lady Louisa —— has been subject to attacks of bronchitis for several winters, the last attack, pneumonic, proving very serious. Her husband wrote to ask which of the biochemic remedies should be given. *Ferric phosphate*, a dose every hour, and a few doses of *Potassium phosphate*, for her exhausted condition, were taken steadily for a few days, and then *Ferric phosphate* and *Potassium chloride* alternately. Shortly after this I received a letter dated London, 6th of October, in which she says: "I must write to thank you more than I can say, for your remedies have done me untold good. The doctor who has called yesterday states all the bronchial symptoms are gone! My only very slight trouble now is a tendency to gout in my ankle. I should be glad to get rid of this, as the doctor thinks it adds to my bronchial attacks. Would you be so kind again to prescribe, and send me the address? Is it Sanger and Son, 489, Oxford Street, where I can get the medicines in London?

"Again thanking you a thousand times.—I am, etc."

Miss Edith M. had an attack of rheumatism, excessive pain in her joints, and several much swollen. She was not able to move, *worse when warm in bed*, and fevered, unable to sleep. *Ferric phosphate*, a dose every hour for one day, and *Potassium chloride* in alternation removed all pain in two days. She continued the remedies for a little time longer, and made a rapid recovery.

Those pains which increase with the warmth of the bed seem always to yield to *Potassium chloride.*

Miss Margaret S. suffered from neuralgia, true nerve-fibre pain, darting through her head along the nerves. She had suffered intermittently for three days. Two doses of *Magnesium phosphate* cured her completely.

The following is an extract from the letter of a medical man in large practice in America:

"I have been trying the new remedies here in the hospital for the past few months, and for two months have used them almost entirely in the female medical ward, with the consent of the two physicians on duty, who have left the cases in my hand for the experiment. Have used them both in acute and chronic cases, and feel well satisfied with them.

"*Potassium chloride* I find is frequently considered by the Pharmaceutists to be the *Chlorate*, instead of *Chloride*, as directed by Schüssler. I thought you might like to know the above.—I am, etc."

Miss M., the daughter of the late Dr. M., has been suffering since her eighteenth year from occasional attacks of aberration of the mind. But as years passed on these attacks of insanity became *worse and more frequent*, until it was deemed advisable by Captain M., her brother, to make arrangements with the doctor of a lunatic asylum in the district to have her removed there. As a last resource a friend called to see if the new remedies could be of any service in such a hopeless case. Having assured him that *Potassium phosphate* would do her good, they gave it very steadily—four doses daily for weeks. This was four years ago. The result was most satisfactory. After taking it she never had another attack, and is completely cured. Able to superintend home duties, receive callers, and make calls, which she had not been able to do for many years, on account of feeling so nervous and shy during the intervals of the attacks.

Several cases of a similar nature have been treated equally successfully—two of these Puerperal Mania—and in all these *Potassium phosphate* was the only remedy given.

The following letter was received from a French lady at Beyrout, Syria, to express her grateful thanks. The case was one of very distressing mania, with suicidal attempts. The remedies given were *Potassium phosphate* and *Calcium phosphate*, with complete recovery; and after two months her friend was again able to take up her vocation as teacher:

"To Mr. Smith, Newport.

"Monsieur,—Pardonnez-moi de ne pas avoir écrit plus vite. Premièrement il semblait que les remèdes envoyés n'avaient aucun effet. Enfin, on a pu faire partir, mon amie elle ne demeure plus à Beyrout, mais Dieu merci *elle se porte bien*. Je n'ai pas voulu le dire, les premiers mois, afin d'être bien sure que le mieux continuerait. Je suis très reconnaissante que le Seigneur ait fait miséricorde. Veuillez je vous prie, Monsieur, communiquer la bonne nouvelle aux personnes qui ont pri tant d'intérêt en mon amie, et je pense que maintenant elle voudrait bien aussi se joindre à moi pour rendre grâces à Dieu, de son exaucement, d'une maladie aussi terrible.

"J'éspère que vous comprendrez, Monsieur, le français de ces quelques lignes, et veuillez je vous prie recevoir mes salutations chrétiennes.

"Beyrout, 8th April, 1884. P. ALLMAND."

Mrs. Forbes, a widow, was lying very ill with erysipelas, high fever, and quite prostrate. The members of her family thought her dying, as she had become delirious. Her head and face so swollen that her eyes were literally closed—suffering intense pain. *Sodium phosphate* and *Ferric phosphate* alternately, a dose every hour and oftener, was given. After the second dose of the former she ejected a great quantity of bile. The severe symptoms subsided; this was on Saturday night. The medicine was continued; *Ferric phosphate*—now only intercurrently, as the pulse had become less frequent. To the astonishment of all her friends, on Wednesday morning she was so well that she went out to her work as usual.

Statistics show a death-rate of 2,000 per annum from this disease. In a similar case of erysipelas in a lady of eighty-seven years of age, these remedies and a few doses of *Potassium phosphate* cured her, when the usual treatment, painting with iodine, brandy, etc., had had no effect in arresting the disease.

Case of a lady who had been bedridden for nine months. Mrs. M'H. was given up by four doctors as beyond medical treatment. The Professor's diagnosis ran thus: Both lungs diseased, especially the right lung. The heart is greatly dilated, especially the right cavity. The lung disease produced by neglected cold. When her case was brought under treatment by biochemic measures four years ago, she was also suffering from dropsy. At this stage she came under the new treatment; it took sometimes an hour and more before she could find the right position to rest in. She would often rather spend the night on the sofa than venture to go through the fatigue of going to bed. Her cough and expectorations very bad, breath extremely short, and palpitation constant. She did not know what it was to have a good night, and rarely slept. By patiently adhering to Dr. Schüssler's remedies she has recovered greatly, her lungs are wonderfully healed up, and her dilatation of heart almost removed. She lives now in comparatively fair health, so that she was able to nurse her husband during a severe illness where night watching was necessary.

To reassure all concerned a diagnosis was made by Dr. H., a specialist, who concurs in the statement that her right lung, of which a large portion is gone, is now fairly healed up, and dilatation of heart has almost disappeared.

Below is another extract from a letter received, which shows the favourable way in which the New Treatment is received by some members of the medical profession:

"Allow me to thank you for the copy of Dr. Schüssler's new edition, received a few days since through the hands of my brother, Dr. H. R. The work is much improved, and several of my medical friends to whom I have shown it are much pleased with it. For myself I find them invaluable, and their usefulness increasing both in acute and chronic cases. In acute rheumatism there is nothing that will cut short the disease as effectually. Recently I had the opportunity of trying it in a severe case of membranous croup with great success. In skin affections it also is superior to other forms of treatment in the majority of cases. Thanking you for your contribution to knowledge,

"Believe me, yours sincerely,

"S. E. S., M.D."

In a severe epidemic of Diphtheria, most cases terminating fatally, a well-known medical man lost every case under the usual treatment until he resorted to the new remedies, after which every case treated by him recovered satisfactorily, all of them being of a severe type.

In fourteen cases of diphtheria, the biochemic measures left nothing better to be desired, *Potassium chloride*—rapidly making a change, the whitish gray exudation being diminished, shrivelling and coming away with the gargle and mouth wash made with *Potassium chloride*—also occasional doses of *Ferric phosphate*. The treatment worked splendidly. In three cases the patients laboured under prostration from the first, and *Potassium phosphate*—had to be given intercurrently. In two cases *Sodium chloride*—alternately with *Potassium chloride*—the chief remedy. In the latter cases there existed considerable flow of saliva, heavy drowsiness, and watery stools. No secondary affections resulted, such as frequently arise under ordinary treatment, as paralysis, defective vision, or neuralgia.

A young gentleman, J. G., the son of a landed proprietor, had been subject to severe attacks of asthma for several years, and all the various usual remedies had failed. Shortly after commencing with the biochemic remedies his sister writes:—"My mother wishes me to say that she provided herself with a small store of the German remedies, and my youngest brother having an attack of asthma on Saturday and yesterday, he tried the *Potassium (phosphate and chloride)*—with, we think, *very* great success, relief having been experienced more quickly than by any other remedy he has tried. He goes abroad with my father and mother this week, and it is comforting to think he will have such a portable and effectual remedy in case of suffering."

The following is from an elderly gentleman, Mr J. M., who had suffered from a prolonged attack of acute and subacute inflammation of the brain. He recovered slowly, but symptoms of softening of the brain set in. He was anxious to give the new remedies a trial. His speech was affected, he seemed to lose momentary consciousness, could not hurry though he saw himself in great danger of being run over, or stop walking when dangerously close to the quay, and could not be trusted out alone.

"I think it is time I were again informing you I still continue to improve, indeed I have little to complain of except occasionally—only occasionally—a feeling of mental stupor, the best remedy for which I have found to be *Potassium phosphate*—which you recommended to me."

Archibald Herbert, suffering from chronic bronchitis, had an attack of pneumonia. An iron moulder by trade, he was exposed to great heat, he had lain down on a form in a state of perspiration, took a severe chill, and inflammation in the right lung was the result. His case was a bad one, complicated by bronchial affection, fever high, cough distressing, a pain deep-seated in the right side, expectoration tenacious, rusty coloured. *Ferric phosphate*—in alternation with *Potassium chloride*—a dose every half-hour was taken for 24 hours, then every hour. For his prostration and sleeplessness a few doses of *Potassium phosphate*—were taken now and then. The improvement every way was very marked in two days. As the colour of the sputa changed to yellow, he took *Potassium sulphate*—instead of *Potassium chloride*; and as this condition was remedied, *Sodium chloride*—and *Calcium phosphate*—completed the cure in little more than ten days. He returned to work free from inflammation and bronchitis, as will be seen from his letter, which is given at his own request, as follows :—

"No. 3 Kincardine Street,
Dundee, March 6th, 1886.

For eleven years back at various times, save this last year, I have been an unfortunate sufferer from bronchitis and occasionally inflammation of the lungs; as a rule I had the best medical advice within my reach, everything was done as usual in such cases, being laid bedfast from eight to ten weeks at a time, generally once, sometimes twice, each year; then I was parboiled with poulticing, cough mixtures wholesale, which destroyed my stomach, could scarcely walk on my legs, my existence was a burden. I was now told no more could be done for me, so that was a blue look out for me. Fully twelve months ago I was again seized with bronchitis and inflammation of the lungs. A friend advised me to consult you. With Dr. Schüssler's biochemic treatment of disease, and God's blessing, and without a single poultice or nauseous drug, in three weeks and three days' time I was at my usual employment, and have since been, and seem likely to continue healthier, happier, and heavier than in any period during the best days of my life. I sincerely hope you may use, and others may see, this brief note, and be resurrected as I have been by this simple, safe, and sure New Treatment of Disease. Life is now worth living for.—I am,

Your much benefitted and grateful Servant,

ARCHIBALD HERBERT."

Case of an old lady about eighty years of age.—Mrs M., a doctor's widow, took a cold three weeks ago. Cough hard, worse at night, little spit, incessant irritation at windpipe, pain under left breast, occasional palpitation. Had taken some *Ferric phosphate*—latterly. Sputa is copious now after much straining, appetite fairly good, but very much inclined to constipation, sleep very much broken by the severe fits of coughing. *Potassium chloride*—for the cough and sputa, and *Sodium chloride*—for the constipation, were now taken regularly every hour, a dose alternately. A letter was received written on the evening of the second day, in which the gentleman writes :—

"You will be pleased to hear that my old mother had a good night and scarcely any cough after following your prescription. Mother says that she might have slept more, but her mind was unsettled, always expecting the cough to return. I left her this morning very cheerful, and of course more than ever a firm believer in the New Treatment of all diseases."

No other remedies were required, the lady recovered in a few days.

A gentleman who had suffered from great sleeplessness, depression, and occasional tendencies to suicidal mania, writes :—"I do not know how to thank you for the medicine you gave me, it has done me so much good. I have taken the *Potassium phosphate*—and occasional doses of *Potassium chloride*—very faithfully, and will continue to do so, as it keeps me right."

In the case of a poor orphan girl fourteen years old, *Silica* saved her having her foot amputated. She had been under treatment a long time for bone disease. Her medical man saw no alternative, as the evil only grew worse, to make arrangements with the infirmary surgeon to have it taken off. This was agreed on, six days before removing her. Her friends were greatly distressed and applied for the New remedies. *Silica*—a dose every hour, was steadily taken, and lotion on lint externally applied. On the fifth day the ankle bone and surrounding tissues presented such a healthy appearance that all cause for amputation was removed. She continued the treatment for a short time longer, and her case was pronounced perfectly cured.

A young lady had been treated by two physicians for several months without being much or permanently benefitted. She had a pricking pain near the shin-bone, and had irritated a raised spot like a pin head, and ulceration set in. Her general health had been good, but being ordered to recline a great deal for relief and even keep to bed, as she suffered pain and lamed on walking, her health began to give way. Mrs G., her mother, applied for the New Remedies, as the doctors seemed puzzled with the case. The appearance of the limb seemed quite normal except the ulcer. This led me to give *Calcium fluoride*—externally as lotion on lint, and every two hours a dose internally. On very minute enquiry it turned out that she suffered from menstrual colic with cramp in the legs; also for the cramp, *Magnesium phosphate*—was taken, giving rapid relief, and special attention to be paid that none of her garments were tight. The sore, a *varicose* ulcer, healed in a very short time, and has not troubled her since a lapse of three years.

The following is a copy of a letter from a lady :—

"Owing to the benefit we have received from Dr. Schüssler's medicine, recommended by you, we thought it our duty to acknowledge, in writing, our thanks. For a long time my daughter was troubled with a very bad cough, for which several doctors had given a great many remedies, but without success. We were advised to consult you, and after taking the medicine prescribed by you for about two months, the cough entirely disappeared, and since then she has enjoyed excellent health. On seeing the benefit she received from it, we bought Dr. Schüssler's book with a therapeutical index by yourself, to which I can easily refer when required. I have recommended the medicine to different persons, and it always proved *very* beneficial. One case in particular was that of an old lady afflicted with gouty rheumatism; her body was so very much swollen that she could do not work at all. I recommended *Sodium chloride*—and *Sodium sulphate*—to her, and after using it for a time the swelling in her body had decreased so much that she was able to knit with ease and go about the house. I have given the remedies in cases of common cold, coughs, inflammation of tonsils, &c., in my own family, and have found them *very* beneficial. Wishing you every success in your noble work.

I remain,

Yours gratefully,

M. V. S."

Extract from a letter by a medical man in a large practice:—"I do not see how the new system can fail to gain headway. If it is thoroughly investigated by the Professors at the Universities, it must do so. But it is hard to overcome old prejudices, and to lift up those sunk into deep ruts. Yet for the sake of suffering humanity these barriers ought to be laid aside when a new method of scientific treatment appeals so strongly to all who are engaged in so noble a purpose as healing the sick."

E.H., M.D.

Case of a gentleman suffering much pain, his hand having been severely cut with a piece of glass. A surgeon near at hand had extracted it, but could do nothing for the intense pain in the wound. This kept him from sleeping, and he was unable to attend to his duties in consequence. *Ferric phosphate*—was applied as a lotion to saturate the dressing, and the doses were taken frequently for one day. Next morning a note reached me as follows:—My hand is nearly well already. I had a good night, and I beg to thank you for the benefit I received from your medicine and advice. In a few days the ragged wound was quite healed.

Annie Allan, aged 18 years, had been under treatment five weeks for rheumatic fever. Little progress was made, and complications grew worse. I was consulted on the 8th March. She was then suffering intensely. One of her legs was swollen to nearly double its size, and perfectly stiff. Neuralgic pains darting periodically through her body, arms, head, etc. The paroxysms were frequent and most exhausting. Morphia pills had been given with little effect. *Magnesium phosphate*—for these agonising attacks acted like a charm. As she had a great itching all over her body, and the symptoms of articular rheumatism were still there, tongue creamy, mouth also sore, *Sodium phosphate*—the chief remedy for these, was given in alternation with *Potassium chloride*—for the synovitis with all its marked symptoms, swelling of knee and leg. Improvement set in at once, and in five days all the severe symptoms had subsided. The leg became normal in size, she had regained the power of moving it, and though the ankle was still swollen, she soon made a rapid recovery, and was able to resume her duties in a very short time. A similar case of synovitis treated on the old system left the young lady a cripple for life.

The following is a most striking case showing what has been done with one Remedy — *Sodium chloride* — in Pemphigus, pronounced incurable. The son of a gentleman came under my treatment at the age of fifteen with this disease, which he had since his childhood ; he was little and stunted in growth. He had never been able to wear ordinary clothes, but wore sandals and a loose garment with a girdle. He had a tutor, as he could never go to school. The whole body, face, and feet, were covered more or less with the vesicles and incrustations in their various stages. All the highest authorities on skin diseases had been consulted and their medicines tried without any lasting effect. The whole of the symptoms and pathological conditions pointing so clearly to *Sodium chloride*—he received this the only remedy to take internally and also for outward application. The effects were such that in less than three months he wore his first tailor-made suit, and has since then (now 8 years ago) enjoyed good health, and is quite the strongest and tallest of the family.

From India reports have reached us through the Sheriff of Madras of the cure of two cases of Diabetes with Dr. Schüssler's remedy—*Sodium sulphate.*

From Melbourne a doctor expresses himself highly satisfied with the results of the twelve Cell-Salts. In New Zealand many are using the New Remedies with the most satisfactory results. In consumption most gratifying recoveries have been achieved with the remedies, selected according to the pathological state of the lung tissues.

Extract from another medical man's letter:—"I wish to say that I possess a copy of your translation of Dr. Schüssler's Biochemic Treatment of Disease, which I have now extensively used in my practice over a year. Indeed I must say I have had the best results from the said system of anything I have yet tried.

When diagnosis (not mere guess work) is properly made, and the Biochemic Remedies are used direct in the pathological conditions pointed out in your therapeutical index; then, they become specific certainties, and will cure all curable diseases, and the practitioner is no longer left to grope his way in the dark. The Biochemic system of practice established on rational basis is a demonstrated truth, and let him who doubts the assertion candidly, and without prejudice, investigate for himself and be convinced; thereby profit by it himself, and benefit suffering humanity at large.

I admit it is easier to practice under the old system, as that is a routine way, hit or miss. But the modern scientific physician seeking after truth is, and must be a diligent worker and a thorough student of the laws of nature, reaching after truth wherever found regardless of "Pathies," and "isms," and medical orthodox dogmas.

Doctor, allow me to thank and congratulate you for your toiling hours of labour spent in the translation of Dr. Schüssler's method and your systematic arrangement of the Therapeutical Index."

T.G.W., M.D.,

Extract from a letter received from George W. Carey, M.D. :—

"Our success has fully sustained Dr Schüssler's theory in "our daily practice. We have recently treated 31 cases of "typhoid fever during 60 days without a failure. Yes, "your name will be inseparably connected with the success of "Biochemistry throughout the world. The certainty of "success encourages us to renewed efforts in our calling and "determined march towards the goal of all medical science. "This, we feel sure, will be reached by those in the near "future, although we both may have laid down our "burdens to rest. All over our great America are spring- "ing up bright minds who refuse to be bound by the "barbarous practices of the past, or allow their minds to "be chained to the cruel wheels of error, and when we shall "have passed to that realm of knowledge where all science "will be understood, the seared torch that falls from our "grasp will be seized with eager hands, and carried for- "ward to lighten the pathway of our fellowmen."

In all cases of disease, molecules of certain salts are required. But deficiency of a certain salt does not imply want of it in the whole system, but want of it in certain abnormal parts only. In fact. a disease is often recognised by an excess of the salt, and its organic substance or basis by the various channels of excretion, in fæces, urine, etc. In diseases where certain salts are thus prevented from being used in the economy of the body, they are often excreted in a manner unchanged. See Albuminuria, Bright's disease, etc.

Bio-chemic Remedies, which act in perfect harmony with Nature's laws, have achieved such notable cures that thousands of thinking minds have already accepted this method by which health is so certain to be restored, even in almost hopeless cases, if Providence be pleased to grant ever so small an amount of vitality or powers for the further continuance of the processes of life.

The Clinical cases given are only a few of the many which are constantly treated with great success at my Dispensary and Consulting Rooms here and in London.

M. Docetti Walker, M.D.,
2 Airlie Place, Dundee.

THERAPEUTICAL INDEX.

The Twelve Inorganic Cell-Salts.

The Tissue Cell-Salts as specially prepared for DR. SCHÜSSLER, *act as* MOLECULAR-CELLULAR THERAPEUTICS.

Modern English Terms.	*Terms as used in German.*
I. Calcium phosphate, $Ca^3(PO_4)_2$.	1. Calcarea phos.
II. Calcium sulphate, $CaSO_4$.	2. Calcarea sulph.
III. Calcium fluoride, CaF_2.	3. Calcium fluor.
IV. Ferric phosphate, $Fe_3(PO_4)_2$.	4. Ferrum phos.
V. Potassium chloride, KCl.	5. Kali mur.
VI. Potassium phosphate, K_2HPO_4.	6. Kali phos.
VII. Potassium sulphate, K_2SO_4.	7. Kali sulph.
VIII. Magnesium phosphate, $MgPHO_4,1H_2O$.	8. Magnesia phos.
IX. Sodium Chloride, NaCl.	9. Natrum mur.
X. Sodium phosphate, $Na_2HPO_4 12H_2O$.	10. Natrum phos.
XI. Sodium sulphate, Na_2SO_4.	11. Natrum sulph.
XII. Silica, SiO_2.	12. Silicea.

The chemical formula appended to each of the cell-salts, with the number of molecules and their atomic composition respectively, suggest the variety of combinations and isomeric positions they may assume in the living tissues. It also shows that each has a certain number of molecules which individually take part in the process of elaborating the various cells and tissues of the body. Each molecule represents the variety of isomeric conditions it can assume in those chemical allotropic combinations which are constantly taking place in the human economy. According to the number of these inorganic molecules which enter into combination with certain organic molecules, both in the process of synthesis and analysis (splitting up), and according to their relative isomeric conditions, or arrangement, they determine the differentiation of cells. Hence it will be possible to explain how the protoplasmic substance changes under the favourable conditions necessary to form the variety of the differentiated organic substances we meet with in the tissues. Protoplasm, by reason of such molecular arrangements, changes, and we have albumen, albumenoids, etc. The basis of the cells, the water or gaseous solutions or combinations as such, have each the power of attracting and taking up their respective cell-salts individually, and will attract by the law of affinity the proper complement of molecules it requires if at all favourably placed.

Thus each combination, general, definite, and special, according to a numeric law, will be found to have changed the nature of the original substance into another by isomerism, *i.e.*, substances with same percentage, composition and molecular weight, but different properties, namely, metameric and polymeric. These two states are due to difference of relative position which the molecules in the cell-substances, etc., occupy. (See Lehman and Ponton.) Molecular motion is aided by heat and cold. All these laws in chemistry, exhibited in nature, play their part also in living things, and are summed up in the term Bio-chemistry (Th. Carnelly, Dr. Sc.). Ex. We know of the molecular movement of iron, the expansion of its molecules by heat and contraction by cold. These influences (magnetic and electric) act on the molecules of iron, which are visibly susceptible to their influence. This same property is inherent in the molecules of Ferric phosphate, and their action in the living body is determined thereby in the same manner. By cold, contraction sets in, and the free movement of the iron molecules (atomic) is checked. This example may serve to show and explain why a person whose circulation (blood containing iron) has suddenly suffered a check through chill will often be able to correct such an abnormal condition by the application of heat alone, which relaxes and will permit the molecules of displaced hydrogen to return; expansion and molecular motion of the iron molecules will resume their function. The function of the Phosphate of iron in the body has been well defined by Dr. Schüssler.

But if heat alone is not adequate to overcome the contraction or cohesion, a deficiency occurs in the number of available molecules or atoms for the general welfare of the economy of the body, which will be felt in some cells. Other causes over irritation or stimulation may also cause a lack by excessive expenditure of molecules of Phosphate of iron. This lack, Schüssler tells us, must be made up for by the physician, who, recognising the general—definite—and special symptoms, *selects*, by a general, definite, and special guiding system, and supplies the salt requisite to restore normal equilibrium in the diseased parts. If this were only a theory made up to coincide and fit in so beautifully with the natural laws, it might as a theory be set aside. But experience has proved and esstablished the curative effects of the biochemical action of the twelve cell-salts, which are brought about by careful study and reasonings and scientific means. Nature acts in obedience to the laws laid down by the great Lawgiver.

The proof of the success these remedies have in the cure of disease is seen by the profession adopting them very largely in England, Germany, the Colonies, and America. In America, in the State of Washington, already two Biochemic Colleges have been established. This shows what hold this new scientific system of medicine has on the profession. There Virchow's "Cellular Pathology" is one of the chief text-books for the medical students.

DIRECTIONS.

THE DOSE.—Dissolve from 3 to 5 grains of the powder (a quantity about the size of a pea) in say a dessert or tea spoonful of water for a single dose. For convenience, take as much powder as will lie on a sixpenny piece, dissolve in half-a-tea-cupful of water, and make 6 to 8 doses or sips of this quantity. In the case of Magnesium phosphate, where warmth is agreeable and grateful, *hot* water may be advantageously taken. If from any reason the patient cannot readily take the remedy in water, the powder may be taken dry upon the tongue, though this is not the preferable or most effective way.

TIME.—A dose should be taken every hour, or even oftener if the case be very acute. In less urgent cases, a dose every two hours. In chronic cases 4 doses daily.

ALTERNATION.—When two remedies have to be taken alternately, each must be kept in a separate cup or phial, the one to be taken in turns or time about with the other.

THE INTERCURRENT REMEDY.—To be taken occasionally, in any disease, between or in place of the chief or principal remedy or remedies, such as *Ferric phosphate* or *Potassium phosphate*, as symptoms may arise in complications. For *chronic* cases, the *intercurrent*, such as *Calcium phosphate*, a dose every day, night, and morning, or only every second day.

EXTERNAL APPLICATION.—This must always be accompanied by the remedy internally. Dissolve a good pinch of the powder prescribed, in half a tumblerful of water. This *lotion* can be used tepid or cold as may be required or preferred, for bathing the parts with; or, if to be applied on lint as a compress, with oilskin over it; or a poultice may be moistened with it, though a compress is preferable to it. It may be used as a *gargle*. Wetted and mixed with either Olive Oil, Glycerine, or Vaseline, it may be applied like ointment, or the parts may simply be moistened with the lotion as often as desirable under existing circumstances. Any of these ways of application may be adopted whenever *external use* is prescribed.

THE TONGUE and its appearance in disease forms, as a rule, a very important index to the remedy required. Different salts when deficient in function, cause a peculiar appearance of the tongue (for which consult page 69). The best time to examine the tongue is *before* and not after meals.

N.B.—**ON SELECTING A REMEDY,** read always the first two paragraphs under each Cell-Salt in this index, as these are of importance.

See that each remedy as given above has its own number affixed on the phial or box in which it is contained, as it facilitates the reading.

TRITURATIONS.—The same trituration which Dr Schüssler recommends for ordinary use, as well as the 12th, 30th, and 100th, can be obtained in boxes at the Biochemic Dispensary. The latter are, however, only for chronic cases, or where the 6th trituration does not act. This arises from some abnormal and altered state of the cells themselves, or of those surrounding the seat of the diseased cells. The molecules of ordinary size being impeded in their passage, do not reach therefore the places where they are required for the completion of the chemical molecular arrangement.

This solves the much vexed question why high or fine triturations act best in old chronic cases and with little children, and are not so well suited in acute and ordinary cases.

1.—Calcium Phosphate = Calcarea Phosphorica.*
Calc. phos.

The Diseases forming this group must be healed or treated with *Calcium phosphate*, as they may have their seat in any of the cells or the intercellular fluids. The *Calcium phosphate* has a chemical affinity for albumen, which forms the organic basis for this salt in the tissue-cells. It is required in all cells, as also in all intercellular fluids, and when albumen or albuminous substances are found in the secretions or effusions, it is clearly shown to be necessary.

All Ailments which are obstinate and do not yield to their own remedy, may require a few doses of *Calcium phosphate*. More particularly is this required with growing young people or old persons in the decline of life.

Abdomen, glands of the bowels enlarged in children, chronic condition.

Ailments in which heat or cold increases the pain. Also Silica.

Albuminuria—Albuminous urine calls for the use of this cell-salt and Potass. phosphate as an alternate remedy in the more chronic stage.

Amenorrhœa in anæmic (bloodless) conditions.

Anæmia (poverty of red blood)—To supply new blood cells, this salt as first remedy, also Sodium phosphate.

Anæmia, with waxy appearance of the skin.

Appetite, loss of, if the patient is emaciated, alt. remedy Sodium phos.

Atrophy, wasting of the body or organs, this the chief remedy, to be alternated with certain others. See the characteristics of these salts.

Backache, when the spine seems weak.

Back, pain across the loins on awakening in the morning. Also Sodium phosphate.

Blisters, eruptions, this as an after course.

Blisters, when the contents are albuminous and clear.

Bone diseases, see Rickets; bone earth not being proportionally extracted from food, or dissolved too freely.

Bones, broken, surgical aid is necessary, and for the uniting of the fractured ends this cell-salt is essential.

Bones when weak, yielding and soft.

Bowed legs in children, to strengthen the weak bones.

Bright's disease (of the kidneys) for the albumen; alternate remedy, Potassium phosphate.

Bronchial asthma, this cell-salt as an intercurrent remedy when the secretion is clear and tough.

Bronchitis, also bronchial catarrhs, chronic or acute, when the expectoration is clear, tough, and contains albumen, this remedy is also useful as an after course by itself.

Bronchocele, goitre, Derbyshire neck; for the cystic enlargement. Also Sodium phosphate and Sodium chloride as lotion.

* These chemicals are all specially prepared to Dr. Schüssler's prescriptions to enter the cells readily.

Cancer, in scrofulous constitutions.

Catamenia, see Menstruation.

Catarrh, chronic, with characteristic expectoration ; obstinate, and in anæmic conditions.

Catarrhs, colds, chronic, of anæmic persons ; as an intercurrent remedy, and when the secretions are albuminous.

Chorea (St. Vitus Dance), when the lime salts are deficient as intercurrent remedy, with Magnesium and Potassium phosphate.

Chlorosis ("green sickness") of young females ; complexion waxy, greenish-white.

Clergyman's sore throat, in ; as an intercurrent remedy.

Cold in the head, with albuminous (white-of-egg-like) discharge from the nose.

Constitutional weakness, in ; as a tonic for delicate persons.

Consumption, in, to lessen the emaciation. Also cream, small doses of cod-liver oil and carbonacious food.

Consumption of the bowels, in ; as an intercurrent remedy.

Convalescence, during ; after all acute diseases, as a restorative.

Convulsions, from teething, without fever, if Magn. phos. fails.

Convulsive twitchings, spasmodic actions are frequently benefitted by this remedy, when Magn. phos. and Potass. phos. fail.

Cornea inflamed, at periphery, a vesicle forming the apex of a triangular network of distended blood-vessels, alternate remedy Calcium sulphate.

Cough, expectoration of albuminous mucus, not watery, (transparent elastic film ?)

Cough, in consumption ; as an intercurrent remedy.

Cramps, or spasms of all description, if Magnesium phosphate fails.

Craniotabes, wasting of the skull ; chief remedy.

Creeping, crawling or numb feeling in the limbs.

Croup, when not yielding to Potassium chloride, alternate this remedy, and when deeper structures are involved.

Crusta lactea, scald head, of children, when the patient is weakly and anæmic.

Cysts, sac, containing morbid fluid ; internally and externally ; this the chief remedy to absorb the albuminous fluid, no operation required.

Cysts, cystic tumours to absorb the albuminous secretion found in the sac.

Debility, general ; with emaciation ; weakness after acute disease ; or delicacy generally.

Delicacy in growing girls and boys, delicate pale appearance when breeding second teeth.

Delicate young infants are much benefitted by the use of this constitutional remedy.

Dentition, teething is promoted by the use of this cell-salt.

Diphtheria, when wrongly treated or when complications of the larynx have already set in, second remedy Calcium phosphate, or eventually Calcium fluoride.

Diphtheria, after effects of, as a tonic.

Development, deficient, of young people, stunted growth.

viii. I.—Calcium Phosphate = Calcarea Phosphorica. Calc. phos.

Diarrhœa, in teething children ; as an alternate remedy.
Dropsy, from non-assimilation, anæmia, or from loss of blood.
Dulness of hearing, deafness, when from nerve disturbances.
Eczema, eruptions of the skin, with yellow-white scabs, or vesicles, (with albuminous white-of-egg-like contents).
Eczema, with anæmia (bloodlessness) ; as an intercurrent remedy.
Effusions, serous, rich in albumen.
Emaciations, without special ailments.
Emaciations, in, accompanying other ailments. This remedy intercurrently. Diet of carbonacious food, cream or small doses of cod-liver oil after food.
Enuresis, wetting the bed ; as an intercurrent remedy.
Eruptions, the same as under Eczema.
Eyelids, spasmodic affection of, if Magnesium phosphate fails.
Exhaustion, weakness, after disease, or a lowered state of the system, generally this remedy in alternation with Potassium phosphate.
Expectorations, albuminous, clear, transparent, stringy, tough.
Exudations, effusions on serous linings of an albuminous nature, as in Hydrocephalus, water on the head, cysts, or mucous membranes.
Exudations, secretions on the skin, of an albuminous nature, clear, transparent, like white of egg.
Face sallow from bloodlessness, pale gums, anæmic conditions.
Face-ache (neuralgic, rheumatic), commences or is worse at night.
Fits, during development in childhood, youth, or old age, where the lime salts are at fault. See also Sodium phos. for worms.
Fits, in anæmic patients with pale waxy complexion.
Fits, in the strumous and scrofulous.
Fontanelles, or opening of the head, sutures of the skull in the infant remaining open too long.
Fractured bones, to promote the formation of new-bone substance.
Freckles are generally lessened by it, and the constitutional want of this salt corrected.
Fungoid, inflammations, white swellings of joints, this remedy internally and externally.
Gall-stones, to prevent the re-formation of new ones ; and Sod. sulph.
Gastric, enteric or typhoid fever, after ; a course of this remedy.
Glands, enlarged, chronic ; as intercurrent remedy.
Goitre, cysts, enlargement on the fore part of neck. See Bronchocele.
Gonorrhœa, with anæmia.
Gout, rheumatic, worse at night and in bad weather. Also Sod. phos.
Gravel ; after Sodium phosphate, for the calculous, phosphatic deposit in urine ; as an intercurrent remedy.
Gums, painful in teething children, and if inflamed, alternate doses of this cell-salt and Ferric phosphate.
Gums, pale appearance, sign of anæmia ; a course of this remedy to be followed by Ferric phosphate.
Hands, involuntary shaking of, as an intercurrent remedy, toning up the tissues.
Hæmorrhoids, chronic, in anæmic or weakly patients ; intercurrently with Calcium fluoride.

Headache, a cold feeling in the head, and the head *feels* cold to the touch; also Ferric phosphate.

Heart, weak; with anæmic sounds.

Hernia (rupture) in anæmic patients; as the intercurrent remedy.

Hooping-cough, in weakly constitutions, or in teething children, and obstinate cases; as an intercurrent remedy.

Herpes, eruption on the skin, with itching, acute or chronic; intercurrent remedy.

Housemaid's knee; acute or chronic; also as lotion, chief remedy to absorb the albuminous effusion, causing the swelling.

Hydrocele, if Sodium chloride fails.

Hydrocephalus, water in the head, acute and chronic; chief remedy.

Hydrocephaloid condition; fontanelles, opening of the head, flat, depressed.

Hydrops genu, dropsical swelling of the knee; white swelling.

Hydroma patella, to reduce the effusion under the knee-cap.

Inflammations of all kinds, and parts of the body with sero-albuminous effusions or discharges.

Inflammation of the eyes, dry, during dentition; intercurrently with Ferric phosphate.

Intermittent fever, chronic, of children; as intercurrent remedy.

Kidney disease, with albumen in the urine; also Potassium phosphate.

Lactation, during; when the milk is poor and unsatisfying.

Lameness, rheumatic, obstinate; intercurrently with Potass. phos.

Laryngismus stridulus, spasm of the windpipe, sudden closing, threatening suffocation; occasional doses between the chief remedy, Mag. phosphate.

Leuchæmia, morbid condition of the blood, excess of white corpuscles.

Leucorrhœa ("Whites"): as a constitutional tonic, and intercurrent, with the chief remedy.

Lumbago; alternately with Ferric phosphate, effects a rapid cure.

Lung disease, expectoration sero-albuminous, clear, starchy.

Lupus, if a partial manifestation of scrofulosis; see also Potassium chloride and Sodium phosphate.

Menstruation delayed in young females, with waxy complexions and bloodlessness, alt. remedy Potassium chloride.

Milk, secretion of; when poor (hungry) and deficient in quantity.

Mucous membrane, affection of the, excrescences, chalky concretions as on the tongue, also Sodium phos., or secretions of an albuminous nature.

Neuralgia, commencing at night, recurring periodically, deep-seated as if on the bone. Also Silica; with beating pain, Ferric phos.

Numbness of the limbs and coldness or a sensation as of ants creeping on the part affected, affection of the nerves.

Pains in cancer, this as constitutional tonic is helpful for connective tissues.

Pains paroxysmal, or like fits, when Magnesium phosphate does not suffice, where the lime salts are abnormal in the young and in old age.

Pains in the head, worse with heat or cold.

I

Pains, neuralgic, deep-seated on the bone. Also Silica ; beating pain, Ferric phosphate.

Pains, rheumatic, with a creeping feeling in the parts affected ; also Sodium phosphate.

Pains, which are worse in the night require this salt intercurrently with the other remedies specially called for, see Potassium chloride, Silica.

Paleness of gums, when there is anæmia, blood poverty, excess of white corpuscles, waxy complexion.

Perspiration, too frequent or excessive, especially if perspiring too much about the head.

Recovery during, after illness ; this remedy is a restorative.

Rheumatic neuralgic headaches, of gouty origin, as an occasional remedy.

Rheumatism, which is worse at night.

Rheumatism, muscular, aggravated with heat or cold. Also Sodium phosphate.

Rheumatism, worse with change of weather, as alternate remedy.

Rickets in delicate children, caused by soft sponginess of bone, from want of the phosphate of lime molecules.

Scabs, crusts forming afterthe discharge of vesicles, blisters, or pimples which are of yellow colour.

Sciatica, as an alternate remedy with Potassium phosphate, in lessening pain, and when the symptoms correspond with any given in this chapter.

Secretions from mucous membrances, albuminous (white-of-egg-like) require this remedy.

Scrofulosis and struma, in, as intercurrent remedy with Sodium phos.

Skin affections, eruptions, vesicles, blisters, and albuminous contents.

Skin affections, eczema, with yellow scabs or crusts.

Sores, discharging serous-albuminous humours.

Spinal cord, softening of, as an alternating remedy.

Spina ventosa must be treated with this bone remedy. Magnesium phosphate as an intercurrent remedy.

Spinal curvature weakness ; also mechanical supports.

Spina bifida.

Stone in the bladder, to check re-formation of the same ; buttermilk as a dietary help, and probably Sodium phosphate.

Sweat, perspirations abnormal, lack of lime salt, to strengthen the connective tissue (padding).

Tabes mesenterica, wasting of the bowels as an alternating remedy.

Teeth, too rapid decay of, strumous conditions.

Teeth when breeding or cutting, if accompanied with teething ailments, fretfulness.

Teething, convulsions in ; alternately with Magnesium phosphate.

Teething disorders ; as chief remedy. See Dentition.

Teething too late ; to hasten development of.

Teething troublesome, little ailments caused by it.

Tic, neuralgia worse in the night, or recurring at night, pain in the bone, see Ferric phosphate.

Tonsils, chronic swelling ; as an intercurrent remedy.
Toothache, worse in the night, alternately Silica.
Tubercules of the skin, see also Sodium phosphate.
Typhoid, Enteric, or Gastric fevers, after, as the disease declines.
Ulceration of bone substance (true bone) ; as intercurrent remedy.
Urine, with secretion of albumen, chief remedy.
Weakliness in children ; slow development.
Whites, discharge of albuminous mucus.
White swellings, in, the chief remedy.
Whooping-cough in obstinate cases, and with emaciation, as an intercurrent remedy.

N.B.—ON SELECTING A REMEDY, read always the first two paragraphs under each Cell-Salt in this index, as these are of importance, so as to grasp the sphere of action of each Cell-Salt and its function.

2.—Calcium Sulphate = Calcarea Sulphurica.
Calc. sulph.

The Diseases forming this group must be healed or treated with *Calcium sulphate*, as it is curative in suppurations, due to lack of this salt in the intercellular fluids—at that stage in which mattery discharges are continuing to ooze after the infiltrated places have discharged their contents of pus, it cures mattery discharges of the mucous membranes, and in serous sacs as in the pleura, tubercular ulcerations of the intestines, and ulcerations of the cornea, etc.
All Ailments in which the process of discharge continues too long and the suppuration and the intercellular fluids are abnormal.
Ailments, with discharge of pus (matter) and blood.
Abscess, this remedy will shorten the suppurating process, and limit the discharge of pus. If the abscess be treated with this salt after Silica, it will bring the process to a close.
Bladder, inflammation of ; in the chronic state, pus forming.
Blisters, this remedy in cases where pus (matter) is forming.
Blows, kicks, falls, injuries, to prevent pus (matter) forming, also when blood and matter is discharging from the wound or contused parts.
Boils, to reduce and control suppuration as above.
Bowels, stools mixed with matter from ulcerations, etc., this the chief remedy.
Bowels, tubercular ulceration of, with matter in the stools.
Breasts, inflammation of, " Weed," when the matter continues to ooze, and the parts are slow to heal up, for heavy odour, Potassium phosphate.
Bronchitis, also bronchical catarrhs, chronic or acute, when the expectoration is yellow, thick, and mattery, and sinks in water.

II.—*Calcium Sulphate = Calcarea Sulphurica. Calc. sulph.*

Bruises, when neglected and suppurating, discharging pus.
Bubo, to control suppuration, in alternation with Silica.
Burns and scalds, which are suppurating; as second remedy after Potassium chloride.
Carbuncles, to control the discharge of pus. See Potassium phosphate.
Catarrh, with abundant secretion, yellow or greenish.
Chilblains, after Potassium phosphate, when in a suppurating stage.
Cold in the head, with thick mattery secretion.
Consumption, sputa, mattery, sanious, mixed with blood.
Cornea, abscess of, deep-seated; also Silica.
Cough, with irritation, yellow secretions.
Cough, with mattery spit, mixed with blood.
Crusta lactea, "scald head" of children, after Sodium phosphate, mattery discharge, or yellow mattery crusts.
Cuts, suppurative, to control the discharge of matter.
Cystitis, chronic (inflammation of the bladder), when there is pus (matter) present in the urine. See Sodium phosphate.
Deafness, with discharge of matter from the ear, sometimes mixed with blood; after Silica.
Diarrhœa, mattery, mixed with blood.
Discharges of mattery secretions on the mucous lining of any part.
Discharges of matter or sanious pus from the skin of mucous linings.
Dysentery, stools mattery, sanious (mixed with blood).
Ears, discharge of matter and blood. See under Silica.
Eczema, skin diseases or affections, when crusts, scabs, tops of yellow matter form on eruptions, Silica when the base is infiltrated.
Effusions, when pus forms.
Empyæma, pus forming in cavity of lung, or pleura.
Enteric, see gastric, typhoid fever when ulceration of the bowels has set in; for the blood poison, rise of temperature, Potassium sulphate.
Eruptions, eczema, when mattery crusts form.
Eruptions, pustular, mattery pimples, or scabs, require this remedy internally and externally.
Expectoration of matter, mixed with blood, or greenish; disagreeable sweetish taste.
Expectoration, yellow mattery, or greenish, sometimes sweet tasted.
Expectorations or discharges, chronic, greenish.
Exudations, mattery, mixed with blood.
Exudations, with matter, in serous sacs.
Eyes, inflammation of, with discharge of thick yellow matter.
Festers (common term for suppurations), are cured by this remedy after the use of Silica, and when there is no more infiltration or collection of pus.
Furuncles (boils), when pus is discharging.
Gathered breast, "Weed," to heal the parts, when the matter has freely discharged under Potass. chloride and Silica.
Gathered finger, for the last stage when the suppuration is continuing and only superficial; externally also on lint.
Glands, lymphatic, discharging pus (matter.) See also Silica.

Gonorrhœa, with bloody mattery discharges.

Hip-joint disease, for the discharge of pus (matter). This dreaded disease requires only Ferric phosphate and Calcium sulphate to effect a complete cure. Rest is useful.

Hypopion, to absorb the effusion of pus in the eye ; after Silica.

Inflammatory swelling of the external part of the ear.

Injuries (from accidents), neglected cuts, wounds, bruises, if suppurating.

Lung disease, with expectoration of mattery sputa.

Mastitis, "weed," gathered breasts, when matter is discharging ; after Silica.

Matter, or blood and matter, discharge of, from any part of the body requires this remedy, when the infiltrated parts have disappeared under the use of Silica, and the intercellular fluids only are at fault.

Mattery discharges from sores or pustules.

Mucous membrane disease, affection of the ; with secretion, discharge of matter, or blood and matter mixed.

Ophthalmia purulent. For mattery discharge from the eyes, thick, sometimes mixed with blood.

Pimples, if matter forms on the head of these.

Pustules, nodules, when suppurating, mattery.

Pustules in smallpox, when matter forms.

Pustules, with mattery heads.

Quinsy, abscess, discharging yellow matter, see Sodium phosphate.

Scabs, mattery, forming on heads of nodules and pimples.

Scalds, burns, when suppuration sets in, internally and externally.

Sebacious glands, at root of hairs suppurating, for the mattery secretion.

Secretions, when mattery, not slimy, on any of the mucous membranes lining the throat, eyes, etc.

Skin affections, "scalled heads" of children, with yellow mattery scabs.

Skin affections, with yellowish scabs ; after Potassium chloride.

Skin, suppuration of, and discharge of matter, after inflammation.

Smallpox, with pustules discharging matter, require this as an alternate remedy.

Sores discharging pure pus or blood and matter ; also on lint, see Directions ; but discharges of unhealthy pus, with heavy odour, require Potassium phosphate as intercurrent remedy.

Suppurations, articular (of the joints) ; also Silica.

Suppurations in general, after discharge continues too long.

Swelling of the Cheek ; after Potass. chlor., if suppuration threatens.

Syphilis, chronic, suppurating stage.

Throat, sore, suppurating.

Throat, ulcerated, with yellow matter, last or suppurating stage.

Tongue, inflammation of the, when suppurating.

Tonsilitis, last stage, when matter discharges on the tonsils.

Tubercular ulceration of the intestines, stools mixed with matter.

Ulceration of Glands. If matter is discharging, this remedy after Silica will assist to cleanse and heal the sore. Externally also on lint. The scar left will be very insignificant if treated in this way.

Ulcers, open mattering sores, which may result from abrasions, pimples, wounds, burns, scalds, or bruises. External use, page i.
Ulcers, of lower limbs ; with yellow or sanious matter.
Whitlow, felon, with discharge of matter ; after Silica.
Wounds, suppurating ; when yellow or sanious matter is discharging.

N.B.—**ON SELECTING A REMEDY**, read always the first two paragraphs under each Cell-Salt in this index, as these are of importance, so as to grasp the sphere of action of each Cell-Salt and its function.

3.—Calcium Fluoride = Calcarea Fluorica. Calc. Fluor.

The Diseases of this group must be healed or treated with *Calcium fluoride*, as they have their seat in the substance forming the surface of bone, enamel of teeth, and part of all elastic fibres, whether of the dermis, the connective-tissues, or of the walls of the blood-vessels, etc.
All Ailments which can be traced to relaxed conditions of any of the elastic fibres, including dilatation of blood vessels, arterial and venous blood tumours, incisted tumours and piles, and those also which arise from a disturbed balance of the molecules forming the enamel of teeth and of bone surface.
After-pains, if too weak, contractions too feeble.
Anus, itching at, or pricking from piles, this remedy internally and externally.
Aneurism, at an early stage, may be reduced or kept in check with the use of Ferric phosphate and this, the chief remedy, provided that Iodide of Potass. has not been taken.
Back-ache, simulating spinal irritation.
Back-ache, weak back with dragging pain, down-bearing.
Back, pain in the lower part of the back (sacrum), with a sensation of fulness or burning pain, and confined bowels.
Blood tumours on the head of new-born infants.
Blood tumours, internal piles ; blood around fæces.
Boils, when slow to heal, with hard callous edges ; to be used also externally as lotion on lint.
Bone diseases, in, Calcium fluoride is one of the cell-salts present in bone, especially on the smooth surface ; it is always helpful as an alternating remedy in bone diseases with bony excresences.
Bowels, costive, constipated, relaxed fibres, pain over sacrum (lower part of back) as with piles. Use also in cold enema after stools.
Bruises on the surface of the bone, the shin, etc., with hard, rough, and uneven lumps.
Bubo, for stony hardness of the enlarged glands, alt. Potassium chloride, also externally.

Catamenia, excessive, with bearing-down pains, flooding, to tone up the relaxed fibres.
Cataract, this remedy in 30th trituration in early stage, Sodium chloride chief remedy.
Cephalhæmatoma, blood-tumours on the parietal bones of new-born infants, on a rough, bony base.
Chancre, for hard infiltration, or callous edges of the sore.
Chaps, cracks of the skin ; this remedy also externally with vaseline, alt. remedy Sodium phosphate.
Cheek, hard swelling, with pain or toothache.
Cold in the head ; stuffy cold, dry coryza.
Constipation, with torpidity of lower bowel, and sensation of inability to expel fæces, with Silica as alternate remedy.
Coryza, stuffy stopped up condition of the nares (anterior and posterior nostrils).
Cough, with expectoration of tiny yellow tough lumps of mucus.
Cough, with tickling and irritating sensation, on lying down, from elongation of uvula, or drop at the back of the throat.
Cracks, chaps, fissures, this the chief remedy, also Sodium phos. for acetone of the blood.
Croup, in, if Potassium chloride and Calcium phosphate do not suffice.
Cutting of teeth, greatly eased by this remedy.
Deafness, when caused by a hardened exudation, alt. remedy Silica.
Dentition ; cutting of the teeth is facilitated by the use of this cell-salt.
Dilatation, enlargement of blood-vessels ; chief remedy to restore the contractility to the elastic fibres.
Dilatation of the heart, with palpitation, Potassium phosphate to invigorate the nerves of the heart as an alternate remedy.
Diphtheria, when the affection has gone to the windpipe through mismanagement ; this remedy and Calcium phosphate alternately.
Displacement of uterus.
Displacement, prolapsus, falling of the uterus.
Displacement, down-bearing of the uterus.
Dragging pains in the region of the uterus and in the thighs.
Dropsy, caused by heart-disease ; dilatation of any of the cavities.
Dyspepsia, see Vomiting.
Enamel of teeth, rough deficient.
Enlargement of the heart.
Enlargement of blood-vessels.
Excrescences, hard, on the bone surface.
Exostosis ; bony growths, excrescences and enlargements, rough corrugated.
Expectorations ; tough, small lumps hard to cough up, yellowish grey.
Exudations on the bone surface, hard, rugged (corrugated), pointed elevations.
Eyelid ; drooping, abnormal conditions, elastic fibres relaxed, as nerve stimulant, alt. Potass. phos. ; for swelling, Potass. chloride.
Fissures, or cracks in the palms of the hands, or hard skin.
Fissure, intensely sore crack near the anus (lower end of the bowel) ; also external applications, and Sodium phosphate when acidity is present, and sour smelling stools.

Flatulence, when due to distension and inactivity of the elastic fibres.

Flooding ; to tone up the contractile powers of the uterus.

Ganglion, round swelling or incisted tumours, such as on the back of the wrist, from strain of the elastic fibres.

Gouty enlargements of the joints of the fingers ; also Sodium phosphate.

Glands, chronic enlargement, stony hardness, when not yielding to the usual remedies.

Growths, small hard lumps seated on the cheek bone or other bony surfaces, if arising from an injury or a bruise ; also outward application if desirable.

Gumboil, with hard swelling on the jaw, and against predisposition to same.

Hæmorrhage uterine ; chief remedy internally and locally ; see also under flooding.

Heart, dilatation of, or valvular insufficiency to tone up the elastic fibres.

Heart, weak and dilated, with anæmic sounds. Also Calcium phosphate—for the muscular fibres, Ferric phosphate.

Heart, weak action of ; with Potassium phosphate acts as a heart tonic.

Hæmorrhoids. See Piles. One of three remedies may have to be selected to alternate with this the chief remedy.

Indigestion, with vomiting of food.

Indurations, hardening, as of glands, or edges of wounds, or of exudations on bony surfaces.

Itching at anus (seat), from piles, this remedy internally as a lotion and in enema.

Knots, kernels, hardened glands in the female breast.

Looseness of the teeth, without pain, and when the slightest touch to the loose tooth is felt painful.

Ozæna, affection of the nose. See also Potassium phosphate.

Piles bleeding ; alternately with such remedies as are specially indicated by the colour, etc., of the blood and coating of the tongue. External application. See Directions, page i.

Piles, internal or blind, frequently with pain in the back, generally far down on the sacrum ; note the appearance of the tongue, etc., indicating the alternating remedy.

Piles, with pressure of blood to the head ; Ferric phos. alternately.

Piles, internal, blind, with constipation, confined state of the bowels, itching.

Prolapsus uteri, falling or bearing down of the uterus.

Relaxed condition of elastic fibres in general.

Relaxed throat, with tickling in the larynx, when caused by elongation of uvula ; also Sodium phosphate.

Secretions from mucous membranes, tough yellowish grey small plugs.

Skin, harsh, dry, cracked.

Skin, hard, horny, also of the palm of the hand.

Spina ventosa, this remedy and Magnesium phosphate.

Suppurations, with callous hard edges.

Swellings, hard, having their seat in fascia and capsular ligaments, or on tendons.

Swelling, stony hard, on the jaw bone.
Syphilis; note pathological condition for the use of this remedy.
Teeth, if becoming loose in the sockets, it not being the period of teething.
Teeth, too rapid decay of; when the enamel is thin and discoloured, also Sodium phosphate.
Testicles, induration of.
Throat, irritation of; short cough from a tickling of the elongated uvula (drop) at the back of the throat, sometimes causing a desire to swallow something obstructing; alternate remedy, Sodium phosphate; with much saliva, Sodium chloride.
Throat, sore, see Uvula.
Tongue, cracked appearance, with or without pain.
Tongue, for induration of, hardening after inflammation.
Toothache, with pain if any food touches the tooth.
Toothache, with a looseness of the teeth.
Tumours, hard.
Tumour of the breast, hard, with Potassium chloride and Potassium sulphate as alternate remedies, also externally applied.
Tumours, vascular, with dilated blood-vessels.
Ulcerations of bone (on bone surface, enamel), injected.
Uvula, relaxed, causing irritation, tickling, and cough, much saliva calls for Sodium chloride.
Varicose ulceration of veins; also as a lotion on lint. Calcium sulphate, may also be applied for discharge of matter.
Varicose veins; this salt as chief remedy internally, and also externally as a lotion on lint. See Directions.
Veins, enlarged (varicose), this remedy internally, and externally as lotion on soft cotton below a flannel bandage.
Vomiting of undigested food, if Ferric phosphate does not suffice.
Whitlow, gathered finger, also lotion on lint; if deep-seated and the bone is implicated, see also Silica.

N.B.—ON SELECTING A REMEDY, read always the first two paragraphs under each Cell-Salt in this index, as these are of importance, so as to grasp the sphere of action of each Sell-Salt and its function.

4.—Ferric Phosphate = Ferrum phosphoricum.
Ferr. phos.

The Diseases forming this group must be healed or treated with *Ferric phosphate*, as they have their seat in the red blood corpuscles or in the vascular system, *i.e.* in the muscular fibres which are circularly arranged around the walls of the blood-vessels. Iron possesses the chemical property or affinity of attracting oxygen, and by this means carries and distributes the oxygen to all the tissues, including the brain and spinal cord.

xviii. *IV.—Ferric Phosphate = Ferrum Phosphoricum.* *Ferr. phos.*

All Ailments arising from a disturbed circulation, or abnormal condition of muscular fibres of blood-vessels, deficiency of iron (red blood corpuscles). These include all febrile conditions and disturbances of the vascular system, all inflammations, congestions, and irritations caused by local stasis, *i.e.*, blood accumulating in some of the blood-vessels by reason of an enfeebled or relaxed condition of the muscular fibres of the walls of these blood-vessels.

Ailments of an inflammatory or congestive nature. The inflammatory stage is recognised by being attended either by heat, pain, redness, irritation, throbbing, fever, or quickened pulse. The tongue is generally red, or has a red line along the centre. If a deposit forms, Ferric phosphate has then to be given in alternation with the remedy selected for the coating of the tongue.

Abscess, the first remedy to reduce fever, heat, throbbing, pain, and congestion (or excess of blood) in the parts.

Albuminuria (acute kidney disease), for the febrile conditions, heat and pain, active congestion, also tent vapour baths at first.

Anæmia, blood poverty, want of red blood; after Calcium phosphate give this remedy to colour the new blood-cells red, and enrich them.

Aneurism, to establish normal circulation, and remove those complications arising from excessive action of the heart, it should be early resorted to. Calcium fluoride, chief remedy.

Anger, causing nervous derangement, excitement or depression interfering with the proper digestion of food; also Potassium phos.; but when the liver is disturbed, alternate the former remedy with Sodium sulphate, a dose every half hour.

Angina Pectoris (breast pang), when there are feverish symptoms present.

Appetite, loss of, with uneasiness soon after meals, and symptoms of indigestion, or vomiting of food.

Back, pain in the, in the loins and over kidneys.

Back-ache, pains in the loins and back, rheumatic, felt only on moving.

Bleeding. See hæmorrhage.

Bleeding from wounds, Ferric phosphate internally and externally; tight bandage, strapping plaisters, and surgical aid if severe.

Bleeding of the nose, whether from injury or otherwise; this generally suffices. See also Potassium phosphate.

Bladder, spasmodic action of, with heat and feverishness, this as an alternating remedy.

Bloodlessness, anæmia, requires a course of this remedy; after Calcium phosphate.

Blood, loss of, if bright red, and coagulating readily.

Blood, rush of, to the head.

Blows, or falls, or kicks. This remedy internally and externally as speedily as possible; for swelling, Potassium chloride.

Bone diseases, in, when the soft parts are red and hot and painful.

Boils, at the commencement to reduce heat, blood accumulation, pain, and throbbing.

Brain fever, phrenitis, this remedy for the inflammatory conditions, high pulse, delirium.

Breathing, short, oppressed, and hurried, at the beginning or during the course of any ailment, accompanied by heat and feverishness.

Bright's disease, when feverishness is present.

Bronchial irritation, with heat or burning soreness ; any expectoration or secretion will require its special alternating remedy.

Bronchial asthma, this remedy when there is feverishness present, also when the patient suffers readily from pain soon after food. Asthma is closely connected with indigestion.

Bronchitis, acute inflammatory stage ; and after exudation takes place, see remedies.

Bronchitis, in, chronic ; occasionally to be taken when a fresh aggravation sets in, or in alternation with the remedy indicated by the expectoration.

Bruises, first remedy.

Bubo, with heat, throbbing, or feverishness.

Carbuncles, where there exists feverishness, heat, or throbbing ; to reduce the swelling, Potassium chloride.

Cancer, in, to modify the pain of congestion.

Catarrhs, colds, for heat and irritation.

Catarrh, bronchial ; the intercurrent remedy, to be used for inflammatory irritation.

Catarrhal fevers, with quickened pulse.

Cheek, sore and hot, to relieve the pain, congestion, throbbing, and heat ; first remedy, where cold applications are grateful.

Chicken pox ; this remedy alone or alternately ; note tongue.

Cholera, in the first stage, for the vascular disturbance, in alternation with Potassium phosphate.

Circulation, rapid feverish, when too rapid from want of nervous power of the heart, Potassium phosphate, lack of inhibition.

Cold in the head, first stage ; for the circulatory disturbance.

Cold in the chest, with soreness or feverishness.

Colds, a predisposition to catching cold ; a course of this remedy in alternation with Calcium phosphate.

Colic at the periods, with heat, flushing of the face, and quickened pulse.

Congestions of any organ or part of the body yield to this remedy, as it tones up the blood-vessels, dispels the excess of blood in those parts, and relieves the tension.

Concussion of the brain, with high pulse and feverish symptoms, alt. Potassium phosphate.

Constipation, with heat in the lower bowel, weak muscular action.

Constitutional tonic ; this remedy increases muscular activity and strength of the tissues and the circulatory channels.

Convulsions (fits), with fever, of teething children.

Consumption of the bowels, for the fever which accompanies this disease.

Cornea, abscess on, of the eye ; for the heat, pain, or redness, first stage ; and as intercurrent remedy.

Coryza, cold in the head, this remedy when there is congestion of the mucous lining, with heat or feverishness.

Cough, acute, painful, short tickling ; also Calcium fluoride.

Cough, at the commencement, for irritation.

Cough, short, from cold, without spit, spasmodic; and Potass. chlor.

Cough, short, sore, or tickling from irritation of the windpipe.

Cough, hard, dry, with soreness.

Cough, very painful, short, spasmodic. In true spasmodic use Magnesium phosphate.

Cough, with feeling of a soreness of lungs.

Conjunctiva, hyperæmic, congested red.

Creaking of the sinews at the back of the hand and arm on moving, met with in craftsmen; at first this remedy.

Croup; this remedy alternately with Potassium chloride; under special conditions a few doses of Potassium sulphate.

Cuts; chief remedy internally, and the dressing to be saturated with the lotion. See first page of Therapeutical Index.

Cystitis (inflammation of the bladder), first stage, with heat, pain, or feverishness.

Deafness from inflammatory action or suppuration, when there is cutting pain, tension, throbbing, or heat.

Delirium in fevers, this for quick pulse in all inflammatory fevers and congestions and high temperatures.

Diabetes, when there is a quickened pulse, or when there exists pain, heat, or congestion in any part of the system, as an intercurrent remedy.

Diarrhœa, from a relaxed state of villi or absorbants of the intestines, not taking up the usual amount of moisture.

Diarrhœa, stools of undigested food.

Diarrhœa, caused by a chill.

Dilatation of heart, or of blood vessels; in alternation with Calcium fluoride, the chief remedy.

Diphtheria; as alternate remedy, at the commencement of the disease, this will lessen the fever. See Potassium chloride.

Diphtheretic throat, falsely so called, yellow deposit; for any feverish symptoms.

Dizziness, giddiness from blood pressure to the head, worse on stooping.

Dryness of skin with fever; should this remedy not promote natural perspirations, Potassium sulphate is required as a stimulant to the epithelial cells.

Diseases of any kind, if ushered in by rigors (shivers), or heat, accompanied by fever, with quickened pulse, or pain; for any or all of these symptoms when they occur.

Dropsy, from loss of blood or draining of the system; as alternate remedy, with Calcium phosphate.

Dysentery; this remedy suffices in most cases with Potassium chloride alternately.

Dysmenorrhœa; pain, at the monthly periods, with hot, flushed face and quick pulse.

Dysmenorrhœa, with vomiting of undigested food, sometimes acid tasted.

Dyspepsia, with flushed, hot face; epigastrium tender to touch. If there is no coating on the tongue.

Dyspepsia, indigestion with beating or throbbing, pain, heat, redness or flushing of face, or vomiting of undigested food, the tongue being clean.

Dyspnœa, short laboured breathing, as in feverishness, etc.

Ear-ache, inflammatory (from cold), with burning or throbbing pain.

Ear-ache, with sharp, stitching pain.

Ears, noises in the, arising through blood pressure from relaxed condition of the veins, not returning the blood properly.

Enuresis, involuntary flow of urine at night, when arising from weakness of the sphincter muscle, this remedy will suffice.

Epilepsy (fits), with blood rushing to the head. See Potass. chlor.

Epistaxis (bleeding of the nose), generally; in children this suffices; if from nervous debility, Potassium phosphate.

Eruptions, eczema, skin affections; when there is feverishness present, it is useful as an intercurrent remedy.

Erysipelas, "rose," and erysipelatous inflammations of the skin, for the fever if high.

Expectoration, rusty coloured, as in inflammation of the lungs, or bright red blood. Ferric is a useful alternate remedy when there is pain in cough or feverishness, or new aggravation of cold and cough.

Eyes, inflammation of, with acute pain, without secretions of mucus or pus.

Eyes, neuralgic pain, or gouty, with inflammatory symptoms, red eyes or bloodshot, or pain worse on stooping, feeling as of sand in the eye, dry heat, also Sodium phosphate.

Eyes, pain in the eyeball, made worse by moving the eyes.

Eyes, inflamed and red, with burning sensation.

Eyes, sore and red looking. See also Sodium chloride.

Face-ache, with flushing and heat, quickened pulse.

Face-ache, worse on moving, with throbbing or pressing pain.

Febrile, inflammatory and catarrhal conditions, require this remedy.

Festers, gatherings, to relieve heat, pain, congestion, and inflammation, first stage.

Feverishness in all its various degrees is met by this salt.

Feverish state, catarrhal, at the commencement or during the course of any disease, calls for the use of this remedy alone, or in alternation with such remedies as co-existing symptoms may require.

Fevers, all, may require Ferric phos. alone, or in alternation with those remedies which the accompanying symptoms require.

Fevers, inflammatory, not contagious; the chief remedy.

Fevers, catarrhal (from cold), require this remedy.

Finger, inflamed or painful.

Fits, convulsious, with blood pressure to the head, heat, redness and fever, quick pulse.

Fits, see convulsions.

Flatulence, bringing back the taste of food partaken of.

Flushed face, accompanied by headache or fulness in the head.

Flushed face, when a precursor of recurring headaches.

Flushed face, when accompanying a sensation of coldness in nape of neck.

Fractures; (besides mechanical aid) to meet the accompanying injuries to the soft parts, first remedy.

Gastric, enteric, or typhoid fever, for the chilly stage; Potassium phosphate for languor; Potassium chloride for loose ochre-coloured stools, white tongue, and Potassium sulphate for rise of temperature. The course of the disease will be cut short by this treatment. See to escape of sewage gas.

Gastric ulcerations, for febrile symptoms and pain, as an intercurrent remedy.

Gastritis (inflammation of the stomach), with much pain, swelling, tenderness at pit of stomach, especially if vomiting of food occurs.

Giddiness (vertigo), from rush of blood to the head, with flushing, throbbing, or pressing pain.

Glands, enlarged, with symptoms of feverishness, also Sodium phos.

Gums, when sore, red, hot, and inflamed.

Hæmoptisis, spitting of blood, blood bright or in streaks, this remedy in alternation with Sodium phosphate.

Hæmorrhage (bleeding, loss of blood), bright red fluid, but with tendency to coagulate readily.

Hæmorrhoids (piles), inflamed; alternately with Calcium fluoride, the chief remedy; and as lotion, cold, externally.

Hæmorrhoids, bleading piles, blood bright red fluid, but with tendency to form a thickened soft mass.

Hay-fever, as an intercurrent with the chief remedy Potassium phos.

Headache, from gouty predisposition, in alternation with Sod. sulph.

Headache, from cold, a bruising, pressing, or stitching pain.

Headache, pains which are worse on stooping and moving.

Headache, with vomiting of undigested food.

Headache, congestive, with pressing or stitching pain, and soreness to the touch; pressing a cold object against the spot seems to ease the pain. If there is also a furred tongue. See page 38.

Headache of children generally requires this remedy only.

Headache, with a throbbing sensation.

Headache, with red face and suffused redness of the eyes.

Headache, sick, with vomiting of food as taken, undigested.

Heart, with anæmic sounds—for the muscular fibres of the same and the blood-vessels.

Heat and feverishness at the beginning of any disease or ailment.

Hip-joint disease; for pain, throbbing, heat, and the inflammation of the soft parts, etc.; matter forming, Silica.

Hoarseness, painful, of singers or speakers, from over-exertion of voice.

Hooping Cough, with vomiting of food; for the hoop or spasm, Magnesium phosphate.

Hyperæmia; blood accumulated in any of the blood-vessels (Stasis). Cause; want of proper balance of the iron-molecules in the *muscular fibres*, which are circularly arranged around these vessels; thus relaxed they lose their tonicity, and do not support normal circulation.

Incontinence of urine, enuresis, if from weakness of the sphincter muscle, p. 51.

Indigestion, from relaxed condition of the muscular fibres of the blood-vessels of the stomach, with burning, tenderness, pain on pressure, or flushed face, and pain after taking food.

Inflammation of any part of the body.

Inflammation of the skin, when there exists either fever, heat, pain, throbbing, or redness.

Inflammations, all, as well as all *congestions* and all *inflammatory irritations*; they are caused by excess of blood in the blood-vessels, or in the capillaries of any of the tissues. They require first Ferric phosphate, and Potassium chloride as second remedy. Such as :—

Bronchitis,	inflammation of the	Bronchi (windpipe).
Carditis,	,,	heart.
Cerebritis,	,,	brain.
Cystitis,	,,	bladder.
Duodenitis,	,,	duodenum.
Encephalitis,	,,	membrane covering the brain.
Enteritis,	,,	intestines (bowels).
Gastritis,	,,	stomach.
Hepatitis,	,,	liver.
Laryngitis,	,,	larynx.
Meningitis,	,,	cerebro spinal membrane.
Mastitis,	,,	breasts, commonly called "weed."
Metritis,	,,	uterus (womb).
Nephritis,	,,	kidneys.
Otitis,	,,	ear.
Pericarditis,	,,	sac. enclosing the heart.
Peritonitis,	,,	membrane lining the belly; also called inflammation of the side.
Periostitis,	,,	periosteum, or membrane covering the bone.
Perityphlitis,	,,	
Phlebitis,	,,	veins.
Phrenitis,	,,	brain, or brain fever.
Pneumonia,	,,	lungs.
Pleuritis,	,,	pleura, covering of the lung, also called Pleurisy.
Stomatitis,	,,	mouth.
Spleenitis,	,,	spleen.
Synovitis,	,,	synovial membrane.
Tonsilitis,	,,	tonsils.
Tympanitis,	,,	drum of the ear.
Typhlitis,	,,	cœcum.

Injuries, cuts, fresh wounds; this remedy prevents pain, congestion, swelling, or feverishness. Use also external applications. Surgical aid if severe.

Intermittent fever, with vomiting of food.

Irritations of throat, or other parts, with redness or heat.

Ischuria, suppression of urine, of recent date, with heat; also for little children.

Kidney, all inflammatory pain is relieved by this remedy.

Lameness, rheumatic, with feverish symptoms. See Potas. phos.

Lumbago; this remedy in frequent alternation with Calcium phos.

Lungs, inflammation of; first stage, until free perspiration is established, and until health is restored. See expectoration.

Lungs, congestion of, with debility and oppression.

Mastitis, "Weed," inflammation of the breasts; for the heat, pain, redness of the mammæ, and feverish symptoms.

Measles, in all stages; and the symptoms of inflammatory affections of chest, eyes, or ears.

Menstrual colic, with severe frontal headache; pain on stooping, and with heat or feverishness, or sharp stitching, cutting or dull pain.

Menstruation (monthly period), excessive congestion, blood bright red; this remedy must be taken as a preventative before the periods, if these symptoms are recurrent.

Milk leg; for the inflammation of the veins, alt. remedy Potass. chlor.

Morning sickness in pregnancy, with vomiting of food as taken; with or without acid taste the food returns undigested.

Mucous membrane, irritation of, with redness, or heat, or dryness.

Mumps, this remedy, should the fever be high, as an alternate remedy until it abates.

Neck, stiff, from cold, requires this remedy internally, also some dissolved in hot water, and steadily rubbed into the part.

Neuralgia, congestive or inflammatory, from cold, with pain as if a nail were being driven in; blinding pain, one sided in the head, temples, or over the eye; or in the jaw bone. If this does not suffice, Sodium phosphate, and note tongue.

Neuralgic pains, caused by congestive conditions, pressure of blood in the blood-vessels, heat, pressure, throbbing, soreness.

Noises in the head, rushing, throbbing.

Ophthalmia, for all inflammatory symptoms.

Ostitis, with painful and inflamed surrounding soft parts.

Ovarian neuralgia, when increased by congestive conditions and blood-vessels pressing on the nerve fibres, also Sodium phosphate.

Pain of any kind, if accompanied by flushed face, burning or diffused heat.

Pain, soreness in every part of the body, especially the joints.

Pain in any part, when caused by movement, or made worse by moving.

Pain in cancer, inflammatory and congestive.

Palate, when sore and inflamed.

Palpitation of the heart. See also Potassium phosphate.

Periostitis, with painful, inflamed soft parts.

Pharyngitis, for the inflammatory conditions, pain, redness, etc.

Phlebitis, inflammation of the vein; this remedy internally and as fomentation, when the veins are red, inflamed and knobby, also Calcium fluoride; when the tongue becomes white coated, Potassium chloride in alternation.

Piles, pressure of blood to the head, inflamed ; bleeding, bright, readily coagulating into a gelatinous mass.
Pimples ; for the redness, heat, or congestion of the skin.
Pleurisy ; for the fever, pain, stitch in the side, catch in the breath, and short cough till when these abate, Sodium chloride second remedy.
Pleura-Pneumonia ; the principal remedy at first; to be followed by Potassium chloride, or other remedy according to the appearance of the tongue, etc.
Polyuria simplex, excessive secretion of urine, and Sodium sulphate.
Pneumonia, inflammation of the lungs ; first and chief remedy.
Pulse, quick, rapid, full, feverish ; to strengthen the circular muscular fibres of the blood-vessels, to sustain the extra flushing of the vessels set up by nervous stimuli, to supply cell-salts to the diseased cells, or by exerting the vascular system to throw off some effete substances, poison, or some noxious intruder.
Quinsy ; at first alone, then alternately Potas. chlor. and Calc. sulph.
Retinitis, inflammation of the retina at the back of the eye ; for exudation, see Potassium chloride and Calcium sulphate.
Rheumatic, neuralgic, gouty headaches ; as an alternate remedy.
Rheumatism, muscular, when any movement sets up the pain, and all movements tend to keep up or increase the muscular pain.
Rheumatism, muscular, pain felt only during motion, or caused by motion.
Rheumatism, muscular, acute or sub-acute, worse on moving, as alt. remedy.
Scarlet fever, in simple cases; this remedy in alternation with Potas. chlor.
Scalding of skin, as in children, also Sodium chloride.
Shivers, chills, shaking with cold.
Shortness of breath, flapping of nostrils, oppression with feverish symptoms, or from chill.
Skin affections, in the first or inflammatory stage.
Skin affections, inflamed, sore and painful.
Sleeplessness, from blood pressure.
Smallpox, if the fever be high, occasional doses of this alternately with Potassium chloride, the chief remedy.
Sore throat. See throat.
Sores, to reduce heat, pain, and congestion of the parts.
Sprains ; to be used as soon as possible, externally and internally.
Stiff neck, if simply from a chill.
Stomach-ache, from cold or chill, frequent occurrence in children.
Stomach-ache, inflammatory, if pressure aggravates the pain.
Stomach-ache, from chill, with loose evacuation caused by insufficient absorption of moisture, from relaxed condition of villi.
Strains of tendons or ligaments ; this salt alternately with Calcium phosphate and Silica.
Teething troubles, with feverishness.
Temperature high, with fever ; high pulse and great heat, which do not increase regularly at night, indicate congestive or inflammatory conditions, for specific fever poison, Potassium phosphate and Potassium sulphate.
Tenalgia crepitans. See creaking of the sinews.

K

Thread worms. Also Sodium phosphate.
Throat, ulcerated; this remedy reduces congestion, heat, fever, pain, and throbbing.
Throat, sore, dry, red, inflamed ; with much pain, very frequent doses.
Throbbing pulsations in any part of the body, with or without pain.
Tic-dolourcux, congestive or inflammatory, in which the pain is beating, or stitching with burning soreness, and often pressing and intolerable. If not yielding, use also Calcium phosphate.
Tinnitus aurium (noises in the head), when from excessive flow of blood to the head.
Tongue, inflammation of, dark red, with much swelling; also Potas. chlor.
Tonsils, the glands on each side in the throat, when red and inflamed, Sodium phosphate, when swollen, Potassium chloride.
Toothache, with hot cheek, inflamed gum or root of tooth.
Toothache, worse with hot, better with cold, liquids.
Typhoid, Enteric, or Gastric Fever, when commencing, initiatory stage, for chilliness ; Potassium phosphate for langour and weariness.
Typhus, in the first stage, in alternation with Potassium phosphate.
Ulceration of glands, to relieve the throbbing pain, soreness, redness, heat, and congested condition ; for swelling, Potassium chloride.
Ulcers; if there is fever or heat, redness and congestion of parts, at any stage.
Urine, incontinence of ; involuntary flow of ; from weakness of the sphincter muscle.
Urine, retention of ; stoppage, with inflammatory conditions of the bladder or neck of the same.
Uterus, inflammation of, first stage, to remove the fever and pain.
Uterus, womb, congestion of.
Vaginismus, inflammation of the vagina ; also Magnesium phosphate.
Voice, loss of, or huskiness after singing or exertion of speaking. See Potassium phosphate.
Vomiting of blood, bright red blood, with tendency to form a gelatinous (liver-like) mass.
Vomiting of the food with sour fluids.
Vomiting of food, the food returning undigested, sooner or later after taking it.
Wetting the bed, when arising from weakness of the muscles of the neck and sphincter of the bladder. See Potassium phosphate.
Windpipe, inflamed condition, with soreness, irritation, and pain.
Windpipe, irritation of, with burning of the throat, and pain.
Wounds, all, will be benefitted by the use of this remedy internally and externally.
Wounds, if severe, surgical aid and Ferric phosphate, externally and internally.
Worms, intestinal; predisposition to passing undigested food.

N. B.—**ON SELECTING A REMEDY,** read always the first two paragraphs under each Cell-Salt in this index, as these are of importance, so as to grasp the sphere of action of each Cell-Salt and its function. Note always the appearance of the tongue.

5.—Potassium Chloride=Kali Muriaticum.
Kali mur.

The Diseases forming this group must be healed or treated with this cell-salt. Fibrinous exudations, glandular infiltration, and inflammatory infiltration of the skin, causing swelling of the part, arising from a disturbed balance of the organic (albuminoid) basis in the cells and of the molecules of Potassium chloride or muscle salt, which stands in biological relation to the albuminoid substances in fibrin, and those forming the basis of the cells constituting the brain and spinal cord. It is contained in the blood corpuscles, muscle, nerve, and brain cells, and in the intercellular fluids. Diseases which arise from a want of this salt are marked either by fibrinous exudations (swellings), torpor of liver, casting off of effete albuminoid substance, as seen in a white coating of tongue, or whitish secretions and expectorations, which call for the use of Potassium chloride, which acts as a solvent upon the fibrin by reason of the chlorine when split off forming Hydrochlorid acid.

All Aliments which have as a principal symptom a *white or gray coating* or fur at the back of the tongue (deposit) ; *exudation* of a white or gray substance on the mucous lining, tonsils, &c. ; *swellings* caused by intersitial plastic exudations ; *discharges* or *expectoration* of a thick white fibrinous slime or phlegm from any of the mucous membranes, &c., or flour-like scaling of skin.

Abdomen, enlargement of, glandular alteration with Sodium phos. Attention to diet.

Abdomen, swelled from enlargement of the glands of the bowels, wasting.

Abscess, second stage, when swelling (interstitial exudation) takes place.

Abscess, mammary, of the breast, to reduce the swelling.

Acne, pimples on the face, with thick, white contents.

Adhesions, recent, consequent on inflammations, fibrinous exudations arising from excessive blood pressure on the walls of the blood-vessels.

Amenorrhœa (suppressed periods), this remedy is often helpful where the river is sluggish, and where there is frequently a white coated tongue, the glandular system inactive, in lymphatic constitutions.

Anœmia, in, this remedy may be required as an intercurrent should there be an eczema, skin affection, present.

Apthœ, thrush, white ulcers in the mouth of little children or nursing mothers, with great flow of saliva, Sodium chloride.

Articular rheumatism, acute, for the swelling or grayish-white coated tongue, in alternation with or after Sodium phosphate, the chief remedy.

Asthma, with gastric derangement, tongue whitish or grayish furred ; and mucus white and hard to cough up ; for the depression of breathing, Potassium phosphate alternately.

xxviii. *V.—Potassium Chloride = Kali Muriaticum. Kali mur.*

Asthma, bronchial, treatment as above, for much frothy mucus, Sodium chloride.

Backache, pain across the kidneys, and swelling.

Bilious derangement, gray or white coated tongue.

Bladder, inflammation of, acute cases require this remedy; alternately with Ferric phosphate.

Bleeding, hæmorrhage, when the blood is dark, black, clotted, or tough.

Blepharitis, cibiaris, inflammation of the hair follicles, of the eyelids, discharge of matter, agglutination, and hard crusts on the edges of the same. Apply also a wash and sweet oil at night to prevent the lids sticking together.

Blisters, arising from burns; also lotion on lint externally.

Blood, loss of, hæmorrhages, or discharges; when the blood is thick dark clotted.

Blows, after effects, swellings; this remedy after Ferric phosphate.

Boils; to blight the swelling before matter forms; also externally.

Bones, diseased, broken, dislocated, this in alternation with the chief remedy when there is swelling of the parts. See page i.

Bronchitis, second stage, when thick white phlegm forms.

Bruises, if swelling, after the use of Ferric phosphate.

Bubo, for the soft swelling, also externally.

Bunions, also externally after Ferric phosphate; and if hard, use Calcium fluoride.

Burns of all degrees must be treated with this remedy internally and externally. Moisten the lint with a strong solution of the remedy, and apply the lotion frequently without removing the lint.

Canker, ulcers of the mouth.

Cattarrh, cold, with phlegm, when white, thick, not transparent, and for stuffy cold; if yellowish, small lumps, also Calcium fluoride.

Carbuncles, for the swelling at first; also as lotion on lint dressings alternately with Ferric phos. if there is much inflammation.

Chancre, soft; principal remedy throughout, 3rd trituration; and externally as a lotion.

Cheek, swollen; to control and reduce the swelling.

Chicken-pox, for swelling, should they assume a severe type; should matter form, a dose of Calcium sulphate morning and evening.

Choloraic diarrhœa, this remedy for symptoms of lack of bile, white coated tongue, etc.

Congestion, second stage, of any organ or part of the body, when there exists a white coated tongue, or expectoration of white mucus; and if there is interstitial exudation present, causing swelling of the parts.

Cold in the chest, with gluey thick white spit.

Cold, with a whitish or gray coated tongue.

Cold, stuffy, in the head, with whitish-grayish tongue; also Calc. fluor.

Cold in the head, with white non-transparent discharge.

Colds, any of the above, not yielding to this remedy may require Calcium phosphate as an intercurrent.

Constipation; light coloured stools, through want of bile from sluggish liver.

Constipation occurs frequently in consequence of some primary disturbance; if the symptoms of this are carefully looked for, no purging need be resorted to. The proper remedy will make the bowels move naturally, as Potas. chlor., Sod. chlor., Potas sulph.

Consumption of the bowels, tubercular, for the enlargement of the intestinal glands and weakness of the lymphatics.

Costiveness, which is accompanied by a white coated tongue; also when fat and pastry disagree; torpid liver. Also Sod. phos.

Cornea; an ulcer on the cornea of the eyeball when flat, not deep seated, requires this remedy internally and externally.

Cornea, inflamed, exudation white, whitish grey.

Coryza, dry, stopped; this remedy and Calcium fluoride.

Cough, in consumption, with thick milky-white spit or white coated tongue.

Cough, loud, noisy, stomach cough, with grayish white tongue.

Cough, with irritation of the larynx (windpipe), true spasm, Magnesium phosphate; short, acute and spasmodic, like Whooping cough, very painful, requires this remedy; also Ferric phosphate.

Cough, with thick milky-white gluey albuminoid phlegm.

Cough, stomachy, noisy, with protruded appearance of eyes, and white or gray coated tongue.

Cough, croupy, hard, with white coated tongue; use also Calcium fluor.

Cough, croup-like hoarseness; persistent, Potass. sulph. in alternation.

Croup, the principal remedy for the membranous exudation; in alternation with Ferric phosphate. If obstinate, Calcium fluor. and Calcium phosphate.

Crusta lactea, milk crust, scurfy eruption on the head and face of little children; principal remedy in alternation with Calcium phos.

Cuts, with swelling; as second remedy. See page i.

Cystitis, inflammation of the bladder, second stage; when swelling has set in (interstitial exudation), and discharge of thick white mucus.

Cystitis, chronic; the principal remedy.

Deafness, inflammatory conditions in second stage, where the exudation is fibrinous, thick and white; drum depressed, ears crack occasionally on blowing the nose or swallowing.

Deafness, from swelling of the internal ear and drum; chief remedy.

Deafness (throat), from swelling of the Eustachian tubes.

Deafness, with swelling of the glands, or cracking noise on blowing the nose, or a white coated tongue; all these symptoms denote a disturbance of the molecules of this salt, Ferric phosphate, for pain and heat.

Diarrhœa, stools of blood and slime.

Diarrhœa, if after fatty food, pastry, &c. Evacuations light coloured.

Diarrhœa, pale yellow, ochre or clay coloured stools; also Potassium sulphate.

XXX. V.—*Potassium Chloride = Kali Muriaticum.* *Kali mur.*

Diarrhœa, in typhoid fever. stools like pale yellow ochre; also Potassium sulphate.

Diarrhœa, white or slimy stools, generally with the characteristic white coating of tongue.

Disease, inflammatory, of the kidneys, for the swelling.

Diphtheria; the sole remedy in most cases in alternation with Ferric phosphate. Use gargle very frequently, 3rd trituration, 10-15 grains in tumbler of water. For prostration see Potassium phosphate; if affecting the wind-pipe, Calcium phosphate and Calcium fluoride.

Discharges of thick, white, slimy mucus from the nose, ears, eyes, or any passage covered with a mucus membrane or lining.

Dropsy, arising from heart, liver, or kidney disease, when there are such prominent characteristic symptoms present, mentioned under ailments.

Dropsy, from obstruction of the bile ducts and enlargement of the liver, there is generally a white coating of the tongue.

Dropsy, from weakness of the heart; this remedy in alternation with Potassium phosphate and Calcium fluoride.

Dropsy, with palpitation; also Potassium phosphate.

Dropsy, in which the liquid drawn off is whitish, or white mucus in sediment of urine; persistent white coating of the tongue.

Dysentery; purging, with slimy sanious stools. In most cases this remedy with Ferric phosphate cures.

Dyspepsia, with a white or grayish coated tongue, pain or heavy feeling on the right side under the shoulder; especially if fatty food disagrees, or the eyes look large and projecting; if there is a dark appearance under the eyes, give Sodium phosphate for this complication.

Ear-ache, with gray or white furred tongue.

Ear-ache, with swelling of the glands.

Ear-ache, with swelling of the throat, Eustachian tubes, or cracking noise in the ear when swallowing.

Ears, ear-ache, with thickening of the drum, or dryness, want of wax or discharge of a white albuminoid substance.

Eczema, skin diseases arising after vaccination with bad vaccine lymph.

Eczema, resulting from suppressed or deranged uterine functions, generally with the characteristic white coating of tongue.

Eczema, skin affections, with dry flour-like scales on the skin, in alternation with Ferric phosphate.

Eczema, if very obstinate, not yielding; use Calcium phosphate.

Eczema, skin affections, of vesicular form, with albuminoid (white) secretions or contents.

Eczema, with albuminoid (whitish) discharge and white coated tongue.

Eczema, with irritation, papular eruption, in alternation with Sodium phosphate.

Embolus; for that condition of blood which favours the condition of clots (fibrinous), which act as plugs; also Ferric phosphate for the circulatory disturbance.

Enteric fever; this remedy for white coated tongue, abdominal swelling, ochre-coloured stools. Also Potassium phosphate for debility and langour.

Epilepsy, occurring with or after suppression of Eczema (eruptions).

Eruptions, acne, pustules, pimples; also when discharging an albuminoid or whitish fatty substance.

Eruptions on the skin (rash), if connected with stomach derangement, and there exists a white coated tongue.

Eruption on the skin, accompanied with deranged menstrual period, with sero-fibrinous secretions.

Eruptions, eczema, skin affections, blisters or pimples, which contain a sero-fibrinous substance, which is generally whitish, and more inclined to be thick.

Erysipelas, vesicular (blistering); the chief remedy. For the fever, Ferric phosphate.

Erythema; after the use of Ferric phosphate, if there be any swelling or white coated tongue.

Evacuations, motions loose or constipated, light coloured, denoting sluggish liver, want of bile.

Expectorations, secretions, sputa, where the mucus phelgm is thick, white, and lumpy; not transparent, and sometimes hard to cough up, coming as it were from low down.

Exudations, after inflammation with effusion of lymph (effete albuminoid substance).

Exudations, fibrinous, in the interstitial connective-tissues, causing swelling or enlargement of these parts.

Exudations, fibrinous, when not becoming absorbed, or already hardened when come under treatment, require Calcium fluoride.

Eyes, affection of the; discharge of white mucus.

Eyes, affection of the, with discharge of yellow-greenish matter, also Potassium sulphate.

Eye, inflammation of the cornea; exudation, white or grayish.

Eyes (sore), on the lids, specks of matter.

Eyes (sore), on the lids; yellow mattery scabs; in alternation with Potassium sulphate.

Eye, superficial flat ulcer; arising from a vesicle.

Face-ache, with swelling of the gums or cheek.

Festers threatening in any part require this remedy for the swelling; also externally, to blight the suppuration.

Fever, puerpural, chief remedy for the exudation. When pressure on the brain perverts the function of the thought-cells, gray nervous substance, Potass. phosphate in alternation.

Flatulence with sluggishness of the liver, and gray or white coated tongue.

Fractures, of bones, when the soft parts are becoming swollen, the interstitial fibrinous exudation will be absorbed by this remedy.

Flooding, should there be much clotted blood, white coated tongue, etc.

Gastric, derangement, and white coated tongue, liver sluggish.

Gastric fever, see Typhoid or Enteric fever.

Gastritis, if caused from taking too hot drinks; this remedy at once.
Gastritis, with white coating of tongue, second stage.
Giddiness, vertigo, when caused by stomach derangement, and when the liver is sluggish, and the tongue coated white or grayish, with constipation.
Glandular swellings, acute, chief remedy, to absorb, but if very hard, Calcium fluoride.
Glandular swellings, chronic; chief remedy, Sodium phosphate.
Glands, follicular; infiltration of, in the throat, etc.
Glands of the neck, swollen, require this remedy; also lotion on lint dressing externally.
Gonorrhœa; principal remedy.
Granular, eyelids.
Gumboil, soft swelling before matter forms; in alternation with Ferric phosphate.
Gums (swollen), soft, or threatening gumboil, this remedy to absorb and carry off the fibrinous exudation in the tissues; bony hard swelling requires Calcium fluoride.
Hæmorrhage, clotted blood, black, thick, or tough.
Hæmorrhoids (bleeding piles), when the blood is dark and thick; for the tumours or relaxed elastic fibres, Calcium fluoride.
Headache, with vomiting, hawking up of milk-white mucus.
Headache, sick, with white coated tongue, or vomiting of white phelgm.
Hearing, dulness of, from swellings of the middle ear.
Hearing, dulness of, deafness, from throat affection, requires a course of this remedy to absorb the effete deposit.
Herpes zona, shingles; vesicles encircling half the body like a belt. Also Sodium chloride.
Herpes, or herpatic eruptions, shingles, when the fluid turns milky.
Hip-joint disease, second stage, when swelling of abscess commences.
Hoarseness, loss of voice from cold; if not yielding, use Potassium sulphate.
Hooping-cough, if there is a white coated tongue, and thick white expectoration; for the whoop, Magnesium phosphate.
Indigestion, with white tongue.
Indigestion, with a sick feeling after taking fat; tongue generally furred gray or white. Also Sodium phosphate.
Indigestion, with vomiting of white opaque mucus.
Indigestion, pain, with water gathering in the mouth, if Sodium chloride does not suffice and the tongue is coated, gray or white.
Inflammations, all, with swellings, in the second stage (with fibrinous exudations), in whatever organ or part of the body, require this salt, after or in alternation with Ferric phosphate, the chief remedy.
Inflammation of skin, with subcutaneous swellings, *i.e.* second stage.
Inflammation of soft palate, catarrhal, with white spots or patches.
Influenza, for the rheumatic pains, and when the tongue is coated white or gray; for the depression, Potassium phosphate in combination with this.

Injuries, from falls, .blows, &c., with swelling of the parts; second remedy.

Intermittent fever, when the fur at the back of the tongue is of grayish or white appearance, in alternation with Sodium sulph.

Irritation of the skin, similar to chilblains.

Iritis, inflammation of the iris, also Sodium chloride, should this remedy not suffice, and watery secretions &c., do occur.

Kidney inflammation, with tenderness and pain across the kidneys in back, immediately below the waist. Urine milky, turpid, or dark; alternate this remedy with Ferric phosphate frequently when acute.

Jaundice, if the disease has been caused by a chill resulting in a catarrh of the duodenum, a white coated tongue; stools light coloured.

Lameness, chronic, caused by rheumatism of the joints, in alternation with Potassium phosphate.

Liver, sluggish action of, sometimes pain in the right side, light yellow colour of the evacuations, denoting want of bile; use Potassium phosphate if the nervous system is depressed.

Liver, sluggish action of, generally accompanied by a white or grayish furred tongue, and constipation.

Lung disease, if the expectoration is whitish and thick. The tongue is frequently coated with white fur at the back.

Lungs, inflammation of, in the second stage; the tongue is generally white coated when this remedy is required, and mucus white and viscid.

Mastitis "weed" (gathering breast); second remedy, to control the swelling.

Measles; for the hoarse cough, for all glandular swellings, and furred tongue, white or gray deposit; second remedy.

Measles, after effects of; diarrhœa, whitish or light coloured loose stools, white tongue, deafness from throat swellings, &c.

Menstruation, the monthly period, too late or suppressed, checked; white tongue or other characteristic symptoms.

Menstruation, if too early. Also Potassium phosphate.

Menstruation, period, excessive discharge, dark, clotted, or tough, black like tar.

Menstruation, period, lasting too long, if other symptoms detailed in this section accompany it. Also Potassium phosphate.

Menstruation, courses or periods suppressed. As above, or Potassium sulphate.

Menstruation, courses or periods too frequent. A course of Calcium phosphate to follow.

Mucous membrane, disease of, when the secretions are of a fibrinous character; plastic, thick, white, gluey, or stringy.

Mumps; this remedy will cure alone, unless there be fever. With much saliva or swelling of testicles, occurring as metastasis with mumps, Sodium chloride will also be required.

Morning sickness in pregnancy, with vomiting of white phelgm.

Mouth, excoriation of, with white coated tongue.

Neck, glands of, swollen. Also Sodium phosphate.

Neuralgic pains, caused by pressure on the nerve fibres from pressure of the surrounding tissues upon the nerve filaments, interstitial exudations causing often swelling. These pains are worse with the warmth of the bed.

Neuralgic, pain of the teeth, with swelling, teeth feel longer; frequent doses of this remedy, especially if the warmth of the bed makes it worse.

Orchitis; primary remedy, if from suppressed Gonorrhœa; also Calcium phosphate.

Palpitation, from excessive flow of blood to the heart, in hypertrophic conditions; also Ferric phosphate.

Palpitation, connected with indigestion, and liver disturbance, flatulence, etc.

Pericarditis; this second remedy may complete the cure

Peritonitis; this second remedy, following Ferric phosphate, generally completes the cure. See exudations.

Pharyngitis, with swelling of the throat, gray or whitish exudation (spots or pustules); as second remedy.

Phlegm, mucus, discharge of, from any cavity lined with a mucous membrane, such as bronchi, throat, nasal cavity, vagina, &c., must be treated with this remedy when the secretion is milky white, thick, or slimy. It reduces the plastic exudation or waste matter there, accumulating for want of this cell-salt, thus restoring normal function.

Pimples on the face, neck, etc., caused by disturbed action of the follicular glands; if the skin is much inflamed, also Ferric phos.

Proud flesh, exuberant granulation, generally requires this remedy only, internally and externally.

Quinsy, second remedy, as soon as there is any swelling in the throat.

Rash, eruptions, pimples, with white contents; tongue coated white, or constipation from sluggishness of liver.

Retinitis, with exudation setting in.

Rheumatic fever, second stage, when exudation takes place, seen as swelling around the joints; this cell-salt will help to remove the swelling by restoring the non-functional cells of the excretory and absorbing structures to normal action, when the acids of the blood have been reduced by Sodium phosphate.

Rheumatic pains, if there is swelling of the parts, or white or gray furred tongue; alternately with Sodium phosphate.

Rheumatic pains, which are only felt during motion, or increased by it, if Sodium phosphate does not remove them altogether.

Rheumatism, chronic, with swelling, or when all movements cause pain; there is generally a gray or white coated tongue, or white discharges, chief remedy Sodium phosphate.

Scald-head, milk-crust, in children, for the sero-fibrinous exudation (whitish), also white coated tongue, sluggish livers, &c.; for acid conditions, Sodium phosphate.

Scalds, from boiling water; chief remedy.

Scales, white, floury, proceeding from blisters.

Scarlet fever; in mild cases it alone may suffice; alternately with Ferric phosphate for the febrile disturbance.

Scarlatina, remedies same as above; if the temperature be very high a few doses of Potassium sulphate also to develop the rash. This treatment applies also to Scarlet fever.

Scrofulous enlargement of the glands, enlarged abdomen with occasional diarrhœa, especially in the young. Also Sodium phosphate.

Scurvy, hard infiltrations; the want of this salt is the cause of scurvy; it is readily cured by its use.

Secretions, white or albuminoid, fibrinous.

Shingles, with white coated tongue; and alternately Sodium chloride.

Sick headache, arising from a sluggish liver, when the tongue is furred at the back, looking gray or white; with want of appetite.

Skin affections, eczema, with white, fibrinous contents of vesicular eruptions, hard pimples, blisters, &c.

Skin affection, with flour-like covering or scales.

Smallpox; the principal remedy; controls the formation of pustules. Mattery pustules, Calcium sulphate.

Sore throat, when swelling of glands or tonsils sets in, this remedy in alternation with Ferric phosphate.

Sores or Ulcers, with whitish flour-like coating; when the parts are hard, swollen, and callous, Calcium fluoride.

Sprains; second remedy, if swelling remains.

Stiffness, mobility defective, when parts are swollen and the tissues infiltrated with sero-fibrinous, or fibrous substance.

Stomach, derangement of, with white or grayish coating at back of tongue.

Stomach-ache, with constipation, and a thick white fur on the tongue.

Stomatitis, thrush, white ulcers of the mouth, with dribbling of saliva, alt. Sodium chloride.

Strumous conditions are benefitted by the use of this remedy and Calcium phosphate.

Swellings, interstitial, plastic exudations, in general, are controlled by it.

Swelling, in the cavity of the middle ear, causing dulness of hearing.

Sycosis (eruption on bearded part of the face); primary remedy.

Syphilis, chronic stage. Note pathological conditions calling for the use of this remedy.

Tabes dorsalis. Wasting of the spinal cord.

Tenalgia crepitans; creaking of the muscles at the back of the wrist or arm on movement; second remedy.

Throat (sore), ulcerated, with white or grayish patches or spots; generally with the characteristic white tongue, which requires this remedy to heal the processes of exudation.

Throat, ulceration of, white ulcers; also where much swelling exists in sore throat

Throat, with swelling of tonsils and glands, and white deposit.

Thrush. See Stomatitis.

Toe-nail, ingrowing; also surgical aid.

 V.—Potassium Chloride = Kali Muriaticum.
Kali mur.

Tongue, coated grayish white, dryish or slimy, indicating that this cell-salt is required to restore the balance between the organic (albuminoid) and the inorganic substance (Potassium chloride).

Tongue, inflammation of, for the swelling.

Tonsils, inflammation of, when spotted white or gray.

Tonsilitis (Quinsy), chronic or acute, with much swelling. Also Sodium phosphate.

Toothache, neuralgic, worse when getting warm in bed.

Toothache, with swelling of the gums. See also Neuralgic pains.

Toothache, with swelling of the cheek, this remedy to resorb and carry off the exuding effete albuminoid substance.

Trachom, granular eyelids, this remedy also externally.

Typhoid, Gastric, or Enteric Fever, for gray or white coated tongue, and looseness of the bowels, with light yellow ochre-coloured or floculent evacuations, and for abdominal tenderness and swelling. Rise of temperature in the evening, Potassium sulph.

Typhus, for constipation, stools light coloured; also Potassium phosphate.

Ulcerations, all, when there is a swelling or a dirty white tongue, or a mealy flour-like scaly surface, or a fibrinous white discharge. See also Calcium sulphate.

Ulceration of the cs and cervix uteri, with the characteristic discharge of thick white mild secretions (glandular or follicular) from the mucous membrane (alkaline).

Urine, milky, muddy, with white coating of the tongue and sluggish action of the liver; also Sodium phosphate, night and morning, for the excess of bile acids.

Urine, retention of, when due to inflammatory conditions after Ferric, this remedy, when the white coated tongue, etc.. indicate it.

Urine, dark coloured; deposit of uric acid; when there exists torpor and inactivity of the liver. See also Sodium phosphate.

Uterus, congestion of, chronic; hypertrophy, second stage; to heal or reduce this condition. See also Calcium fluoride.

Ulcers, with fibrinous discharges; callous edges, Calcium fluoride.

Ulcers, flat, of the cornea.

Ulcers, flour-like scabing or coating, also whitish discharges.

Voice, loss of, hoarseness from cold, often with a white deposit on back of tongue.

Vomiting, hawking of thick, white phlegm.

Warts, on the hands; this remedy externally also.

"*Weed*," for the swelling of a gathering breast; this remedy in frequent alternation with Ferric phosphate. Also external application.

Whitlow, also phlegmon, must be treated with this cell-salt, to reduce the swelling and blight, or reduce the process of matter-forming.

"*Whites*" (Leucorrhœa), discharge of milky-white mucus, thick, mild, non-irritating.

Wheezing, rale or rattling sound of air passing through thick tenacious mucus in the bronchi, difficult to cough up, hard cough.

Whooping-cough, with expectoration of white mucus; also the short spasmodic cough like whooping-cough requires this remedy.

Worms, small white thread worms, causing itching at anus, white tongue; Sodium phosphate in alternation.

N.B.—ON SELECTING A REMEDY, read always the first two paragraphs under each Cell-Salt in this index, as these are of importance, so as to grasp the sphere of action of each Sell-Salt and its function.

6.—Potassium Phosphate=Kali Phosphoricum.
Kali phos.

The Diseases forming this group must be healed or treated with *Potassium phosphate*, as they have their seat in some portion of the gray nervous substance either of the brain, spinal cord, or of the nerve centres (nervous system), the muscles, or the blood corpuscles, of which this cell-salt is a constituent.

Physical or mental stimuli proceed from the brain (gray nervous matter), whether they be ideational, emotional, or volitional, or are sometimes induced by external causes, and sometimes originate primarily in the great nervous centres, from the operation of the instinct, the memory, the reason, or the will; but by deficiency or absence of stimulus, from want of nervous force of the gray nervous matter, paralysis may be induced. The remedy for such abnormal conditions as: mental excitement, depression, or suspension of function in the receptive substance, or the true seat of thought and volition, is Potassium phosphate.

All Ailments, which arise from or denote a want of nerve power, hence nervous prostration, exhaustion, nervous rigours; and also all those affections in which the brain, and consequently the faculty of thought or the mind, shows want of vigour. Alternation of this remedy may often be required whenever symptoms of exhaustion, depression, or want of mental power or response of sensation occur; or in those cases where there is rapid decomposition of the blood corpuscles and muscle juice, causing foul putrid conditions, mortification, and septic conditions; and ailments inclining the patient to rock body or limb, or move about.

Adynamic conditions for all; depression of vital powers.

After-pains, when too weak from want of nervous involution, not stimulus, vigorous, or normal, alt. Calc. fluor.

Abscess, when the puss becomes ichorous with heavy odour.

Agoraphobia, disease of the eye.

Amenorrhœa, retention or delay of the monthly flow, with depression of spirits, lassitude, and general nervous debility.

Anæmia, poverty of blood, from influences continuously depressing the mind and the nervous system.

xxxviii. *VI.—Potassium Phosphate = Kali Phosphoricum.*
Kali phos.

Anæmia, cerebral; anæmic morbid conditions of the brain, causing undue nervousness.

Anxiety, nervous dread without special cause, gloomy moods, fancies, taking dark views of things, dark forebodings.

Aphthæ, thrush offensive breath, with white ulcers of the mouth.

Asthma; in often repeated, large doses, this is the chief remedy for the breathing and the depressed condition of the nervous system.

Asthma, bronchial, treatment same as above; for expectoration.

Atrophy, wasting disease, when putrid-smelling stools occur.

Bladder, paralysis affecting the sphincter, causing inability of retaining the urine.

Bleeding from the nose, in weak or delicate constitutions; also Ferric phosphate.

Bleeding of the gums, predisposition to, red seam on the gums.

Blood, loss of, if dark, blackish thin, like coffee grounds, not coagulating.

Blood, putrid, causing symptoms of decomposition.

Bloodlessness, pale sickly sallow complexion, with nervous depression and low spirits, timidity.

Boils, when becoming putrid, and the matter has a heavy odour, externally and internally.

Bowels, heavy putrid-smelling stools; also looseness, from excitement.

Brain-fag, from over-work, with loss of appetite, stupor, depressed spirits, irritability or great impatience, loss of memory or sleeplessness.

Brain-fever, phrenitis, for the high temperature, excitement, sleeplessness, or intense stupor.

Breath, offensive, fœtid; tongue coated like stale brownish liquid mustard.

Breathing, short, on exertion, with palpitation from weakness, when the nervous system is lowered.

Bright's disease (of the kidneys); for the great functional disturbance of the nerve centres, in alternation with Calcium phosphate for the albumen.

Cancer in, of the breast, in hard tumour, for the nervous depression of the system.

Cancrum oris, mortification of the cheek, with ashey-gray ulcers; also Potassium chloride.

Carbuncles, require this as chief remedy, internally and externally.

Catamenia, premature and profuse in nervous subjects, discharge bright or dark, but thin, and continues with heavy odour.

Canker, ulcers of the mouth; fœtid breath.

Chancre, phagadænic.

Chattering of the teeth, nervous, not from cold.

Chilblains, for, chief remedy.

Cholera, when the stools have the appearance of rice water.

Chilliness, blueness of skin and fingers from weak circulation, with symptoms of acidity of blood; also Sodium phosphate.

Chorea, St. Vitus dance, involuntary twitchings and jerkings of the face and body. This remedy should Magnesium and Calcium phosphate not suffice.

Circulation, sluggish, temperature persistently sub-normal.
Coldness, sluggish circulation, nervous shivers, require this remedy.
Collapse, with livid, bluish countenance, and low pulse.
Concussion of brain; asthenic conditions, dilated pupil. Optic illusion, Magnesium phosphate; for febrile disturbance, Ferr. phos.
Constitutional tonic, this remedy increases tone of the nervous system, and rouses mental activity and normal action.
Crossness and irritability in children, ill temper often arising from nervous disturbances.
Croup, if treatment is delayed till last-stage, syncope; for nervous prostration, pale or livid countenance; in alternation with Potassium chloride.
Crying or screaming in children from undue fear or fretfulness.
Cystitis, inflammation of the bladder; in asthenic condition, with prostration.
Deafness, from want of nervous perception, noises in the head, with weakness and confusion.
Deafness, with weakness, exhaustion of the nervous system in general.
Debility, general, with nervousness and irritability or timidity.
Delirium, or stupor, in brain or typhus fever requires this remedy, also in typhoid conditions of this nature.
Delirium tremens, the horrors of drunkards; fear, sleeplessness, restlessness, and suspiciousness, rambling talk, endeavours to grasp or avoid visionary images. Sodium chloride must be given alternately for the purpose of restoring the normal consistency of brain substance, which in this disease is disturbed.
Depression of spirits and lassitude.
Diabetes; the symptoms for which this remedy must be given intercurrently is nervous weakness, sleeplessness, and voracious hunger; to establish normal function of the medulla oblongata and pneumogastric nerve, which latter acts on the digestion or stomach, and on the lungs. Sodium sulphate is the remedy for the liver derangement, causing the sugar to pass through the system and into the urine, Sodium phosphate for the acetone of the blood.
Diarrhœa, foul; often accompanying other diseases, to heal the conditions causing putrid evacuations.
Diarrhœa, with heavy odour, occasioned by fright and other causes.
Diarrhœa, with depression and exhaustion of the nerves.
Diphtheria, after effects of; weakness of sight, nasely speech, or paralysis in any part.
Diphtheria, in the well-marked malignant gangrenous condition.
Diphtheria, for exhausted prostrate conditions at any stage.
Dispiritedness, low spirits or feeling of faintness.
Discharges, putrid, heavy smelled, unhealthy, ichorous.
Dizziness, swimming of the head, when from cerebral or nervous causes.
Dread of noise, over sensitiveness to noise, nervousness.
Dropsy, which is caused by heart disease; may be benefitted by occasional doses of this nerve salt.

Dulness, want of energy ; alternating Potassium chloride.

Dysentery, when the stools consist of blood only, and the patient becomes delirious (brainish), abdomen swollen ; or when the stools have a putrid odour, this remedy must be given.

Dysentery, with putrid, very offensive stools, and great dryness of tongue.

Ears, noise in the, from nervous exhaustion.

Eczema, if nervous irritation and over sensitiveness accompany it ; this salt may be taken as an intercurrent remedy.

Empyema, pus (purulent matter) forming in cavity of lung after inflammation, or after pleurisy in plura, with symptoms as of hectic fever and nervous exhaustion.

Energy, want of, timidity.

Enteric, Typhoid, or Gastric Fever, for debility, weak action of the heart, langour, or nervous condition and sleeplessness, offensive breath, putrid odour of stools, stupor ; also Sodium chloride.

Enuresis, when arising from a weakness of the nervous system (shock), paralytic conditions, also in old people ; Sodium phosphate as an intercurrent remedy.

Epilepsy, sunken countenance, coldness and palpitation after the fit ; for chief remedy Potassium chloride.

Epistaxis, bleeding of the nose, weakness and predisposition to ; also Ferric phosphate.

Eruptions, rash, as in typhus and typhoid fevers, indicate this remedy, if suppressed alt. Potassium sulphate.

Evacuations, putrid, very offensive smell.

Excessive hungry feeling, soon after taking food, a nervous disturbance, depression or weakness, "gone feeling."

Exhaustion and weakness, from any cause, which has lowered the nervous system.

Expectoration, heavy fœtid odour.

Exudations, serous, mixed with blood.

Exudations, ichorus, foul. offensive, sanious.

Exudations, from any of the mucous linings which are corroding, chafing ; also Sodium chloride.

Eyes, dread of light, without special symptoms, or after over exertion.

Eyes, excited, staring appearance, a symptom of nervous disturbances during the course of a disease.

Eyesight, weak, from an exhausted condition of the system.

Face-ache, neuralgia, with great exhaustion after the attack, feeling of prostration.

Face, livid and sunken, with hollow eyes.

Fainting, from fright, fatigue, and also when from weak action of the heart.

Faintness, feeling of, in nervous people.

Faintness, feeling of, or dizziness without gastric derangement.

Faintness, feeling of, from weak action of the heart.

Fainting, from want of blood in the brain.

Febrile conditions, with excitement or great depression, and exhaustion, stupor.

Felon, when the matter becomes fœtid.

Fevers, typhus, typhoid, malignant for excitement, great depression and exhaustion, stupor.

Fits, attacks, from fright, with pallid or livid countenance.

Flatulence, with distress about the heart, or simply on left side of pit of stomach.

Flatulence, with a weary pain in the left side ; weakness of heart.

Flooding in, when there are symptoms of exhaustion as an intercurrent remedy.

Fright, effects of, on the nerves ; nervous substance.

Grangrenous conditions, mortification in the early stages, to heal those pathological conditions which give rise to it.

Gastric ulcerations, when the substance ejected is dark brown like coffee grounds ; circular ulcers.

Gastritis (inflammation of stomach), if it comes too late under treatment, with asthenic conditions.

Giddiness, vertigo, nervous causes, depletion, not gastric derangement.

Gonorrhœa, with discharge of blood.

Gums bleeding easily ; paleness, and when there exists a red line or seam on the edges.

Hallucinations.

Hay-asthma, for the depression and asthmatic breathing ; in alternation with Sodium chloride.

Hay fever, in, for the nervous irritability ; for watery secretions, Sodium chloride.

Headache, nervous sensitiveness to noise, irritability, confusion.

Headache, which is relieved by gentle motion.

Headache of students and those worn out by fatigue, when no gastric symptoms are felt, but the tongue is sometimes found to be coated brownish yellow, like stale mustard ; bad breath.

Head, pains, and weight at the back of the, with feeling of weariness and exhaustion ; to be taken after Ferric phosphate.

Headache, nervous, inability for thought ; loss of strength ; irritability, restlessness, sleeplessness, or despondency.

Headache, with weariness ; yawning and stretching ; prostrate feeling, hysteria.

Headache, with a weary, empty feeling, "goneness" at the stomach ; also if the headache be a precursor of an attack connected with bilious vomiting.

Headache, neuralgic, humming in the ears, feeling of inability to remain up, yet better under cheerful excitement.

Hæmorrhage, blood not coagulating, blackish or bright red, but thin, or like coffee grounds.

Hæmorrhage from the nose, when arising from debility, weakness, or old age. Also Ferric phosphate.

Hæmorrhage, uterine, with dark thin blood and great exhaustion.

Hæmorrhage, bleeding, when the blood is dark, thin ; exhaustion and nervous depression.

Hands, involuntary shaking, to tone up the motor powers of the nerve centres, and Ferric to strengthen the muscular fibres.

L

Hearing, affected, from want of nerve power; alt. Calcium phos.
Hearing, dulness of, with noises in the head.
Heart complaint, functional, intermittent, with palpitation.
Heart complaint, palpitation after rheumatic fever, with exhaustion.
Heart, intermittent action of the, with morbid nervous sensitiveness, effects of violent emotions, grief or care.
Heart, weak or intermittent action of; also Calcium fluoride.
Hoarseness, with exhausted feeling from over-exertion of voice, and with nervous depression; or if rheumatic affection.
Hooping cough, in the highly nervous, or with great exhaustion.
Home sickness, morbid activity of memory, haunted by visions of the past, and longing after them.
Hunger, excessive, nervous affection.
Hypochondriasis, melancholy; when accompanied by liver complications, see Sodium sulphate or Potassium chloride.
Hysteria in females, nervous attacks, from sudden or intense emotion, or from smothering passion, in the highly nervous and excitable; also a feeling as of a ball rising in the throat.
Hysterical fits of laughter and crying.
Ill humour, from nervous exhaustion.
Illusions, mental, an abnormal condition of the gray nervous system.
Impressions, false, fancies.
Incontinence of urine from paralysis of the sphincter of the bladder.
Indigestion, with great nervous depression.
Infantile paralysis, recent; also Magnesium phosphate; with teething, give Calcium phosphate.
Influenza, severe type, whenever suspected this remedy and throughout to keep up the nervous system; also as an after course.
Irritability, mental, undue, after exhausting diarrhœa or long-continued use of purgatives.
Insanity, mania, or other mental derangement; all arising from exhausted or depressed condition of some brain cells, of the gray nervous substance, showing itself in perverted function of the brain. Also Sodium sulphate in gouty subjects.
Intermittent fever, fœtid, debilitating, profuse perspiration; also Sodium sulphate.
Labour pains, if feeble and ineffectual; also against spurious labour pains.
Labour, tedious, from constitutional weakness; this remedy gives vigour and helps materially.
Lameness, recent, paralytic, from exhaustion of the nerves, with stiffness after rest, yielding a little to gentle exercise.
Lameness, rheumatic, affection of nerve centres, the pain alleviated by gentle exercise.
Lassitude, depressed state, want of energy.
Leucorrhœa, "whites," scalding acrid; also Sodium chloride.
Lung, œdema of, acute; spasmodic cough with frothy serous masses being brought up in excess, and threatening suffocation.
Lung, inflammation of, exudations; expectorations fœtid, with heavy odour, or fœtid breath.

Madness, fancies, loss of correct reasoning faculty, requires a steady course of this remedy.

Malignancy, arising in any disease.

Mania in its various degrees, requires a steady course of this remedy.

Mastitis, if the pus is brownish, dirty-looking, with heavy odour, to heal the adynamic condition. See also page i. for external use.

Melancholia and other similar ailments, which arise from deranged mental function, caused by over-strain of the mind.

Melancholia, accompanying exhausting drains affecting the nerve centres of the spinal cord.

Memory, bad or loss of; Calcium phos. as an intercurrent remedy.

Menstrual colic, or great pain at the time of the periods in pale, lachrymose, irritable, sensitive females.

Menstruation, too late, in pale, irritable, sensitive lachrymose females; to heal the pathological conditions which give rise to this.

Menstruation, too scanty, in similar constitutions.

Menstruation, too profuse discharge, deep red, or blackish red, thin, and not coagulating, sometimes with heavy odour.

Mental aberrations, abnormal conditions of some of the nervous (gray) substance.

Miscarriage, threatening of, in nervous subjects; also Calcium fluoride intercurrently.

Mortification, grangrene, requires this remedy alone or with other remedies, to heal complicating symptoms.

Motor nerves, spasmodic disturbance of; this remedy to invigorate the nerve stimulus, as an intercurrent remedy.

Nausea, sickness with brain disturbances.

Nervous affections, when occurring without reasonable causes, such as: impatience, irritability, dwelling upon grievances, merriment, becoming oppressive, shedding tears about trifles, making "mountains out of mole hills."

Nervousness in its various manifestations requires this salts.

Nervous sensitiveness, feeling pains very keenly, better during pleasurable excitement, standing or walking.

Nettlerash, apply also as lotion.

Neuralgic headache, with confusion and nervousness, tearful mood, better during eating; but if better on lying, and keeping the head still, it is congestive, and requires Ferric phosphate.

Neuralgic headache, with depression; pain worse on stooping, or moving the eyeballs, requires Ferric phosphate.

Neuralgic pains in any organ, depression, failure of strength, feeling of inability to rise, or to remain up, yet pain felt less when standing or walking about.

Neuralgia, with ill humour, sensitiveness to light or noise, improved, or even not felt at all, during pleasant excitement; requires this remedy to tone up the gray nervous substance.

Neuralgic headache, with sleeplessness, nervousness; pain worse on stooping, moving the eyeballs; or tearing gnawing pain, requires Ferric phosphate.

Neuralgic pains, seat of pain in the nervous substance, threatening paralysis, with a feeling of lameness or numbness. Also Calcium phosphate alternately.
Neuralgic pains, better with gentle exercise, worse on rising.
Neuralgic pains, which are most felt when quite alone.
Neuralgic pains, and humming in the ears, failure of strength.
Night terrors, in children awakening in a great fright and screaming ; note also coating of tongue.
Noises in the head on falling asleep, feeling as if a rocket had passed through the head.
Noises in the head, ears, when from nervous causes.
Noma, water canker, grangrenous canker of the mouth.
Nose, nasal disease, with offensive odour, fœtid discharge ; when the seat of disease is located in the mucous lining. Also Silica.
Numbness and blueness (dead fingers) ; this arises from weakness of the nervous impulses of the heart, and requires Potassium phosphate, also Calcium phosphate.
Œdema pulmonarium, spasmodic cough, threatening suffocation ; for dyspnœa and livid countenance ; excessive accumulation of watery mucus in the lining and bronchi, Sodium chloride.
Ozœna, foul offensive discharge from the nose. Also Silica. Sod. phos.
Pain during rest, actual movement gradually relieving pain.
Pain in the left side, with flatulent pressing on the heart.
Pain, morbid sensibility, or a bruised and painful feeling in the part affected, and discolouration.
Pain in cancer is greatly subdued by this remedy, and offensive odour from discharges, also discolouration is lessened.
Pains, neuralgic, paroxysms of, with subsequent exhaustion.
Pains, great sensitiveness to ; depression and alternating with great vivacity ; malaise better under excitement and in company.
Pains, laming, which are worse on rising from a sitting posture, better with gentle exercise, but are increased by exertion ; to heal the abnormal condition of nervous cells.
Palpitation, from a weakened condition, or direct nervous excitement.
Palpitation, from conditions resembling anæmia ; this remedy and Calcium fluoride.
Palpitation, on ascending stairs, etc., with shortness of breath.
Palpitation, with nervousness, anxiety, melancholia.
Palpitation, with sleeplessness and restlessness.
Paralysis, facial, loss of stimulating power over some muscles. "The mouth is distorted, being drawn over to the opposite side by the unparalysed muscles."—*Marshall.*
Paralysis, creeping, in which the progress of the disease is slow, and there is a tendency to wasting, with loss of the sense of touch, &c.; also Magnesium phosphate.
Paralysis, locomotor, loss of motor force or stimulating power (evolved in gray nervous matter) finds its remedy in Potassium phosphate. "The nerve force is, as it were, nourished from the physical force, as the living substance of the nervous tissues is fed from the *inorganic* material of the dead world."—*Marshall.*

Paralysis of the vocal chords; loss of voice, through *relaxed* or paralysed condition of the laryngeal muscles.

Paralysis, atrophic, in which the vital powers are reduced, and stools have a putrid odour.

Paralysis, all the varieties require this the chief remedy, as partial, paraplegia, hemiplegia, facial, or merely of the upper eyelid. Paralysis usually come on suddenly. "It is shown by experiment that the conducting power or force is greater in the central part of the gray matter of the spinal cord than in the cornea."—*Brown Séquard.*

Pemphigus malignus. Blisters and blebs over the body, sanious watery contents, skin wrinkled and withered looking.

Perspirations, excessive, exhausting, with heavy odour.

Perspirations, during meals, with a feeling of weakness at the pit of the stomach.

Powerlessness, conductile force deficient, causing stiffness or lameness. "The conducting power of the gray nervous matter seems now to be well established."—*Chauvau.*

Prolapsus recti, protrusion of the lining of the bowel. Also Ferric phosphate.

Puerpural (child-bed), fever in; this is the specific remedy.

Puerpural mania, when illusions absurd notions, or violent madness, set in; convulsions, Magnesium phos. and Calcium phosphate intercurrently.

Pulse, intermittent, irregular, from exhausting causes.

Pulse below the normal standard from enfeebled nervous system.

Purpura, "land scurvy," to heal the adynamic processes.

Pus, matter, when ichorous or with fœtid odour.

Restlessness and irritability, gray nervous matter abnormal.

Rickets, atrophy, with putrid smelling discharges from the bowels.

Rheumatism, muscular, acute and chronic, with pains disappearing on moving about, severe in the morning after rest, and on first rising from a sitting position; alt. Sod. phos. for all rheumatic ailments.

Rheumatism, muscular, very painful, the parts feel stiff, on first attempting to rise up, improves slowly, but is increased by all exertion and fatigue; alternate remedy Sodium phos.

Rheumatism, with stiffness, paralytic tendency; also Sodium phos.

Scabs, greasy, with offensive smell.

Scarlet fever; putrid condition of throat, and symptoms of exhaustion, stupor.

Sciatica, affection of the sciatic nerve which extends down the back of the thigh to the knee, dragging, laming pain, torpor, stiffness, great restlessness and pain, nervous exhaustion, lack of motor stimulus, moving gently for a little time gives relief; also Sodium phosphate where symptoms of constitutional gout exist.

Scurvy, with gangrenous conditions.

Secretions on the mucous linings; excoriating, or when having an offensive odour, also when mixed with blood.

Secretions on the skin, irritating, causing soreness of the parts.

Sensitiveness, too keen, want of nervous balance.

Septic-Hæmorrhage (bleeding), blood putrid.

Sighing and depression, with inclination to look at the "dark side" of things.

Sighing or moaning, also when occurring during sleep.

Shortness of breath, asthmatic, or with weakness of heart, or exhaustion, or in fatty degeneration.

Shortness of breath when going up a stair, or on the least exertion, with any symptom showing exhaustion or want of nerve power.

Shyness, excessive blushing, from emotional sensitiveness, lack of controlling force over the nerves of the coats of the blood vessels.

Skin affections; greasy scales, heavy odour, or blood in the vesicles (blisters).

Sleeplessness, after worry or excitement, showing the source of such condition to be a want of this cell salt in the nervous centres.

Sleeplessness, wakefulness. "Arises from loss or want of contractile stimulus to the vessels of choroid plexus to diminish the quantity of blood in the gray matter of cerebrum."—*Durham.*

Sleeplessness, from nervous causes; to restore those brain or nerve cells which do not act normally.

Sleeplessness, pathologically is an abnormal condition of the brain cells, kept vivified or awake by the blood supplied to them, when it should be lessened by the contracting of the vessels supplying the brain, and shows loss of stimulating power of the nervous centres to cause muscular contraction of the vessels and diminished supply of blood to the brain. During sleep the brain is anæmic and pale, and should be so. Sleeping draughts, Morphia, etc., dangerous, deadening in effect, and can produce death. Potassium phosphate, the true remedy, restores normal stimulating power in the gray nervous matter, and consequent contractions of the artery, which diminishes the flow of blood to the brain, and natural, healthful sleep results. Sometimes a course of the remedy is needed.

Sluggish circulation, in emotional or nervous subjects; to strengthen the heart's action.

Smallpox, with putrid condition, heavy odour, exhaustion, and stupor.

Softening of the brain, early stage, if connected with hydrocephalus or water on the brain, then give also Calcium phosphate.

Softening of the brain, as the result of inflammation; Potassium chloride must also be given. This kind of softening may be very insiduous in its strength.

Somnambulism, walking in sleep, of children, requires a steady course of this remedy.

Spasms of all descriptions, when Magnesium and Calcium phosphate fail, there are generally symptoms present for this salt.

Speech, slow and becoming inarticulate, frequently connected with creeping paralysis.

Spinal cord, softening of, idiopathic, with gradual molecular deadening of the nervous centres. This remedy must be given to arrest its progress.

Spleen affections are much benefitted by the use of this remedy.

Starting on being touched, or at sudden noises.
Stomach-ache, from fright or excitement.
Stomatitis (ulcers of the mouth), with fœtid offensive breath. "Thrush."
Stools, offensive, or when in dysentry pure blood is passed.
Strabismus, not spasmodic, squinting setting in after Diphtheria.
Stumbling, tripping over trifles, when the person has difficulty in guiding himself, or loss of the power of movement.
Stupor, low delirium, as in typhus fever, or when occurring during any disease, brain chiefly affected.
Suppurations, dirty foul ichorous matter, with offensive odour.
Temperature below the normal from weakness, depressed condition, this remedy when from a chill, alt. Potassium sulphate.
Temperature, high, in disease; to strengthen those nerves which control the function of the blood-vessels. See Potassium sulphate.
Temperature, high, in disease with great nervous excitement or depression from specific blood poison as in Typhus, etc.
Throat, gangrenous sore throat.
Tongue, coated, like stale brownish liquid mustard, offensive breath.
Tongue, excessively dry in the morning, feeling as if it would cleave to the roof of the mouth.
Tongue, inflammation of, when excessive dryness of tongue occurs, or exhaustion sets in.
Toothache, of highly nervous, delicate, or pale, irritable, emotional persons; also Magnesium phosphate.
Toothache, with easily bleeding gums.
Toothache, in the highly nervous, and when the gums have a bright red seam or line.
Toes, chilblains on, or on hands or ears, require this remedy externally and internally instead of Potassium chloride, for the tingling or itching pain. Calcium sulphate for broken chilblains.
Typhoid fever, or symptoms malignant; when affecting the brain, causing stupor, during the course of a disease, or with symptoms of putrid blood; see blood-poisoning.
Typhus fever, malignant fever, putrid fever, camp fever, nervous or brain fever, farm fever; chief remedy; (not to confuse with enteric or typhoid fever; brown tongue, petechia, sleeplessness, abnormal brain functions, stupor, delirium; also Sodium chloride.
Ulcers of stomach, circular ulcers caused by a functional disturbance of the trophic fibres of the sympathetic plexus.
Ulcerations, when the discharge is unhealthy, heavy odour.
Urination, frequent, or passing much water, frequently scalding; nervous weakness.
Urethra, bleeding from, Potassium phosphate.
Urine, incontinence of, from nervous debility. In children Ferric phosphate suffices generally.
Vertigo, giddiness from nervous exhaustion and weakness, and not from gastric derangement.
Vomiting of blood, thin, dark, black, like coffee grounds.

Water on the head; this remedy as an intercurrent, when nervousness or putrid smelling stools set in.

Weakness, constitutional, in, from a lack of activity in the gray nervous tissues.

Weakness in the left side, under the heart.

Weakness of sight from exhaustion; to restore nervous vigour.

Weakness, from exhaustion of the nervous system, and depression.

Weakness of sight, loss of perceptive power, if in the optic nerve, also Magnesium phosphate.

Weakness of sight if after diphtheria.

Weariness with pain in left hypochondrium.

Whining and fretful disposition in children and adults.

" *Whites,*" discharge, acrid, scalding; also Sodium chloride.

Whooping cough; in very nervous, timid, sensitive children this is an intercurrent remedy, and when general exhaustion sets in.

Writers, cramp, as an intercurrent remedy.

Yawning, stretching, weariness, when arising from nervous causes, sometimes accompanied with a sensation of emptiness of the stomach although food has been partaken of.

Yawning, hysterical.

N.B.—ON SELECTING A REMEDY, read always the first two paragraphs under each Cell-Salt in this index, as these are of importance, so as to grasp the sphere of action of each Cell-Salt and its function.

7.—Potassium Sulphate = Kali Sulphuricum.
Kali sulph.

The Diseases forming this group must be healed or treated with *Potassium sulphate,* which is the functional remedy of the epidermis and epithelial cells; but it is also a remedy for intercellular fluids. A want of this constituent cell-salt causes yellow slimy deposit on the tongue, slimy thin, decidedly yellow or greenish discharges and secretions of watery matter from any of the mucous membranes, epithelium, conjunctive, etc., and epithelial desquamation.

All Ailments which favour development of bacilli, connected with typhoid condition, blood poison, where the ailments become worse in the evening, or show a rise in the temperature of the blood-heat at night. Also when worse in a heated atmosphere, and better in a cool or open atmosphere. Ailment accompanied with desquamation, peeling of the skin, yellow scales, also all which are caused by sudden retrocession of eruptions (rash); When Ferric phosphate does not suffice to produce free perspiration, this cell-salt assists as a useful intercurrent remedy.

Abdomen, stomach swelled from chill, pain over the ovaries.

Kali sulph.

Ague, in ; with persistent evening rise of temperature.
Amenorrhœa, see Menstruation.
Articular rheumatism, shifting from one joint to another, alternate doses with Sodium phosphate the chief remedy.
Asthma, when the yellow mucus is easily coughed up.
Blood heat, temperature, rising in the evening and on till midnight, then falling again, sign of blood poison, typhoid conditions, which favour Bacteria are met with this cell-salt.
Bowels, motions from, evacuations yellow, slimy, or constipated, see also coating of tongue.
Bronchial—asthma, with yellow expectoration, and worse in the warm season or in a hot atmosphere. Also Potassium phosphate.
Bronchitis, if the mucus is distinctly yellow, or greenish, slimy, or watery.
Bronchitis, yellow watery matter and profuse.
Cancer, epithelial. See Epithelioma.
Cancer of the tongue, in ; for the epithelial cells involved.
Catamenia, see Menstruation, periods.
Catarrh, chronic, of the stomach ; when there is a yellow slimy coated tongue.
Catarrh of the stomach, sense of pressure, weight, and fulness, yellow coated tongue, or pains and uneasiness, worse on lying down, alt. Potassium phosphate.
Catarrhs, colds, with yellow or greenish slimy secretions or expectorations of watery matter ; patient feels generally worse in the evening, or in a heated room, when not yielding, alt. Potassium sulphate.
Catarrh, of the stomach, if with a yellow slimy coated tongue.
Cataract, dimness of the crystaline lens of the eye. Also Sodium chlor.
Chills, skin inactive ; this remedy taken in hot water to induce gentle perspiration.
Chills, with check of perspiration feverish in hot close air, worse in the evening.
Cold, in the head, with decidedly yellow or greenish slimy discharge ; note tongue ; also Calcium sulphate.
Colds, with dry skin, when perspiration does not set in freely under the use of Ferric phosphate.
Constipation, costiveness, when the fæces are covered with yellow stringy threads, and are large ; tongue coated yellow slimy.
Coryza, cold in the head, this remedy taken at night often, assists in throwing it off more rapidly.
Cough, with yellow spit, or watery mattery. Worse in a heated room, or in the evening.
Cough, worse in the evening, with heat, mucus slips back, and is generally swallowed, hard hoarse cough like croup, weary feeling in the pharynx.
Croupy hoarseness and cough, if not readily yielding to Potass. chlor.
Dandriff, yellowish or white scales on the scalp.
Dandriff, on the scalp, requires this remedy topically as a wash, and internally also ; it not yielding, Sodium chloride.

1. VII.—*Potassium Sulphate = Kali Sulphuricum.*
Kali sulph.

Deafness, when worse in a heated room; with yellow slimy coated tongue. Desire for cool air.

Diabetes, in; alternately with Sodium sulphate when symptoms for its use exist.

Discharges from any of the mucous linings of any part, nose, mouth, throat, etc., when of a yellow slimy or greenish appearance, or turn green on exposure to the air.

Diarrhœa, yellow-slimy, or watery-mattery stools; note also coating of tongue.

Dropsy, kidney disease after scarlatina.

Dropsy, in; dry harsh skin, to produce gentle perspiration, when this is salt tasted, also Sodium chloride.

Dropsy of the kidneys after scarlet fever; this remedy produces action of the epithelial cells when there is dryness and harshness of the skin.

Dryness of skin, from suppressed skin disease, with other symptoms as above.

Dryness of skin, perspiration not induced by Ferric phosphate.

Dyspepsia, indigestion, with decidedly yellow coated tongue, feeling of pressure and fulness.

Ear-ache, with discharge of watery matter, or yellow water.

Ears, with secretion of thin yellow or greenish fluid, after inflammation. See also directions, page i.

Ears, pains under the; sharp, cutting pain, stitches, tensive and piercing, below the mastoid process.

Eczema, skin affections; when the characteristic abnormal conditions present denote a disturbed function of the cells containing this salt, there will be a casting out of effete matter; a discharge of yellow or greenish slimy matter.

Eczema, skin affections; when suddenly suppressed, if any characteristic symptoms are present for which this remedy is given.

Effusions, serous pus (watery matter).

Epithelioma, cancer on the skin near a mucous lining, with discharge of thin yellow serous mattery secretions. External use, see clinical cases, Nos. 33, 34.

Eruptions, when suddenly receding either through a chill, or from other causes, a few doses of this remedy.

Erysipelas, blistering; to facilitate the falling off of scabs, scales.

Evening aggravations, when persistent in any ailment, requires this as an alternate remedy.

Exacerbations, of ailments in the evening.

Expectoration, yellow mucus, as soon as loosened, slips back, and cannot be expectorated, or yellow slimy, and easily coughed up in the morning.

Exudations, serous matter.

Eyelids, with yellow crusts.

Eyes, *discharge from*; yellow or greenish matter. Also Potass. chlor.

Eyes, yellow mattery slime, or yellow watery secretions.

Face-ache, aggravated in a heated room and in the evening; improved in cool or open air.

Febrile condition, sensation of inward heat and feverishness, extremities, chilly, oppressed in close air, temperature rises in the evening up till midnight, then falls again.

Fevers in the onset caused by blood poison (microbes) in the cold stage.

Fevers, in, when the blood heat rises in the evening; it assists in producing perspiration, and warm coverings should be applied for a time, and this remedy given very frequently. This applies also to fevers from blood poisoning.

Flatulence, pain, pressure, and fulness of the bowels in left side of the groin, ovarian complication.

Fungoid, inflammation of the joints.

Gastric fever, see Typhoid.

Gonorrhœa; slimy, yellow, or greenish discharge.

Hair, of the head, etc., when falling out, this remedy as a wash, and internally.

Headache, which grows worse in a heated room and in the evening, and is better in cool or open air.

Hearing, dulness of, with one or other of the characteristic derangements of function, for which this cell-salt is required.

Heart, palpitation, traced to the effects of hot or close air.

Heat, of climate or rooms, increasing slight ailments.

Hæmorrhoides, see Piles.

Hoarseness, from cold. If not removed by Potassium chloride.

Hooping-cough; for decidedly yellow slimy expectoration; for the whoop, Magnesium phosphate.

Indigestion, see pain.

Indigestion, dyspepsia, with sensation of pressure as of a load, and fulness at the pit of the stomach, and yellow coated tongue.

Indigestion, with pain, and water gathering in the mouth, should Sodium chloride or Potassium chloride not suffice.

Inflammation, with yellow watery, serous watery secretions.

Influenza, severe type, temperature rising in the evening; to promote perspirable activity to throw off the poison.

Jaundice, secondary remedy, when the symptoms correspond with the special indications for its use.

Kidney, disease, post scarlatinal dropsy.

Leucorrhœa, "Whites," discharge of yellow greenish slimy or watery secretions.

Lips, dryness and desquamation of the lower lip, peel in large flakes.

Lungs, inflammation of, with wheezing; if yellow loose rattling plegm be coughed up, or watery matter.

Matter, pus in; when unhealthy greenish or turns greenish on the lint after exposure to the air.

Measles, in; when the rash is slow to develop or has receded again, this cell-salt stimulates the epithelial cells, and throws the blood to the skin.

Measles, the discharges are yellow, thin, slimy.

Menstruation, too late and too scanty, with a feeling of weight and fulness in abdomen, yellow coated tongue.

Menses, excessive flow, caused by heat of too warm covering at night.

Nails, for diseased condition of, shown in interrupted growth. See also Silica.

Ophthalmia, purulent greenish discharge from the eyes.

Ovarian neuralgia, or pains which are located chiefly on the left side of the pelvis.

Pain after food, indigestion, with a feeling of pressure, a load, bruised feeling, and with yellow tongue ; or when heat or lying down is oppressive or aggravate the symptoms.

Palpitation, caused by heated atmosphere, or with yellow slimy tongue.

Pains, behind and under the ear, over carotid artery.

Pains, resembling colic, the abdomen feels cold to the touch, and Magnesium phosphate does not relieve the severe pains.

Pains in the abdomen, resembling flatulent colic, caused sometimes by great heat from excitement, and sudden coldness of the part shortly after ; gas passing from the bowels has a sulphurous odour.

Pains, neuralgic or rheumatic, in the back, nape of the neck, or in the limbs, if periodical, worse in the evening, or in warm room, and if decidedly better in a cool or open atmosphere.

Perspiration, when checked, to promote it.

Perspiration ; when not well established under the use of Ferr. phos.

Piles, internal and external, may require this remedy in alternation with Calcium fluoride the chief remedy, when the tongue has a yellow slimy coating, or discharges or secretions, of the characteristic type are present.

Pulse quick. with dull, low, throbbing, boring pain over crest of ileum, disinclination to speak, pallid face ; also Ferric phosphate.

Rash, of measles or other erruptive febrile diseases, when suppressed or suddenly receding, with harsh and dry skin. This remedy will assist the returning of the rash.

Rheumatic fever, when articular pains are shifting, wandering, or flitting.

Rheumatic headaches, always beginning in the evening, and in a heated atmosphere.

Rheumatic pains in the joints, shifting, wandering, flitting, chronic, or acute.

Rheumatism, acute, articular, when of a shifting nature, settling in one part and then settling in another; neuralgic pains require Magnesium phosphate.

Rheumatism, chronic, of the joints, with characteristic symptoms pointing to this remedy.

Scales, yellow tinged, as on the scalp.

Scarlet fever, desquamation, *i.e.*, skin peeling off, the cause of infection in scarlet fever, etc. ; this salt assists desquamation, and formation of new healthy skin.

Secretions, from the mucous membranes, of eyes, nose, throat, vagina, etc., when yellowish or yellow-greenish slimy.

Ulcers of the lower limbs, yellow, slimy discharge and flaking of skin.

Skin, dry, burning; itching in the evening ; yellow coated tongue or palate ; dread of hot drinks, disinclination to perspire, call for this remedy.

Skin scaling freely on a sticky base in large flakes.

Skin, sores on, with yellow, watery secretions on limited portions, or discharges of thin watery matter, sometimes with peeling of the surrounding skin.

Smallpox, in ; to promote the formation of new healthy skin, and the falling off of the crusts.

Stomach, pains in ; fixed in the abdomen just above the angle of the crest of the ileum, in a line toward the umbilicus, deep within, beside the right hip.

Stomach, pains in ; colicky pain, when Magnesium phosphate gives no relief.

Suffocating feeling in a hot atmosphere or during a disease, desire for cool air.

Syphilis, with the characteristisc symptoms, yellow slimy secretions, evening aggravation, etc..

Temperature of the blood rising regularly in the evening during any disease is a sign of a typhoid condition and special poison in the blood. The white and gray nervous substances, according to the latest researches, contain, besides the cell salts mentioned, traces of Potassium sulphate, Oxide of iron, Silica, and Sodium chloride, etc.

Tongue, coating of, yellow, slimy, sometimes with whitish edge.

Toothache, aggravated in the warm room and in the evening, but better in the cool open air.

Torpidity and oppression of the system, when a rash or other disease seems unable to make rapid headway.

Typhoid, Enteric, or Gastric fever, rise of temperature at night, and fall in the morning, requires this remedy in particular.

Vitality depressed, nocturnal exacerbations, absence of pain, paleness of face, at the onset of a disease, especially of miasmatic origin (microbes).

Voice, hoarse, hard cough as in croup, speaking is fatiguing, yellow coated tongue or palate.

Wheezing, yellow slimy expectoration.

Wounds, not healing readily, with yellow slimy thin matter or scaling of skin.

" *Whites*", see Leucorrhœa.

N.B.—ON SELECTING A REMEDY, read always the first two paragraphs under each Cell-Salt in this index, as these are of importance, so as to grasp the sphere of action of each Cell-Salt and its function.

8.—Magnesium Phosphate=Magnesia Phosphorica. Mag. phos.

This salt, termed muscle and nerve earth, is a constituent part of all white nerve fibres ; these act as conductors of the *external* and *internal* stimuli. whether sensory, motor, or reflex. The fibres may become abnormal in their conducility and excitability. Magnesium phosphate is also met with in the tissue of bone.

Stimuli applied to the white nerve fibres or conductors may not only excite sensation, but also contraction or motion, by direct conduction along a nerve, or else by the conduction of a stimulus to a nervous centre (gray matter) whence it is reflected along another nerve to the muscles. Sensory impressions have different channels, special paths by which they travel ; touch, pain, the sense of heat or cold, and the muscular sense, each having its own channel. Tactile sensibility. its own path is in the white columns of the cord.—*Schiff.* Abnormal condition of these conductors require Magnesium phosphate chiefly.

The Diseases forming this group must be healed or treated with *Magnesium phosphate*, as these diseases have their seat in the muscle, nerve fibre, and bone cells

All Ailments with intensely sharp pain, which are of a darting, crampy, spasmodic nature, often accompanied with a feeling of constriction. This is the true anti-spasmodic remedy. When warmth is soothing it may be taken in hot liquids.

After-pains, excessive, cramp-like.

Angina pectoris, breast pang, for the neuralgic spasms. The remedy had best be given in hot water.

Asthma millari, spasmodic croup in ; as an intercurrent remedy for the cramping.

Asthma, when flatulence is troublesome.

Back, neuralgic pains in, very acute, darting, boring, shifting about, and remittent.

Bladder, spasms of the, spasmodic, retention of urine.

Bowels and stomach, gnawing pains in, with flatulent detension, slight short belching of gas (wind) giving no relief.

Cancer, this remedy when there are excruciating pains of a neuralgic nature occurring.

Chattering of teeth, nervous ; also Potassium phosphate.

Choleraic cramps

Chorea, St Vitus dance, involuntary movements and contortions of the limbs, if worms symptoms exist Sodium phosphate.

Chromatopsia, spasmodic vision of sparks or of rainbow colours, abnormal condition of optic nerve fibres. Also Sodium phosphate.

Closing of the windpipe, a spasmodic sudden attack, shrill voice, suffocating cough ; also a dose of Potassium phosphate.

Colic, flatulent, of children, with drawing up of legs.

Colic, forcing the patient to bend double, pain eased by friction, warmth, and belching of gas.

VIII.—Magnesium Phosphate = Magnesia Phosphorica. Iv. *Mag. phos.*

Colic, in umbilical region, forcing the patient to bend double, muscular contractions.

Colic, remittent, gripes, crampy pain, if associated with acidity; also Sodium phosphate.

Concussion of the brain, with contracted pupils; an intercurrent remedy.

Constriction of chest and throat, with spasmodic, dry, tickling cough.

Convulsive twitching of the corners of the mouth, abnormal action of motor nerve fibres.

Convulsions, with stiffness of the limbs or of the body, thumbs drawn in, fingers clenched; if convulsions occur in children, give Calcium phosphate alternately. Over stimulation of nerve fibres.

Cough, true spasmodic, coming in fits paroxysms; if accompanied with a spit, see Expectoration.

Cramp, of the fingers, or writers' cramp.

Cramp in any part of the body requires this remedy.

Cramp, of the legs, or indeed in any part of the body. Nerve disturbances of the posterior roots of the spinal nerves, afferent fibres, conveying sensation, causing feeling of cramp, &c.

Crampy pain, in stomach or bowels, with a feeling as if tightly grasped with a band.

Cramp, spasm of throat, closing of the larynx.

Deafness, arising from weakness or disease of the auditory conducting nerve fibres.

Dulness of sight or vision, from weakness of the optic nerve (conductor).

Dysentery, with crampy pain, muscular spasms, eased by bending double, by warmth, or friction.

Epigastric pains at pit of stomach, nipping, griping, with short belching of wind giving no relief, and clean tongue.

Epileptic fits, sometimes the result of vicious habits, which must be restrained; for spasms, stiffness of the limbs, clenched fists or teeth, alt. chief remedy Potassium chloride; Calcium phosphate may have to be given as an intercurrent.

Epigastric spasms, cramp in the stomach, with clean tongue, crampy pain as if a band were tightly laced or drawn round the body.

Eyelid, drooping of, also Potassium phosphate.

Eyelids. spasmodic action, twitching, note also if symptoms of acidity can be traced, and alt. Sodium phosphate.

Eyes, affection of the, with contracted pupils.

Eyes, neuralgic pain in, or over the eye, sharp and darting; alt. Calcium phosphate if not yielding.

Eye, violent boring pain; in gouty patients Sodium phosphate.

Eyes, vision affected, seeing sparks, colours before the eyes, also Sodium phosphate.

Face-ache (neuralgic, rheumatic), stinging, shooting like lightening, darting about, and remittent; if with watery secretions, Sodium chloride.

Fits, for the muscular contractions, twitchings, and spasms, intercurrent remedy.

 VIII.—Magnesium Phosphate = Magnesia Phosphorica. Mag. phos.

Flatulence, with nipping pain, and short belching of gas, giving no relief; clean tongue.

Glottis, spasm of the, causing contraction of the opening of the wind-pipe, a struggle for breath, and a feeling of suffocation, sometimes with stiffness of the limbs.

Gravel, windy pain ; deposit in urine, Sodium sulphate.

Hands, involuntary shaking of, affection of the muscles.

Headaches, very excruciating, with tendency to spasmodic symptoms.

Headaches (neuralgic, rheumatic), shooting or stinging, shifting pain, and intermittent.

Headache neuralgic, as if a band were drawn tightly round the head.

Hiccough, convulsive and spasmodic.

Hooping cough, beginning as a common cold, Ferric phosphate as first remedy, but for the convulsive fits of nervous cough ending in a whoop, give Magnesium phosphate steadily.

Illusions, optical, Diplobia, Spectra, &c.

Indigestion, with spasmodic cramping pain, and a clean tongue.

Intermittent fever, with cramp of the calves.

Labour pain, spasmodic, with cramp in legs.

Labour pain, crampy, excessive expulsive efforts.

Laryngismus stridulus, cramp of spasm of the larynx (windpipe), occurring sometimes in the young ; also called "child crowing :" suffocation threatening; frequent doses, even dry when swallowing is impossible.

Limbs, pains in, (neuralgic rheumatic), very vivid, darting about, shifting and remittent.

Menstrual colic ; the chief remedy.

Menstruation, painful, or pain preceding the periodic flow.

Mobility, power of motion, or locomotion, spasmodic.

Motor nerves, spasmodic disturbances of, require this remedy.

Nape of neck, pains in, very sharp, shooting, boring, shifting, and remittent, relieved by warmth.

Nerve fibres (white), when in an abnormal condition do not propogate the motor impulse sent by them in an equal or regular manner, and cause by sudden irregular interrupted action on the muscles, intermittent reflex action, spasmodic muscular contractions. Hence spasms, cramps, lockjaw, shaking of the hands, palsy, neuralgia with sudden darting pain, and all such ailments find their remedy in this salt, the natural constituent part of the conductors of white nerve fibres. Mechanical influences may also act as a stimulus to the nerve fibres, and if it be excessive, or unequal in strength, they interfere with the normal action of the fibre, and spasmodic and persistent contractions may result. In scientific experiments, sudden excessive motor stimuli applied to the ends of the white nerve fibres produce similar phenomena, whether mechanical or chemical. (Idopathic and traumatic.)

Neuralgia, intercostal (between the ribs), of a drawing, constrictive kind ; spasms from cold, without fever.

Neuralgia in the head, pains darting and very intense. If inflammatory or congestive, with feeling of weight or pressure, give Ferric phosphate alternately.

Neuralgic pains in any part of the body.

Ovarian neuralgia, pains darting.

Ovarian neuralgia, for acute darting spasmodic pains shooting along the course of the nerve, and where heat is soothing. A few doses of Potassium phosphate when the patient seems to be nervous and weak.

Pains, bodily, when the phenomena of sensation is too acute, and pain excruciating, or spasmodic. Pain in ends of nerve fibres.

Pains coming on periodically, very acute.

Pains, improved by pressure, but worse by slight touch.

Pains, neuralgic, in any parts, when darting or shooting along the nerve.

Pains, spasmodic, in the stomach or bowels, griping, cutting, drawing, so as to bend the body double, increased on the slightest muscular movement, and clean tongue.

Palpitation, sudden, of the heart, when a purely spasmodic affection.

Palsy, agitans, involuntary shaking and trembling of the hands or limbs, or of the head; an affection of the muscles. Also Calcium phosphate, Potassium phosphate.

Palsy, muscular paralysis, caused by a disturbed or diseased condition of the efferent nerve fibres, which convey the motorial stimuli to the muscles. Also Potassium phosphate.

Paralysis, of white nerve fibres. Also Calcium phosphate.

Photophobia, intolerance of light, this remedy internally, and externally by tepid syringing.

Piles, pains cutting, darting, very acute, neuralgic, often like lightning so sharp and quick; in external piles, also as tepid lotion.

Puerpural convulsions in, an intercurrent remedy.

Retention of urine, inability to pass water from spasmodic constriction; after use of catheter, a sensation as if the muscles did not contract; for fever, if present, Ferric phosphate, also Calc. phos.

Rheumatic pain, excruciating spasmodic pain, this as an intercurrent remedy, with Sodium phosphate the chief remedy.

Sciatica, in, with the peculiar spasmodic pains for which this remedy is given, darting, shooting &c.

Sciatica, excruciating darting pain in hip and leg.

Sensibility, want of, deadening of the white nerve fibres as of the eye, &c., requires this cell-salt.

Shaking of the hands, trembling, even when caused by alcoholism.

Shaking, spasmodic trembling of the muscles in any part of the body; also Calcium phosphate.

Skin itching.

Smell, loss of; or pervertion of the sense of smell, under certain conditions, not connected with cold; a course of this remedy.

Spasmodic affections of the eyelids (twitching).

Spasmodic cough, coming in fits, severe, shaking, windy, or like whooping-cough; Calcium phosphate as an intercurrent remedy.

M

lviii. *VIII.—Magnesium Phosphate = Magnesia Phosphoricæ.* *Mag. phos.*

Spasmodic cough at night, with difficulty of lying down, constrained feeling.

Spasmodic pains and affections of almost any kind.

Spasmodic pains of the abdomen, as in dysentery, ameliorated by pressure and doubling up.

Spasm of the throat, on attempting to swallow liquids, sensation of choking.

Squinting, spasmodic, in children ; give also Calcium phosphate.

St. Vitus' dance ; chief remedy.

Stammering, spasmodic ; to strengthen the white nerve fibres and remove the spasmodic action of the muscles ; Potassium phosphate for nervousness. Begin your speech with the teeth closed.

Stomach, cramp in, intensely painful constriction of the muscles of the coat of the stomach. This remedy and hot applications.

Strabismus, spasmodic squinting. When in children, give Calcium phosphate alternately. If caused by worms ; Sodium phosphate.

Stricture, spasmodic, of the bladder.

Teething, convulsions, cramps, without fever ; in alternation with Calcium phosphate.

Tetanus (lockjaw) ; this remedy must be moistened and rubbed into the lower gums *very* frequently.

Tetanic spasms, abnormal condition of nerve fibre, which may be induced by sudden abstraction of moisture from the fibre cells.

Toothache, if hot liquids ease the pain ; but if the application of cold ease the pain, it is inflammatory, and must be treated with Ferric phosphate.

Toothache (neuralgic, rheumatic), very intense and shooting, eased by warmth.

Toothache, pain eased by pressure, but aggravated by slight touch.

Tonic spasms, violent contraction and rigidity of muscles during longer or shorter intervals.

Urine, spasmodic retention in, abnormal conditions of the molecular constitution of the nerve fibres. On injecting water into the vessels of a muscle, strong contractions take place, due to the effect of the fluid on the *terminations* of the nerves.—*Schiff.*

Vaginismus, spasmodic contraction of the passage, also Calcium phosphate ; this condition may also require Ferric phosphate.

Windpipe, spasmodic closing of.

Writers' cramp, or cramp of the fingers of violinists and pianists.

Yawning, with excessive spasmodic straining of the lower jaw.

N.B.—**ON SELECTING A REMEDY,** read always the first two paragraphs under each Cell-Salt in this index, as these are of importance, so as to grasp the sphere of action of each Cell-Salt and its function. Note always the appearance of the tongue.

9.—Sodium Chloride = Natrum Muriaticum.
Nat. mur.

The diseases forming this group must be healed or treated with *Sodium Chloride;* they arise from a disturbed balance of the molecules of this salt, which is a constituent of all solids and fluids of the body. Its presence regulates the proper degree of moisture of solids and proper amount of water of the fluids in the organism. It has its function in the epithelial cells of the peptic gastric glands, and assists in forming hydrochloric acid, the essential of the gastric juice. It is present in the mucous membranes, and acts on the mucin.

All Ailments of any kind when the epithelial cells of the salivary glands are affected — excess of watery secretions, also of the mucous membranes. Ex. The tongue has a clear slimy appearance, or small bubbles of frothy saliva extend along its sides, salt taste—also when there exists an involuntary flow of tears or watery discharge; and when there are increased watery secretions, discharges from any of the mucous membranes, sometimes scalding and chafing, with co-existing want of moisture, *i.e.*, diminished secretions, in some other portion of the mucous linings, including constipation. It includes gastric catarrhs, indigestion, and anæmia, from lack of normal gastric juice.

Adynamic conditions, weakness with drowsiness, watery vomiting, etc.

Ague, or intermittent quartan fever, in, with vesicular eruptions on the lips, and other corresponding symptoms.

Ague fever, veiled, taking the form of neuralgia of the face or head.

Anæmia, bloodlessness caused by catarrh of the stomach. Salt taste in the mouth.

Anæmic conditions, blood thin, watery.

Anasarca, accumulation of serum (water from the arterial blood) in the areolar tissues of the body; general dropsy.

Aphthæ, thrush, with flow of saliva; this remedy and Potass. chlor.

Asthma, with profuse frothy mucus; in alternation with Potass. phos.

Atrophy, wasting disease, when the blood is decidedly watery and patient chilly.

Back-ache, when there is poverty of blood, wateriness of blood, excess of saliva, etc.

Blood, loss of, hæmorrhages, or discharges, when the blood is watery, thin, or pale red.

Blisters, vesicles, eruptions, with clear watery contents, leaving thin scabs.

Bowels, costive; with drowsiness, or waterbrash, dribbling of saliva from the mouth during sleep, crumbling stools, etc.

Brain fever, as an alternate remedy when there is too much moisture in the brain pulp, and great drowsiness, or watery secretions set in; also Calcium phosphate as an alternate remedy.

Bronchitis, acute inflammation of the windpipe, with frothy and clear watery phlegm, loose and rattling, and sometimes coughed up with difficulty.

 IX.—Sodium Chloride = Natrum Muriaticum.

Nat. mur.

Bronchitis, chronic, bronchial catarrh, "Winter Cough," with any of the above symptoms.

Cataract, opacity of the crystaline lens, to dissolve the deposit ; Calc. fluor. for contractile fibres when relaxed.

Catarrhs, chronic, of bloodless patients, the mucus has sometimes a salty taste.

Catarrhs of any of the mucous linings, as of mouth, nose, windpipe, bowels, and other passages, with watery, transparent, frothy discharges. Also Calcium phosphate.

Cerebritis, for effusion ; also Calcium phosphate.

Chicken-pox, to limit the effusion in the vesicles.

Chilliness, not arising from having newely taken a cold, wateriness of the blood, and almost habitual feeling of coldness in the back, with characteristic appearance of tongue, etc.

Chlorotic conditions, like "green sickness," if any of above symptoms are present.

Circulation sluggish in certain conditions when the blood is poor, hygromic ; slow pulse in disease or after having passed through a disease, requires Potassium phosphate to stimulate the nervous vigour.

Cold in the head, with clear, watery discharge. Calcium phosphate as an intercurrent remedy.

Colds, causing vesicular eruptions with watery contents, which burst and leave thin crusts or scabs.

Coldness, feeling of, principally in the back ; clear, watery spit.

Conical Cornea; vision of the one eye limited to five inches; was cured by this remedy alone.

Constipation, this as chief remedy, when arising from want of moisture, dryness of the mucous linings of the bowels ; or watery secretions in other parts, watery vomiting, watery eyes, excess of saliva in the mouth or on the tongue ; inability to expel the fæces, requires Calcium fluoride. Silica.

Cornea, blister on the, of the eye.

Coryza, "running cold," with watery, clear, frothy discharge.

Cough, with excess of watery secretions, frothy, clear, or tough, alt. Calcium phosphate.

Cough, in consumption, chronic, frothy spit.

Cough, with irritation on the windpipe ; mucus frothy and watery. When clear, but difficult to detach, Calcium phosphate in alternation.

Cough, with frothy, watery expectoration, salt tasted.

Dandruff, white scales on scalp, sometimes co-existing with watery secretions from the mouth, nose, or eyes.

Deafness, from swelling of the tympanic cavity, with watery condition of tongue as above, or watery secretions.

Deafness, throat, with catarrh of the throat ; secretions watery, or other symptoms of this class co-existing.

Delirium, occurring at any time, with starting of the body, wandering delirium, and muttering, frothy tongue ; inflammatory fever requires also Ferric phosphate.

Delirium tremens (alcoholic), for the molecular disturbances, watery condition of brain substance, or lack of moisture, which Sodium chloride, being hygromic, will overcome when sent to the brain.
Diarrhœa, with watery, frothy, slimy stools.
Dimness of sight, as if mist or gauze before the eyes, and after suppression of coryza, with watery secretions.
Diphtheria, if face be puffy and pale, with drowsiness, watery stools, flow of saliva, or vomiting of water ; if the latter be greenish, Sodium phosphate.
Discharges from the mucous or serous linings of the throat, nose, &c., when clear, frothy, watery.
Dropsy and dropsical swellings of any of the subcutaneous areolar tissues of the body, perspirations salt tasted. Also Sodium sulphate.
Drowsiness, excessive and unnatural sleep, sometimes with saliva dribbling from the mouth.
Dyspepsia, causing waterbreak, or much clear frothy mucus.
Ear-ache, with a watery secretion, or singing in the ears ; alt. Ferric phosphate.
Eczema, white scales. See external application, page i.
Eczema, eruptions with watery contents.
Effusions, serous, poor in albumen ; note also if other symptoms characteristic of a disturbed condition of this cell-salt are present.
Eruptions of small vesicles or blisters, with colourless watery fluid, forming into thin scabs or crusts, which fall off and readily form again.
Epilepsy, with froth at the mouth, bloodlessness.
Expectoration, serous, as in cough, when clear, transparent, frothy, watery, sometimes salt tasted.
Exudations on the skin or mucous lining, occurring after inflammations, when watery, serous, poor in albumen.
Eye, blister on the cornea.
Eyes, discharge of clear mucus from, or flow of tears with obstruction of the tear duct. Also Ferric phosphate.
Eyes, neuralgic pains in the, periodically appearing, with flow of tears.
Eyes, watering.
Eyes, affection of, with secretion of water, and flow of tears, causing scalded skin or eruption of small vesicles ; sensitiveness to light may require Magnesium phosphate.
Eyes, white spots on the cornea ; this remedy also externally, daily syringing the spot.
Eyelids, granulated, with secretions of tears, also Potass. chloride.
Face-ache, with constipation ; tongue showing a clear mucous slime, and little frothy bubles at its edge.
Face-ache, with vomiting of clear phelgm or water.
Fevers, accompanying acute diseases ; also in scarlet and typhus fever, diphtheria, smallpox, when drowsiness, dryness of tongue, or vomiting of water occur, and this cell salt is lacking in some tissue cells.
Flatulence, bringing back the taste of the food, "repeating."

Flatulence, connected with watery secretions, waterbrash (tasteless fluid), deficiency of normal gastric juice.

Flooding, in, as intercurrent remedy, watery blood, drowsiness.

Fingers, blistering festers on, containing watery fluid, often used by arsenical wall papers.

Glands, salivary, chronic inflammation of, with corresponding symptoms, excess of saliva, &c.

Glands, lymphatic, chronic swelling, if with corresponding watery symptoms.

Glands, sebaceous, swelling of.

Gleet ; this remedy and Calcium phosphate.

Gonorrhœa, with scalding, the characteristic secretions for which this salt has to be given. Also Calcium phosphate.

Gonorrhœa, chronic ; transparent watery slime.

Hay Fever, for the watery discharge from the eyes and nose ; the lotions may also be syringed up into the nostrils ; for the feverishness. Ferric phos. ; the depression of breathing, Potass. phos.

Headache, dull heavy, with profusion of tears, and drowsiness, sleep not refreshing.

Headaches, with constipation, from torpor and dryness of a portion of the internal mucous membrane ; when the tongue is clean, or covered with clear watery mucus, or frothy edges, much saliva.

Headaches, with vomiting of transparent phlegm or water

Hœmorrhage, bleeding ; blood pale red, thin, watery, not coagulating.

Hearing, dulness of, deafness, with singing or whizzing noises.

Herpetic eruptions, blisters, occurring alone or during the course of a disease.

Herpes or tetter, an inflammation of the skin, accompanied by small blebs, blisters, or watery vesicles.

Herpes-zoster, as second remedy.

Hooping-cough, if the mucus is frothy, clear, and stringy.

Indigestion, gastric juice, abnormal ; weak.

Indigestion, with vomiting of clear frothy water, or stringy saliva.

Indigestion and pain, with water gathering in the mouth.

Influenza, with watery, frothy expectoration, running at the nose, great sleepiness. For the fever and bruised feeling in the back, the limbs, or the bones, give Ferric phosphate alternately.

Intertrigo, soreness of skin, also of children with watery secretions, Sodium phosphate, with acidity, Sodium sulphate with bilious exudations.

Iritis, in ; after Potassium chloride, or in alternation with it when symptoms exist to indicate it.

Jaundice, with drowsiness, and any of the symptoms present, peculiar to this group of ailments.

Leucorrhœa, "whites," a watery, scalding, irritating discharge.

Legs jerking, involuntary, fidgets, or jerking, starting during sleep

Lethargic state, excessive drowsiness, with jerking or starting of the limbs, falling asleep constantly when a symptom of disease.

Liver complaint, when watery secretions occur, and such symptoms as denote a lack of this salt.

Looseness of the bowels, with watery stools ; avoid excessive use of salt.
Lungs, inflammation of, if there is much loose rattling phlegm, clear, serous, and frothy ; sometimes coughed up with difficulty.
Malignant symptoms, with drowsiness, &c.
Measles, if there is an excessive secretion of tears or saliva ; as an intercurrent remedy.
Meningitis, when watery secretions supervene, and drowsiness, &c. ; also Calcium phosphate.
Menstruation, returning, after ceasing a day or more.
Menstruation, discharge thin, watery, or pale.
Mental aberrations, with tendency to dejection and hypochondriasis, alt. with Potassium phosphate.
Morning sickness, with vomiting of stringy, frothy phlegm, or watery fluid.
Mucous membrane, diseases of, when the secretions are clear, frothy, or watery, or watery blisters form.
Mumps, with much salivation.
Neck, pains in the nape ot the, with creaking on moving ; generally flow of saliva, or tears, or watery secretions.
Nerve pains, neuralgic, recurring at certain times, with flow of saliva or involuntary tears.
Neuralgia, periodic, with great flow of saliva or tears ; also Mag. phos.
Neuralgia, darting, shooting along the nerve fibres, but accompanied by flow of saliva or involuntary tears, or clear watery mucus.
Noise in the head, singing, whirring noises in the head, ears, hearing the pulse.
Œdema of lungs, acute ; excessive, serous, frothy secretions.
Pain after food, with watery secretions.
Pains, neuralgic, caused by irritation of the fifth or facial nerves, dilatation of the nutrient vessels of the glands, increased activity and watery secretions.
Pains in the eyes, also when occurring periodically, with flow of tears, sometimes smarting.
Palpitation, with anæmic condition ; small fluttering pulsations felt ; watery blood ; also in dropsical swellings, &c.
Pemphigus, skin disease, blisters, blebs, fluid clear like water, and scabs.
Piles, in ; alternately with the chief remedy when secretions are watery, saliva dribbling in sleep, general chilliness and constipation (crumbling stools), which does not yield to Calcium fluoride.
Pimples, see vesicles.
Pleurisy, when serous effusion has taken place during and after its course.
Pleuro-pneumonia, when effusion of water has taken place in the pleura.
Polyuria, if the symptoms correspond, waterbrash acid, Sod. phos.
Præputial œdema. Also Sodium sulphate.
Ranula, a tumour, swelling of the glands below the tongue.
Rheumatic gouty pains, if symptoms of tongue, or watery discharges, or secretions, &c., correspond, after giving Sodium phosphate.
Rheumatism of the joints, chronic ; after Sodium phosphate, the chief remedy, if tongue or other symptoms correspond, and if joints crack.

Rupia, blisters, not pustular eruptions.

Salivation, excess of saliva, whether existing alone or accompanying any other disease.

Scarlet fever, with drowsiness, twitchings, or vomiting of watery fluids.

Scales, white, on the scalp ; Potassium sulphate chief remedy.

Scrotal œdema, with serous infiltration. Also Sodium phosphate, with erysipelatous condition.

Sebacious glands, swelling of, small glands at the root of the hairs.

Secretions, discharges, if frothy, clear, watery.

Secretions, if clear, transparent, serous ; but rich in albumen, Calcium phosphate.

Secretions on the skin, watery, not sticky, with other corresponding symptoms ; if not yielding to this, use Sodium sulphate.

Secretions, which cause smarting and soreness, excoriation of the parts. Also for those of mucous linings.

Shingles, with the characteristic symptoms of this group, indicated at the heading of this remedy blisters ; for nerve pain, neuralgic, Magnesium phosphate.

Shortsightedness, also from conical cornea.

Sick headache, with vomiting or coughing up of clear watery or stringy mucus. Also Calcium phosphate.

Skin affections, eczema, blisters, serous sacs filled with clear, watery secretions.

Skin affections, herpes, with watery contents bursting readily, and crust form repeatedly. Note also if symptoms of acidity are present.

Skin affections, with white scales, chief remedy. Note palate and tongue.

Skin, chafing of, in infants ; generally with watery secretions ; also Sodium phosphate.

Sleep, excessive, is traced to an excess of moisture in the brain substance.

Sleepiness, natural amount of sleep unrefreshing, feeling tired in the morning on awakening.

Sleepiness, constant and excessive inclination to sleep, when accompanied with one or other above characteristic symptoms.

Small-pox, with salivary flow, confluence of pustules, and drowsiness.

Softening of the brain, this remedy, especially when the symptoms predominate which are indicated at the head of this chapter as the characteristics which this cell-salt meets. Calcium phosphate to strengthen the brain pulp.

Sores, excoriations of skin, with clear watery oozings.

Stings of insects. Apply the lotion externally as soon as possible ; the remedy may also be taken internally.

Stomach-ache, with much saliva, water gathering in the mouth ; if this remedy does not suffice, the coating of tongue may indicate Potassum chloride or Potassium sulphate.

Stomach, catarrh of ; with watery secretion and vomiting.

Sunstroke. The pathological conditions of this affection arise from sudden abstraction of moisture in the tissues at the nape of the neck. Sodium chloride is the chief remedy in these conditions.

Swellings, dropsical, puffiness, much saliva, or skin peeling in flakes.
Sycosis (affection of the bearded part of the face), if the (watery) symptoms correspond.
Syphilis, chronic. Serous exudations, etc.
Teething, with much dribbling and flow of saliva, caused by disturbed condition of this cell-salt, which, if acting normally, regulates such secretions.
Throat enlargement, goitre, if with watery secretions; Sodium phos. chief remedy.
Throat, inflammation of the mucous lining, with transparent frothy mucus covering the tonsils.
Thrush, with salivation.
Tongue, slimy, clear, and watery, or when small bubbles of frothy saliva cover the sides, this remedy may be required.
Toothache, with involuntary flow of tears.
Toothache, with great flow of saliva.
Typhoid or malignant conditions, during the course of any fever, such as twitchings, with great drowsiness, watery vomiting, etc.
Typhus fever, when the stupor and sleepiness are very great.
Ulcers, when the discharge is watery.
Uterine hæmorrhage when bright red, thin, watery.
Uvula, inflamed, relaxed, when there is much saliva. See also Calcium fluoride.
Vesicles, pimples, small blisters, when moisture oozes, clear watery.
Vomiting of transparent, watery, stringy mucus.
Vomiting of mucus, with constipation.
Vomiting of watery fluids (not acid) or froth.
Water brash, watery fluid coming up the throat, not acid tasted; often accompanied by constipation.
Wheezing, râle, rattling of loose phlegm, frothy, clear.
"*Whites*," Leucorrhœa, watery, smarting discharges, after or between the periods.
Whooping cough, for the glands, and serous secretions, also frothy expectoration.
Winter cough, bronchial, transparent secretions, also Calcium phos.

N.B.—ON SELECTING A REMEDY, read always the first two paragraphs under each Cell-Salt in this index, as these are of importance, so as to grasp the sphere of action of each Cell-Salt and its function.

10.—Sodium Phosphate=Natrum Phosphoricum
Nat phos.

The Diseases or pathological conditions forming this group may have their seat in blood corpuscles, muscle, nerve, or brain cells, or in the intercellual fluids, and must be healed or treated with *Sodium phosphate;* they arise mainly from excess of lactic acid, composed of carbonic acid and water. This cell-salt decomposes, splits up, the lactic acid in venous blood, and fixes or takes up the carbonic acid, and carries it to the lungs to be exhaled. It has an affinity for acid albumen, and hence is able to cause resorption of the same. By its presence the uric acid is held in solution in the blood when the latter maintains its normal warmth ; but when chill causes a precipitate of uric acid, gout and acute articular rheumatism will set in. It assists also in the emulsion or saponifying of fats. It is most important in diseases with albuminous deposits.

All ailments in which there are any symptoms of acidity ; deposit on the tongue of a thin, moist, creamy coating (gold coloured) like honey, sometimes covering the tongue as if with moist yellow sugar ; or the soft palate has a yellowish creamy look. It is a most important factor in many diseases caused by excess of acids, a most useful alternating remedy. Where fatty substances are not saponified, causing dyspepsia. In Lupus, tubercular diseases struma and scrophulosis where certain acids are found in excess in the tissues. Tox albumen.

Abdomen, enlargement of, glandular ; with acidity.

Abrasions, gastric ; portions of the coatings of stomach or intestines corroded, superficial ulceration. Pain after food, sour risings.

Acidity, sour risings ; a course of this remedy to correct the excess of lactid acid. Attention to diet. A course of this remedy in alternation with Ferric phosphate to strengthen the digestion.

Ague, intermittent fever ; will be useful when the perspirations are acid.

Albuminuria, in ; when there are acid taste and sour risings. Take this remedy before all meals.

Anæmia, in ; to reduce fermentative processes.

Angina tonsilaris, quinsy, tonsilitis.

Anus, itching at, from worms, especially at night when warm in bed. Also injections of the solution.

Aphthæ, thrush, for the bile acids, invariably in excess as an intercurrent remedy before meals.

Appetite, loss of, indigestion felt slightly ; on rising in the morning the tongue has a thin moist creamy deposit at the back, or as if raw or yellow sugar had been partaken of, acid conditions.

Arthritis, articular rheumatism, acute. Chief remedy.

Back, pain across the loins on awakening in the morning.

Bilious conditions, so called, with acid, sour risings.

Bladder, catarrh of ; with irritation.

Bladder, irritation of ; frequent desire, when the urine is acid.

Bowels, motions from, sour smelling, greenish, loose, or reddish-brown, or fluid like oil.

Bronchocele goitre, Derbyshire neck, for the cystic enlargement.
Catarrhs, with symptoms of acidity.
Cancer of the tongue, as an intercurrent remedy.
Catarrh of the stomach, with acidity alternately; Ferric phos.
Chafing of the skin. See ailments above.
Chorea, St. Vitus' dance; if worm symptoms exist, this remedy kills the worms by degrees. A forcible worm expellant may also be given.
Chronic rheumatism of the joints.
Colic, flatulent with acidity.
Colic, of children, with symptoms of acidity, such as green, sour-smelling stools, vomiting of curdled milk, etc.
Constipation or diarrhœa, when with creamy palate, creamy golden yellow moist tongue, or deep red furrow in the centre, sour smelling motions.
Consumption, in the early and later stages, to control the excess of acids; see also expectoration.
Consumption of the bowels; the alternating remedy for the mischief underlying this disease, the excess of acids, which dissolves the lime salts out of the tissues and leaves them weak and unhealthy, causing coldness and want ot warmth or healthy thermal stimulation in the body.
Cough in tuberculosis, as chief remedy.
Cystitis, inflammation, acute and chronic, of the bladder from stone and other causes; this as first remedy.
Diarrhœa, caused by excess of acidity, stools sour-smelling, green, or liquid like oil.
Diphtheritic throat, falsely so-called (not true), when the tonsils are covered with a *yellow* creamy coating, and the back part of the roof of the mouth looking creamy yellow, or coating of the tongue moist creamy or gold coloured.
Discharges from the mucous linings, creamy looking, they arise generally from some acid condition, and denote lack of oxygen of the blood; excess of lactic acid in the first instance.
Dyspepsia, indigestion, severe burning spot in the region of the stomach, pain often going through to the back. Abrasions of the coat of the stomach.
Dyspepsia, with acid risings, either occasionally or frequently; this remedy, and Ferric phosphate before food.
Ears, sore; the outer part of the ear about the seam, with slight thin cream-like scabbing, and the deposit on the tongue looks as if yellow raw sugar had been eaten.
Ears, one ear red, hot, and frequently itchy, accompanied by gastric derangement and acidity.
Eczema, vesicles forming yellow white crusts.
Eczema, with irritation, papular eruption and itching.
Eczema, with symptoms of acidity, secretion, creamy, yellow, honey coloured.
Enuresis, when arising from irritation and acid condition of urine, also when caused by worms.

lxviii. *X.—Sodium Phosphate = Natrum Phosphoricum.* *Nat. phos.*

Erythema, "rose rash," this remedy and Ferric phosphate.
Epilepsy requires this as chief remedy.
Epileptic fits, falling sickness in ; this as chief remedy.
Expectoration, secretion creamy, honey coloured.
Exudations from the mucous linings, red and raw appearance of these, with soreness and chafing.
Eyes, pain, deep seated, often thought neuralgic, at the back of the eyes, but of gouty origin ; this as an alternate remedy.
Eyes, pain in, of a severe boring nature, often gouty.
Eyes, *affection of ;* in the scrofulous people.
Eyes, discharge of golden yellow creamy matter.
Eyes, *inflammation of*, conjunctivitis, discharge of yellow creamy matter, the lids glued together in the mornings ; note also conditions of tongue, and back of palate, or if sour risings occur.
Face red and blotched, yet not feverish, with gastric derangement and acidity ; see tongue and palate.
Face white about the mouth or nose ; yellow creamy look of palate or tongue.
Fatty food when causing dyspeptic troubles ; Sodium phosphate to reduce the fatty acids.
Flatulence, with sour risings
Gastric derangements, with symptoms of acidity.
Gastric ulcerations, pain and indigestion, sour taste in the mouth.
Giddiness, with gastric derangement, acidity, and want of appetite, or thin gold coloured creamy coating on the tongue.
Gout, acute, chief remedy.
Glands, lymphatic, chronic swelling, as of the neck, etc.; this as chief remedy.
Goitre, cystic tumour in front part of neck, for the acid conditions underlying this dissolving of lime out of connective tissues.
Gouty enlargement of joints, this the chief remedy. Occasionally Sodium phosphate.
Gravel in the kidneys or ureters.
Headache ; the after effect of taking wine, etc. Acetone in the tissues.
Headache, when after taking thick sour milk, containing excess of lactic acid.
Headache on the crown of the head ; on awakening in the morning, creamy appearance of the back part of the palate, yellow moist tongue.
Headache, severe pain, as if the skull were to fall, frontal or occipital, with nausea or sour slimy vomiting.
Headache, very severe, with intense pressure and heat on the top of the head, as if it would open, if Ferric phosphate does not suffice.
Heartburn, if with symptoms of acidity ; note the tongue.
Herpes, zoster, shingles, blisters, occurring in patches ; for the acetone existing in the blood.
Hunger, irregular, excessive, in children, generally connected with an acid condition of the food in the intestines and worms, Potas. phos. for nervous weakness.
Hydrocele, in ; this remedy is indicated after Calcium phosphate.

Nat. phos.

Indigestion, with characteristic tongue indicating this remedy.

Indigestion, and severe pain after food, or coming on two hours after, with acid (sour) risings.

Indigestion; depraved appetite, tongue creamy coated at the back, raised papilla (round or oval elevations).

Influenza, severe type not fluent, for acid condition; before and after all food.

Itching at lower orifice of the bowels from worms.

Intermittent fever, with vomiting of acid, sour masses.

Knee, dropsical swelling from acid, gouty conditions, effusion; also Calc., phosphate.

Lupus and other tuberculous deposit, chief remedy.

Lupus; secondary remedies, Potassium chloride and Calcium phos.

Morning sickness, with vomiting of sour masses or fluids, heartburn.

Mucous membrane, disease of, with dry feeling and itching, brownish scabs forming, as in the nose.

Nails, habit of biting the same; this cell-salt will remove the irritating cause.

Nape of neck, pains in when with stiffness; alt. Ferric phosphate, and hot lotion to be rubbed into the parts.

Nausea, sick feeling, of a morning, feeling of weakness, with creamy looking tongue or soft palate, acid risings.

Nausea, sickness, with sour risings.

Nose, picking at the, generally associated with acidity and worms.

Ophthalmia, infantile, purulent discharge from the eyes of new born children, so difficult to deal with, finds its remedy in this single cell salt.

Ophthalmia, when the mattery discharge from the eye is creamy.

Ozoena, ulcer in the nose; purulent fœtid discharge.

Pain after food, cramps, spasms with acidity, sour risings, or creamy appearance of the back of the palate.

Pains, various, if the tongue, tonsils, or the palate has a golden-tinged deposit like cream, and honey coloured.

Palate, with redness and soreness from an acid condition with the peculiar symptoms in lack of Sodium phosphate.

Paleness of face or bluish florid complexion, and sour risings after food.

Perspirations, acid, and when sour smelling.

Piles, this remedy to correct acidity underlying this trouble, caused by excess of acid in the blood.

Quinsy, in, chief remedy.

Rheumatic fever, this remedy is generally the only one required if taken very frequently and steadily throughout.

Rheumatic pains, acute, of the joints.

Rheumatism, articular, this the chief remedy for the acetone in the blood, special symptoms may require some alternate remedy according to their aggravations, as indicated under each cell-talt. Careful dieting, liquid foods.

Scabs, if golden yellow, like honey; scrofulous affection.

Secretions, discharges of creamy consistency, and acid.

Secretions, discharges yellow like honey, and if acidity exist.

Secretions, discharges, causing soreness of skin.
Sickening headaches, ejection of sour froth, etc.
Skin affections, eczema ; with much heat, redness, and irritation.
Skin, soreness, chafing in little children, also Sodium chloride.
Sleeplessness, wakefulness, when connected with an acid condition of the stomach or the blood, this remedy in alternation with the chief remedy, Potass. phos.
Sore patches on skin, red ; sometimes itchy, and moist, loose stools ; if offensive, putrid smelling, Potassium phosphate alternately.
Sores, with yellow, creamy discharge. This effete organic substance is thrown out for want of Sodium phosphate.
Sores, excoriations of skin, when corrosions from an acid conditions of the blood ; creamy or dark-yellow honey coloured moisture oozing.
Sparks before the eyes.
Spasms, from an acid condition of the system, also convulsions and fits come under this head, calling for this salt as an alternating remedy.
Spinal cord, softening of ; for acid conditions of the blood.
Sterility, with acid secretions from vagina.
Stomach-ache, accompanied by acid risings.
Stomach-ache, when worms are present.
Stomach, ulceration of ; pain in one spot after food, and sometimes sour risings, loss of appetite.
Struma.
Squinting, occasionally, if caused by intestinal irritation from worms ; there are often acid risings, or symptoms peculiar to this group of ailments.
Tabes mesenterica, consumption or wasting of the bowels ; for the acid condition of the blood or secretions.
Tape-worm. By a lengthened course of this cell-salt, the acid condition of the contents of the intestines having been corrected, tape-worm, as well as other worms, have been destroyed.
Teeth, grinding of, in children during sleep.
Throat affection, the tonsils being coated with a deposit, having a yellow creamy or gold-coloured tinge.
Throat and tonsils, inflamed, ulcerated, with a creamy golden-yellow covering, or loaded mucous membrane.
Throat, sore, raw feeling, with a moist deposit on the tongue in the morning on rising, looking yellow as if raw (brown) sugar had just been partaken of. For feverishness, Ferric phosphate.
Tongue, coating at the back, moist creamy, or golden-yellow. When Sodium phosphate is medicinally required, and excess of lactic acid has to be reduced in the venous blood, and the tongue has generally its characteristic appearance, or there is an acid taste in the mouth.
Tonsilitis, inflammation of tonsils, swelling excessive.
Tonsilaris, augina, requires this remedy ; also the chronic swellings of the tonsils.
Tonsils, catarrh of, covered with a golden-yellow tinged exudation, with acid condition of stomach.

Tubercular deposit.
Ulcers, all, when the secretion is yellow and creamy.
Ulcers, ulceration of stomach, vomiting of sour fluids, or a dark substance like coffee grounds; also Ferric phosphate before and after meals and rest. Circular ulcers, Potassium phosphate.
Ulceration of the bowels; Potassium sulphate may also be required alternately.
Urine, frequent desire to pass water with irritation of the bladder.
Urine, incontinence of, in children, with acidity.
Uterus, discharges from the, acid, sour smelling.
Vomiting of acid (sour) fluids, not food. This remedy to remove the acidity, and a course of Ferric phosphate to follow.
Vomiting of blood.
Vomiting of curdled masses and acid fluids.
Water-brash, with acidity.
White swelling, fungoid, inflammation of the joints, also Cal. phos.
"*Whites*," discharge creamy or honey coloured, or acid and watery.
Worms, intestinal, long, or thread worms, with characteristic symptoms of acidity, or picking of the nose, occasional squinting, pain in the bowels, restless sleep.
Worms, causing irritation about the anus, depraved appetite, offensive breath, picking of the nose, disturbed sleep, grinding of the teeth, biting of the nails, etc.; this the chief remedy.

N.B.—ON SELECTING A REMEDY, read always the first two paragraphs under each Cell-Salt in this index, as these are of importance, so as to grasp the sphere of action of each Cell-Salt and its function.

11.—Sodium Sulphate=Natrum Sulphuricum.
Nat. Sulph.

The Diseases forming this group must be healed or treated with *Sodium sulphate.* They arise from a disturbance in the molecular motion of this salt in the inter-cellular fluids of the tissues, preventing elimination of such water from the tissues produced by oxidation of the organic substances and the analysis of lactic acid by Sodium phosphate.
All Ailments, in which there is accumulation of water in the inter-cellular tissues, greenish or yellow watery secretions on the skin or mucous membranes, or yellowish scales forming on eruptions of vesicles, including those ailments marked by excessive secretion of bile and derangement of the liver, gravel, sand in the urine etc., and those characterised by a dirty greenish-gray or greenish-brown coating at the root of the tongue.

 XI.—Sodium Sulphate = Natrum Sulphuricum. Nat. Sulph.

Ague, the quotidian (daily recurring) the Iertian (recurring every other day) require to be treated with this cell-salt.

Anasarca, simple dropsy.

Arthritis, or gout, acute ; this remedy and Ferric phosphate.

Asthma, where the phlegm is green, watery.

Bile, vomiting of, with bitter taste, headache, giddiness, and lassitude.

Biliousness, excess of bile, bitter taste in the mouth, vomiting of bitter fluids, greenish-brown or greenish-gray tongue, or greenish diarrhœa, dark bilious stools. White or gray coated tongue requires Potassium chloride, and marks the *want* of bile.

Bilious colic, with bitter taste in the mouth, and grayish or brownish green coating at the root of the tongue.

Bilious fever, remittent. See intermittent fever.

Bowels, heat in the lower, with green bilious discharges, knotty stools.

Bowels, motions from the, evacuations loose, bilious, green, or very dark stools.

Bronchitis, acute and chronic, in gouty bilious subjects, as an intercurrent remedy, or when the expectoration is greenish and does not yield to Potassium sulphate.

Condyloma, a soft fleshy excresence at anus, of syphilitic origin. This remedy externally and internally.

Constipation, connected with biliousness, bitter taste in the mouth, etc.

Diabetes ; chief remedy. If sac lactis is objected to, use tincture. In health the liver so elaborates the chemical property of the sugar that it is turned into lactic acid, passing to the heart and by the vena cava inferior to the lungs. In diabetes the function of the liver is perverted, and sugar passes unchanged into the blood, and is excreted in the urine (glycosuria), causing great waste and destruction of tissues and emaciation. Use also Potassium sulphate, a carrier of oxygen.

Diarrhœa. stools dark, bilious, or of green bile.

Diphtheria, in, vomiting of green water ; as intercurrent remedy.

Dizziness and bile in excess, greenish-gray coating of tongue, bitter taste in the mouth, or greenish bilious secretions.

Dropsy, simple, invading the areolar tissues of the body.

Drowsiness, often the precursor of jaundice, when there exists a grayish or brownish-green coated tongue, or other decided bilious symptoms, this remedy and Sodium chloride alternately.

Eczema, affection of the skin, vesicles, containing yellow eruptions, moist watery secretions.

Erysipelas ("rose") ; smooth, red, shiny, tingling or painful swelling of the skin ; for fever. Ferric phosphate.

Expectorations, green, sometimes slimy, watery.

Exudations, watery, moist yellow, greenish, with bilious symptoms.

Face, sallow, or jaundiced, with biliousness.

Herpes tonsurans, blisters, eruption from shaving.

Gastric derangement, with bitter taste in the mouth.

Giddiness, with bilious coating on the tongue, or bitter taste in the mouth.

Gout, in acute attacks after Sodium phosphate. Also chronic gout, this remedy alternately.

Gravel, in bilious subjects; also Sodium phosphate as chief remedy.

Headache, sick, with bilious diarrhœa, or vomiting of bile; bitter taste, colicky pain.

Headache, with giddiness, greenish gray coated tongue.

Influenza, chief remedy, to increase secretion of urine, and diminish the excess of intercellular fluids.

Intermittent fever, veiled, suppressed, appearing as neuralgic face or headache requires this remedy, or Sodium chloride when the symptoms correspond to the special action of this cell-salt.

Intermittent, remittent, febrile conditions, but when perspirations are acid, turning blue test paper red, and palate or tongue are creamy, Sodium phosphate; Calcium phosphate as an intercurrent remedy for children.

Jaundice, arising from vexation, with bilious green evacuations or greenish-brown coated tongue, or sallow skin, yellow eyeballs. This remedy should be given at first in all cases.

La Grippe. See Influenza.

Lead colic, this remedy frequently; 1x or 2x trituration.

Liver, irritable, bilious attack, too much bile; if after excessive study or mental work, also Potassium phosphate.

Mental aberrations, suicidal tendency, in gouty subjects, also Sodium phosphate. Chief remedy Potassium phosphate.

Milk, when the secretion is to be reduced, weaning.

Morning sickness (in pregnancy), with taste of bitter ejecta, bilious stools.

Mouth, excoriation of, sore at the corners, sometimes moist blisters, or moist cracks. Potassium phosphate in weak or debilitated persons.

Nausea, feeling of sickness, bilious greenish gray coating of the tongue, bitter taste in the mouth.

Œdema; smooth swelling, infiltration. Dropsical accumulations.

Pemphigus, watery vesicles or blebs over the body, wheals containing a yellow watery secretion and scales. If bloody matter, Potassium phosphate.

Piles, internal and external, as an alternate remedy with Calc. fluor. for bilious symptoms, bitter taste, much bile, greenish-yellow coating at the root of the tongue, stools greenish or dark, forming small balls.

Pimples, vesicles, small blisters with yellow moisture exuding.

Podagra, gout in the feet, acute and chronic cases. Abstinence from wine and malt liquors.

Polyuria simplex, excessive secretions of urine, if diabetic.

Preputial œdema; this remedy and Sodium chloride.

Scales, yellow, forming after the breaking of vesicles or blisters on the skin.

Sciatica, this remedy with the chief remedy alternately, when there seems kidney trouble present, gravel, red deposit.

Scrotal œdema, also Sodium chloride.

N

Secretions, in ; when the mucus is greenish.
Secretions, with or without vesicles (blisters), which are yellow watery, with irritable liver.
Sick headache, with bad or bitter taste in the mouth, giddiness, or vomiting of bilious matter.
Skin affections, moist, with yellowish scales, and predisposition to bilious derangements.
Skin affections, with vesicular eruptions containing yellowish water.
Skin, chafing of, with bilious symptoms.
Skin, œdematus inflammation of, erysipelatous.
Sleeplessness, marked drowsiness in bilious diseases ; this remedy in alternation with Sodium chloride.
Tongue, coating of the ; dirty, brownish green coating, or grayish green.
Ulcers, with bilious symptoms, secretions green or watery.
Urine, suppression of.
Urine, sandy deposit, or sediment, gravel, also Sodium phosphate.
Urine, deposit brick-dust-like colouring matter in the water, and associated with gout. Uric acid, requires also Sodium phosphate.
Vertigo, giddiness, dizziness, gastric derangement, with excess of bile.
Vomiting, bilious.
Vomiting, morning sickness, and bitter taste in the mouth.
Vomiting of bile, with bitter taste in the mouth.
Vomiting of greenish water ; also if it occurs during acute fevers, etc.
Yellow fever. If it assumes the form of severe bilious remittent fever, and there is excess of bile ; vomit greenish yellow, brown or black. Ferric phosphate for the fever in alternate doses.

N.B.--ON SELECTING A REMEDY, read always the first two paragraphs under each Cell-Salt in this index, as these are of importance, so as to grasp the sphere of action of each Cell-Salt and its function. Note always the appearance of the tongue.

12.—Silica = Silicea.

The Diseases forming this group must be healed or treated with this cell-salt, as they have their seat either in the connective-tissues, the periosteum, the skin, the hair, the nails, or the sheaths, of the nerve fibres, of which this salt is a natural constituent.
All Ailments with *suppurations* require this remedy at first to mature the discharge of pus, and is required till all *infiltrated* parts are reduced. Also those ailments which are connected with the periosteum (the fibrous skin covering all bones) or those affecting the connective-tissue sheaths covering nerve-fibres ; also all suppurations which do appear deep-seated, and the pus (matter) thick and yellow. With those seated on ligaments and tendons, there is often very little pus. It promotes painlessly the process of suppuration, and maturing of pus., and evacuation. It is re-

quired as long as there are infiltrated parts present. Also indurations, conditions in which swellings with accumulated matter undergo a process of hardening; also in some reflex affections connected with the nerves as in toothache.

Abscess, for, if Potassium chloride has not blighted the swelling, and matter has formed, the chief remedy to promote the discharge of pus, matter. For the throbbing, Ferric phosphate.

Abscess, glandular. if Potassium chloride has not blighted it, and matter forms, this remedy to bring the matter forward to discharge externally. If continuing to ooze, Calcium sulphate.

Boils, suppurating small inflamed tumours, swellings owing to formation of pus (matter). To shorten and alleviate this process, Silica is the best remedy; for the throbbing, Ferric phosphate.

Boils, little lumps. not mattering, blind.

Bone diseases, where splinters are suspected it is most helpful in bringing them away, alt. Calcium fluoride.

Bone diseases, where the periosteum (membrane investing the bone) is injured.

Bones, suppurating, ulcerating; to limit and mature the pus. Apply also externally.

Bowels, constipated, confined, with inability to expel fæces.

Breasts, inflammation of the, "weed," this remedy after Potassium chloride, should matter threaten. Also Calcium sulphate.

Bruises. This remedy should the case have been neglected and matter is forming.

Carbuncles, this remedy and Potassium phosphate alternately for the malignant symptoms. External use, page i.

Cataract, initial symptoms with flickering before the eyes.

Cheek, swollen, where matter forms.

Chilblains, festering, require Calcium sulphate; for itching, Potassium phosphate, Sodium sulphate.

Constipation, with inability to expel, fæces receding.

Cornea, abscess on the horny membrane of the eye-ball, when deep seated and matter is forming.

Deafness, from a hardened deposit or exudation swelling, or when matter is discharging, suppuration.

Dulness of hearing, with swelling and catarrh of the eustachion tubes, and of the cavity of the drum of the ear.

Ears, outer ear swollen and inflamed, also Calc. sulphate.

Ear, inflammatory, swelling of the external meatus.

Earache, suppuration, matter forming.

Eczema, inflammatory skin affection, when pustules form with crusts of pus (matter). Also Calcium sulphate.

Eye, deep seated, ulcers, matter.

Eyelids, indurated, nodules, styes.

Faceache, with concurrent appearance of small nodules, lumps the size of a pea appearing on the scalp.

Feet, habitual perspiration of; suppression thereof. followed by other ailments.

Glands, suppurating, to shorten this process. If all the infiltrated parts have discharged their contents, and matter still oozes, give Calc. sulph.

Gumboil, the remedy for the swelling is Potassium chloride, when matter is formed, and can be felt on pressure, then Silica will hasten the breaking and discharge of the gumboil painlessly, as a rule, if not, a slight incision should be made.

Gums, swollen, matter forming, fluctuation on pressure, to hasten the process of suppuration and discharge.

Headaches, with concurrent appearance of small lumps or nodules the size of a pea on the scalp.

Hip-joint disease, to prevent or control suppuration and heal the parts.

Hypopion, disease of the inner eye, for the effusion of pus.

Indurations, hardening, as of a "stye on the eyelid," the hardening of substance in a part after the acute stage of matter forming.

Injuries, neglected cases, if festering, threatening to suppurate.

Mastitis, "weed," for the suppuration, when matter has formed to mature the discharge, and to control the formation of pus.

Nails, interrupted growth of the, or for ridged thickened nails, also as a lotion.

Neuralgic pain, toothache, pain deep seated in the jaw.

Ozæna with fœtid, offensive discharge from the nose. when the affection is seated in the sub-mucous connective tissue or periosteum this remedy is required, with Sodium phosphate; Potassium phosphate may also be necessary for the heavy odour. Also syringing with a solution of the remedies.

Perspiration of the feet, when excessive, with heavy odour, Potassium phosphate.

Perspiration of the feet, when suppressed by a chill.

Pustules, when matter has formed, and has become hardened.

Scabs, crust yellow, as of pure matter dried.

Sciatica, when the nerve sheats are affected.

Sebaceous, fatty glands at root of hairs, suppuration of.

Secretions, mattery, bloody mattery; fœtid and unhealthy pus, Potassium phosphate.

Stye on the eyelid, also as a lotion to remove it, and to hasten the discharge painlessly. If there is much inflammation about the eye, give also a few doses of Ferric phosphate.

Styes on the eyelids, hardened nodules, induration of the lids.

Suppurations, excessive, and when continuing after the infiltrated portions have discharged their contents, Calc. sulph.

Suppuration slow and torpid, to bring the matter to maturity; phlegmon, Potassium chloride.

Suppurations (festers) having their seat in the cell substance of the connective tissues. All deep-seated suppurations, including those on tendons, ligaments, and bone.

Suppurations of joints, to control the formation of pus.

Sweat about the head, in children.

Swellings, lumps, which become hard after threatening to suppurate.

Syphilis, chronic, with suppurations or indurations.

Tongue, induration of (hardening).

Toothache, when very violent at night, when neither heat nor cold gives relief, and when caused by chilling of the feet.

Toothache, when the pain is deep-seated, and in the periosteum or fibrous membrane covering the root, and abscess forming.

Toothache, caused by sudden chill to the feet, when damp from perspiration. (Reflex.)

Twitching, jerking of limbs, wakening the patient out of deep sleep, twitching on falling asleep, requires Sodium cholride.

Ulcers of the lower limbs; if this does not suffice to arrest discharge of matter, after all soft and infiltrated parts are emptied, give Calcium sulphate. Unhealthy looking matter, Potass. phos.

Ulcerations of bone, also Calcium fluoride.

Ulcers, when deep-seated and the periosteum is affected.

Ulcers of the cornea, deep-seated.

"*Weed*," gathered breasts, mastitis, when matter has formed, to hasten the suppuration and discharge of "laudable pus." Potassium chloride to disperse swelling, and prevent matter forming.

Whitlow, to assist and control the formation of pus, and to stimulate the growth of new nails.

Wounds, when discharging thick yellow matter, and the suppuration deep-seated; if discharge of matter continues after all infiltrated parts have emptied their contents, Calcium sulphate will heal the sore. Fœtid or brownish matter requires Potassium phosphate.

Wounds, suppurating, as first remedy, Calcium sulphate if not healing from torpidity of tissues, and excess of intercellular fluids lacking the latter salt.

N.B.—ON SELECTING A REMEDY, read always the first two paragraphs under each Cell-Salt in this index, as these are of importance, so as to grasp the sphere of action of each Cell-Salt and its function. Note always the appearance of the tongue.

The great advantages and simplification of medicaments by the new treatment with bio-chemic remedies, their safety and certainty, may be shown by a few examples; and their relative position to such remedies as are used in Homœopathic and Allopathic treatment.

The great desideratum in medicine is certainty as to *the* right remedy. The more drugs to choose from, the more uncertain the success.

SMALL POX.

NEW TREATMENT.	*Homœopathic treatment.*	*Allopathic treatment.**
IV. Ferric phos. V. Potass. chloride.	Primary fever, Aconite, Bell, Verat Vir., Bry.	Saline laxatives, Opium, Henbane, Sarracenia, Effervescent Citrate of Magnesia,
V. Potass. chloride.	Eruptive stage, Ant. Tart., Thuja., Sulph.	Compound Rhubarb Powder, Astringents, Quinine, Bark and Nitric Acid, Ale, Wine,
VII. Potass. sulph.	Retrocession, Camph., Sulph., Cupr. Acet.	Mercury, Actea. Pustules to anoint with Olive Oil, Glycerine, and Lime Linament,
VI. Potass. phos. IX. Natrum mur. IX. Sodium chlor.	Secondary fever, Confluent cases, Ars., Bapt., Hydrast., Opi., Lachesis., Bry., Rhus., Sulph., Phos., Merc., etc.	Nitrate of Silver, Puncturing, Collodion, Gutta Percha and Collodion, Mercurial Ointment, Tincture of Iodine, Sulphur Linseed or Yeast poultices,
II. Calc. sulph.	Suppurative stage, Ant. tart., Merc., Apis.	Oxide of Zinc Ointment.

Complications, such as Pneumonia, Pleurisy, Erysipelas, Glossitis, or Glandular Swellings will rarely occur if Ferric phosphate be more or less frequently alternated with the chief remedy given for each stage. External applications of the remedies as lotion, warm or cold, are admissable.

* The latest text-book of Lauder Brunton, Examiner in Materia Medica, London, dispenses with *all* prescriptions for this disease, and gives no treatment.

ERYSIPELAS.

Mortality in England, 2000 annually.

NEW TREATMENT.	*Homœopathic treatment.*	*Allopathic treatment.*
	Erysipelas, smooth, non-vesicular. Simplex, phlegmonous, idiopathic, or traumatic, in all its stages,	No distinction in the treatment of vesicular and non-vesicular Erysipelas.
XI. Sodium sulph. IV. Ferric phos.	Acon., Bell., Bry., Puls., Apis., Ars., Carbo. Veg., Nit. Ac., Lach., Sulph., Verat. vir., etc.	Castor Oil, Aloes, Senna Magnesia, Rhubarb Pills, Blue Pill, Comp. Rhubarb Powder, Carbonate of Ammonia, Tincture of Perchloride of Iron, Iodine, Belladonna, Sulphurous Acid, Digitalis, Rhus toxicodendron, Tartar Emetic, Chlorate Potash, Quinine, Turpentine, Colchicum, Port Wine, Porter, Brandy, Fomentations, Poultices, Inunction with lard, Dusting with flour or ground rice powder, Collodion, pencilling boundary lines with Nitrate of Silver or Iodine Tincture, Incisions to evacuate pus.
V. Potass. chlor. IV. Ferric phos.	Erysipelas, vesicular (blistering), Acon., Rhus., Bell., Merc., Verat., Vir., Nux. Vom., Canth, Sulph.	

Under either the Allopathic or Homœopathic treatment it is and cannot be but hazardous or difficult to select the right remedy among so many. And if the wrong one be chosen, what then? The loss of time and protracted sufferings of the patient must be a source of anxiety to the physician.

SCARLET FEVER. SCARLATINA.

NEW TREATMENT.	*Homœopathic treatment.*	*Allopathic treatment.*
V. Potass. chlor. IV. Ferric phos.	Scarlatina simplex, Bell., Acon., Coffea, Sulph. Ars., etc.	Carbonate of Ammonia, Acetic Acid or Vinegar and water, Inunction of hot lard.
V. Potass. chloride. II. Calc. sulph.	Scarlatina anginosa, Acon., Bell., Gels., Apis, Ammon. carb., Rhus., Merc. Biniod, Ac. Nit., Verat. Vir. etc.	Emetics of Ipecacuanha, Saline effervescing draughts, Carbonate of Ammonia, Sponging with tepid water and vinegar, Cold affusion, Inunction with lard, Scalp to be shaved if there be delirium.
VII. Potass. sulph.	Suppressed rash, evening rise of temperature.	
VI. Potass. phos. IX. Sod. chlor.	Scarlatina maligna. Ailan, Ac. Carbol., Ars., Lachesis, Hydr. Tabacum, Ac. Mur., Opi., Baptisia, Ac. Cup., Stram., Zinc., Hydrocyanic Acid, Sulph., Apis., Hellebore.	Maligna Demands stimulation from the first, Carbonate of Ammonia, Bark, Port Wine, Brandy, Quinine, Chlorine, Aconite, Hydrochlor-Acid and Ether, Acid drinks, Chlorate of Potash drinks, Cold affusion, Astringent gargles, Nitrate of Silver to throat, Salycilic Acid, Brandy, Ferric Perchloride, Digitalis, Mercury or grey powder.
V. Potass. chloride.	Sequelæ, Glandular swelling, croupy cough, and deafness. Mer., Iod., Mur. Ac., Calc. Carb., Aurum, Sulph., Lyc., Sil., Hep. Sulph., Spong., Hyos., Hydras., Phos., Merc., Iod., Brom.	

Complications or Sequelæ rarely occur if Ferric phosphate be frequently alternated with the chief remedy, and the latter be administered until perfect recovery set in, no "dregs" are left. The remedies for sequelæ are, however, given, when, under the use of *other* therapeutics, they have set in.

PNEUMONIA, INFLAMMATION OF THE LUNGS.

NEW TREATMENT.	*Homœopathic treatment.*	*Allopathic treatment.*
IV. Ferric phos.	Acute & chronic stage, Aconite, Verat V., Phos., Bry., Chelid., Ant. tart.	Castor Oil, Aconite, Ammonium carbonate, Belladonna, Small doses of Opium, Bry., Acetate of Ammonia, Copper Acetate, Digitalis, Iodide of Potassium, Iodide of Ammonium, Phosphorus, Quinine, Tartarated Antimony, Calomel, Veratrum viride, Leeches, Blisters, Salicylate of Soda, Senega, Serpentaria, Turpentine, Stupes, Wine or Brandy, etc.
IV. Ferric phos.	Congestive stage, Gels., Bell., Phos., Verat. Vir., Bry., Cactus.	
IV. Ferric phos.	Pleuritic complication Acon., Bry., Phos., etc.	
V. Potass. chloride. IX. Sodium chlor.	Hepatization,	
V. Potass. chloride. IX. Nat. mur. IX. Sodium chlor.	Bronchial complication Sputa white; frothy. Puls., Phos., Calc., carb., Hep., Sulph., Ant., Tart., Ipecac., Merc. sol., Sulph., Squilla, Ars., Chin., Spongia, Bryonia, Cham., etc.	
VII. Potass. sulph. II. Calc sulph.	Sputa yellow, greenish; purulent. Hydrastis, Kali bich., Sulph., Dig., Puls., Calc. carb, Bry., Lyc., Merc., Nux. vom., Phos., Carb. veg. etc.	

With the New Remedies this disease in its typical form can be cut short very rapidly by the use of only one remedy, Ferric phosphate; and Potassium chloride, as seen above, meets early secondary conditions.

TYPHUS FEVER.

NEW TREATMENT.	*Homœopathic treatment.*	*Allopathic treatment.*
IV. Ferric phos. VI. Potass. phos.	Febrile symptoms, Aconite, Bryonia, Gelsemium, Cimic	Avoidance of active remedies at first especially. No specific known to cut short the disease. An emetic of Ipecacuanha wine, 30 to 60 grains of Compound Rhubarb Powder, diluted drinks of mineral acids, Hydro chloric, Phosphoric Acid, Chlorate of Potash. When the powers of life begin to fail, stimulants.
VI. Potass. phos.	Cerebral symptoms, Hyos., Bell., Verat Vir, Strammonium	
VI. Potass. phos.	Sleeplessness, Gelsemium, Belladonna, Coffea Ignat	
VI. Potass. phos.	Prostration, Ac. Mur., Ac. phos., Arsen., Rhus., etc.	
IX. Sodium chlor.	Stupor, twitchings, Opium, Rhus. toxicodendron	
VI. Potass. phos.	Partial paralysis, Rhus. tox., Strych., Galvanism	
VI. Potass. phos.	Putrescence, Carbo. veg., Arsen., Rhus. tox., Baptisia.	

The specific remedy for this serious disease is easily recognised, and no difficulty presents itself in the choosing of *the* remedy, which meets the whole group of symptoms, which have so often baffled the efforts and anxious care of the physicians.

PUERPERAL FEVER AND MANIA.

NEW TREATMENT.	*Homœopathic treatment.*	*Allopathic treatment.**
	Fever,	
VI. Kali phos.	Acon., Bell., Bry., Merc., Hyos., Stram., Ars., Bapt., Puls., Nux. vom., Lach.	Aconite, Ammonia, Bromide of Potassium, Bark, Quinine, Phosphoric Acid, Cod Liver Oil, Brandy, Wine.
	Mania,	
VI. Kali phos.	Cannabis, Ind., Merc., Corr., Opi., Platina, Aurum, Actea Racemosa, Verat. Vir., Ac. Phos., Ignatia, China, Verat. Alb., Cimic, etc.	Extract of Stramonium, Extract of Opium, Morphia, Indian Hemp, Subcutaneous Injections of Morphia, Chloroform inhalations, Chloral, Separation from family and friends†, Alkaline, Sulphate, Columba Tincture, Opium, Permanganate of Potash, Turpentine.

Puerperal fever, so much dreaded on account of its subtle infectiousness, and very fatal under Allopathic treatment, requires but one remedy for its cure.

Puerperal Mania under the use of the biochemic measures becomes at once amenable to treatment, and in the simplest form, or in its various degrees of severity, a proportionally speedy cure may most reasonably be looked for. The cases of recovery have all been permanent and rapid throughout.

* Some text-books have no treatment for the "childbed" fever, only for the mania.

† Puerperal Fever Treatment, Lauder Brunton's Text-book.

NEURALGIA.

NEW TREATMENT.	*Homœopathic treatment.*	*Allopathic treatment.*
True neuralgia, darting, paroxysmal, VIII. Mag. phos. Lachrymation or flow of saliva, IX. Sod. chlor. Inflammatory, Tic, IV. Ferric phos. Worse in the evening and heated atmosphere, VII. Potass. sulph. Worse in the night or only felt at night, I. Calcium phos. With depression, VI. Potass. phos.	Bell., Ars., Ver. vir., Acon., Spig., Coloc., Merc. S., Cham., Coff., China, Sulph., Quinine, Chelid., Cimicifuga, Gelsem., Sticta, Nit. of Strychina, Mag. sulph., Nux. vom., Staph., Verat. alb., Ran. bulb., Rhod., Arn., Bell. liniment, Phos., Ignatia, etc.	Aconitia Ointment, Acupuncture, Alcohol, Ammonium chloride, Ammon. valerianate, Amylonated nitrate, Aquapuncture, Atropine, Belladonna, Bebeeru bark, Blisters, Brom. of Potassium, Caffeine, Connatis indica, Capsicum, Carbonic Acid, Chalmugara Oil, Chamomile, Chelidanium, Chloral and camphor, Chlarate of Potash, Chloroform, Ciminifuga, Cod Liver Oil, Croton chloral, Digitalis, Electricity, Ergot, Gelsemium Ignatia, Iodides, Iron, Iodoform, Morphia, Mustard Poultices, Marcein, Nux vomica, Nitro glycerine, Oil of Cloves, Peppermint, Pulsatilla, Pyrethrum, Quinine, Salicysilic Acid, Stavesacre, Sumbul, Thermo-cautery, Valerian, Valerianated Zinc.

Seeing that the action of the New Remedies is so exact and well-defined, and so certain, surely every Medical man who desires the good of his patients will select from these for the scientific and rapid cure of the sick; and all patients will be anxious to be treated, restored to health, in the new way, with safe and truly rational remedies.

INDEX OF DISEASES AND REFERENCE TABLE OF THE NEW TREATMENT.

In this Reference Table *numbers only* are appended to each disease for the sake of brevity. They refer to the twelve sections of the Therapeutical Index, and represent the remedies from No. 1 to No. 12 in the numerical order in which they are arranged, as seen from page i. to lxxvii.

The Dose, the Time of taking, and Directions for external applications, etc., will be found on page i.

The **numbers** show *which* remedies may have to be given in the different ailments, and must be looked up under the *corresponding number* in the Therapeutical Index as to *when* and for which special symptoms they ought to be given. For the special reason *why*, see Dr. Schüssler's explanations referred to in the pages indicated. A careful study of the "**Characteristics**" from page 18 to 27, and of each section in the Therapeutical Index, will familiarize with the Pathology and leading symptoms of a disease, and the range of action of each of the cell salts. It is hoped this will form a Key to a correct selection of the required remedies for the treatment of the various diseases and their characteristic symptoms. Many diseases are found to pass through three evolutions or stages. With the appropriate cell salts, the intensity and duration of the malady in each stage can be greatly reduced, as may be noticed in inflammation of the lungs, etc., and health soon restored. If the treatment of **first** stages be prompt, **second** and **third** stages may often be prevented, and the disease thus cut short, and suffering averted. Cases often become chronic and sometimes very tedious; not so here, where nature is supplied with the natural substances and direct means of repair for the cells of the blood or of the tissues.

In cases where the **mucous** *membrane or linings* are affected, the characteristics of the secretions or discharges may be very various in colour or consistency, which explains the great number of remedies after such ailments.

Ferric phos. is recommended to be given alternately with any of the remedies specified, since these ailments incline to have inflammatory, congestive, or febrile tendencies. When a person is not able to judge of the exact length of time a remedy should be taken for a certain stage or certain symptoms, and cannot decide between two remedies if there are symptoms for both, he need not hesitate, but give both alternately until one or other symptom subside, for which they are given.

They are the safest medicines ever yet prescribed.

Dr. SCHÜSSLER wrote his Therapeutics for the use of medical men, and with their knowledge of symptoms and pathological conditions, without the aid of the Therapeutical Index, they can get all information in the concisely written pages of the book itself. But for others, the addition of my Therapeutical Index, with frequently repeated details, names of diseases, and characteristic symptoms, may be a help, as well as my alphabetical arrangement of the Reference Table.

M. D. W.

EXPLANATION REGARDING NUMBERS GIVEN AFTER A DISEASE.

The numbers after each disease represent the Medicines which may be required at the *different* stages of the disease. If there is any uncertainty which to choose, read up the chapter with the corresponding number in the Therapeutical Index, p i. to lxxvii., compare the symptoms, and select one or other of the remedies which have those symptoms clearly defined which the patient complains of.

Those numbers *preceding* the dash represent the chief remedies, or those most likely to be required at the commencement (first stage) of an ailment.

When 4 stands *first*, symptoms for its use will predominate; if *after* other numbers or after a dash (—), it may be advisable to alternate it with *any* of the preceding numbers, not with the last only.

A

B

C

o

D

E

F

G

H

I

J

K

L

M

N

O

P

Q

R

S

T

U

V

W

Y

GLOSSARY.

A.

Abdomen. The lower belly, or that part of the body which lies between the thorax and the pelvis.

Aberration. A term applied in cases of partial insanity, in respect to the mental faculties.

Abscess. A collection of pus (purulent matter) in some tissues of the body, generated by suppuration or festering; a purulent tumour.

Absorbents. Vessels which absorb or drink in, as the lacteals and lymphatics.

Acetic acid. The pure acid of vinegar, composed of two atoms carbon, with four of hydrogen, and two of oxygen ($C_2H_4O_2$).

Acid. Sharp; sour to the taste.

Acini. Granulations; compound berries.

Aconite. Extract of the poisonous monk's-hood, acting on the heart and circulation, the nervous system, etc.

Aconitum napellus. A plant, the wolf's-bane or monk's-hood, from which the preceding is obtained.

Acrid. Sharp; pungent; bitter; of a hot, scalding nature.

Acute. Opposed to chronic; an acute disease is one which is attended with symptoms of certain degrees of severity, and comes speedily to a crisis.

Addison's disease. A peculiar form of anæmia, with a brownish discoloration of the skin.

Adenitis. Inflammation of a gland.

Adynamic. Weak; destitute of strength through disease.

Æt., Ætas. Aged.

Ætiology. The science of the causes of diseases.

Affinity, chemical. The innate, inherent power which different bodies have of combining or uniting.

Agglutination. A glue-like adhesion of the eyelids.

Ague. An intermittent fever, attended with cold shivering and outbreaks of heat alternately at certain defined periods.

Albumen. A substance existing abundantly in the white of an egg, and forming a constituent principle of the animal organism, consisting of carbon, hydrogen, oxygen, nitrogen, and sulphur; hence Albuminous, pertaining to albumen.

1

Albuminoid. Like albumen; that substance in the blood which forms the organic basis of the cells, and is composed of proteine, and constitutes part of fibrin; hence Fibrinous or Fibrous.

Albuminuria. A disease of the urinary organs, denoted by the presence of free albumen in the urine.

Alimentary. Having the quality of nourishing. The alimentary canal is the great duct or intestine by which aliments are conveyed through the body, and the useless parts excreted.

Allopathic, Allopathist, Allopathy. Terms applied generically to the treatment of disease, those who treat it, and the system of treatment, by which the cure or prevention of disease is assumed to result from a special, rather than a general, mode of operation: opposed to homœopathy, which professes to treat all diseases on the principle of the production, on a modified scale, of the same disease—*similia similibus curantur* being the motto of this system. Except by contrast, the term *allopathy* is indefinable. Literal signification, "other treatment."

Alopecia. Partial baldness; falling-off of the hair of the head.

Alopecia. The fox sickness or mange, the fox-evil or scurf; any kind of baldness.

Alopecia areata. The hair falling off, leaving bald patches.

Alveolus. Connected with the alveoli, or sockets of the teeth.

Amaurosis. An affection of the optic nerve, by which the recognition of external objects is rendered impossible; a kind of optic paralysis.

Amblyopy, or **Amplyobia.** An incipient stage of amaurosis (which see).

Amenorrhœa. Suppression or delay of menstruation.

Ammonia. A chemical compound, otherwise called volatile alkali, which in its uncombined form exists in the state of a highly pungent gas, one part nitrogen and three parts hydrogen (N_1H_3).

Amorphous. Irregular in shape; not having a determinate form.

Anæmia. A deficiency of red blood; bloodlessness; incipient loss of the vital proportion of the blood.

Analogue. One thing which resembles or corresponds with or bears great resemblance to another.

Analysis, quantitative. It consists in the determination not merely of the component parts of a compound, but their relative proportions.

Anasarca. Species of dropsy, indicated by an effusion of serous (watery) fluid in the areolar tissues.

Anatomy. The art of dissecting, or artificially separating, the different parts of an organic body to discover their situation, structure, and economy. Morbid anatomy deals with the structure of diseased parts.

Anchylosis. A contraction or stiffening of the joints.

Aneurism. A preternatural dilatation of an artery by the enclosed blood, causing a soft red sac or tumour; a dilated artery.

Angina. A quinsy; Ang. generally applied to diseases affecting the throat and chest: as A. faucium, a sore throat; A. gangrænosa, a gangrenous sore throat; A. pectoris, contraction or spasm of the chest; A. membranacea, croup; A. tonsillaris, soreness of the throat with swelling of the tonsils; A. uvularis, soreness affecting the uvula.

Angina pectoris. Spasm of the heart; extremely painful contracting sensation in chest about the region of the heart.

Ani prolapsus. Protrusion of the membrane of the rectum, attendant on piles.

Anterior chamber of the eye lies between the cornea, the iris, and pupil behind.

Anus. The fundament, or lower opening of the body, by which excrement, evacuations, or stools are passed out of the body.

Aphonia, Aphony. Loss of speech; dumbness.

Aphtha. The thrush, a disease which shows itself in small white ulcers upon the tongue, gums, inside of the lips, and palate; common to infants and nursing mothers.

Apoplexia. Apoplexy, of which there are several varieties, as sanguineous, pulmonary, cerebral, etc.; characterized by loss of power of motion, and of the exercise of the mental faculties.

Areolar tissue. The small (spaces) interstices of cellular tissues.

Areotic. Opening the pores, a term applied to medicines promoting perspiration.

Arsenic. A virulent metallic poison. Arsenious oxide, or *white arsenic*, is composed of three parts oxygen to two parts arsenic (A_2O_3).

Arteries. Those bloodvessels which convey the red blood from the heart to all parts of the body, having valves only at their origin, and in this being unlike the veins, which carry the blood back to the heart.

Arteritis. Inflammation of an artery.

Arthritis. The gout, or analogous diseases of the joints. A. articularis, rheumatic gouty affection; A. nodosa, knotty concretions, arising from the gout, chalk-stones, etc.

Articular rheumatism. Rheumatism of the joints.

Arytenoid cartilages. Pyriform cartilages situated at the back of the larynx on the upper border of the cricoid cartilage.

Ascarides. A genus of intestinal worms; thread-worms.

Assimilation. The taking up and converting of nutritive substances into flesh, etc., of animal bodies; the production of flesh, fat, bones, etc., from the substances supplied by food.

Assimilation, vegetable. The process of elaboration of plant tissues from carbonic acid gas, water, ammonia compounds, and salts.

Asthenic. Results of disease attended with great bodily debility; a condition of asthenia, or weakness.

Asthenopia. Weakness of vision; fatigue readily induced, with a tendency to confusion of the lines and words of a book, after reading for a few minutes.

Asthma. An affection of the breathing organs, characterized by difficulty of breathing, recurring in paroxysms, commonly attended with cough, wheezing, and constriction of the chest.

Atonia, Atony. Defective power of muscular action.

Atrophy. Wasting away of the body, arising from defective nutrition.

Atropine. An alkaloid derived from the deadly nightshade, or Atropa belladonna.

Attenuation. Subdivision; the reduction of a drug by dilution or pulverization.

Axilla, Axil. The armpit; hence axillary, pertaining to the armpit. Axillary plexus, a fold of nerves in the armpit.

B.

Balanitis. Inflammation of the glans penis.

Balano-posthitis. Inflammation of the foreskin.

Balanorrhœa. Inflammation of the glans penis, with discharge.

Barber's itch (Tinea sycosis). Inflammation of the hair follicles of the beard, causing an eruption of small pustules.

Base. In chemistry that substance with which an acid unites to form a salt; the leading substance of compounds.

Basedow's disease. Abcess of the orbit or tumour somewhere behind the eyeball, causing the protrusion of the eyeball.

Belladonna. Deadly nightshade.

Bile. A thin yellow bitter liquid, separated from the blood in the liver, collected in the gall-bladder, and thence discharged by the common duct.

Bilious. Subject to excessive secretion of bile; an overflow of bile causes a bitter taste in the mouth, and is usually accompanied by drowsiness or severe vomiting. In extreme cases, when the liver is affected, the eyeballs become yellow, and the disease takes the form of jaundice, often with suppression of this secretion.

Bio-chemic. Pertaining to the chemistry of life; the chemical actions taking place in the body in life, by which one class of substances conjoin with certain others, by the laws of combination and chemical affinity, to form new compounds, such combinations acquiring new properties. This takes place only between dissimilar particles, as seen between certain organic and certain inorganic substances.

Biology. The science which investigates the phenomena of animal and vegetable life.

Bladder, paralysis of the. Applies to the sphincter muscles, causing inability of retaining the urine, generally of old people.

Blephari is. Inflammation of the eyelid.

Blind boil. A swelling, attended by inflammation of the part, containing little pus, and mostly blood.

Blood-plasma. The colourless fluid part of the blood in which the corpuscles float.

Bone-earth. Phosphate of lime ; the earthy substance of bone.

Borborygmus. Rumbling noise of wind in the bowels.

Bright's disease. A disease of the kidneys, with albumen in the urine; has acute and chronic stages. Urinary organs not affected.

Bronchi. The ramifications of the trachea or windpipe ; the bronchial tubes which branch from the trachea and carry air into the lungs.

Bronchitis. An inflammation of the lining membrane of the windpipe or bronchial tubes.

Bronchocele. Enlargement of the thyroid gland at windpipe ; goitre ; cellular sarcoma, cyst.

Broncho-pneumonia. Inflammation of the bronchial membrane, extending to that of the lungs.

Buboes. Hard swelling of the glands of the groin and armpit through venereal or other causes.

Bursa. A small serous sac found between bony or other surfaces moving upon each other, and thus ensuring their free and easy movement.

Bursæ Mucosæ. Mucus-bags, situated about the joints, secreting a fluid that lubricates them.

Butyric acid. A colourless acid found in butter, and also occurring in the gastric juice, perspiration, urine, etc. It consists of four atoms of carbon, eight of hydrogen, and two of oxygen ($C_4H_8O_2$).

C.

Cachexia, Cachexy. A deranged state of the body, arising from vitiated blood.

Cacoethes. An incurable ulcer.

Cacosis. Indisposition ; illness.

Cacothrophy. Inadequate or bad nutrition.

Calcareous. Partaking of the nature of lime ; containing lime.

Calcium. The metallic base of lime.

Callus. The new growth of bony matter between the extremities of fractured bones, serving to unite them.—**Callous.** A hardness of any part of the body from friction or from swelling, which should be soft in its natural condition.

Cancer, scirrhous, hard fibroid tumours, frequently occurring in the female breast.

Cancrum oris. Mortification or gangrene of the cheek.

Canker. Certain small corroding white ulcers in the mouth, particularly of children or nursing mothers.

Cantharides. The Spanish fly, used, when dry, for making blisters, etc.

Capillaries. Small hair-like tubes; minute bloodvessels existing in almost all parts of the body, of which there are many so minute as to be only the 5000th part of an inch in thickness. Through these the blood corpuscles have to circulate.

Capsular ligament. A cup-like arrangement of connective tissue, usually found surrounding ball and socket joints.

Carbon. Pure charcoal, an elementary combustible substance, black, brittle, light, and inodorous. It may be obtained from most organic matters, animal as well as vegetable, by ignition in close vessels.

Carbonate. A compound formed by the union of carbonic acid with a base.

Carbonic acid gas. A compound of one atom of carbon and two atoms of oxygen (CO_2); it is gaseous and colourless; given off from the lungs in breathing, and if allowed to accumulate in a confined space inducing suffocation. Red blood corpuscles deteriorate when brought in contact with it. Hence the necessity of breathing pure air.

Carbuncle. An inflammatory suppurating tumour, or malignant boil discharging from several openings.

Cardiac. Pertaining to the heart.

Carditis. Inflammation of the muscle or substance of the heart.

Caries. Mortification, ulceration, etc., of a bone; hence **Cariosity** and **Carious.**

Cartilage. Gristle; solid elastic substance attached to bone, softer than bone.

Cartilage salt. Sodium chloride, met with in the cells of cartilage or gristle, which is a smooth solid substance or tissue, softer than bone, but harder than a ligament, without cavities, for marrow, etc.

Caseine. A proximate principle of animal and vegetable.

Catalysis. The influence which induces changes in the composition of substances by their mere contact with another body or power; destruction.

Catamenia. The menses; monthly flow; menstruation.

Cataract. A disease of the eye, non-transparency or opacity of the crystalline lens, causing loss of sight.

Catarrh. Inflamed state of the mucous membrane of the air-passages, more particularly of that portion which lines the nostrils, producing, amongst other symptoms, an increased defluxion of mucus from the nose.

Catarrh, common, is popularly called a cold.

Catarrh, epidemic, is termed influenza.

Cathartis. Purging, evacuation of the alvine discharges; hence Cathartics, medicines that promote purging.

Catheretic. A mild caustic, for destroying granulations on wounds, ulcers, etc.

Catheter. A tubular instrument introduced through the urethra into the bladder, to draw off the urine; a bougie.

Caustic. A substance which burns or disorganizes animal bodies when brought into contact with them.

Cauterizing. The act of burning with a cautery or caustic.

Cavity. A hollow in the body, as of the mouth, throat, a bone, etc. —*Pleural cavity.* The cavity of the pleura or sac covering the lungs.

Cell. A little bag or minute bladder containing fluid or other substances.

Cellular. Consisting of an infinite number of minute cells, as the cellular tissues, and membranes in animal bodies.

Cell-salts. The inorganic mineral or saline substances which are the essential component parts of the cells, of which tissues consist, and may, therefore, be called tissue cell-salts, or simply tissue salts.

Centigramme. The hundredth part of a gramme. The gramme is the unit of weights in the metric system, and is equal to 15·432 grains.

Cephalalgia. Headache; hence Cephalalgic, producing or relating to headache.

Cephalic. Pertaining to the head, as cephalic remedies.—*Cephalic vein.* The jugular vein, or carotid artery.

Cephalalgic. Relating to headaches.

Cephalitis. Inflammation of the brain.

Cephalotomata. Blood tumours; soft vascular tumours on the parietal bones of new-born children.

Cerebral. Pertaining to the brain.

Cerebritis. Inflammation of the brain.

Cervix uteri. Neck of the womb.

Cervical. Belonging to the neck, as *cervical* vertebræ, vessels, muscles, etc.

Chalk stones. Deposit of sodium urate, forming whitish concretions on the joints in the hands and feet of persons afflicted with gout.

Chancre. A venereal or syphilitic ulcer.

Chemical affinity. The force which determines the combination of different substances to form compounds, and which holds together the elements in a compound, an operation exemplified in the absorption of the tissue salts into the particular cells where they are required, and where in a state of perfect health they are found to exist in proper proportions.

Chemistry is an extensive science, the objects of which are to investigate the composition of all kinds of matter, and their mutual actions, combinations, and decompositions.

Chicken-pox. A mild eruptive disease common to children.

Chilblains. Slight frost-bites with redness, sometimes with swelling, on the hands or feet, from cold in winter, giving rise to tingling, itching, and pain.

Chloride. A compound of chlorine with another element, such as sodium, potassium, etc.

Chlorine. A greenish-yellow gas obtained from common salt.

Choris retinitis. Inflammation of the retina, with separation of a lamina, forming a scale or doubling of the retina.

Chloroform. A fluid obtained by distilling chloride of lime with alcohol or methylated spirits, and now largely employed to produce insensibility to pain during an operation. It contains carbon, hydrogen, and chlorine in these proportions ($C\,H\,Cl_3$).

Chlorosis. The green sickness, a disease incident to young females, giving them a pale, greenish hue; excess of white blood corpuscles.

Chlorotic condition. Affected by chlorosis, or green sickness, a disease similar to the above.

Cholera, English. A disease characterized by vomiting and purging, with great pain, debility, and crampy pain.

Cholera, Asiatic. Known in Europe since 1817. All the symptoms are more violent than the former, with violent choleraic cramps, biliary disturbance, purging, stools like rice-water, great prostration, and collapse.

Chondroma. A cartilaginous growth seated in the periosteum covering the bone.

Chorea. St. Vitus' dance, a disease which manifests itself in convulsive motions of the limbs, causing strange and involuntary gesticulations.

Cholerine. Choleraic dysentery.

Chromatopsia. Spasmodic visions of rainbow colours.

Chronic. Of long continuance; lingering; in contradistinction to acute.

Chyle. A milky fluid formed by the action of the pancreatic juice and the bile on the chyme after leaving the stomach, which, being absorbed by the lacteal ducts, is poured into the blood.

Chyme. The condition of food after being dissolved by the gastric juices, and before it is converted into chyle.

Cicatrization. The process of healing or forming a cicatrice; a scar; the state of being healed, cicatrized, or skinned over.

Cilia. The hairs on the edge of the eyelids; eyelashes; hence Ciliary, belonging to or like the eyelashes or eyelids.

Cinchona officinalis. Peruvian bark, produced from various species of cinchona, and invaluable as a tonic, producing quinine (which see).

Cinchonina, Cinchonine, Cinchonia. An alkaloid obtained from species of cinchona, and valued as an active tonic, etc., but inferior to quinine.

Clavicle. The collar-bone.

Clinical. Applied to a discourse on the disease of a patient at his bedside to students; also to notes of a case so visited, and subsequently read or published.

Coagulate. To solidify, as when blood changes into a liver-like mass.

Coccygodynia. Pain and congestive condition of the coccyx, with tenderness.

Coccyx. A small bone joined to the lower end of the os sacrum, at the lower extremity of the spine; so named from its resemblance to the bill of the cuckoo.

Coition. A coming together; conjunction; the act of generation; copulation.

Colic. A spasmodic painful disorder of the bowels (various kinds), attended with severe crampy pain.

Collapse. Sinking; a sudden and extreme depression of strength; failure of vital power; utter prostration.

Colon. The largest of the intestines, or the largest division of the intestinal canal.

Colonitis. Inflammation of the colon.

Commotio-cerebri. Disturbance of brain functions.

Compress. Folds of soft linen, cloth or lint, used to cover the dressings of wounds, etc.

Concomitant. Accompanying; conjoined with.

Condylomata. Warty excrescences, or soft, fleshy, indolent excrescences.

Congestion. An accumulation of blood in capillaries or other blood-vessels in any part of the body; a relaxed condition arising from want of normal tension in the muscular fibres of the blood-vessels, caused by insufficiency of iron.

Conjunctiva palpebrarum. The fine sensitive membrane which lines the eyelids, and is joined on to the ball of the eye.

Conjunctivitis. Inflammation of the lining membrane of the eyelid covering front of the eyeball.

Connective tissue is found in the animal body as a supporting framework and investment to various organs, besides being intimately interwoven with all the textures of the body. It is composed of cells and intercellular gelatine-yielding substance.

Constipation. Costiveness; defective excretion of fæces or stools.

Contra-functional. Out of working order.

Convalescence. The slow recovery of health and strength after disease.

Convulsions. Violent and involuntary contractions of the muscular parts of an animal body; spasm; agitation; commotion.

Co-ordinating. All parts of a machine working towards the same object and keeping up the cosmic order of the body.

Cornea. Transparent horny membrane in front of the pupil of the eye.

Corpuscle. A minute body or physical atom seen only by the microscope. There are nearly 3,000,000 corpuscles in one droplet of our blood. These globules carry the iron (cell-salt) to all parts of the body by the circulation of the blood; hence the reasonableness of using minimum or infinitesimal quantities of cell-salts. One corpuscle does not exceed the 120,000,000,000th of a cubic inch.

Corrugated. Wrinkled ; furrowed ; uneven.

Coryza. A catarrh with a limpid, ropy, mucous discharge from the nose, generally caused by cold in the head.

Cramp. A spasmodic contraction of the muscles, attended generally with much pain, arising from various causes.

Craniotabes. Wasting away of the bones of the skull, found in rickets and congenital syphilis.

Creeping paralysis. Wasting palsy.

Croup. Inflammation and exudation of thick, tough phlegm at the top of the trachea or windpipe, accompanied by a hoarse cough and difficult respiration ; especially incident to children.

Croup, hysterical, is attended with spasms of the muscles of the windpipe.

Crusta lactea. Scald-head of children ; scabs.

Crystalline lens (in the eye). A double convex, transparent, solid body, with a rounded circumference, lying behind the iris in the partition between the aqueous and vitreous humours.

Cupped. Bled ; blood taken from the body by means of the cupping-glass.

Cuticle. The scarf-skin ; the thin outer coat of the skin, also called epidermis.

Cyst. A sack or bag which contains morbid matter.

Cystitis. Inflammation of the bladder.

Coxarthrocace. Disease of the hip.

D.

Dandruff. A white or yellow scurf which forms on the head, and comes off in small scales or particles.

Decomposition. The breaking up of a chemical compound into its elements, or into two or more less complex compounds.

Defecation. Removal of impurities from the body. See Fæces.

Defluxion. A flowing off or discharge of humours, as from the nose.

Delirium. A state in which the ideas of a person are wild, irregular, and unconnected ; a wandering of the mind ; disorder of the intellect.

Delirium tremens. An affection of the brain, with illusions of the mind, trembling of the body, produced by excessive use of spirituous liquors in large or repeated small doses, which gradually deprive the brain pulp of its proper softness and moisture, and harden it.

Dentition. The breeding or cutting of first or second teeth.

Dermis. The true skin or lower layer of the skin.

Desquamation. Free scaling of skin ; the separation of the outer skin in small scales.

Diabetes. An excessive and morbid discharge of urine ; characterized as D. insipidus, when the urine is insipid, and D. mellitus, when it possesses abundance of saccharine matter ; hence Diabetic, pertaining to diabetes.

Diabetes mellitus. An excessive and morbid discharge of urine containing saccharine matter (sugar).

Diagnosis. Distinguishing one disease from another by its symptoms.

Diaphoresis. Perspiration or sweat ; increased secretion of the skin ; hence Diaphoretic, applied to medicines that increase the insensible perspiration, and differing from sudorifics, that act more violently.

Diarrhœa. Violent purging.

Diathesis. Particular disposition of constitution.

Dilatation. Extension or relaxation of muscular fibres.

Diphtheria. Diphtheritis, a disease of the throat, in which there is a formation of a false membrane, in fatal cases ending in suffocation or exhaustion.

Diplopia. Seeing double ; an affection of the eye.

Disarticulation. Out of joint.

Dissipated. Scattered ; dispersed.

Diurnal. Applied to diseases whose exacerbation or sharpest attacks occur in the day.

Dolor. Pain ; hence Dolores osteocopi, pains in the bones.

Dorsal. Pertaining to the back; hence Tabes dorsalis, wasting of the spinal marrow.—*Spinal dorsi.* A fold or plexus of veins around the processes of the vertebræ.

Drooling. Drivelling or dropping saliva.

Dropsy. A morbid collection of water in the cellular tissues or other cavities of the body.

Duodenal. Relating to the duodenum, the first of the small intestines immediately following the stomach ; the twelve-inch intestine. It is capable of considerable distension.

Duodenitis. Inflammation of the duodenum, the first part of the intestines, commencing at the small or pyloric end of the stomach.

Dynamic. Relating to dynamics.

Dynamics. The science which treats of the law of force, moving power, matter in motion, mechanics.

Dyscrasy or **Dyscrasia.** Depraved condition of the animal fluids, producing, generally, a morbid state of the system.

Dysentery. A flux in which the stools consist chiefly of blood and mucus, or other morbid matter, accompanied with griping of the bowels, and followed by tenesmus (straining, a painful feeling for evacuation).

Dysmenorrhœa. Difficult or painful menstruation or period.

Dyspepsia. Bad digestion ; indigestion ; the imperfect conversion of food into nourishment.

Dyspnœa. A difficulty or shortness of breath.

Dysury. Difficulty of voiding the urine (different from ischury), or suppression.

E.

Eczema. An eruption of the skin ; sometimes small vesicles on, or morbid redness of, the skin.

Effete. Having lost the power of production ; worn out.

Effusion. The pouring out of serous fluid, mostly the result of inflammation.

Egesta. Vomited matter.

Elastic cells. Those cells which constitute elastic tissues of the living body.

Element. That which cannot be divided by chemical analysis, and therefore considered as a simple substance.

Eliminate. To expel ; to discharge ; to throw off ; to set at liberty.

Emaciation. Thinness produced by a gradual wasting away of the flesh of the body.

Embolism. The clot or other matter which is carried into the circulation of the blood.

Embolus. Clot of blood in bloodvessel.

Embryo. The early stage of the fœtus ; an animal or plant forming from the egg or ovum.

Emmetropia. The defection of the accommodation of the eyes for distinct vision of near objects, due to muscular weakness.

Empiricist or **empiric.** An experimentalist who prescribes remedies by guess and traditional experience or trial regardless of scientific theory and even common-sense. Empiricism is, notwithstanding, acknowledged to be the character of the every-day medical practice, in as far as it is a system of trial (from *perariō*, I try).

Empyema. A collection of purulent matter, chiefly in the cavity of the pleura, a thin membrane which covers the exterior of the lungs.

Eucalyptus. An interesting class of trees, from some of which tannin is obtained.

Encephalitis. Inflammation of the brain.

Enchondroma. A tumour somewhat smooth on its surface, essentially consisting of cartilaginous structure.

Encysted. Enclosed in a cyst, bag, or bladder.

Endocarditis. Inflammation of the lining membrane of the heart.

Enteralgia. Nervous pain in the stomach or bowels.

Enteritis. Inflammation of the bowels.

Enuresis. Incontinence of urine; involuntary flow of urine at night.

Epidermis. The upper layer of the integument, the cuticle or scarf skin of the body.

Epididymis. A worm-like body, forming part of the vas deferens of the testes.

Epididymitis is inflammation of the epididymis, a part of the testicle.

Epigastralgia. Pain in upper part of stomach, where digestion takes place.

Epigastrium. The upper part of the abdomen, or epigastric region.

Epilepsy. The falling sickness, a disease characterized by spasms or convulsions and loss of sense.

Epiphysis. Abnormal growth of a bone, by which one becomes joined to another without proper articulation; a part of bone growing into another, previously separated by cartilage; hence Epiphytal, in botany, applied to plants that are parasitical.

Epistaxis. Bleeding from the nose; nasal hæmorrhage.

Epithelial sheathings. Portions of the layer of cells forming the inner membranous surface of the bladder, etc.

Epithelioma. Cancer on a cutaneous surface, or at the union of the skin with the mucous membrane, with discharge of thin yellow mattery secretions; epithelium scaly.

Epithelium. The cuticle covering the lips, nipple, etc.; such parts as are not covered with thick skin, and specially liable to excoriation, etc.

Erethism. Acute sensibility, irritability, or energy; morbid energetic action.

Erosion. Eating away; corrosion.

Eructations. Ejection of gas or wind from the stomach through the mouth.

Erysipelas. Rose; St. Anthony's fire; an inflammatory affection of some part of the skin, smooth or blistering.

Erysipelatous. Eruptive; resembling erysipelas, or partaking of its nature.

Erythema. Morbid redness of the skin; hence Erythematic.

Eustachian tubes. Small canals or ducts running from cavities of the middle ear into the upper part of the pharynx.

Exanthema. An eruption of the skin, as in small-pox, scarlatina, etc.; generally confined to such eruptions as are attended with fever.

Excitation. Increased action of any part of the body, as by friction, electricity, or any other cause.

Excoriation. Abrasion, ruffling, or destruction of the skin, causing soreness.

Excretion. The throwing off of effete matter, etc.

Exfoliation. Scaling or peeling off; separation of carious or decayed bone from a living one.

Exophthalmic goitre. Great prominence of the eyes, with large tumour or swelling on fore-part of the neck.

Exostosis. A bony tumour; tumour of the bone.

Extensor. Any muscle of the body that extends or straightens a part; opposed to flexor.

Extravasated blood. The blood of the body escaped from its natural canals, etc., and consequent diffusion in the surrounding tissue, as from the rupture of a bloodvessel.

Exudation. Discharge of some parts of the blood-plasma from the mucous lining and other tissues, in a diseased state.

Ex usu in morbis. From practice in diseases.

F.

Fæces. Feces or fæces, evacuations; stools; discharges from the bowels.

Fasciæ. The thin tendinous coverings which surround the muscles of the limbs, and bind them in their places.

Febrile. Pertaining to fever; feverish.

Felon. Whitlow; abscess of the finger-ends.

Fibrin. A white, fibrous, albuminoid substance obtained from blood; hence Fibrinous.

Figwort. A plant of the genus Scrophularia.

Fissura, Fissure. A groove or opening, as of a bone; F. magna sylvii, a furrow dividing the anterior and middle lobes of the brain; F. umbilicalis, the groove of the umbilical vein.

Fistula. A deep, callous, and narrow ulcer, generally following an abscess, in certain parts of the body.

Fistula in ano. An abscess occurring in some portion of the cellular tissue around the anus.

Fits. Paroxysms of disease; sudden and violent attacks; convulsions.

Flatulent. Windy; affected with air or gas generated in the stomach and intestines.

Flatus. Flatulence; wind generated in the stomach.

Flexor. Applied to such muscles as assist to bend any part of the body.

Flocculent. In the form of flocks, as sheep and cotton wool.

Fluoride. A compound of fluorine with another element—*e.g.*, Calcium fluoride ($Ca F_2$).

Fluorine. An elementary body obtained from fluorine, of great energetic action on most bodies, producing, with hydrogen, hydrofluoric acid, etc.; unites eagerly with silicon to produce fluosilicic acid; Fluorides, compounds of fluorine with bases.

Flux. In pathology, an extraordinary abnormal issue or evacuation.

Fœtid. Having an offensive smell.

Follicle. A bag, gland, or cavity.

Fomentation. External application of hot moist flannels, etc., to ease pain or excite action.

Fontanelles. The soft cartilaginous membrane at the top of an infant's head.

Foramen. Generally a name given to various openings or holes of the body.

Fossa. A cavity in a bone having a large aperture ; as F. hyaloidea, the cavity in which the crystalline lens of the eye rests ; also F. lachrymis, F. navicularis, F. ovalis, etc.

Freckle. A spot of a yellowish colour in the skin.

Frontal. Pertaining to the forehead (Lat. *frons*).

Function. The office of, or purpose subserved by, any given organ or part of an animal or plant.

Fungi. A certain class of vegetable forms characterized by the absence of chlorophyll (green colouring matter), such as met with in the diphtheritic exudation ; microscopic organisms found like bacteria or microbes in unhealthy or decomposing matter.

Fungus. Singular of the preceding ; also an excrescence of a morbid and spongy character, as "proud flesh." F. articulorum, white swelling ; F. hæmatoides, bleeding fungus ; F. medullaris, medullary cancer.

Furuncle. A boil ; a superficial tumour.

G.

Gall-bladder. A small membranous sac, shaped like a pear, which is attached to the liver, and receives from the liver an extremely bitter fluid, called gall or bile.

Gall-stones. Concretions formed from the gall.

Ganglion. A hard, round, indolent swelling, of the colour of the skin, situated on a tendon, varying in size from that of a pea to that of an egg. It consists of a fluid contained in a cyst of greater or less thickness, such as is sometimes met with on the back of the wrist. This term ganglion is also employed to denote an enlargement in the course of a nerve, and constituting a nerve centre.

Gangrenous. Mortified ; indicating mortification of living flesh.

Gastric. Belonging to the stomach.

Gastritis. Inflammation of the stomach.

Gastro-enteritis. Inflammation of the stomach and intestines.

Genital. Pertaining to the organs of reproduction, as the penis, pudenda, etc.

Germ. Seed ; first principle ; the ovum.

Gland. An organ of the body in which a secretion of some kind is elaborated from the blood—*e.g.*, lymphatic sweat glands, salivary glands, gastric glands.

Glauber salt. Sodium sulphate.

Gleet. A watery discharge from the penis, consequent on gonorrhœa.

Globus hystericus. A sensation as of a ball in the throat, produced by air prevented by spasmodic action from reaching the mouth.

Glossitis. Inflammation of the tongue.

Glosso-pharyngeus and lingualis. Nerve connected with the pharynx and the tongue.

Glottis. The narrow opening at the top of the trachea, or windpipe.

Gluten. The nitrogenous proximate element of certain food stuffs, and one of its most nutritive parts.

Glycerine. The sweet principle of oils and fats.

Glycogen. A substance formed by the liver, and capable of being converted into grape-sugar or into glucose.

Gonorrhœa. A contagious inflammation of the genital organs, attended with a profuse secretion of mucus, etc.

Gout. An inflammatory disease of certain joints, chiefly of the hands and feet, with chalky deposits, attacks occuring by paroxysms.

Granule. A small particle ; a little grain.

Gravel. A disease produced by small calculous concretions in the kidneys and bladder.

H.

Hallucination. A diseased state of mind, in which a person has a settled belief in the reality of things which have no existence ; delusion ; error.

Hæmatemesis. Vomiting of blood.

Hæmaturia. Bloody urine.

Hæmoptysis. Spitting of blood.

Hæmorrhage. A discharge of blood through rupture of bloodvessels.

Hæmorrhoids. Piles ; small tumours in different stage of congestion, and inflammation within or outside the anus.

Hangnail. A small piece or sliver of skin which hangs from the root of a finger-nail.

Hawking. Making an effort to discharge phlegm from the throat.

Hay fever or **Hay asthma.** Summer catarrh, caused by the pollen of grasses.

Hectic fever. Exacerbating and remittent fever, attended with chilliness, heat, perspiration, etc.

Hemiopia, Hemopsia. Partial vision, by which the whole of an object cannot be seen.

Hemiplegia, Hemiplexia. A paralytic affection of but one side of the body.

Hepatic. Pertaining to the liver, as *hepatic* gall, pain, artery, ducts, etc.

Hepatization. Conversion into a substance resembling the liver.

Hernia. Rupture.

Herpes. The tetters, an eruption of the skin, as in erysipelas, ring-worm, etc. ; hence Herpetic, as applied to eruptions.

Herpes circinatus. An eruption which disposes itself worm-like in circles.

Herpes tonsurans. Eruption or irritation of the skin after shaving.

Herpes zona. Shingles ; large or small blebs, in patches on the skin.

Herpes zoster. A spreading eruption encircling one-half of the body.

Herpetic eruptions. Pertaining to the herpes or cutaneous eruptions.

Heterogeneous. Of a different kind or nature; unlike or dissimilar in nature.

Hiccup, Hiccough. A convulsive catch of the respiratory organs and larynx, arising from a spasmodic affection of the diaphragm.

Hip-joint disease. Scrofulous affection commencing with inflammation in the hip-joint. The pain is often felt for a long time before swelling sets in, with ultimate discharge of matter from an abscess on the part; the head of the bone also becomes implicated.

Hippocratic. Of the nature of hippocras.

Hippocras. A medicinal drink, composed of wine with an infusion of spices.

Histology. The microscopic study of the tissues of the body.

Hives. The croup, the rattles; also applied to chicken-pox.

Homœopathy. A medical practice the opposite of allopathy.

Homogeneous. Of the same kind or nature.

Hooping-cough. An affection of the bronchi and breathing apparatus, attended with repeated spasmodic, convulsive fits of cough, ending in a characteristic whoop.

Hordeolum. A stye, or small tumour of the eyelid, so called from *hordeum*, a barleycorn.

Housemaid's-knee. A watery tumour; enlargement of bursa or sac on the knee-cap.

Hunterian chancre. Disease of the genital organs.

Hydræmia. Watery blood.

Hydroa. Watery blisters.

Hydrocele (in the male). Dropsy in the scrotum.

Hydrocephalus. Dropsy in the head, or water in the head.

Hydrochloric acid. Muriatic acid, a compound of chlorine and hydrogen.

Hydrogen. One of the constituent elements of water; a colourless combustible gas, and the lightest substance known.

Hydrogenoid. Combined with hydrogen.

Hydrops genu. Dropsical effusion; swelling of the knee.

Hygroma patellæ. A watery tumour under the knee-cap.

Hyperæmia. Excess of blood in any part; accumulation.

Hypertrophy. Unnatural morbid enlargement of an organ of the body.

Hypertrophy. Morbid enlargement of an organ; over-nutrition.

Hypochondriasis. Depression of spirits, with languor, listlessness, and despair of recovery as the result of long-continued indigestion, especially affection of the lining membrane of the stomach.

Hypochondrium. The region on each side of the stomach over the liver and spleen.

2

Hypogastrium. That portion of the belly reaching from the navel to the *os pubis*.

Hypopium. Hypopion ; an effusion of pus into the anterior chamber of the eye.

Hypoxanthin. A peculiar organic compound found in the fluid of the spleen, and in very small quantity in muscle.

Hysteria. A nervous affection of women, attended with involuntary laughter and crying.

Hysteric. Disordered in the region of the womb ; troubled with fits or nervous affections.

Humid. Moist ; damp ; somewhat wet or watery.

I.

Ichor. Thin watery serous fluid oozing from an ulcer.

Idem. The same, or identical.

Idiopathic. An inherent, morbid, or diseased state, not produced by any preceding disease or injury.

Iliac. Pertaining to the ilium.

Ilium. The last portion of the small intestines ; hence the term Iliac region, etc.

Ilium os. The haunch bone.

Imbibition. A drinking in ; the passage of fluid or gaseous matter into and through the tissues ; endosmosis.

Incineration. The act of reducing to ashes.

Incipient. Commencing.

Incontinence. The inability of any of the animal organs to restrain discharges of their contents.

Indication. Any symptom or occurrence in a disease which serves to direct to suitable remedies.

Induration. The act of hardening.

Inertia. That property of matter whereby it tends to continue at rest or to move when in motion ; indisposition to move.

Infiltration. The entering of a fluid into the pores of a body.

Infinitesimal. An infinitely small quantity.

Influenza. An epidemic catarrh, that has often produced as fatal effects as cholera ; so named by the Italians from an idea of its being connected with the "influence" of the stars.

Infraorbital. Situated underneath the orbit, as an artery.

Inguinal. Pertaining to the groin ; as Inguinal glands, hernia, etc.

Inherent. Existing in, so as to be almost inseparable from ; innate ; inborn.

Inorganic. Of the nature of minerals. Devoid of organs ; not possessing the organs or instruments of life.

Insectivorous. Feeding or subsisting on insects.

Insomnia. Restlessness ; want of sleep.

Integument. That which naturally invests or covers another thing, as the skin covers the body.

Intercellular. Lying between the cells or the cellular tissue.

Intercostal. Lying between the ribs.

Intercurrent. Running between or among; intervening.

Intermittent. A term applied to any disease that entirely ceases at certain intervals, and then returns.

Interstice. A narrow or small space between things closely set; hence Interstitial.

Intertrigo. A species of erythema, redness of skin, induced by acridity of the urine; scalded.

Intestine. The canal of the stomach, extending thence to the anus, in which digestion is performed; length from thirty to forty feet. Primarily divided into large and small; secondarily, into the duodenum, jejunum, and ilium; and the latter into cæcum, colon, and rectum, this last ending in the anus; hence **Intestinal.**

Intestinal villi. Minute projections on the mucous lining of the intestinal canal, which are made up of bloodvessels, nerves, and absorbents.

Iodine, Iodium. An elementary body obtained from marine plants, etc., analogous to chlorine and bromine; affords a purple vapour when heated. In combination with a base produces an Iodide; with oxygen produces Iodic Acid, and salts called Iodates; with hydrogen an acid called the Hydriodic. Iodide of potassium is of much use in medicine.

Irritation. The operation of exciting excess. In physiology, a vitiated and abnormal state of sensation or action produced by external or mechanical agents or influences; the morbid super-excitation of vitality or function.

Irritation-Hyperæmia. Excess of blood through irritation or stimulation in any part of the body; often resulting in stasis or stagnation of blood.

Ischury. A stoppage or suppression of urine.

Isomeric. Compounds having the same amount of equivalents of bodies, and yet having different properties.

Itis. To force; urge against; denoting violent action in the bloodvessels; used as a terminal to indicate inflammation, *e.g.*, Bronch-itis, inflammation of bronchial tubes.

J.

Jaundice. A disease of a biliary nature, characterized by yellowness of the eyes, skin, and urine staining yellow, etc.

K.

Keratitis. Inflammation of the keratin, or substance of the horny tissues.

Kidney disease (Bright's). See Bright's disease.

Kidneys. Two organs of the body, the function of which is to secrete the urine, this fluid afterwards flowing from them into the bladder.

King's evil. Scrofula.

L.

Labia. The lips of the mouth; the red part is called the prolabium; the sphincter, orbicularis labiorum; the cuticle, epithelium. Labia leporini, hare-lip; Labia pudendi, the exterior parts of the female genital organs; hence Labial.

Labyrinth. That part of the internal ear consisting of the cochlea vestibulum, and semicircular canals.

Lachrymal. Pertaining to the tears, as Lachrymal glands, etc. *L. duct*, tear duct.

Lachrymose. Readily shedding tears; tendency to crying.

Lactation. Giving suck.

Lacteals. The lymphatics of the intestines; minute vessels which absorb the chyle and convey it to the thoracic duct, and so into the blood at the junction of the left subclavian and jugular veins.

Lactic acid. An organic acid present when milk has turned sour.

Laryngeal. Pertaining to the larynx.

Laryngismus stridulus. Miller's asthma of children; child-crowing, from partial obstruction of the windpipe; rickety children are especially liable to such attacks, or spasms.

Laryngitis. Inflammation of the larynx.

Larynx. The upper part of the windpipe, a cartilaginous air passage.

Lassitude. A morbid sensation of languor, frequently preceding and accompanying disease.

Lead colic. An affection produced by lead, as in newly-painted rooms, etc.

Lepra, Leprosy. A cutaneous scaly disease, with eruptions of circular spots on the skin, attended with violent itching. The leprosy of ancient writers was, most probably, elephantiasis.

Leucæmia lienalis. Excess of white blood corpuscles in the spleen.

Leuchæmia, Leukæmia, or **Leucocythemia.** Excess of white blood corpuscles.

Leucocytes. The white blood corpuscles, of which there should be one in every four hundred of red corpuscles in healthy or normal blood.

Leucorrhœa. A discharge from the uterus or vagina; the 'whites.'

Leucosycosis. Occurring in conjunction with sycosis.

Leucocytosis. An increase in the number of white corpuscles in the blood, in several morbid conditions.

Lichen. A papular cutaneous eruption of red pimples, like goose-skin, reddened pricking sensation and itching.

Ligaments. Tough flexible bands of connective tissue which bind the bones together at the joints.

Lithic. Pertaining to stone. *Lithic acid*, uric acid, produced from urine.

Liver. A large abdominal organ, of a deep red colour, lying under the false ribs on the right side ; its principal use is to secrete the bile.

Local. Limited or confined to a spot or place.

Lockjaw. A violent rigid contraction of the muscles of the jaw, by which its motion is suspended ; tetanus.

Locomotor ataxy. Want of co-ordination in the movements of the arms or legs, or both, depending upon fascicular echrosis of the posterior column of the spinal cord.

Locomotor paralysis. Paralysis of the limbs.

Lumbago. An acute pain in the loins and small of the back ; a rheumatic affection of the muscles of the loins.

Lumbar region. That portion of the back between the false ribs and the upper edge of the haunch-bone.

Lumbo-abdominal. Loins and abdomen.

Lunar caustic. Fused nitrate of silver.

Lungs. The organs of respiration, which with the heart completely fill the thoracic cavity or chest ; the right is divided into three, the left into two, lobes. The upper lobes most prone to tubercular disease.

Lung idiopathy. A morbid state or condition of the lung not produced by any preceding acute disease.

Lupus. A tubercular disease of the face and nose.

Lymph. Watery humour, or a colourless fluid allied to the serum of blood, and carried through the body by vessels called lymphatics.

Lymphangitis. Inflammation of the vessels carrying lymph.

M.

Macrocosm. The infinitely large or visible horizon.

Macula (*pl.* **Maculæ**). Coloured spots on the body

Magnesium. The metallic base of magnesia.

Mal. A prefix denoting bad or evil.

Malaise. An indefinite feeling of uneasiness ; being ill at ease, not at all well.

Malaria. Exhalations from marshy districts, producing fevers, agues, etc.

Malleolus. The ankle.

Malignant. Virulent ; dangerous.

Mammæ. The breasts of a female.

Manganese. A hard, brittle metal, of a grayish-white colour.

Mania transitoria. Temporary insanity, due to an excess of blood on the brain.

Marasmus. Atrophy, wasting away from various causes.

Marrow. A soft oleaginous substance contained in the cavities of animal bones ; spinal marrow or spinal cord.

Mastitis. Inflammation or suppuration of the breasts of women.

Mastoid. Having nipple-like processes; as the Mastoid process of the temporal bone.
Masturbation. Self-abuse.
Materia medica. That branch of science treating on the articles used in medicine and pharmacy.
Maxilla. The jaw; the lower jaw is termed M. inferior; the upper, M. superior; hence Maxillary, pertaining to the jaw.
Measles. A contagious disease (rubeola) indicated by a pinkish rash upon the skin. Ushered in, like influenza, with catarrh, and frequently accompanied by a watery discharge from the eyes.
Meatus. A passage, as that leading to the ear, called the Meatus auditorius.
Megrim, Migraine. A neuralgic pain in the side of the head, *i.e.*, one-sided, often periodical.
Melancholia. Lowness of spirits; mental depression; often accompanied by irritability of the liver.
Membrane. A thin, white, flexible skin, formed by fibres interwoven like network, and serving to cover some parts of the body.—**Mucous membrane.** Inside lining of hollow cavities, such a mouth, throat, etc.
Meninges. The two membranes that envelop the brain.
Meningitis. Inflammation of the coverings or membranes of the brain or spinal cord, also called meninges.
Menorrhagia. Excessive menstrual discharge; flooding.
Menstrual colic. A spasmodic and painful affection of the bowels, but especially the colon, during the monthly period.
Menstruation. Menses; the catamenial period or monthly discharge of women.
Mercury. Quicksilver; a metal used in medicine, a very subtile and powerful drug.
Mesentery. A membrane in the cavity of the abdomen attached to the vertebræ in the loins. It encloses and sustains the bowels; hence Mesenteric.
Metabolism. Chemical changes in the living body; pertaining to vital affinity.
Metameric. Chemical substances having same age, composition, and molecular weights.
Metamorphosis. Change of condition, form, or shape.
Metastasis. Removal of disease from one part of the body to another.
Metritis. Inflammation of the womb, attended with pain, swelling, tenderness, vomiting, difficulty of passing water.
Metrorrhagia. Hæmorrhage of the womb.
Microcosm. The infinitely small; the miniature world.
Micturition. Passing urine.
Migraine. The brow-ague, a painful disorder generally on one side of the head.

Miliaria. Miliary fever, having an eruption like millet-seeds; Miliary glands are the sebaceous ones of the skin.

Milligramme. The thousandth part of a French gramme, and equal in Imperial weight to about $\frac{15}{1000}$ parts of a grain. Though small, yet even this quantity of cell-salt has effect.

Minimals. Smallest quantities.

Molecule. A name given to the minute particles of which bodies are composed; means strictly the smallest quantity of an element or a compound that can exist in a free state.

Monomania. Derangement or mania on one particular subject.

Morbid. Diseased; sickly; unhealthy; unsound.

Morphia. The chief narcotic principle of opium.

Mortification. Death of one part of the body while the rest is alive; gangrene.

Mortify. To destroy the organic texture and vital functions of some part of a living animal.

Motor. A mover; in anatomy applied to certain nerves which control certain muscles and their movements.

Mucous lining. A membranous lining of the canals and cavities of the body, as the throat, stomach, intestines, etc.

Mucous membrane. The lining of the internal parts of the body, exposed to the action of air or solid matter.

Mucus. Phlegm, a viscid fluid that lubricates the surfaces, secreted by the mucous membrane lining the nose, air passages, etc.

Multiple cheloid. Flat tender excrescences of skin, usually found on the chest.

Mumps. A swelling of the parotid glands, situated below the ear.

Muriatic acid, or Hydrochloric acid. A strongly corrosive acid, composed of one equivalent of hydrogen and one of chlorine.

Muscæ volitantes. An affection of the eye, attended with the appearance (to the patient) of dark spots floating on the cornea.

Muscles, flesh. Such parts of the fleshy portion of the body as perform movements by contracting or relaxing. Voluntary muscles, those subject to the will, as of the face, arm, leg, etc. Involuntary muscles, as the heart, stomach, etc.

Myelitis. Inflammation of the brain and spinal marrow.

Myodesopsia. A disease of the eye, producing the effect of Muscæ volitantes (which see).

Myosin. An albuminoid body extracted from muscular fibre; muscle-juice.

Myositis. Inflammation of the muscles.

N.

Nasal. Pertaining to the nose.

Nævi. Spots; moles.

Nævus. A natural spot upon a child at birth ; hence N. maternus, a mark on a child, supposed to have been produced by a maternal impression during gestation.

Nausea. Originally sea-sickness ; disposition to vomit.

Nebulous. Cloudy ; hazy.

Necrosis. Mortification ; gangrene ; inflammation of bony matter, ending in decay.

Nephritic. Pertaining to the kidneys ; medicines alleviating disease of the kidneys.

Nephritis. Inflammation of the kidneys.

Nettle-rash. An eruption of the skin, much resembling that produced by the sting of a nettle.

Neuralgia. A painful affection of the nerves, generally of one system of nerves, but occasionally of several ; hence N. facies, tic douloureux ; N. sciatica, etc.

Neurasthenia. Nervous debility.

Neurilemma (Nerve Sheath). The membrane which invests the substance of the nerves, and forms for each filament a distinct sheath which may be easily separated in the form of a tube.

Nidus. A nest.

Nitrate of silver. Nitric acid, saturated with pure silver.

Nitrogen. An elementary gas which forms the base of nitric acid, and composes four-fifths of our atmosphere, acting as a diluent of the oxygen.

Nocturnal. Occurring at night, as Nocturnal perspiration, etc.

Node. A hard circumscribed tumour, proceeding from a swelling of the periosteum of the bone.

Nodules. Rounded little lumps or tumours, sometimes from swelling of the periosteum or membrane covering the surface of the bone.

Noma. Water canker ; eating, corroding, or cancerous sores attacking the cheek and skin, and the vulva of women.

Nomenclature. A vocabulary of names or technical terms of things in any art or science.

Non-assimilation. Food taken and not converted into nourishment nor absorbed by the tissues of the body.

Non-functional. Not performing its functions ; not in working order.

Normal. Natural ; according to rule ; not deviating from the ordinary structure ; in anatomy, healthy.

Nutrition. Process of promoting growth, or repairing the loss of the animal and vegetable system, attending vitality ; hence Nutritious, etc.

Nyctalopia. Faculty of seeing best at dusk or dark, attended by defect of vision by day.

Nymphomania. A morbid female affection, attended with extraordinary sexual desire.

Nystagmus. Involuntary winking, or nictation.

O.

Occiput. The back of the skull.

Odontoid. Tooth-like.

Œdema. Swelling or tumour proceeding from pituitous matter.

Œdema of the ankles. A local dropsical swelling; hence Œdematous.

Œdema pulmonarium. Swelling or infiltration of the lungs with serous phlegmy humour.

Œsophagus. The gullet; the canal through which food and drink pass to the stomach.

Ophthalgia. Pain in the eye.

Ophthalmia. Inflammation of the eye; hence Ophthalmic, etc.

Ophthalmia-neonatorum. Disease of the eye in new-born children.

Opusculum. A small work.

Orbits. The two cavities in which the eyes are placed.

Orchitis. Inflammation of the testicles, the seminal glands in the male.

Organic. Relating to all structures possessing organs or instruments through which natural activities are made manifest.

Organism. A living thing having organs, *e.g.*, any animal or vegetable forms.

Organic substance. A living or organized substance which is readily subject to change in its structures from putrefaction, decomposition, or otherwise. It thus differs from the substances of the mineral kingdom or inorganic matter, such as lime, iron, etc.

Orgasm. Immoderate excitement.

Os. The mouth, as the Os uteri, the opening of the womb, etc.

Osseous. Composed of bone; resembling bone.

Osteophytes. A term denoting a great variety of bony growths which are formed, for the most part, in an inflammatory exudation.

Osteosarcoma, sarcosis. A tumour of a fleshy nature, connected with bone; also called Mollites ossium.

Ostitis. Inflammation of the bone.

Otalgia. Earache.

Otitis. Inflammation of the ear.—*Otitis, suppurative.* Second or suppurative stage.

Otitis catarrhalis internus. Inflammation of the inner ear with discharge.

Otorrhœa. Discharge of blood or matter from the ear.

Ovaria (*pl.* of **Ovarium**, ovary). Two flat oval bodies, an inch in length, situate behind the uterus, and a little below the Fallopian tubes. The female source of reproduction, concomitant with the exercise of the male power, in generation, amongst all mammalia, or suck-giving animals; hence Ovarian, Ovarial, etc.

Ovaritis. Inflammation of the ovaries.

Ovarian. Relating to the ovaries and womb.

Oxidation. The burning away of any substance in oxygen; that is, oxygen entering into mechanical combination with another substance.

Oxygen. An electro-negative, basifying, and acidifying elementary principle; the vital part of the atmosphere, and the supporter of ordinary combustion.

Ozæna. An ulcer of the nose, discharging fœtid purulent matter, and sometimes even affecting the bone; met with in scrofulous constitutions.

P.

Pabulum. Food.

Palpebral. Pertaining to the eyebrows.

Palpitation. Excessive beating of the heart.

Palsy agitans. Trembling paralysis.

Panaritium. Whitlow.

Pancreas. The sweetbread, a glandular organ situated between the bottom of the stomach and the vertebra of the loins, reaching from the liver to the spleen. It secretes the pancreatic juice, which is essential to the formation of chyle, and to the process of digestion generally.

Papilla. The nipple; also applied to various elevations of the body, as the papillæ of the tongue, skin, etc.; hence Papillary, Papillous, etc.

Papulæ. Pimples; an eruption of the skin, accompanied with pimples either containing a fluid or suppurating; hence Papular, Papulose, etc.

Paralysis. (Palsy synonymous with paralysis.) Loss of motion or sensation, affecting the nerves of one or more parts of the body.

Paralysis agitans. Shaking palsy.

Paraplegia. Paralysis of the body transversely.

Parasitic. Growing and living upon some other organism.

Parenchyma. The substance contained between the bloodvessels of the viscera, of a spongy texture; in botany, the green juicy layer of the bark of plants, immediately under the epidermis; hence Parenchymatous, etc.

Paresis. Slight paralysis.

Parietal. Pertaining to or within the sides of anything; thus, the parietal bones form the sides and upper part of the skull.

Paronychia. A genus of plants, so named as supposed to cure whitlow.

Parotid. Pertaining to the two glands, one on each side of the ear, which secrete a portion of the saliva.

Paroxysm. Intermittent fits of a disease; hence Paroxysmal, etc.

Patella. The knee-pan or knee-cap.

Pathology. That part of medicine which treats of the cause, nature, and symptoms of diseases.

Pathogenetic. Treating of the causes of disease.

Pelvis. A bony cavity, open above and below, and forming the lower cavity of the belly; bounded in front by the os pubis: at the back by the os sacrum and os coccygis; laterally by the ilia above, and the ischia below. P. renum, a membranous bag receiving the urine, and passing it to the bladder; P. cerebri, the infundibulum in the brain.

Pemphigus. An eruption of bullæ; vesicles or blebs filled with watery fluid, attended with feverishness.

Pericarditis. Inflammation of the membranous covering of the heart.

Periosteum. Fibrous membrane which covers all bones.

Periostitis. Inflammation of the periosteum.

Peristaltic. Spiral, worm-like; applied to the motion of the intestines, caused by the contraction of the fibres, both assisting digestion and the evacuation of the fæces.

Peritonitis. Inflammation of the peritoneum, or thin serous membrane lining the internal surface of the abdomen; also called inflammation of the side, inflammation of the bowels.

Perturbation. Agitation; disturbance.

Perityphlitis. Inflammation around the cæcum, or part of the large intestine situated below the entrance of the ilium.

Petechia. Purple spots, common on the skin in some malignant fevers.

Phagedenic. A spreading, sloughing ulcer; gangrenous.

Phalanges. The small bones of the fingers and toes; hence Phalangeal, etc.

Pharmacology. Science of preparing medicines.

Pharyngeal. Pertaining to the pharynx.

Pharyngitis. Inflammation of the pharynx, or upper part of the gullet.

Phenomena. Appearances; usually applied to those appearances or symptoms of disease of which the cause is not immediately obvious.

Phlebitis. Inflammation of the veins, tenderness, heat, redness, and knots in their course. It may follow wounds, operations, or labour.

Phlegm. Mucous matter; watery fluid; bronchial mucus; viscid matter ejected from the throat.

Phlegmonous. Tendency to cutaneous inflammatory tumours.

Phlyctæna. A vesicle containing serous fluid; hence Phlyctenoid.

Phosphate. A salt of phosphoric acid; a combination of phosphoric acid with a base, such as lime, potass, etc.

Phosphoric acid. An acid composed of one equivalent of phosphorus, three of hydrogen, and four of oxygen ($H_3\ P\ O_4$).

Phosphorus. An elementary substance contained in all the phosphates, of a wax-like consistency, highly combustible, of a yellowish colour and semi-transparent.

Photophobia. Dread of light, owing to the extreme sensibility of the retina.

Phrenitis. Inflammation of the brain, attended with fever and delirium; frenzy.

Phthisis. Consumption, an affection of the pulmonary organs or lungs, marked by cough, expectoration, sweats, hectic fever, etc. P. pulmonaris, pulmonary consumption ; P. laryngeal, consumption in the larynx ; P. abdominal, consumption in the intestines ; P. tuberculous, tubercular consumption ; P. florid-hectic, decline ; P. tracheal, consumption in the trachea ; P. mucosa.

Physics, applied. Practical application of the properties of matter ; the laws of motion as found to exist in nature.

Physico-chemical. Natural or material productions in the body by natural agents, in harmony with the principles of chemistry.

Physiology. The study of the operations which take place in living or organized beings.

Piles. Hæmorrhoids, a disease arising from a morbid dilatation of the veins of the lower rectum on the edge of the anus.

Pin-worms. Thread-worms.

Plasma. The colourless fluid part of the blood in which the corpuscles float ; liquor sanguinis ; contains most of the chlorine and soda of the blood.

Plastic. A mass of matter capable of being moulded into a definite form, as the diphtheritic (albuminoid) exudation.

Pleurisy. An inflammation of the pleura, or thin membrane which covers the lungs and lines the inside of the chest or thorax.

Pleuritis, Pleurisy. Inflammation of the pleura, or membrane which invests the lung ; hence Pleural. P. plastica, pleurisy, with adhesion of the pleura to the lung.

Plexus. Network ; in anatomy applied to bloodvessels, nerves, or fibres ; a close network of nerves or bloodvessels.

Pneumonia. Inflammation of the lungs.

Pneumogastric nerve. A nerve arising from the medulla oblongata joining the brain.

Podagra. Gout in the feet.

Polymeric. Chemical substances, containing same composition, but different molecular weights.

Polypus. A tumour of morbid growth, attached to the interior of a mucous canal, occurring in the uterus, nose, larynx, fauces, etc. ; divided into vesicular, gelatinous, fibrous, and malignant. So called from being supposed to have many feet.

Polyuria simplex. An excessive passing of urine, as in diabetes insipidus, which is devoid of sugar.

Posterior nares. The back of the nostrils.

Post-scarlatinal dropsy. A morbid collection of water in any part of the body after scarlatina.

Potash, Pearlash. See Kali.

Potassium. The metal of which potash is an oxide ; kalium (see Kali).

Potassium. The metallic base of potash.

Pott's disease. Pott's curvature of the spine ; the angular curvature is produced by caries of the vertebræ, or ulceration of the substance between the vertebræ, followed by more or less loss of power over the lower extremity.

Precursory. Preceding; the forerunner, a precursor.

Premonitory. Stage in which occur forewarning symptoms.

Prepuce. The præputium, or foreskin of the penis, of the cutis of which it is a prolongation.

Preputial. Pertaining to the foreskin.

Prodromic. Forerunner.

Prognosis. The foretelling the result of any disease, based upon a consideration of its signs and symptoms.

Prolapsus. Falling down, as of the uterus, P. uteri, or P. recti, of the rectum.

Prolapsus recti. Falling down of lower end of bowel.

Prolapsus uteri. Falling down of the womb.

Proliferous. Bearing abnormal buds.

Proptosis. See Prolapsus.

Prosopalgia. Pain in the face; facial neuralgia.

Prostate. Situated in front.—*Prostate gland.* A large gland situated between the neck of the bladder and the bulb of the urethra. *Prostatic juice.* The secretion of the prostate gland.

Prurigo. A papular eruption of the skin, causing itching; distinct from the itch.

Psychology. The science which treats of the mind, or thinking faculties, as distinguished from *physiology*, which treats of the visible body.

Proud flesh. The name of a spongy excrescence formed in wounds.

Pruritus. Itching; a skin disease (prurigo).

Pruritus senilis. A skin disease of old people, the itchiness varying much at particular times.

Pruritus vulvæ. Itching of the female genital organs.

Pseudo-catarrhal. Spurious catarrhal affections.

Psoas. Two inside muscles of the loins, P. magnus and P. parvus, the former moving the thigh forward, and the latter bending the spine on the pelvis.

Ptosis. Falling of the upper eyelid, with want of power to raise it; also called Blepharoptosis.

Pubescence. Puberty.

Pudenda. The external parts of the organs of generation, but especially of the female (literally, "parts of modesty").

Puerperal. Belonging to child birth; hence puerperal fever, child-bed fever occurring soon after parturition.

Punctæ lachrymosa. Tear-punctures, small apertures which perforate each papilla lachrymale, or minute soft prominence in the corner of the eye near the nose.

Purgative. Purging, cathartic, drastic; hence to purge. The term Purging is at times substituted for diarrhœa, dysentery, and looseness of the bowels.

Purpura. Land-scurvy.
Purulent. Consisting of pus or corrupt matter, contained in ulcers, etc.
Pus. Yellowish-white matter, found in abscesses or boils, etc.
Pustule. An elevation or rise of the cuticle, with an inflamed base, and containing pus ; hence Pustulous and Pustular.
Pustules. Little pimples or blisters, containing matter.
Putrescence. The state of decomposing.
Putrid. In a state of decomposition or disorganization ; corrupt, rotten.
Pyæmia. A disease supposed to be due to the introduction of pus into the blood, or of some morbid poison ; is often accompanied with inflammation of one or more veins, and the formation of abscesses in other parts of the body than those originally affected ; blood-poisoning.
Pylorus. The lower and right orifice of the stomach, guarding the entrance to the bowels ; hence Pyloric, as the Pyloric artery.
Pyrosis. A derangement of the stomach, attended with a sensation of burning ; the waterbrash ; heartburn.

Q.

Quinsy. A suppurative inflammation of the tonsils of the throat, with yellow matter forming.

R.

Rachitis. Soft state of the bones in children, called rickets.
Raisonnement. Reasoning.
Râle. A rattling or wheezing in the throat ; every kind of noise attending the breathing in the bronchia and vesicles of the lungs different from the sound of breathing in health.
Ramify. To divide into branches.
Ranula. A tumour under the tongue.
Reflex. Directed back.
Resolution. In medicine, the dispersion and disappearance of inflammatory affections of the system.
Retching. Attempt to vomit.
Retinitis. Inflammation of the retina, the pulpy expansion of the optic nerve, resembling network, in the interior of the eye.
Rhagades. Cracks or fissures in the skin.
Rheumatic fever. Acute rheumatism, accompanied by intense fever.
Rheumatism. A painful disease affecting the muscles and joints, acute, called articular rheumatism. There are other varieties, as lumbago, which occurs in the loins.
Rickets (see also Rhachitis or Rachitis). A disease of children, characterized by arched legs, a bulky head, or deformed spine,

tumid abdomen, flabby flesh, etc.; partially a scrofulous affection, but stimulated by non-nutritious food in early infancy; hence Rickety.

Rose-rash. The popular name in Scotland for erysipelas.

Rupia. An eruptive disease, characterized by broad, flat vesicles, the scales being easily rubbed off, yet recurring

S.

Sac. A small bag or cyst.

Saccharated. Mixed with or containing sugar.

Sacrum (os). The bone which, in the human being, forms the basis or lower end of the spine.

Salicylic acid. An acid obtained from the distilled products of willow-bark (salix), poplar-bark, and other similar sources, and largely used as an antiseptic. It is composed of carbon, hydrogen, and oxygen, in these proportions—$C_7 H_6 O_3$.

Saliva. Spittle; the fluid secreted by the salivary glands.

Salivation. An excessive flow of saliva, sometimes from the bad effects of mercury.

Salt. A compound resulting from the mutual action of an acid and an alkali, or a base.

Sanguineous. Abounding with blood; of the nature of blood.

Sanies. A thin, often purulent, discharge from wounds or sores; hence Sanious, pertaining thereto.

Sarcoma. Any fleshy tumour; hence Sarcomatous.

Scald-head. An eruption of the scalp; ringworm.

Scapula. The shoulder-blade; hence Scapular, pertaining thereto.

Scarlet fever. Scarlatina, a febrile disease characterized by an eruption of crimson-red patches appearing on the third day, first on the fauces and breast.

Scarlatina. Generally applied to mild scarlet fever.

Scarlatina anginosa. Scarlet fever, with inflammatory affection of the throat.

Scarlatina maligna, with danger to life.

Sciatica. A rheumatic affection of the hip joint and sciatic nerve, pain darting often along the whole course of the sciatic nerve from the hip to the knee.

Scirrhus. A hard tumour on any part of the body; the induration or hardening of a gland ending in cancer.

Sclerosis. The hardening of a part by an increase of its connective tissue, resulting from inflammatory action.

Scorbutic. Affected or diseased with scurvy.

Scrofula. A disease affecting the glands; the king's evil.

Scrofulosis. King's evil; morbid affection of the glands.

Scrotum. The sac containing the testicles; hence Scrotal.

Scrotal œdema. Dropsical swelling of the testicles.

Scurvy. A disease attended by livid spots, debility, spongy gums, etc., occasioned by a limited range of food deficient of potassium chloride.

Sebaceous glands. Fat glands.

Secondary symptoms. Sequelæ: morbid affections following acute diseases.

Secretion. A separating of the animal fluids by various organs; hence Secretory glands.

Senile. Pertaining to old age.

Septic. Having power to promote putrefaction.

Septicæmia. An acute disease, resembling pyæmia, supposed to be caused by the absorption into the blood of putrid matter from the surface of a wound or ulcer.

Sequelæ. Attendant complications, or consequences resulting from diseases.

Serum. The watery liquid part of the blood, like whey, which separates from the blood corpuscles on coagulation.

Shingles (Herpes zoster). An eruption round the trunk or round the armpit, characterized by vesicles or small blisters, attended by inflammation of the parts and considerable pain.

Sigmoidal. Resembling the Greek letter sigma; hence applied to designate several forms in the body.

Silica. An important constituent of rocks. Quartz, flint, and sand are natural forms of silica.

Similia. Similar or like; refers to drug action, and the law homeopaths select their remedies by.

Simplex. A general name for uncomplicated conditions.

Sinapism. A mustard poultice.

Sinew. Tendon; that which unites muscle to bones.

Singultus. Hiccough, caused by convulsive motions of the diaphragm.

Sloughing. The dead structure of flesh that separates from the living parts, as from a wound or sore.

Small-pox (Variola). An infectious febrile disease, accompanied with eruption on the skin, which is at first hard, red, and pointed, and at the third day assumes a bladder-like appearance.

Sodium. The metallic base of soda.

Sodium hydroxide. Oxide of sodium combined with water.

Sodium sulphate (Glauber's salt). First discovered as a separate salt by Glauber by the distillation of common salt over the oil of vitriol. It is found in a natural state in many localities efflorescent on the soil, or dissolved in mineral springs, salt lakes, and salt-mines. The following is the composition of this substance found in its artificial separation—$N_2 S O_4$. All the separate chemical component parts which go to make up this salt are found in the tissues of the body, and in essential ood stuffs.

Sodium urate. A compound of soda and uric acid—a white, tasteless, and inodorous acid carried off in urine; when deposited about the joints gives rise to gout.

Sopor. Sleepiness; drowsiness; a heavy sleep.

Sordes. Foul, dirty deposit on the teeth during disease.

Spasms. Sudden and violent contractions of one or more muscles; cramps.

Spavin. A swelling or bony excrescence in some of the joints of a horse.

Spectrum analysis. The art of ascertaining the character and composition of bodies when in a state of combustion, by causing rays of light from the body desired to be so analyzed to pass through a prism, each substance having its own characteristic system of lines. This method is adopted to ascertain the qualitative or quantitative analysis of minerals, etc., when the presence of extremely minute quantities of different bodies has to be determined.

Spermatic. Consisting of animal seed; seminal.

Spermatic cord. A cord made up of the vessels and nerves which pass to and from the testes.

Spermatorrhœa. Involuntary flow of semen.

Sphincter. A muscle that contracts or shuts an orifice or opening round which it is placed.

Spina bifida. A congenital swelling situated over some part of the spine, due to the deficient or arrested growth of the posterior arches of one or more vertebral bones.

Spina ventosa. A morbid condition of bone, in which the cellular structure between the external and internal walls of a bone are abnormally distended into a cavity, which may contain air.

Spinal cord. The grayish-white matter, a continuation of the brain substance or matter lodged in the interior of the spinal column or backbone.

Spinal neurasthenia. Weakness of the nerves of the spine.

Spine. The backbone; hence Spinal.

Spleen. The milt, situated on the posterior of the left hypochondrium, near the large end of the stomach; a ductless gland composed of areolar tissue.

Splenitis. Inflammation of the spleen.

Spondylitis. Inflammation of the vertebra; generally followed by anchylosis of two or more of the vertebræ.

Sprain. To overstrain the muscles or ligaments of a joint.

Sputum. Expectoration.

Stasis. Stagnation of the blood, or accumulation of the blood.

Status quo ante. The condition in which the tissue was previous to disease.

Sterility. Barrenness.

Sternum. The breast-bone; hence Sternal.

Stertorus. Applied to the loud snoring of apoplexy and diphtheria.

Stimuli. That which excites to increased action.

Stomach, proper, is the membranous bag and principal organ of digestion, into which the food passes from the mouth. Pain in the stomach proper, however, is termed indigestion pain.

Stomach ache. Conventional term referring to pains in the lower region of the abdomen or belly.

3

Stomatitis. Inflammation or ulcers of the mouth.

Strabismus. Squinting.

Stricture. The narrowing of a channel or canal of the body, as of the gullet, bowel, or urethra.

Strumous. Scrofulous; having struma; a tendency to swelling and suppuration of the glands in various parts of the body.

Stye. An inflamed tumour on the edge of the eyelid.

Subcutaneous. Situated under the skin.

Submaxillary. Applied to glands under the jaw.

Sub-paralytic. Somewhat paralyzed; a not clearly defined effect of paralysis.

Sui generis. After its own race or genus.

Sulphate. A salt formed by the union of sulphuric acid, composed of hydrogen, sulphur, and oxygen in these proportions, $H_2 S O_4$, with a base or elementary substance, such as lime, potassium, or sodium, etc.

Sulphur. Brimstone; one of the elementary substances.

Sulphuric acid. An acid composed of one equivalent of sulphur, two of hydrogen, and four of oxygen ($H_2 S_1 O_4$).

Sunstroke. Ictus solis.

Suppurating. Mattering, festering; accumulating of pus, yellow matter.

Suppuration. Formation of pus; process of producing purulent, corrupt matter.

Supracostal. Above the ribs.

Supraorbital neuralgias. Neuralgia above the orbits or cavities in the skull containing the eyeballs.

Suprasternal fossa. Cavities or depressions above the sternum or flat bone of the breast to which the ribs are attached in front.

Suture. The junction of bones by their edged margins; hence Sutural, Sutured.

Sycosis. A tubercular eruption upon the scalp or bearded part of the face; chinwelk.

Sycosis menti. A cutaneous eruption which affects the follicles of the hair on the face.

Sympathetic. Dependent on sympathy or irritation.

Sympathetic nerve. It consists of nerves having one or more ganglia, which are nucleated nerve-cells, and centres of nerve power to the fibres connected with them.

Sympathetic nerve system. A secondary nervous system, supposed to control the involuntary muscles and processes of alimentation or nutrition, a fact now generally accepted.

Symphysis. Union of bones by cartilage.

Symptom. A sign of disease or phenomenon which indicates disease, and especially the kind of disease.

Symptomatology. A treatise on the symptoms of disease.

Synchondrosis. Articulation of bones by cartilage.

Synocha. Simple continuous fever.

Synovia. A lubricating fluid secreted at the joints of the bones; hence Synovial.

Synovitis. Inflammation of the synovial membrane of the joint.
Synthetic. Pertaining to synthesis, or the uniting or building up of elements into a compound; the reverse of analysis.
Syphilis. The venereal disease; a virulent and specific disease, the result of contagion.
Systaltic. Contractile.

T.

Tabes. A wasting away; atrophy; emaciation.
Tabes dorsalis. Wasting of the spinal cord.
Tabes mesenterica. A tubercular disease of the mesenteric glands; generally a disease of childhood. A wasting with loss of appetite, tenderness and distension of the abdomen.
Tarsus. The instep; hence Tarsal.
Telangiectasis. The expansion of the remote vessels; a disease of the capillaries, called "aneurism by anastomosis" or "erectile tumour"; a congenital affection, presenting a cutaneous swelling of a circumscribed form.
Tenalgia crepitans. Crackling of the tendons.
Tendons. Fibrous cords attached to the extremities of certain muscles, and attaching them to the body or other firm textures.
Tenesmus. Painful but useless urging to evacuation.
Tenonitis. Inflammation of the tendons.
Tentacle. A handle or filiform process of insectivorous plants; also found in animals for the purpose of prehension, touch; for example, the feelers of a snail.
Tertiary syphilis. Third stage of syphilis.
Tetanus. Tonic spasms; a spasmodic contraction of the muscles of voluntary motion with tension, rigidity, and stiffness.
Tetter. A common name for skin diseases; herpes.
Therapeutics. That branch of pathology which has for its object the treatment and cure of disease.
Thoracentesis. The operation of tapping the thorax (chest) for fluid or pus.
Thorax. That part of the human trunk, situated between the neck and the abdomen, containing the heart, etc.; the cavity of the chest.
Thread-worms. Small thread-like intestinal worms.
Thrush. A disease with minute ulcers in the mouth.
Thyroid. Resembling a shield.—*The Thyroid cartilage.* Adam's apple. *Thyroid gland*, lying on the thyroid and cricoid cartilages of the trachea.
Tibia. The largest of the two bones of the human leg: it articulates with the fibula; the shin bone.
Tic douloureux. Neuralgia of the face.
Tinea. Scald-head; ringworm, as T. capitis, etc.

Tinnitus aurium. Ringing in the ears; often merely nervous, or the result of indigestion; sometimes indicative of brain or functional disturbance of the heart; or it may be connected with deafness.

Tissue. The texture or minute structure of which organs are composed. Animal tissues divisible, according to Virchow and others, into three groups. These are: I. Cellular tissues, exclusively consisting of cells, such as the skin, nails, etc. II. Intercellular tissues, in which one cell is regularly separated from the others by intermediate or intercellular substance, such as connective tissues, etc. III. Various tissues, in which the cells have attained specific higher forms of development, such as nerves, etc. Virchow also places blood with its blood cells or corpuscles in this group.

Tissue-salts. The cell-salts of cellular and intercellular tissues and fluids.

Tonic. A medicine that increases the strength, and gives vigour of action to the system.

Tonsils. Two oblong glands situated on each side of the fauces at the root of the tongue.

Tonsillitis. Inflammation of the tonsils; a form of sore-throat.

Tormina. The gripes.

Torpid. Having lost the power of exertion and feeling, or of muscular action.

Torpor. Inactivity; loss of motion.

Tox albumin. Poisonous albuminate body.

Trachea. The windpipe.

Tracheitis, Trachitis. Inflammation of the windpipe.

Transosmose. The passing of a fluid through a porous body, such as the products of chemical change through the porous porcelain jar of a Bunsen's battery, or the nutritive components of the blood through the walls of the bloodvessels in certain parts of the body.

Transude. To pass through the pores.

Traumatic. Pertaining to wounds or applied to them.

Trigeminus. Three branches of the fifth pair of nerves.

Triturate. To rub or grind to a very fine powder; to reduce.

Tubercle. A small nodule or tumour on animal bodies, of the size of a hemp-seed or a pea, having a tendency to form into caseous or calcareous deposit; hence Tubercular disease of the lungs.

Tumour. A swelling; a morbid enlargement.

Tumor albus (White swelling). Fungoid swelling.

Tunic. A membrane that covers some organ.

Tympanitis. A flatulent distension of the abdomen.

Tympanum. The drum of the ear.

Typhlitis. Inflammation of the cæcum, or little sac formed in the course of the intestines.

Typhoid or **Enteric fever.** A lingering fever, with great prostration, languor, stupor, in which the bowels are implicated.

Typhoid. Relating to or resembling typhus.
Typhus. A form of low nervous fever, malignant, infectious, attended with irregular and weak pulse, delirium, etc. T. abdominalis, abdominal; T. biliosus, bilious; T. cerebralis, brain; T. gastricus, gastric; T. hepaticus, liver or bilious; T. puerperalis, puerperal; T. putridus, putrid; and T. rheumaticus, rheumatic—fever.

U.

Ulcers. Sores on any part of the body discharging morbid matter.
Umbilicus. The navel; hence Umbilical.
Urea. A crystalline substance obtained from urine.
Urethra. The canal by which urine is voided. See Urine.
Uric acid. A white tasteless and inodorous acid, contained in urine.
Urine. An animal fluid secreted by the kidneys, from whence it is conveyed to the bladder by the ureters, and discharged through the urethra.
Urticaria. Nettle-rash.
Uterine. Pertaining to the uterus, or womb.
Uterus. Womb.
Uvula. A small nipple-like body or projection drooping from the middle of the arch of the palate.
Uvulitis. Inflammation of the uvula.

V.

Vaccination. The act of inoculating with cow-pox.
Vaginal. Resembling a sheath; pertaining to the vagina, the canal which leads from the external orifice to the uterus.
Vaginismus. Congestion or inflammation of the vagina.
Varices. Dilatations of veins.
Varicocele. Swelling of the veins of the spermatic cord; also of those of the scrotum.
Varicose. Preternaturally enlarged or dilated, as applied to the veins.
Variola. Small-pox.
Vascular. Full of bloodvessels.
Vaseline. Obtained from petroleum, used as an ointment.
Vaso-motor. That which gives motion in the veins, etc.
Veins. Vessels in the animal body which receive the blood from the extreme arteries through the capillaries, and return it to the auricles of the heart.
Velum. The back part of the mouth.
Velum pendulum palati. Hanging down of the membrane which surrounds and partially closes the mouth of the disc of the Medusa, or jelly-fish.
Vermicular. Resembling the motion of a worm.

Vertebræ. The individual bones forming the backbone or spine, the foramen of which serves to protect the spinal cord.
Vertebrated. Having a spine with joints; a backbone.
Vertex. The crown of the head.
Vertigo. Giddiness; dizziness, or swimming of the head.
Vesicle. A little bladder, or a portion of the cuticle separated from the skin, and filled with fluid.
Villi. Minute thread-like projections, like velvet pile; on the mucous lining of the smaller intestine they act as absorbents.
Viscera. Internal organs; the contents of the thoracic and abdominal cavities, the heart, lungs, liver, etc.
Vitreous humour. A pellucid (clear, transparent) delicate jelly, which fills the bulb of the eye behind the crystalline lens.
Volatilize. To cause a substance to pass off by evaporation.
Vomiturition. An unavailing effort to relieve the stomach by vomiting.
Vulva. Part of the female organs of generation.

W.

Warts. Hard excrescences on the skin.
Waterbrash. Heartburn. Belching up of a watery or acid fluid.
Water canker. Noma, or cancrum oris; destructive ulceration of cheek and mouth, found generally in badly-nourished children.
Wheals. Red and white marks on the skin, seen in cases of nettle-rash.
Whitlow. Inflammation about the root of the nail of a finger, commonly terminating in suppuration.
Whooping-cough. A disease of children, attended with repeated spasmodic cough.
Worm. See *Vermes*, Tapeworm, *Tænia*, *Platyelmia*, etc.—*Worm-grass.* A species of *Spigelia*. *Worm-seed.* A species of *Artemisia*, etc.
Writer's cramp. A cramp or contraction of the fingers to which writers and violin players are subject.

Y.

Yolk-fat (Vitellin). The oil containing phosphorus found in minute globules in the yolk of an egg, also in the brain, nerves, and blood corpuscles.

Z.

Zona or **Zoster.** The shingles.
Zygomatic bones. The temporal and cheek bones; Zygomatic muscles, two muscles of the face rising from the Zygomatic bone; Zygomatic processes, processes of the temporal and cheek bones; Zygomatic suture, the suture joining the zygomatic processes.
Zymotic. Contagious, infectious; such diseases as may be occasioned by an organism or a diseased principle acting on the system like a ferment.

Dr. SCHÜSSLER'S

"BIOCHEMIC TREATMENT."

ARRANGED AND COMPILED

BY

Drs. DEWEY AND BOERICKE.

ENGLISH EDITION,

With Corrections and Annotations.

Contains much New Matter, and Additional Testimony to the Great Value of the Remedies.

8vo., post free, 6s. 9d.,

By M. DOCETTI WALKER, M.D.,

The Biochemic Dispensary, 9 Perth Road, Dundee.

"In its present state the book represents the complete presentation of the Biochemic Treatment of Disease by means of the twelve tissue Cell-salts. If any Physician wants to study up Biochemistry, he has the whole of it as far as can be gathered up to date in this volume. Biochemistry has a vitality so remarkable as to indicate that it is far more than a medical fad—in fact, Biochemistry has reached that point where it cannot be ignored. It is practised with remarkable success by many Physicians of both schools."

"The general title of the work is comprehensive."

"Each of its four parts is a special monograph upon these remedies, and each and all of them will prove of real value to the physician. The more we have used them the more we have been impressed with their therapeutical scope and utility."—Ed., *The Hahnemanian Publishing House.*

"This fairly embodies the attitude of the Press and the Profession towards the book, or rather, what it represents—Biochemistry."—*The Clinique.*

"The writer can say that he has been surprised by the effects of these remedies in a number of cases."—*Californian Medical Journal.*

"NEW TREATMENT OF DISEASE."

SCHÜSSLER, Dr. med.—Abridged Therapeutics founded upon Histology and Cellular Pathology. With an Appendix. Biochemic Method of successfully treating Disease. By Dr. MED. SCHÜSSLER, of Oldenburg. Authorised translation by M. DOCETTI WALKER, M.D. Eighteenth edition. London: Aug. Siegle, 30, Lime Street. Dundee: Biochemic Dispensary, 9, Perth Road. 8vo. . . . Post Free 5s. 9d.

OPINIONS OF THE PRESS.

"This work, from the pen of the celebrated Dr. Schüssler, will attract great attention. Though written for the study of the learned, it is perfectly plain to the lay reader as a book of domestic medicine, and full of interest."—*Courier and Argus.*

"Dr. Schüssler must be credited with a great amount of success. *A priori* it must be admitted that he has laid down a scientific basis for his treatment of disease which is well worthy the attention of the adherents of recognised systems of Therapeutics."—*Aberdeen Journal.*

"For this tissue-remedy side light on our pharmacology we shall be ever grateful to Dr. Schüssler. Many a good cure have we wrought with the aid of these remedies."—*H. World.*

"That much may be done for the simplification of Therapeutics on the lines which Dr. Schüssler lays down, can hardly be doubted; and perhaps the principal value of his work is, that it is a contribution to the attainment of that end."—*Scotsman.*

"That large proportion of mankind who are not practitioners, but merely patients, and who know how defective is still our powers to heal the diseases which afflict us, will welcome every thoughtful suggestion that points towards improvement, and will demand for Dr. Schüssler's method a fair trial."—*Dundee Advertiser.*

Now ready, paper covers, post free 1s. 6d.

DR. SCHÜSSLER'S New Cure for Diphtheria by Biochemic Treatment, with the Enlarged Glossary of Medical Terms. The remedies may be termed specifics from the unprecedented success in the treatment of diphtheria. This Brochure was written by Dr. Schüssler at the request of, and on condition that it would be published in English by the Translator.

Opinion of Dr. MOLESCHOTT, Professor of Physiology and Senator of Rome: "I am pleased that my views of the part which the inorganic substances play in nutrition has induced Dr. Schüssler to issue this treatise."

"This Brochure, a translation of which by M. Docetti Walker has just been issued, upon 'The Cure of Diphtheria,' treats not only of this special disease, but gives a brief account of the system."—H. A. MILLER, M.A.

WALKER, M. D.—Domestic Guide to the ready Use of Dr. Schussler's New Remedies, the more Common Diseases and their Treatment. With Medical Glossary, Notes on Digestion and Foods. Biochemic Dispensary, Dundee. 8vo. . . . Post Free 3s 3d.

"The 'Domestic Guide' I find most useful, and medical men are very pleased with it, as it saves time, especially to beginners. No doubt it will be welcome to all who use the remedies."—W. G. C., *M.D.*

THE SCHÜSSLER REMEDIES.

Wrong and useless, and even injurious substances having been sold in place of these preparations, it may be well to mention the Natural Tissue Cell-Salts are to be had as specially prepared for Dr. Schüssler at:

LONDON—FRANCIS NEWBERY & SON, Wholesale Chemists, 1, King Edw. St., E.C.
,, JOHN SANGER, 489, Oxford Street, W.
,, WILLIAM WHITELEY, Westbourne Grove, W.
SHEFFIELD—P. N. ORR, Abbeydale.
BRIGHTON—CHURCHILL, East Street.
EDINBURGH—INMAN & Co., 8, Shandwick Place.
GLASGOW—MURDOCH BROS., Sauchiehall Street.
DUNDEE—W. DOIG & SON, High Street.
,, THE SUPPLY CO., Commercial Street.
,, THE BIOCHEMIC DISPENSARY, 9, Perth Road

Complete Case of Half Boxes, 5s. 9d.; Whole Boxes, 10s. 9d. Post Free. Dilutions in Bottles, 1s.; in Complete Cases, 11s. 9d. Post Free. Also the 3rd and 30th Triturations to be had at THE BIOCHEMIC DISPENSARY, 9, Perth Road, Dundee.

Zeitfracht Medien GmbH
Ferdinand-Jühlke-Straße 7
99095 Erfurt, Deutschland
produktsicherheit@kolibri360.de